SWIFT SHADOWS - BOOK 1

# OF RIOTERS & ROYALS

m.l. greye

http://www.mlgreye.com

ISBN: 9781793141804

Edited and Cover Design by Heather Austin
Map by Hillary Goryl

*For Palmer —*

*Always fight for what
you know to be right*

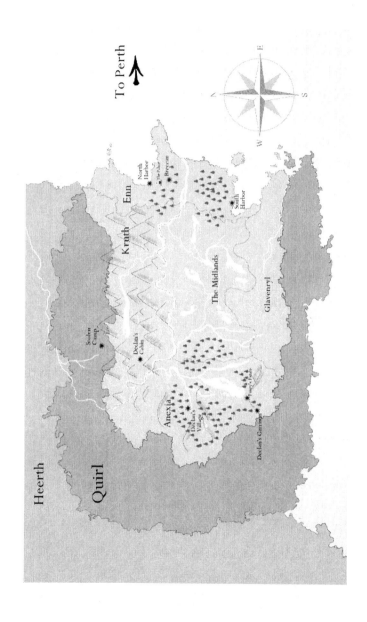

# PROLOGUE

## *A Brief History of The Feud of Enlennd*

*Enlennd is a medium-sized country of our world, located in the Southern Hemisphere. It juts out slightly into the Sea of Dridd on its Eastern side and is bordered by the nation of Quirl on all its others. Historically, fortune has favored our country in that our harbors have become some of the largest and most successful in the world. We have all manner of exports and imports that have prospered our people. However, our prosperity has slowly turned us against one another within the last century.*

*There are five distinct regions of Enlennd: the Kruth Mountains of the North, Glavenryl of the South, Anexia to the West, Enn to the East, and the Midlands in the center. The inhabitants of the harsh Kruth Mountains are a headstrong and eccentric group with a vivacity for life that is unparalleled by any other region. Those who dwell amid the flatlands of Glavenryl, on the other hand, prefer seclusion under their open skies. Anexia is the well-known hilly portion of our land, while the Midlands are the wetlands, saturated by lakes. Enn is the seat of our capital with our vibrant harbors nestled on its eastern shores.*

*Fifty years ago, our regions were at peace. All were content citizens of Enlennd, basking in our fortune. Then, the plague of Heerth – the nation located north of Quirl – reached our borders. It came from Heerth through Quirl to Anexia. The epidemic claimed thousands throughout all of Enlennd, but the vast ma-*

*jority were in Anexia.*

*Our sovereign of the time was the father to our current King Onyx Nylles, named Topaz Nylles. When Anexia became infected with the plague, instead of sending its people supplies to aid in battling the illness, King Topaz had all roads to and from the region blocked. He believed that quarantining an entire region would starve the virus. As we later discovered, however, this only worsened the plague in Anexia. The illness was in the tainted waters of the Vloyd River, which runs through most of Enlennd to empty into the sea. By cutting Anexia off to any outside water supplies, its people were forced into exclusively partaking of the contaminated river. For weeks, Anexia suffered alone, until the Vloyd carried on its disease to the other regions, Glavenryl being the least infected as the river does not pass through its borders.*

*King Topaz also fell victim to the plague. His near death caused him to investigate the epidemic further and learned it originated from the Vloyd. He apologized to Anexia, but it was too late in the eyes of its people. They had begged for assistance, yet their appeals had been ignored. In just two short months, their population that could have once rivaled Enn's had been diminished by more than half. Anexia was unwilling to forgive their king. The Feud of Enlennd had begun.*

*A decade later, when the children of Anexia who had survived were barely reaching adulthood, Enlennd was attacked on its Eastern shores. A fleet of ships from the nation across Dridd's waters – known as Perth – waged war against the capital, seeking to claim the lucrative ports. Enn, being a seaside region, was not fortified with enough food or soldiers to fully defeat Perth's impressive invasion. King Topaz sought reinforcements from his other four regions. All obeyed, except for Anexia, who refused.*

*It was Anexia's responsibility to supply troops to guard the Quirl border. Its people felt they were already working with an inadequate number of youth to fulfill that duty. To send the limited numbers they had into the capital to most likely die at the hands of Perth did not please Anexia. Thus, they chose to disregard Enn's plea as theirs had been unheeded years prior.*

*King Topaz was infuriated, but Perth kept him occupied for three years. During which time Anexia never sent support. Once Perth was finally exhausted, King Topaz sought to punish Anexia. His advisors persuaded him otherwise, urging him to disregard this act of rebellion since Anexia had maintained their protection of the Quirl border throughout the Perth attack. They believed there would be no more blatant defiance.*

*For another decade, the advisors appeared to have been correct in their assumptions. Anexia returned to its place as simply one of Enlennd's regions. When the protests slowly broke throughout the nation, however, they soon realized their imprudence.*

*Even though the meetings were nothing more than a gathering of concerned citizens, they were deemed riots by the capital, as the main topic discussed was to remove the royal family as sovereigns. The treasonous beliefs of the people of Anexia had slowly leaked into the Midlands as well as parts of Kruth and Enn. The only region seemingly unaffected by the political uproar was Glavenryl. Yet, given the secluded nature of its people, one can hardly be certain.*

*The riots continued to grow in frequency and attendance over the next five years. Enlennd's people had been exhausted financially and physically from both the Perth War and Heerth Plague. Many felt their king uncompassionate and ill-fitted to lead. Despite Enlennd's hardships, King Topaz was relentless with his taxes, using his remaining militant forces to deplete what little fortune remained among the regions.*

*It wasn't until King Topaz's health began to decline, some thirty years after the Heerth Plague, that the traitors to the crown gained their name.*

*While King Topaz lay on his deathbed, his eldest son, Prince Helio, was murdered in his sleep. The Captain of the Guard* captured a man supposedly fleeing the capital that night as the culprit for the prince's death. Without so much as a trial, King Topaz had the man hung in front of his palace. The man was a well-known political figure in Anexia. His hasty and arbitrary execution outraged Anexia. In retaliation, six months later, while the captain was traveling through the Midlands, he was beset upon by hooded men and stabbed in the stomach several times. When he was found on the side of the road, the last he said when asked whom had harmed him was 'Rioters.' From then on, those in favor of the uprising were deemed Rioters, and those who honored the crown were Royals.

King Topaz succumbed to his failing health not long after his captain's death. His son, our current King Onyx, took the throne. He has not necessarily followed in his father's footsteps, but he has not changed the course. King Onyx was not a man bred to be a leader, being the younger son. The throne had always been intended for his elder brother. Thus, when his father's elderly advisors instructed him on what to do with the kingdom, he did not refuse their counsel.

For nearly fifteen years, Enlennd lay at a stalemate. Or rather, neither the Royals nor Rioters made any further acts of violence to disrupt the balance. The sporadic riots continued, and the Royals complained of the failing patriotism. Both sides merely existed – none taking the upper hand – until the murder of Onyx's Crown Prince, Jasper Nylles.

King Onyx proclaimed Prince Jasper's death from the hands of bandits along the Kruth border, but there has been much disbelief in this declaration as the prince hadn't been seen in Enn or Kruth for months. During the past three years, theories and rumors surrounding the cause of his demise have circulated in all the five regions. This has created a tumult of anger and proposed vengeance. The Royals blame the Rioters for Prince Jasper's death. Whereas, the Rioters point to the Royals, claiming they were once again framed. The prince was well-loved in both Enn *and Anexia, having parents from both regions. Since the actual perpetrator has yet to be found, the two factions have contented themselves with accusing the other of the crime. It has created a rift within the nation.*

*However, for the first time in almost a century, Enlennd will be holding a Princess's Knight Trials for the Princess Citrine Nylles this very year. Princess Citrine and her sister, Princess Emerald Nylles, are Enlennd's first princesses in three generations. The event will force the five regions to each select one contender to send to The Trials in the capital. The man who wins will be sworn to Princess Citrine as her personal bodyguard until she weds. It will once again be region competing against region, rather than Rioters versus Royals. Perhaps The Trials will be able to, in some way, mend our Enlennd...*

Levric Sharpe lowered the pamphlet he'd found resting on his table. It wasn't current. He'd been a little surprised to see it still in circulation. The trifold had been printed nearly two years prior. He knew because he had participated in the dispersal of these pamphlets throughout the regions. He'd written half of it himself. It had been one of his duties in his position serving The Mistress.

In Enlennd, it was common for political pamphlets to be distributed among the common folk. The pamphlets were supposed to educate, but as they were mostly editorials, they were truthfully used to sway public opinion toward a certain bias. The purpose of this particular pamphlet had been meant to do just that – to cast the Rioters' cause in the light of more historical fact than that of simple, meddling peasants. Sadly, the outcome hadn't been what The Mistress and her Committee envisioned. The Rioters were still seen as power-grasping anarchists by the Royals.

Loosing a pent-up breath, Levric glanced into the dying embers of the fire his table sat near. The fireplace was neither close enough to fully illuminate his table, nor too far that the initial drawing of the eyes to the fire and the following sweep away would end up on himself. He'd blend in with the other patrons without a single glance his way. Thanks to the abilities his brown eyes gave him, the act of going unnoticed was more instinct than conscious thought at this point.

The tavern's front door swung open, bringing with it a frigid, sad excuse for a spring wind. The embers flickered. Levric shifted his gaze ever so slightly to the petite figure who had entered. He recognized her gait at once. The Mistress's dark blue cloak dripped water from the sleet outside. She kept her hood up as she approached the bartender and asked like a Kruth native for something to warm her. Levric feigned disinterest, returning to his study of the fire, while she waited for her steaming, scalding mug of cider – a Kruth favorite on nights like these to keep them warm in the harsh temperatures of the Kruth Mountains.

The keeper handed The Mistress her wooden mug in exchange for a coin. She thanked him then spun toward Levric. She strode directly to him – no fear of hiding her destination. Levric frowned, scratching a hand over his bearded chin. It wasn't until she was seated across from him that she pushed back the hood of her wet cloak, revealing her silvery blonde hair braided on top of her head. A few tendrils had managed to escape the coronet, dangling around her face.

Levric inclined his head in greeting. "I see you've come alone."

She breathed in the steam from her mug with a smirk. "I do believe we chose a night with no moon for a reason. No need for a bodyguard when there's darkness for cover."

"One can never be too careful, my Mistress," he replied slowly. It was a topic they had discussed on more than one occasion before. Levric believed that as an important figure she needed to be more cautious. She, on the other hand, presumed her abilities were protection enough. No matter how much they quarreled, The Mistress still did as she'd originally intended in the end. Levric would have assumed it to be a sign of her youth, if he didn't know better.

Despite the limited years of the woman sitting across from him, she was surprisingly well versed in the ways of the world, having witnessed much evil in it already. While still in her teens, barely into her adulthood, she had fought her way upward among the Rioters to claim the coveted title of The Mistress – the leader of their sect. Although the power of her abilities was great, it hadn't been on might alone that she'd gained her position. No, it had been through meticulous, shrewd plotting with an abundance of patience. For someone her age, she was uncommonly astute. Somehow, she had won the trust of each region's Rioter faction and created her renowned Committee within only a matter of a couple years. It had been The Committee, of which Levric was a participant, that had appointed her as The Mistress of the Rioters a little more than two years before.

"The dark and I are old friends," she finally responded after taking a sip of her cider. "Now, what news from court?"

The Mistress's court was not the same as the Royal Court of the Jewels – the name the Rioters gave the royal family since each member was traditionally named after some precious gem. The court she referred to was seated in Anexia and was filled with The Committee and commoners – those who believed in the Rioters' cause.

He frowned. "I received a letter from Princess Emerald."

Slowly, her eyes lifted from the murky liquid in her mug to meet his. "Did you now?"

"She is petitioning for my son to submit his name for her Trials," he replied. "Even though she hasn't seen him in years, she remembers well his skills."

"Will you submit his name?" She bit the tip of her tongue. Levric didn't miss the hope in her gaze.

"I cannot encourage him. His mother is adamantly against it. The danger concerns her," he said gently.

The Mistress loosed something between a sigh and a moan. It showed just how much she confided in Levric for her to release such a display of emotion around him. "Your son's former acquaintance with the princess, though, would be advantageous to our cause during The Trials. She obviously trusts him."

"Naturally," Levric nodded once. "He is worthy of it after saving her life."

"Is he still ignorant of the identity of the girl he saved?" The Mistress asked, her voice low.

"He is."

She pushed back a few of the strands of hair that had fallen in her face. "And your wife cannot be swayed?"

Levric shook his head. "She will not."

"Well, that's unfortunate," The Mistress grumbled, sounding more like her actual age than he'd heard from her in a long time.

A corner of his mouth edged upward at her reaction. "No need to fret quite yet. Declan came to me just last night informing me of his intention to submit his name, despite his mother's disapproval. As he is an adult, he has the right do so without our blessing."

Genuine surprise lined her eyes. "Declan wishes to become a Challenger of his own accord?"

"He hopes he can be of service to our cause and believes he could win The Trials with the same set of skills the princess admired."

"How egotistically loyal of him," The Mistress scoffed, somewhat fondly. "Do you have as much faith in your son as he does in himself?"

"Declan does not fail," Levric said without hesitation. "When he sets his mind to a task, he always completes it with expertise."

"Good." She smiled. "Then, let us begin to plan for when he becomes Princess Emerald's Knight."

# CHAPTER ONE

*About four months later*

Declan Sharpe tried to stifle a yawn behind his hand. This was his seventh yawn in the past twenty minutes. So, since the meeting began, he'd been yawning once every three minutes. If he wanted the Challenger's selection panel to think what they discussed bored him, then he was fairly certain he'd be succeeding. Unfortunately for him, that was not his goal. He needed the seasoned men and women surrounding him in the front room of his own home to accept him as a plausible candidate for The Mistress's proposed plan. By all the dubious looks he kept receiving, though, he suspected he was failing at impressing any of them.

It was his own fault, really. He'd stayed out late the night before with his friends, trying to catch a Starlit Pig. As the name implied, the delicious animals only ventured their short snouts out of their burrows during the very early hours of the morning.

Despite his formal petition the next day, Declan had agreed to go hunting with Bran Wynpreg – his closest friend in Anexia – because it was something someone his age would have done. The hunt was more an excuse to explore the woods at night with friends than anything. Starlit Pigs were rarely caught. So, Declan had agreed to go in yet another attempt to be an average Anexian.

He'd known that Bran's younger sister, Brielle, was going. She'd been trying to get his attention for months. Since his goal had been to feel like a normal man his own age, he'd kissed her – to prove to himself that it was still possible to feel young and alive. He hadn't kissed anyone since his time in Quirl. Kissing Brielle had been nice, sweet even. Brielle was pretty and was smiling more often than not. Her simple joy in life was what had first caught his eye after he returned from Quirl. There was an innocence to her that he found himself yearning for.

Yet, he was beginning to wonder if staying out for a kiss had truly been worth it as an additional yawn battled to consume him. No attempt at normalcy was worth losing the panel's approval. His father, Levric, was now casting him a critical look. Declan forced himself to sit up straighter in his seat. His father was sticking his position and reputation on the line in support of this opportunity, and he wouldn't let Declan forget it.

*Opportunity.* Declan almost snorted. That was what the panel called it, but really it was closer to suicide. To be a Challenger in The Trials wasn't really an honor as much as it was a burden. Men had died during The Trials in the past. There was a possibility that Declan could as well. Still, Declan wanted to be chosen. It was the means to finally prove his value to the Rioters, rather than be merely seen as the returned, brooding son of one of their leaders. Declan fought the sudden urge to drum his fingers on the arm of his chair. Tension was starting to build up inside of him, causing his shoulders to ache. All of his preparation came down to this meeting.

For the first time in his twenty-three years of life, the Rioters could possibly end The Feud of Enlennd. If Declan's petition were chosen, he'd be thrust into an operation as the key component. It would be an enormous responsibility. If he failed, the Rioters would most likely shun him.

About a year and a half prior, the Anexian candidate – carefully selected by this same panel – for The Trials of Princess Citrine, botched miserably his chance to win the coveted position of her Knight. The poor man was the first to be eliminated. Since his disaster, no one had heard from him. Knowing that he'd disappointed and shamed his region, he'd had the wisdom to not return to Anexia. Somewhere in the back of Declan's head, there was a warning sounding that he could share a very similar fate. Yet, Declan was ignoring the risks. He'd been through far worse. Princess Emerald's Trials didn't scare him.

Declan shifted in his chair. Marlo Vrig – a gray-haired, purple-eyed woman – was reading his petition out loud to the panel. She switched from his written proposal for consideration to his qualifications backing his application. Her continuous monotone voice was luring him to sleep. Declan dug his nails into his palms to try to keep himself awake. As much as his mother used to chastise him when he was younger for calling Marlo boring, Declan held fast to his previous accusation. His eyes were drooping. No one should have made her the speaker.

"Now for the testimonials," Marlo finally finished, gradually returning her old bones into her chair. Declan heard her joints crack with the movement and silently wondered if she'd ever been youthful in his lifetime. His only memories of the woman were of her being ancient.

As previously discussed, Declan's father stood and began to express his pleasure and support that his only son, out of his four children, wished to assist the Rioters' cause. It was a speech Declan had heard the evening before while both he and his father rehearsed what they'd say this morning.

Levric really did have a way with words. It was probably one of the reasons why The Mistress had appointed him to her Committee. As Levric listed off Declan's accomplishments, which were really nothing more than a short list expounded upon in greater depth than was probably necessary, Declan regarded his father's appearance.

The man was always adorned in perfectly tailored clothing, thanks to Declan's seamstress mother. Though Levric's attire was that of a humble blacksmith, he often appeared more imposing than some dignitaries Declan had seen. Levric was rarely found covered in soot or grime outside of his forge. He'd told Declan as a child that one aspect of gaining someone's respect was to portray a figure of cleanliness. Those who were covered in filth tended to be frowned upon by those who could afford to never get dirty. It was simply the way the world worked.

Today, Levric really had outdone himself. He wore his finest buttoned cream shirt, tucked into gray pants, which were stuffed into a pair of black boots. To finish it off, he wore a new black vest Declan's mother had finished just the previous evening. Levric's shoulder length hair – the mature cut of a married Anexian man – had been pulled back at the nape of his neck and tied there by a leather cord. The look accentuated the gray around his temples. His graying beard had been trimmed to be barely more than stubble. Even the eyebrows that hooded his deep-set brown eyes looked neater.

Declan took a deep breath as Levric concluded his oration and motioned for Declan's uncle to begin next. Marsdon Finn was Declan's mother's brother – twelve years her junior. At first glance, though, anyone would mistake him to be Levric's instead. Marsdon had the same thick build as Levric and similar coloring. However, where Levric was tall, Marsdon was more average sized in height. It was his eyes that betrayed him as a relation to Declan's mother, Llydia Finn. They were a vivid teal with flecks of navy blue – eyes that certainly caught one's attention. Even though Declan looked very much like his father – with his raven black hair and height somewhere between Levric's and Marsdon's – he'd inherited the base eye color of his mother and uncle.

And eye color was everything. It was a way to interpret a person's talents. Certain abilities were intrinsic to a person, depending on the shade of their eyes. Base color was inherited from ancestors, while veins and flecks of other colors were developed over the course of one's life. Generally, a person had a base color and only one other color flecked or veined throughout the eyes.

As a Teal, Declan was unnaturally quick. The dark, hunter green specks in his eyes meant he also had some control over nature. Although, all he could really do with the green in them was avoid ever becoming lost. He could always find his way to his destination.

Marsdon's deep voice forced Declan's attention back to the present. His uncle didn't have the same eloquence of Levric, but his words were sincere. Declan was touched that his usually reserved and somewhat shy uncle would stand up in a room full of people to vouch for him. When Marsdon was done and seated once more, Declan knew it was his turn.

Slowly, Declan rose to his feet. It wasn't for dramatic effect – it was simply because it seemed to take an excessive amount of energy. Once standing, he took in the faces watching him. He was in front of his own fireplace, composed from large rocks found along the banks of the Vloyd River, with his father to his left and Marlo to his father's left. Everyone else in the room scrutinized him expectantly. Even his mother had paused at the sink in their kitchen to listen. She'd outright refused to join the meeting earlier as she was adamantly opposed to his petition. But she had stayed within hearing range in the kitchen that was only about twenty feet away from the panel's circle.

Declan offered her a small smile and decided to adjust his memorized speech at the last moment. It was mostly because he was too tired to recall what exactly he'd rehearsed. He had an odd feeling that it didn't matter anyway – that the panel had already made up their minds at this point.

Taking a deep breath that nearly launched him into another yawn, Declan quickly said, "I wish to thank you for hearing my petition, good people of Anexia." It was the customary way to address an assembled group from his region and was typical in beginning an oration. "I also thank my uncle and father for their kind words."

Now he ventured away from his script, "I could say that no matter whom you choose, I'd be satisfied and encourage your decision, but that would be a lie. If you chose anyone other than myself, you'd be making an enormous mistake."

That sent up the eyebrows on some of the faces through the crowd. Declan hurried on, purposely avoiding his father's gaze. "I know what the circumstances require, and I know my strengths. I reach goals. I do not fall short. And there is not another person alive as fast as myself. If you select me, I can promise you that I will bring us significantly closer to ending The Feud or die trying."

With that, Declan sat down again. This time he wasn't able to fight the yawn, and he quickly covered his mouth to block everyone from a glimpse of his mouth gaping open. He told himself it was better to be direct than waste his audience's time. Yet, the gruff look on his father's face was making Declan wonder if he'd later regret his words.

Marlo stood once more and bobbed her head. "Challenger candidate dismissed."

It was time for the panel to discuss his petition, which was why Declan was excused. As the room rose to their feet and bodies began shuffling toward the kitchen so as to sample his mother's refreshments while they talked, Declan happily turned towards the exit, grateful for the chance to get some air.

His father clasped wrists with a few of the panel members, and Declan slipped silently outside. On the back porch, he took a deep breath and turned to the worn path behind his house. It led through the woods surrounding his village to a stream that was a runoff from the massive Vloyd. The stream was where he went to be alone when he stayed with his parents. After the meeting he'd somehow managed to stay awake through, he craved some time to rest by himself.

Keeping a brisk pace without tapping into his speed ability, he passed between the first set of trees. From that place deep inside of him that had urged him to even apply for Anexia's Challenger, he knew. He knew the panel was going to pick him. Even with his blunt delivery. To be honest, it was why he hadn't cared to provide his full speech. Somehow he knew it. Felt it. He would be their choice.

No one was a better swordsman in all of Anexia than he was. And what he'd told them was true – no one was faster than him. He might have even been the fastest Teal in history. That alone should have convinced them. But tied with his family connections, he was sure to gain the position.

What bothered him now was the fact that he'd possibly just agreed to his own demise. He should have been anxious. He was going to be the Rioter's clandestine contender for the Princess Emerald's Knight. In just a week, he'd be on his way to the capital of Enlennd, about to begin The Trials. Any average man would have been nervous…

Declan moaned and raked his fingers through his hair. Unlike Levric, Declan kept his thick, dark locks short. It was a symbol of his age. Once he became established with a wife, then he'd be permitted to grow out his hair. It was the habit in Anexia for the youth to keep their hair shorter than their elders, even the girls weren't allowed to have their hair past their shoulders until they wed. But Declan had spent enough time in Quirl that he'd already decided he'd never let his hair grow beyond his ears. It was customary there for all men to have hair to their shoulders, and he wasn't particularly fond of it.

He reached the stream and, with a sigh, dropped onto the damp pebbles along its bank. He had half a mind to strip down and go for a dip in the icy water.

Perhaps it'd help clear the sleep-deprived haze he was in. Maybe it'd knock some apprehension into him.

Someone cleared her throat behind him.

He whirled. "Brielle?"

The girl was sitting on a log, her high-waist brown dress splayed out around her. He frowned, wondering how he'd not seen her there. Her deep auburn hair was hard to miss, even when pulled up on the crown of her head in a small bun as it was now. She smiled and flushed – pink spreading behind the scattered freckles on her cheeks. She knew it made her appear endearing. "Good morning, Declan."

"Morning," he murmured.

It wasn't that he was upset to see her – it was just … He felt that twang again. The one where he felt as if he'd been expecting someone else. The sensation was much more frequent now. He'd begun experiencing it two years before in random bursts. Lately, it was every day. He frowned as he twisted his body all the way around to face her. These phantom disappointments grated on his nerves. Declan leaned back on his hands, his fingers digging into the pebbles. "What brings you here? I thought you'd still be in bed after the late night."

The sun sprinkled her face with light as it filtered down through the branches of the trees. Her ruby red eyes, ribbed in pink, gazed at him through her eyelashes. He probably would have appreciated the gesture more if her brother had not been born with the same base eyes. Declan had seen Bran flaunt his eyes shamelessly with far too many girls. She and Bran looked too much alike for Declan to not be reminded of his friend's favorite flirting technique. Ruby eyes were somewhat uncommon in Anexia and Bran used that to his advantage.

"I was waiting for you," Brielle replied. "I figured for good or bad, after the meeting you'd end up here."

Declan grunted. "I'm surprised you knew that."

"Of course, I do." She seemed miffed by his comment.

Perhaps that had come out harsher than he'd intended. He offered her a smile. "Sorry. It's good to see you again."

The pleased pink in her cheeks matched the outer ring of her eyes as she stood and joined him. For a girl who blushed so easily, no one would ever guess that she was actually one of the few remaining unwed older girls in their village. At eighteen, she'd tasted her fair share of hopeful young men. It was odd that she hadn't married yet. In Enlennd, women became eligible to wed at sixteen, while men had to wait until eighteen. Most women became betrothed during their seventeenth year. Brielle, being one of the prettier faces in the village, could have been married with a baby by now.

"So?" Brielle's cheerful voice broke Declan's reflections. "How did your petition go?"

Declan tipped his head back, raising his gaze to the treetops. "I think it went well, all in all."

"Then, why do you look so distressed?" She laughed lightly – a sound he'd once mentioned to her that he liked.

He frowned. That was a good question. One he wasn't sure he knew the answer to.

"There you are!" Bran appeared out of the forest, panting. He hunched forward, placing his hands on his knees. He didn't seem surprised to find Declan with his sister. "I've been searching for you everywhere. They just announced who will represent Anexia."

Before Bran even said the words, Declan grimaced and tipped his head skywards again.

: : : : :

"Could you raise your arms, dear princess?"

Emerald Celeste Nylles suppressed a very unladylike roll of her eyes as she obeyed. It wasn't the required movement that annoyed her – it was the incessant formalities of her servants. Whenever she was alone with one of them, she was addressed as *dearest princess*. Since her sister was in the room, they both were simply *dear princess*. She'd been pestering her personal maid, Fanny, to call her by her name for the past four years. Yet, the woman would have nothing of it. Fanny was only nine months older than her. Why must she insist on being so formal when no one else in the room cared to be?

"Emry," her sister said as she flopped onto the extravagant four-poster bed at the center of the room. Their former governess would have gasped had she'd witnessed the display. "Are you certain I should go with cayenne as the color for my ball gown?"

Even though her first name was Emerald – after a precious stone as was royal tradition – she only ever went by that in Court. All those close to her called her Emry.

At the moment, both she and her sister, Citrine Agatha Nylles, were in the process of being measured for their new dresses they were to wear during Emry's Trials, which would take place in a little more than three weeks. Usually Cit's maid, Sadie, dealt with Cit's measurements, but the girl had today off and the deed fell to Fanny.

They were in Emry's quarters – her bedroom to be

exact. Unlike most of the palace, Emry decorated her room in whites and pastels. The walls were a pale sea-foam green with white curtains and matching swabs of cloth strewn over the top of her bed, cascading down on either side. Her comforter and sheets were both white, but the mounds of pillows on top were soft shades of blue and purple. The thick, plush rug beneath the bed was a purposely faded geometric design in cream, gray, and blue – imported all the way from Heerth. The large stuffed chair in the corner was a color somewhere between white and gray. The other furniture in the room were the enormous bed and two nightstands on either side of it. All three items were whitewashed wood, reminding Emry of the driftwood that washed ashore in the nearby North Harbor.

Outside of her bedroom was a sitting room and table with four chairs for when she chose to eat alone or with her sister. The color scheme out there was the same as it was in her room. Faded Heerth rug, white-washed table, pale colored furniture and pillows. It was all just as she'd imagined when she'd redone her room after her first year in Heerth.

"For the last time, Cit, yes." This time Emry did roll her eyes. "It will bring out those miniscule veins of red in your lovely orange eyes." She pressed her lips together to bite back a smile.

Citrine gasped and whirled to her Knight, Freddick Zembe. Her long, midnight black braid whipped around her head. Freddick was lounging in the room's stuffed chair on the opposite side of the bed from Emry. "You told her I thought I found some red?" She demanded.

Freddick's black eyes narrowed briefly at Emry before dipping his head apologetically to his princess. "I didn't realize it was a secret."

Emry couldn't help but laugh, earning her a poke from Fanny. Citrine, named after the stone that matched the shade of her eyes, had always been a little sensitive about which colors her eyes held. The best description Emry had ever come up with was that Cit's eyes were base orange with varying shades of orange, marbled outward from her pupil. It gave her eyes the illusion of a blazing fire. Fitting, considering her abilities.

"All finished, dear princess." Fanny straightened and began gathering the swatches of fabric along with her measuring tape from the low, thin bed just outside the room's door. It was more of a cot, really. The thing was a recent addition to her chambers. Emry was still getting used to seeing it next to her door. It'd only been there a few days, as it was meant for her future Knight.

"Thank you, Fanny." Emry lowered her arms before sitting beside her sister on the edge of her bed.

"Are you really not going to choose which colors to wear?" Citrine asked, one eyebrow raised.

"No, Fanny has exquisite taste. I'll wear whatever she wishes." Usually Emry was meticulous about what she wore, but in the case of her Trials, she needed to give the appearance of nonchalance – to hide her growing anxiety. Letting Fanny pick would show her father's ever-judging Court that she was unaffected by her upcoming Trials. Much better than letting them know how she actually felt – like a loaded cannon about to explode.

The maid's face flushed. "Thank you, dear princess." She gave a small curtsy, her arms full, and then exited Emry's chambers.

Once she was gone, Emry fell backward over her

sister's middle. Cit grunted at her weight. "Tell me again why I must have a Trials," Emry whined to the white cloth above her head. "How about I just take your Knight?"

"Freddick is clearly happy in his current position." Citrine shoved her sister with one hand.

Emry snorted, another unladylike choice that would have sent that governess into hysterics. She and Cit had had only one for less than a year, but the woman had been disgusted with most of what Emry did. Emry really hadn't been fond of her. "Freddick would be glad to be rid of you. The way you lounge about the palace all day must be dreadfully boring."

"Well, I realize the ridiculousness in tearing about the woods everyday," Citrine retorted. "One of these days, you're going to be thrown from your horse or, worse, fall from climbing the palace wall."

"I only ever descend the wall," Emry corrected, sitting up. "I don't prefer to climb up it."

"And you think that Freddick would enjoy following you around?" Citrine shook her head in disbelief.

Her sister grinned. "I'd keep him on his toes. Men like that."

Freddick cleared his throat, as if to remind the girls that he was still present. "I'm sorry to disappoint, Emry, but I like Citrine very much and am quite content to be sworn to her."

Citrine shot Emry a triumphant smirk. "See? He knows that with you his likelihood of death or pain increases significantly."

"You insult him by suggesting he'd choose an easier path over a daringly more rewarding one," Emry objected.

"Daringly more rewarding?" Citrine repeated slowly. "Is that how you intend to describe yourself at The Trials?"

She rose from the bed. "I might."

"Since when did you stop looking forward to having your Trials?" Freddick's deep voice rumbled from his corner.

Emry turned to the dark-skinned Glav. As was typical of those from Glavenryl, Freddick was taller than most men in Enn by two or three inches. In accordance with his region's fashion, his dense, russet colored hair that fell in waves – not quite ringlets – to the middle of his back was braided into a tight bun at the nape of his neck. His thick eyebrows hooded his deep-set almond shaped eyes – base black with flecks of lavender. His oval face, though almost ethereal, was entirely masculine. Citrine had found him striking the first time she'd seen him, and Emry had had to agree with her. Freddick was handsome and exotic. Since the people of Glavenryl maintained a somewhat isolated existence, Citrine had never come in close contact with a Glav until meeting Freddick. Emry had spent a few months there visiting its people, as was expected of the royal family. Citrine, not one for travel since her near-death illness years ago, had not joined her.

Releasing her breath out in a rush, Emry said, "There's the possibility The Trials might not go as I'd hoped."

"What do you mean?" Citrine frowned, her thin, dark eyebrows drawing together.

"Well," Emry sighed and gripped onto one of the thick, squared posts of her bed. "There is a very real risk that I could be stuck with the wrong Knight at the last minute."

Freddick and Citrine exchanged looks for a moment. She blinked. "What?"

"I thought you knew," Citrine pushed herself up.

"Knew what?"

"You make the ultimate decision," she replied. "The Trials narrow the candidates for you to the top two, and you choose between them. That's the last trial – your choice."

"I'm able to choose?" How had she not known this?

"You are the one who will be spending the most time with your Knight, so you have the last say," her sister pointed out. "It stands to reason."

"Oh." Emry frowned. "Why didn't you mention that before?"

"You never asked. But anyway, let's say you have a preference for a certain Challenger. He wouldn't need to be the best to become your Knight, just a finalist," Citrine informed.

"And if he were not a finalist…" Emry let her voice trail off.

Citrine pulled a face. "Then, I'd suggest you find yourself a runner-up."

"You know there's no runner-up." She moaned and tossed the thick braid of her own long, black hair over her shoulder.

In Enn, young, unmarried women wore their long locks in one swooping braid that began at one ear and swirled around the entire head returning to the same ear to dangle down the back or over the front shoulder, except for formal Court events. On those special occasions, their hair was piled onto their heads, with a few lucky strands allowed to escape in soft, short ringlets. While at the palace, Emry was not permitted outside her own chambers without her hair in some sort of braid. Her hair was so long, though, that the braid was actually fairly practical. It kept her thick hair from getting everywhere.

Freddick chuckled, a low, chesty sound. "I fear for your future Knight. The amount of stress you will undoubtedly supply him will lead him to an early grave."

"Me? Dangerous?" Emry blinked. To be teased by the large, ever-serious man was a rare treat. "As if I need a Knight to begin with. His job will be so easy, he'll start to gain weight with all the luxury the position has to offer." Emry stared pointedly at Freddick's middle, repaying his jest.

Her sister was laughing again. "Perhaps we should warn her Challengers before The Trials. Nothing with Emry is easy."

"Or, rather, one of The Trials should be chasing her around the palace for a day." Freddick's lips twitched upward.

"Except, if Father did go that route, the Challengers would never be able to find her." Citrine grinned wickedly. "Or, the men could contest Emry herself in climbing down the palace wall bare-handed. Wouldn't it be splendid to see someone best her?"

"We all agree, *dear princess*, that your Knight must be a hearty fellow with just the right streak of wild in his veins," Freddick said, emphasizing the silly name both sisters loathed.

"I'm not certain there is such a man in existence, but mayhap fortune will finally smile upon your soul and your preference will become a finalist," Citrine added.

"Mayhap fortune?" Emry repeated incredulously. "What's with all the pretty words?"

"We're having tea with that snooty emissary from

Quirl today. I thought I'd practice sounding all lofty to give her a taste of her own flavor of annoying." Cit's smile turned sheepish. "You know ... the woman who has been in our Court for eight months and hasn't shown any sign of leaving anytime soon."

"Have fun with that." Emry grimaced and sank back onto the bed. "I'll be sure to give you plenty of space today."

"You mean, you'll be outside – most likely in the woods today," Cit retorted.

Emry tilted her head to one side and grinned. "Ah, you know me so well."

# CHAPTER TWO

As was required, Declan traveled to the capital in Enn alone. It was a condition for each of the five Challengers to leave their respective regions and arrive at the palace of the Jewels without assistance. Something of a pre-Trial. Since the Challengers carried documents of authenticity from their local leaders as their region's chosen candidate, to overtake them would be advantageous to any bandit wanting to win a life of luxury as the Princess's Knight. Well, to those who were stupid enough to assume The Trials weren't that hard. Either way, it was unwise for any man to tour the country alone in the weeks prior to The Trials. Thieves flocked the highways and paths leading to Enn in hopes of claiming some Challenger papers as their own.

Fortunately for Declan, his teal eyes were speckled with dark green flecks. His speed, mixed with his inability to lose his way, had helped him reach Enn in record time. Coming from Anexia meant that he'd had the farthest to travel. The distance was the reason he'd given his village for departing the day after he'd been proclaimed Anexia's Challenger. It hadn't been the full truth, but it made for a good enough excuse.

He'd heard of the way the last contender for Anexia had been treated before leaving for the capital. The man's relatives and friends had all flocked to him to say their farewells, believing to never see him again. Like he was about to die. Declan had thought their actions ridiculous at the time. But the man had yet to return to Anexia and probably never would. Perhaps his relations had had incredible foresight after all. Not wanting to have to endure a similar scenario, Declan chose to take off early.

Honestly, it really had been an uneventful journey thus far. Almost disappointingly easy. Almost. Declan wasn't an idiot, wishing for a fight. He'd had more than his fill of those. It was why he'd trekked through the Kruth Mountains rather than taking the faster route through the Midlands.

This time of year, Kruth frosted over from the tips of its mountains to the base where it met the Midlands. The cold weather generally cleared the mountain range of visitors and pilferers, resulting in deserted roads. Enduring a little snow was well worth avoiding bringing attention to himself.

Now, as he trotted along the short road through the woods between the capital city, Breccan, and the palace, he couldn't help but smile at his luck. The likelihood of being harassed by bandits here, on the main road to the seat of the Jewels, was highly unlikely. Since he'd entered the region of Enn, the roads had steadily become more populous. Going both to and from Breccan were carriages of genteel citizens, farmer's carts, wagons filled with merchant wares, and the occasional patrolling platoon.

After more than a week of solitary travel, the stench of sweaty bodies and animal feces combined with all the congestion on the road was making him irritable. He'd picked up a hired horse in Breccan a couple hours before, having traveled mostly on foot and figuring that it'd be easier to deal with the throngs of people atop a horse. Yet, even the tame animal seemed to be affected by the crush around them. Apparently, during the day, the palace hosted numerous merchants, who were now all crowded around Declan. They were on their way to sell their goods to their sovereign's housekeeper, cook, steward, gardener, or whoever else was in charge of supplying the palace.

Unwilling to endure them a minute more, Declan groaned and decided to slip off the beaten path into the cover of the trees. It took nearly fifteen minutes of wandering away from the road to no longer hear the commotion of it. With a sigh of relief, Declan tipped his head upwards, breathing in deeply the fresh air. The scent on the road had left him near gagging.

Alone with just the sounds of the forest, he heard the vague gurgling of a nearby brook and permitted his horse to ramble toward the sound. He was in no hurry. As Anexia's champion, his presence wouldn't be expected for at least a few days more, if not a week. He had plenty of time to reach the palace, which was supposedly only twenty or so minutes away, if the merchant he'd asked was to be trusted.

"Is it wise to be out by yourself, so close to The Trials?"

The feminine Enn voice made Declan jump in his saddle. He'd heard no one approach. He spun his head side to side but couldn't make out anyone amid the trees and underbrush.

Before he was able to demand the woman show herself, a light laugh drifted to him and a slim, petite figure dropped to the ground about ten feet away to his left. Well, he assumed the person was a she.

Dressed in boy's clothing with a large cap over her hair that cast most of her face in shadow, the girl had to have been trying not to be recognized. The tight fit of her clothing in certain areas, though, assured anyone who wasn't half blind that the smooth chin peeking out from beneath the brim of the hat belonged to a female.

There was something oddly familiar about the way she held herself – the way she moved. Declan couldn't quite place it. He waited for that usual twang of disappointment from subconsciously expecting someone different, but it didn't come. He blinked in surprise. When was the last time he hadn't felt it? He couldn't remember.

Frowning, he nearly forgot to nod his head in greeting. "Good-day."

"Good-day," she replied.

The girl said nothing more, building an awkward silence between them. Not really wanting to linger, Declan nodded at her once again and urged his mount onward.

But she stepped into his path, a smile playing at the corners of her mouth. The only part of her face he could see. "You sound like an Anexian. Not many Anexians traverse Enn."

Her observation startled him. Unless traveling for The Trials, as he was, an Anexian wouldn't be caught dead in Enn nowadays. Most of the people he'd encountered in Enn confused his accent with that of a Glav, which he'd been grateful for. Even though his hair was far shorter than a Glav's, he could still be assumed to be from the Midlands – the mixing ground for the regions.

"You're mistaken," he told her. "I hail from Glavenryl."

She grinned, as if it was a joke. "Right. Let me just ignore the fact that, first, your hair is far too short for a man your age in Glavenryl." She held up a hand as if he intended to interrupt her and needed to stop him. "No, not even in the Midlands do Glav men cut their hair. Second, you have daggers strapped to your biceps, like an Anexian or someone from Quirl. Then third, your accent, though similar to a Glav, is distinctly different. Anyone who has come in close contact with both could be partially deaf and still notice."

Declan said nothing in reply, stunned. He eyed her warily. As she was a woman, she wouldn't be after his papers since only men became Challengers. Unless she was acting as a distraction for an ambush. Not that an ambush frightened him. It was highly unlikely they'd be able to catch him with his Teal abilities. So, what exactly was she getting at?

He wasn't sure about her exact age. With all her hair stuffed up into that knitted cap and most of her face hidden, she appeared young, barely more than sixteen, which might have been her intention. The way she spoke, however, pointed to a more confident, older woman. From the way *she* sounded, she was clearly an Enn.

When Declan didn't respond, her smile faded slightly. "Are you Anexia's Challenger?"

"I am," he answered, somewhat begrudgingly. It was part of the moral conduct of a Challenger to announce himself as such when questioned. Another stupid rule.

Her grin returned. "Good. I'm glad."

"You are?" He blinked.

"Of course!" She must have noticed the confusion written on his face because her brow furrowed. "Oh, you can't see my face, can you?"

"No, miss. I can't."

She reached up to remove her hat when loud shouts were thrown towards them from between the trees. The girl winced and dropped her hands. "That's my cue to go. Wouldn't want to be caught here with you."

"You're being chased?" Declan stared. Was she some sort of criminal? That thought didn't sit well with him.

"Always. Until the next, Declan." She yanked off her cap and tossed it at his head as she spun away from him. He snagged it before it actually hit him, but he didn't catch a glimpse of her face before she tore off. All he saw was a long braid of black hair bouncing against her back as she ran.

He'd never said his name. He knew he was gaping, but how could she know him? Here? In Enn? He'd never stepped a foot into Enn until this trip. He made to ride after her, but his horse had barely taken a step when she suddenly disappeared beneath the shade of the trees, as if into thin air.

Three men, attired in Enlennd's colors of black, white, and silver, galloped into Declan's sight. He frowned. The girl was being followed by soldiers? Or were they palace guards? Their uniforms were not exactly the same as the platoons he'd ridden by earlier. The men eyed him suspiciously. When one asked if he'd seen a boy or a young woman dressed as one, Declan only shook his head, unable to bring himself to betray her to them. He wasn't sure why – he owed the stranger nothing. For all he knew, she could have been a bandit. Yet, there was something about her that made him hesitate giving the guards information.

Frustrated and visibly exasperated, the men road on.

As Declan urged his horse forward once again, he

racked his mind for when he might have slipped up and mentioned his name back in Breccan. The girl could have come from there, followed him maybe. He hadn't seen her eyes. She could have been a Teal, like himself. But he'd been careful. He'd been using his alias exclusively during the time he'd been traveling. How did she know his name?

Declan no longer desired to visit that brook he could still hear. All he wanted now was to get to the palace as fast as possible and collapse into whatever bed he'd be offered for the remainder of the day. The fatigue of his journey had suddenly caught up to him.

: : : : :

Emry had barely finished fastening the last button at her neck on the back of her day gown – a skill she'd learned to do while moving – when she collided head first into her father's chest. He let out a soft grunt as she bounced backwards off of him, nearly losing her footing. She would've landed on her rear had the king not grabbed her wrists to balance her.

"Hello, daughter," King Onyx greeted, somewhat dryly, releasing his grip once she was steady again.

"Hello, Father," Emry replied instinctively.

If her brother had lived, he would have aged to look just like their father. Same dark hair, deep set eyes, and squared jaw. There'd never been any question who had sired the former Crown Prince.

Vardin Melc, her father's Captain of the Guard, stood a few steps behind Onyx. He bowed silently when Emry glanced at him. Emry could feel her cheeks turning red. She was never this clumsy, and especially not around her father and the captain. Her encounter with Declan had left her distracted and a little disoriented.

Onyx raised an eyebrow as his gaze shifted past her toward the way she had come. It was obvious that she'd just left the stables. Not only were they in the sole hallway that led there, she was certain she reeked of the outdoors. "So, what were you doing today?" His gaze drifted back to her face. His voice was resigned, knowing full well she'd left the palace without authorization.

She licked dry lips, hoping her cheeks weren't smudged with dirt this time. "I was climbing trees."

"Naturally," Onyx said humorlessly.

"I finished my Heerth dialect lessons early today," she hurried to tell him, as if that explained why she'd run off again. The color in her cheeks wouldn't go away. She wanted to put her cool hands over her face to bring down the red, but that would only bring more attention to her embarrassment of being caught. She usually stuck to the shadows in the palace so as to avoid discovery. This was all Declan's fault.

"The Trials cannot come soon enough." Onyx passed a hand across his eyes.

She grimaced. An apology for her actions would've been the appropriate thing to say. Yet, she felt no remorse. She hated being cooped up in the palace. It was no secret.

Vardin laid a hand on her father's shoulder. "Only a couple weeks more, my liege."

Emry's eyes narrowed ever so slightly toward him. The blue-eyed Captain and she had never truly gotten along. The way his oval-shaped eyes held no other color or variation of his base made his eyes look flat to her. There was no depth to them. It seemed so unnatural, especially compared to her own complicated mix. Not that that was the real the reason for their disharmony. There was darkness in him that her father ignored. Emry didn't trust him.

Onyx only nodded once. "I look forward to swearing you to a Knight who will be able to keep you here in your proper place."

"Yes, Father." Emry dropped her gaze to the floor, trying to at least act demure. She wanted no such Knight. She didn't need a cage.

"Sire, we must be on our way," Vardin's voice reminded. The way he spoke always reminded Emry of honey – dark and smooth but sticky enough that you never really wanted to touch it. Ironically enough, the man's hair was the shade of honey. If he didn't slick it back every day, his hair would have reached down to his chin. A somewhat old fashioned style for someone in his mid-thirties.

"Right." Onyx inclined his head toward Emry. "Until the next, daughter."

Emry gave a small curtsy. "Until the next, Father."

She stepped back against the wall to let them pass before continuing on her way. She released her breath out in a rush. With Declan Sharpe as one of her Challengers, the pieces of her carefully planned future were finally falling into place. Yet, he hadn't recognized her. Or rather, he hadn't seen her face.

Tossing a quick glance at her father's back as he rounded the last corner to the stables, Emry tore off down the hall once again at a pace that could hardly be deemed walking. Where was Cit? She desperately needed to tell her sister the news. Fortunately, unlike Emry, there weren't too many places within the palace that Citrine frequented. Emry was able to find her within a few minutes.

Citrine was perched in front of her pianoforte, marking up a sheet of music with some changes she thought sounded better than what the original composer had created. It was a cherished activity of hers.

Freddick lounged in a stuffed armchair near the window of the relatively small parlor. His head was tipped back with his eyes closed, but upon Emry's entrance to the room, he straightened, casting his gaze behind her to see if anyone followed. Emry quickly shook her head to his unspoken question, assuring him he didn't need to rise, and then shut the parlor's thick door. When she turned back to her sister, she noted Citrine had deserted her scribbling and was now facing her.

"Why are you grinning?" Cit asked slowly, her eyes slightly narrowed.

Emry scanned the room to be certain they were alone before responding. "He's here."

"What?" Her sister gasped. "Are you sure? How can you be sure?"

"I saw him." Emry crossed to the window and peered down to the front courtyard, three floors below. Servants and merchants bustled about.

"You did? Where?" Citrine joined her at the window, as if expecting him to be among the servants.

"In the forest, outside the palace."

Cit shot her a doubtful look. "Did you just excite me over nothing?"

"Of course not," Emry retorted. "It was him."

Her sister rolled her eyes and returned to her music. "Seeing a man roaming through the trees who vaguely resembles him is giving into your wishful sentiments."

Emry blinked. "I didn't simply spy a man from a distance. I spoke with him."

"You did what?" Citrine whirled, knocking her papers onto the braided rug.

"I recognized him and decided to drop down to become reacquainted," Emry leaned her shoulder against the window frame, "but he didn't know it was me."

"Drop down?" Citrine frowned. "Were you climbing trees again?"

She smiled sheepishly. "Their shadows called to me."

"Five years can change a young girl dramatically," Freddick spoke up from his seat. "I would have been surprised if he had known you."

"It wasn't that he didn't know my face, he just didn't see it," Emry explained, trying not to bristle at being referred to as a young girl only five years ago.

"It really was him?" Citrine furrowed her brow, still skeptical. "Did you tell him who you are?"

Emry let out a short laugh. "No. The guards caught my scent so I had to disappear."

"Well, I wouldn't hold my breath quite yet." Citrine leaned back onto the keys, releasing a mixed array of notes into the room. "He's not here yet."

She grunted. "A bit pessimistic?"

"You're still certain he's enough of a warrior to merit himself capable of even winning The Trials?" Cit had asked this at least twenty times before.

"Yes," Emry sighed. "I'm not concerned about him failing in the slightest. He's clever enough to make it here early, all the way from Anexia."

"Early?" Cit raised her eyebrows. "Again, he isn't here yet. If he were, wouldn't he have been announced to Father?"

"Not if he was taken straight to the stables," Emry returned. "Father's there now."

Her sister blinked. "Had a run in with Father on your way back into the palace, did you?"

"Yes," Emry grimaced, "and one of your favorite suitors."

"Captain Vardin is *not* one of my suitors," Citrine retorted.

"No?" Emry laughed darkly and lowered herself onto a lilac settee across from Freddick. "The Court and Father believe him to be."

"I'm quite aware of what they think," her sister shot back. "I'm also aware that the man is old enough to be our own father. He's ancient."

"The Court mistakes his nearly forty years for maturity." Emry frowned. "They assume his current responsibilities would have shaped him into the perfect consort."

"You disagree," Freddick stated.

She turned. "You know my opinions on the matter."

Just then, the door to the parlor burst open. All three of them leapt to their feet in surprise. Onyx entered with a smile on his face. Without waiting for a curtsy from his daughters or bow from Freddick, he exclaimed, "The first Challenger has arrived!"

# CHAPTER THREE

The palace wasn't what Declan had expected. It was more like an enormous manor. Or rather several manors joined together to make one massive, elongated building. It was four stories high and crafted of stone in varying soft shades of gray. The roof, which peaked and flattened depending on which part of the palace he was looking at, was copper – aged green from the centuries it had acted as a shield from the weather.

Probably a hundred windows faced him, and that was only on the front. A small section of the palace jutted out in the middle of the structure, with a few steps leading up to at least ten-foot doors that had been painted black. Above the doors, an expansive balcony ran nearly the full length of the palace, along what looked to be the second floor.

On either side of the palace, the pitched roof flattened. These portions were railed with a short stone wall, as if meant for visitors. There was no gate, portcullis, or wall surrounding the palace. That surprised Declan. Anyone could ride up to the paved front courtyard that nearly ran the full expanse of the palace. It was exactly what Declan had done. He'd ridden up to the front before he was directed to the right side of the palace to the stables – around a corner and out of sight from the road.

After arriving at the palace, Declan had not had a

moment's rest, which was incredibly frustrating. The king had been present in the stables with his Captain of the Guard when Declan was ushered in. Following a brief introduction, Declan was whisked away to his temporary chambers, which consisted of a sitting room, an adjoining bathing room, and another room just for his four-post bed and armoire.

Once within his chambers, a maid measured him for what she'd called evening wear. While he was poked and prodded by her, another maid with orange eyes heated his bath. Even though the servants offered him privacy while he soaked his travel-worn muscles, he could hear them rustling about outside the door of his bathing room. When he finally emerged from the bathtub, he found clothes in colors that were only fitting for a woman laid out for him on the bed.

A middle-aged, brown-eyed, manservant with a rather long, flat nose had lingered in his room to help him dress. The man, named Peffun, said that he was to be Declan's valet for the duration of The Trials, unless Declan was expulsed from them.

Peffun wasn't a cheery sort of fellow. He was also very short. Declan wasn't an exceptionally tall man, but Peffun only came up to his shoulders. The volume of Peffun's voice, though, could have been attributed to a man twice his size. As he dressed Declan in more layers than he'd ever worn inside – especially not on an early autumn's day – Peffun instructed him, in a voice that practically rattled the walls, on court behavior and requirements for that evening's events.

There was to be a banquet in his honor, as was expected, where he was to be introduced to the royal family – the Jewels, not that Peffun would ever be caught saying such a name. Declan would be sat beside Princess Emerald so that over the course of the night, they would be able to get to know one another. However, Declan was never to initiate conversation. He was to only speak when spoken to. He was not to touch the food placed before him until, first, the king partook and then his daughters. He was not to discuss The Trials with the princess so as to not upset her emotions, because for some reason it might.

By the time Peffun finished garbing him in the palace finery, Declan was thoroughly dreading an evening of mostly silence beside what sounded like an overly sensitive, spoiled girl. Not to mention, all of Peffun's rules were making his head throb. For the first time, Declan was feeling ill prepared at being a Challenger. It seemed that those months of studying Royal Court protocol had still left him wanting.

The ordeal of dressing had taken so long that when Peffun finally issued his approval of Declan's appearance, a footman was at his door, ready to escort him to the great hall for his banquet. There was no time for rest. It took a great deal of restraint on Declan's part to graciously step past the bed he so desperately wanted to throw himself onto and allow himself to be led out toward the king's Court.

He was instructed to wait outside the hall's massive white doors while the servant went in to announce him. Out of boredom and a little awe, Declan's eyes traced over the intricate carvings within the wood of the doors. They were of the familiar emblems of his country – the crescent and full moon within the same sky above a mighty stallion, standing on three legs, head tilted downward, and its front right leg bent at the knee, bowing to the two faces of the moon. The crescent moon was painted black and the full moon was silver.

The beautiful horse was the palest yellow — almost the same white as the doors.

Inside the hall, the loud rumble of voices had quieted to nothing, in anticipation for the contender. Declan heard the servant clearly ring out, "Thane Dexx, Princess Emerald's Knight Challenger from Anexia!"

Declan's alias reverberated off the walls and out to him as the giant doors that were at least twice his height were slowly swung open, revealing him for the first time to the king and his courtiers. Taking a deep breath to calm his sudden unease at having so many eyes on him, Declan bowed and headed out of the shadows of his hallway into the light of the enormous room.

: : : : :

For a brief moment, Emry panicked when the servant announced Anexia's Challenger to be some Thane Dexx. There had to have been some mistake! She'd seen Declan — she knew she had. Citrine shot her a quick glance across their father, her doubts about whom Emry had encountered clearly resurfacing on her face. Emry dug her fingernails into her palms. She'd seen Declan. He had been sent. It had been him no matter what her sister thought.

Then, the doors were shoved open, and relief washed over her. There he was. Just as beautiful as ever. Straight, angled jaw and nose. Soft lips she'd only ever dared taste once in her dreams. And eyes of brightest teal. His short, black hair gleamed in the light from the candelabras and chandeliers. As for below his face ... Emry tried not to gawk at the wonderfully thick muscles beneath his too-tight tunic. She'd have to thank whoever had measured him incorrectly, making the fit snug.

She accidentally released a sigh in admiration as she, her sister, and her father rose to their feet – a traditional greeting for an honored guest. Declan bowed at the waist, before emerging toward them.

The hundred or so members of the Royal Court remained silent and seated as Declan moved between their four long tables – placed vertically, as opposed to the royal family's horizontal table. Emry wished to catch his eye, but his gaze didn't wander away from her father's face. She nearly rolled her eyes at such strict adherence to protocol. When he was within a few steps of her table, he stopped and went down to one knee on the marble floor, bowing his head.

"Rise," her father commanded.

The entire room stood, followed by Declan. Onyx smiled. "Welcome, Challenger of Anexia. My daughter, Princess Citrine Agatha Nylles and her Knight, Freddick Zembe of Glavenryl," he gestured to his left where Citrine stood with Freddick at her left.

Declan turned his body slightly so as to face Citrine and bowed at the waist again. "A pleasure, dear princess."

Onyx took Emry's hand when Declan straightened, and said, "This, Challenger, is your Princess Emerald Celeste Nylles."

Emry knew the moment he recognized her. Saw it in his face. The absolute shock. As if a stranger had slapped him. He nearly stumbled back a step. His eyes grew large, and his mouth fell open. He forgot to bow. "The– the greatest pleasure, dearest princess," he managed to stammer out the formal address. Only a princess's Knight or Challenger was permitted to address his princess as *dearest* in front of another princess.

His stunned reaction warmed Emry's insides, and she had to bite the inside of her lip to stop herself from grinning. He remembered her. They hadn't seen each other in years, but he remembered her.

Her father didn't seem as impressed. He frowned at Declan. "Join us," he said and dropped Emry's hand after a brief squeeze to extend it toward the empty seat to her right.

Declan obeyed. His eyes never left her face, not even when he lowered himself into his seat. As the guest of honor, he sat first, followed by the rest of the royal table, and then finally the courtiers. When everyone was seated again, conversation returned, and the hall was noisy once more. The servants then began distributing the first course.

Under the cover of many voices, Emry half-whispered to Declan, "So, is Thane a family name?"

He was still gaping. "Emry," he breathed.

The sound of her name on his lips ... Emry took a steadying breath. It'd been so long. Years. It had been five years since she'd last been within arm's length of him, since she could smell him. His scent hit her, and she nearly shut her eyes. Balsam and cedar and some other musk that was entirely his own. He'd been too far away in the woods earlier for her to have enjoyed it. But now, practically brushing elbows with him, it was perfect. Just as she remembered. Exactly as he'd smelled in her dreams – the dreams she'd never admitted to having, not even to her sister.

She held his gaze. "Hello, Declan."

"It was you in the woods." His eyes roamed her face, as if he'd find an answer written on it.

"Yes." She gave him a small smile. "That was me."

"You're the princess," he said it as though he had

to hear himself speak the words in order to believe them.

"What gave it away?" She smirked, taking a sip from her goblet. It was an excuse to glance away from the intensity in his gaze.

Declan watched her every move. Her every breath. "Ewan…"

"He died," she replied quietly.

"Why-" His voice cracked on the word. "Why didn't either of you tell me?"

This was not the place to have this conversation. "I can't answer that," she grimaced, "at least not here."

That seemed to wake him up from his stunned haze. He blinked and swept his eyes around the hall. As if suddenly remembering they weren't alone. He stared down at the plate in front of him for a moment before picking up his fork. He didn't take a bite, though. No, he just sat there, lightly rapping the tines of his fork against the edge of his plate. His breathing was ragged, shallow even.

Emry realized she should have warned him. Someone should have warned him. It wasn't right for him to find out this way, in front of everyone. Without a way for her to explain.

"How have you been?" He asked, so low she almost missed it.

"I've been well." Emry bit the tip of her tongue. "And yourself?"

He loosed a short, almost bitter laugh without lifting his eyes from his untouched food. "Well enough."

She nodded, watching as his fork continued to tap the plate. "Declan, eat," she pleaded. "I promise to answer your questions, just not here. Not now."

The fork paused in the air. He glanced up at her

with such pain in his eyes that Emry drew in a quick breath. But then it was gone in a flash, and he bent his head over his plate. He took a bite. "Your hair is different."

"I know." Her hair had been much lighter then.

"Why do we match?"

"Match?" She blinked.

He waved his hand back and forth between them. "Our clothes are the same color."

"Oh, that." Emry grunted, a little relieved at the shift in topic. "At formal events, such as these, Knights, or Challengers, wear the same colors as their princess. See how my sister and Freddick are both in blue?"

"Are you particularly fond of lavender? Is this a color you wear often?" He'd aimed for nonchalance, but he didn't quite hit the mark.

Emry's smile spread slowly. "No, my maid picked this for me. She said it would make my eyes shimmer."

"Well, she's right about that." He nodded his head once as he took another bite. "*You* look lovely in it."

She tilted her head to one side, silently accepting his compliment. Ignoring the warmth that once again swept through her. "Do you lack self-confidence in lavender?"

Declan actually flushed a little, and Emry chuckled. "You have nothing to fear," she assured him. "No woman mistook you for anything but absolutely masculine when you walked in."

With the way that tunic fit him, it was the truth. During the five years they'd been apart, his features had shifted from that of a fresh-faced youth to an experienced young man. Emry found her gaze wandering to his mouth as he ate. At those lips ... She forced herself to pry her eyes away only to find him smirking at her.

He'd noticed where her attention had lingered.

"Did you like what you saw?"

A younger Emry would have blushed. But now, she merely said coyly, "It would be rude of me to injure your self-esteem during your special night."

"How generous of you." His smile turned crooked, and Emry had to look away again.

Her heart was racing as she raised her fork to her mouth. Her mind barely registered the food her tongue savored. All she saw were images of him that her own subconscious had concocted while she'd slept. She'd been dreaming of him for the past three years. Off and on. Short snippets of conversation by a moonlit pond she'd never visited outside of her sleep. Peaceful walks through mountain forests that smelled of pine. She'd often wake feeling the lines of reality and slumber blurred.

Fortunately, she hadn't had one in months. She'd convinced herself that she was finally over whatever subliminal obsession she might have had with him. Had figured she'd worked him out of her system.

Now, though, once again in his presence, she felt the full force of the lies she'd been feeding herself. She wouldn't be surprised if she started dreaming of him again that night.

: : : : :

Declan couldn't stop staring at Emry. The princess. His princess – the one he was to eventually betray. The shock of seeing her again had worn off, only to be replaced with dread. If he had known Emry was Princess Emerald … he didn't let himself finish that thought. He took a deep gulp from the sweet liquid in his cup instead, as his eyes drank in her features once more.

Raven black hair was twisted up on top of her head in an elaborate braid with several curls escaping their pins in strategically fashionable disarray. The current Enn trend. Shapely dark eyebrows sat high above large eyes – eyes that were silver and gray and black. Complex eyes. Shimmering, ethereal eyes that upon first look were practically impossible to guess her actual base color. But Declan knew what they were – silver. Emry was a silver-eyed. Rare and lovely.

Below her eyes were high cheekbones and plump, rounded pink lips. He forced his gaze not to dwell on them. Between her eyes, her almost straight nose jutted out with an ever so slight bump in it at its bridge. He doubted anyone would even notice that her nose was just barely crooked. He honestly wouldn't have either, except her sister shared the same nose. Princess Citrine's nose upon closer inspection – as Declan now did across Emry and the king – was identical with its crest at its bridge. Yet, it was perfectly centered between her eyes. Emry's must had been broken before. That was new – an addition from the last time he'd seen her in person.

This little revelation drew Declan's brow together. He knew Emry had always been adventurous. Today confirmed that that hadn't changed. She was willing to don boy's clothing and climb trees. Yet, something was different in the way she carried herself.

Gone was the girl he'd first met. Had known years ago. In her place, this poised woman sat before him. Calculating and certain in every word she spoke. It was as if the one mar of her crooked nose, on her otherwise flawless face, had given Emry a confidence her sister didn't quite share. It spoke of courage and failure and experience. Declan decided it was her best feature, even lovelier than her expressive eyes.

"What are you thinking?" Emry asked without turning to him. She'd felt his scrutiny.

He took another swig from his goblet. "When did you break your nose?"

Emry's head snapped around, gawking at him. Her mouth moved as if chewing on her words, but no sound emerged. Finally, "No one has ever noticed. Not even Cit. I had to point it out to her. How did-" she paused, recollecting herself. "You've discovered one of my vain insecurities."

"Come on," he grunted. "Secretly, you must admire it."

She stared at him. "Why would I admire a flaw?"

"Because it was no doubt a token from some past incident that has inevitably made you stronger, or shaped your character." He jerked his chin toward her sister, who was currently conversing with the king. "I doubt your sister has ever done anything to give herself such a mark."

"No," she let out a short laugh, "no, she has not."

"So, how did it happen?" He asked, finishing the last bite on his plate. A servant quickly removed it from the table.

"It was from a tree trunk," she answered softly, her eyes distant. "I was tossed into it."

He frowned. "Who tossed you?"

The pensive look she gave him made him feel as though he should already know the answer. She shook her head. "Not tonight. We can go over that later, too."

The next course was served. It was almost time for the entertainment of the evening – a musical troupe. Discussion during their performance would not only be limited but also considered rude. Declan's window for open communication with Emry was closing. In less than an hour, their opportunity to converse would end until the third Trial – the Challenger's Ball. That was if he lived past the first two Trials. Also, at the Ball, he'd be sharing her with the other Challengers. The thought that this evening was his only chance until after The Trials to speak with her freely grated on his nerves.

Declan grasped at something to say, to break their silence. The best he came up with was, "Any inside pointers on how I might win The Trials?"

"Unfortunately, I am not permitted to know the details of The Trials," she told him. "But even if I was, I don't know if I'd tell you. You must win on your own merit."

He winced. "No need to remind me."

"I don't think you have anything to worry about," she replied. "I've seen you fight. I know you're quick."

"That's just the teal in me," he said, tapping the side of his eye with one finger.

The musicians were setting up their instruments for their performance. Declan's time was running out. The Rioter in him wasn't very accepting of keeping with Trial traditions. He needed more time with Emry. Craved it, even. On impulse, he leaned in, putting his mouth close to her ear. "Do you go into the woods every day?"

Emerald stiffened slightly. Yet, she didn't pull back. Instead, she twisted her head so that her mouth neared his ear as well. "Whenever the opportunity presents itself."

"Will the opportunity be present tomorrow?" If anyone overheard such a bold question, the palace guards would probably have tossed him out.

She didn't seem at all ruffled by it. "It might," she said slowly. "Why?"

Declan wasn't able to respond. The king loudly clearing his throat made them both separate immediately. Onyx narrowed his eyes at Declan before rising to his feet. After a second too long, he peeled his gaze away to the musicians. With one hand, he waved for the troupe to begin and then lowered back into his ebony, high-backed, cushioned chair.

As the music filled the hall, Declan forced himself to focus on the entertainment rather than the princess. It took a great deal of effort. Although the troupe was probably the best he'd ever heard, he hardly enjoyed any of it. Emry distracted him. He felt robbed of finishing their discussion. Frivolous Royals with all their formalities. No Anexian would have thought conversation during a recital rude. Music in Anexia was usually more for background noise rather than the main event, unless dancing was involved.

Almost two hours later, the troupe sang their last tune to much applause. Declan clapped more from relief than anything else. While the musicians removed themselves, dessert was dished out.

"Finally," Emry breathed. "That was the longest concert I think I've ever sat through."

Declan gaped. She'd held the same opinion? "Was it?"

"A new type of torture." She nodded.

"That's being a bit dramatic," he drawled.

"I'm still waiting for you to tell me why."

"I often go riding in the late afternoon."

"During the heat of the day?" Emry blinked. "Most in Breccan nap at that time."

"So I'm told," he replied. "Must make it easy to go

unnoticed."

Mischief flashed in her eyes. "Such an amateur. No, everyone resting makes for many tired and irritable eyes, willing to rip to shreds anyone who accidentally disturbs them."

"When would you suggest then?" He raised an eyebrow.

"During meals," she cast her voice a touch lower, "when the eyes are on the food set in front of them."

"Noted."

The king had finished his dessert. He stood and the rest of the room did the same, whether or not they were done with their own. Declan had barely touched his. Oddly enough, he wasn't upset about it.

"Until the next," King Onyx bid the hall.

"Until the next, my king," came the response in unison.

Those words signaled the end of the banquet. Scattered conversations filled the hall as its occupants slowly exited. King Onyx nodded once to Declan as he passed him. Declan gave a small bow. Princess Citrine and her Knight had disappeared already, leaving Declan alone with Emry beside the table.

"Oh, I'm so full from this evening, I don't think I'll be hungry until lunch tomorrow," Emerald said with a smile.

"Until the next, dearest princess." Declan winked and bowed.

"Until the next, Challenger Dexx." She emphasized the *ck* sound of his alias before finishing with the *s*. "Good fortune at The Trials."

# CHAPTER FOUR

Emry couldn't sleep. She'd been lying in bed for over an hour now. It was almost midnight. She could feel it within her – tingling down her spine, aching. Releasing a groan, she sat up, her comforter pooling onto her lap. She wouldn't be able to sleep much tonight, not with the full moon outside calling to her.

Deciding she'd fought the urge long enough, Emry slid out of her bed and reached for her satin robe. For the hundredth time, she was grateful she'd picked the color black for it, rather than the cream her sister had pleaded with her to choose. The black ankle-length robe, along with her ink black hair, made it easy for her to slip through the palace unnoticed at night without even touching her abilities.

Quickly tying her robe's sash around her, she snatched a pair of black ankle boots before heading out of her chambers, still barefoot. She'd put on the boots when she reached the stables.

Keeping to the shadows, down hallways Emry could have traversed blindfolded, she made it to the stables' door without any unwanted eyes spotting her. She yanked on her boots while still moving and hurried out of the palace into the familiar warmth and stench of the stables. The sleeping animals didn't heed her arrival, and she didn't wish to rouse them.

The night sky summoned, and she accepted its

command. Hot energy welled up inside of her, flushing through her veins, threatening to erupt out of her. She was moving too slowly. Her body, now that she'd finally heeded the call, craved to be outside under the moon. Required it. Like lungs needing air. Emry broke into a run, unable to contain the tension building inside of her.

The two giant stable doors to outside – doors that could fit two carriages passing side-by-side when open – were fastened shut in front of her. Emry didn't decrease her speed, though. There was no need to have them ajar tonight, not while the moon demanded her presence beneath it.

A silvery ray of light shone through the inch-thin rift between the massive doors Emry could never open by herself. The moonlight splayed over the dirt and hay floor as an invitation to Emry. Fully sprinting now with her robe flapping behind her, Emry's laugh bubbled out of her. She loved a full moon, if for no other reason than it allowed her to run on light.

Tipping back her head, Emry lunged into that sliver of illumination. Just when she should have collided into the wood doors, she became shadow, sliding through the doors to emerge a moment later on the other side of them. Without skipping a beat, Emry solidified and continued to run. Now enveloped completely in the moonlight that cascaded onto the world, Emry was able to double her natural speed. She basked in the euphoria of her pace as she watched the land pass beneath her feet. It was only during a full moon that she slid through the world like a Teal.

Once almost to the surrounding woods, Emry came to a stop. She was panting, but not from being out of breath. She felt invigorated – as if she merely survived the days when the moon ran its cycles, never fully living until it was full again. Every month it was this way. Why had she thought to skip it tonight? Sleep could never fill her the way the moon did.

Slowly, Emry stretched her arms wide and angled her face upward, welcoming the light. It bathed her in its beams. Tingling and soothing. Warm and cool, all at once. She breathed it in deeply, storing as much as she could within her. Only when wrapped in moonlight did she ever feel this content, complete, and happy. All her fears, doubts, and troubles seemed to dissipate, leaving her with simple, pure joy.

"Emry?"

Emry nearly jumped out of her own skin. She clamped her hands over her mouth to quiet her shriek and whirled. "D-Declan?" She stammered. Her euphoria was gone. The moon didn't welcome Declan.

He stood there gaping at her. His short hair was plastered to one side of his head, most likely where he'd fallen asleep on it. He wore a plain white linen shirt, the collar open to reveal some of his chest, and gray trousers, partially stuffed into knee-high black boots, as if put on in a great hurry. The disarray of his appearance made Emry suddenly remember that she was in nothing more than her shift below her satin robe.

She quickly folded her arms across her chest, pulling the robe tighter around her. "Were you following me?"

It took him a moment to find his voice again. "You went through the crack between the doors." He stopped, taking a breath. "You disappeared."

"You saw me?" She exclaimed, stunned.

"I've never seen anyone do what you did."

Emry decided to deflect his upcoming interrogation

with one of her own. "What were you even doing in the stables?"

"I might ask you the same thing," he shot back. "I fell asleep in a stall after the banquet and woke to find you heading straight for the doors. But then you..." His voice trailed off. "You ran like a Teal."

"And only a Teal could have caught up with me so fast," she grumbled. "Why were you there?"

His face, cast with a blue tinge from the moonlight, still held unbelief. "Does it matter? Sneaking off during the day is completely different than going out alone at night."

She blinked. Was he worried for her safety? "No one can harm me tonight."

"Tonight?" He stared at her. "Why would tonight be any different than other nights?"

"The moon is full," she said as if that explained it, knowing that it probably only confused him further. She sighed and shivered, finally feeling the chill of the night air. "I think we should head back before either of us are missed."

"Why? Have you suddenly obtained some semblance of caution?" He shook his head, taking a few steps closer to her.

Emry winced. "It's for your sake. My father wouldn't look kindly on us being discovered alone together before The Trials."

He grunted. "I have a feeling his opinion doesn't matter much to you."

It was the truth. Not about everything. But on many things, it was the truth. How he'd figured that out for himself so quickly, though ... She frowned. "What makes you think that?"

"Does your father like it when you wander the

woods alone?" Declan quipped. "Or does he not know?"

She opened her mouth to retort, but he sank onto the grass, as if he didn't need to hear her response to know her answer. He leaned forward over his raised knees and raked his hands through his hair, head bent. His posture – that position – here in the moonlight, it reminded her of how he'd looked in so many of her dreams. Her breath hitched, and she lowered herself to the ground in front of him, flattening the grass beneath her.

They sat there in silence for a moment, until Declan said without lifting his head, "We're alone now. Mind telling me why you and Ewan were pretending to be common in Anexia?"

"We lived in a manor," she grunted. "We clearly weren't pretending to be common."

He stopped scraping his scalp and glanced up. "Ewan's death ... those weren't Rioters."

"I know." She sighed. "Only Cit believed me, though, when I tried to tell my father. He and his advisors thought I was too young, dealing with too much too fast. But I was there," she said bitterly. "Those men that attacked us – they weren't Anexian."

Declan watched Emry. The anger in her eyes. This was the girl he'd carried into the forest that night. Carried because her brother had made him promise to keep her safe. Emry was the reason Declan hadn't been able to help her brother fight. When those men had attacked them, Ewan had shouted for Declan to run as fast as he could with Emry – to make sure she wasn't near the danger. But Declan hadn't known she was the princess. That Ewan was the heir. He'd been a Royal all along. Declan's friend, who had died because he hadn't been there to help. Because of Emry, who had needed his protection. Grief rose up in his throat, leaving him raw inside.

"I was told you'd died," he said hoarsely.

"That doesn't surprise me." She hugged her knees to her chest. "My father never allowed me back into Anexia after Ewan was murdered."

"I broke your nose." Declan just realized the small fact. He'd tripped that night, and she'd flown from his arms. He'd picked her back up so quickly that he hadn't noticed the blood dripping onto his shirt until much later.

"You did." She smiled slightly. "But you also saved me."

"Why go by Ewan and Emry?"

"It was what our family called us," she replied. "Ewan hated his actual name."

"All this time..." His voice faded out. He took a breath. "Ewan was the heir."

Emry nodded, her eyes on her bare feet. "He wanted you to know, but one of my father's stipulations about us living in Anexia was that no one could know our titles. You were the closest friend he'd ever had."

"We patrolled side by side on the Quirl border all those months, and I never even guessed," Declan said more to himself than to her. He furrowed his brow. "All this time I thought it was Royals that had attacked, but he was one. If it wasn't Royals or Rioters, then who?"

She shrugged. "My father never discusses matters of the state with me, so I only have theories."

"Really?" He blinked. "Never?"

"Never." She was now glaring at her feet. He'd apparently struck a nerve.

Declan moaned as a new thought struck him. "I volunteered to be Ewan's little sister's Knight. Now I *have* to win. I can't let anyone else be in charge of little Emry's safety."

"Little Emry?" She blinked. "You do realize I'm an adult, right?"

"Barely," he retorted. "It's been what, a month? Two?"

"You know I can't divulge my actual birthday."

"Right." He rolled his eyes. "Not until your wedding day. Some silly, nonsensical, uniquely Enn tradition."

She smirked. "I've been told men appreciate a woman with a little mystery."

"Have they been feeding you those lies since birth?"

"I spent the first half of my life in Anexia," she shot back, somewhat sourly. "No one ever seems to recall the outright exile of my mother, the king's consort, and her daughters."

Most had forgotten that detail, or chosen to ignore it. Honestly, Declan had been too young to care about the affairs of the Jewels, but he did vaguely remember hearing about how Onyx's father's advisors banished the queen from the capital because she was Anexian. King Onyx, not wanting to ruffle any feathers at the start of his reign, hadn't pushed for his wife's presence. Yet, as time passed he never did correct the wrong toward his wife – never established her by his side. Declan's mother, for some reason, had been especially upset, ranting about it as if it had been a personal offense.

The king's consort had stayed in Anexia until her death, nearly a decade ago. Declan's mother had wept for days. He'd never really understood why. One of his older sisters had suggested it was because the first

Anexian consort they'd had in three centuries was dead before she'd been given the chance to make a difference. That had satisfied Declan's curiosity at the time. Looking back on it, though, his mother wasn't really the type to mourn a stranger as she had. It was a little unsettling that she'd lamented the woman who had married a Jewel.

"So, are you going to tell me why you fell asleep in what I hope was an empty horse stall rather than your own bed?" Emry's voice roused him from his thoughts.

"It'd been a long day." He shrugged. "I went for a run after dinner."

Emry let out a short laugh. "A run? To calm yourself?" She shook her head. "You're such a Teal. No one runs for pleasure."

He raised an eyebrow. "You just did."

"My running was to a destination," she sniffed. "It's different."

"Your destination was to the middle of a field."

"No." She tilted her head upward and spread her arms wide as she had been doing when he'd found her. "It was to be under the moon."

"Why?"

"Because Silvers love a good full moon," she said simply.

He scowled. She knew he didn't understand. "How long were you planning on staying out here?"

"Until I'd had my fill."

Declan stared at her. These weren't really answers. "You're not making sense on purpose."

"I know." She pushed herself to her feet. "I'd better get back to my rooms."

Declan frowned, also rising. "Will I see you tomorrow still?"

"Perhaps," she smirked. Then, "Why do you wish to go riding with me?"

That caught him off guard. "Don't you think we have some catching up to do? I don't think I can wait an entire week or more to talk to you again."

"That's right. You always were impatient."

"*I'm* the one impatient?" He gave her a crooked smile. "I'm not the one who couldn't wait thirty seconds to open a door."

"That door would've taken me far longer to open and you know it," she retorted. "I'm astonished you made it out so fast."

He tapped the corner of his eye. "It's the teal."

A breeze picked up a few stray strands of hair from her braid, tossing them across her face. Emry brushed them behind her ears as Declan offered her his hand to escort her back. "Shall we?"

Emry gazed upward at the moon and shook her head. "No, tonight I'll run like a Teal." With that, she tore off through the meadow, Declan right beside her.

: : : :

The next three days released a torrential downpour onto Breccan and the palace, brought in by a westward wind from the Sea of Dridd. Declan didn't go riding with Emry. On the morning of the planned ride, he received a forbidden note from her that had been slipped under his door, calling off their arrangement due to inclement weather. A storm from the Dridd was like nothing he'd ever experienced before. High winds whistled into the cracks of the palace, while the heavy rain covered it like a blanket, giving the illusion of being under water. It was relentless. Sometimes it would fade to a light drizzle, but no more than for a few minutes before returning to its onslaught. Declan feared flooding, yet, the palace never did. The land surrounding it was surprisingly well drained.

All of the water outside, however, confined him to his chambers and the few rooms in the palace he was permitted to venture. Peffun was kind enough to remind him often that he was not to go near the Jewels. For some reason, the man took it upon himself to follow Declan through the palace during the storm, at a polite distance. Peffun was never too far to steer him clear of ever running into the princesses or their father. Having a constant watchdog at his heels annoyed Declan to the point that he spent little time wandering. At least, not at normal speeds. The man had to be part hound, because as soon as Declan ceased his Teal speed in the palace, Peffun arrived mere minutes later. So, Declan spent much of his time in his room, where he was safely alone. It made for a very dull three days, though.

Declan ate, looked out the window, ate some more, paced, read a few pages here and there from books he'd borrowed from the palace's library, ate again, and slept. And ran. He ran through every inch of the palace, excluding private chambers, and then ran it again and again. For three days. He'd never been so bored in his life. It didn't help, either, knowing that Emry and he were under the same roof and forced to be separate. Left with little to occupy his time, he was alone with his thoughts. And he was going mad.

When he'd volunteered himself as a candidate for The Trials, he'd had no idea that the princess he was to win over and then kidnap was Emry. Ewan's younger sister, Emry. He wanted to believe that it wasn't true —

that girl and the current Emry didn't even share the same hair color. Younger Emry had been an ash blonde, while this Emry's hair was obviously black. To have her hair darken so drastically in only five years seemed almost impossible. But he couldn't lie to himself. That beautiful, exquisite woman was Emry. The one he hadn't been able to forget, even after she'd disappeared from Anexia.

Emry hadn't grown since he'd last seen her. Standing beside each other, she still reached a little above his shoulders. Her face had changed – lost some of its former roundness for sharper angles. Her eyes, though, were exactly as he remembered.

Declan wanted to roar with the unfairness of it all. To have her alive, and near, after believing her dead for over a year, only to have her be ripped away from him. By his own future betrayal. He was sent to Enn by The Mistress herself. To lure Emry into trusting him before he snatched her away to Anexia as a bargaining tool to force negotiations with Onyx. All for the glory of the Rioters.

The Feud had gone on for far too long. The Rioters were willing to seek out a more peaceful solution before resorting to violence. To be used as the Challenger for The Mistress was a great honor. He'd been happy to do it. To help his people through the use of his unique skill set. But now, knowing that Emerald was Emry, the notion nauseated him. How could he bring her to Anexia with the possibility of danger greeting her there? He'd sworn to her brother that he'd keep her safe.

Even though Ewan had been the Crown Prince, deceiving Declan about his identity, he had been his closest friend and ally at the time. Ewan had been brilliant, charming, daring, and fiercely loyal. They'd met the winter after Declan turned sixteen. They were assigned to the same barrack for the required ten-month training program all Anexian-blooded male adolescents were to complete should they ever be required to protect the Quirl border. As there had been peace with Quirl for decades, it was more of a right-of-passage when Declan went through than actually necessary.

The first few weeks of Declan's acquaintance with Ewan weren't anything special. They followed orders and were civil enough to each other. It wasn't until two months later that they really connected – during one night that they both had been posted to the midnight perimeter watch. It was the custom of the fort to use its plebes as guards. Little did Declan know as he began that auspicious shift that he'd be spending it with the young heir to his nation. That night blew by in laughter as Declan got to know Ewan more fully. From that night until the one when Ewan was murdered – almost two years later– Declan was hardly ever separated from him.

For five years, Declan had endured the void of his friend's death. Despite his promise, it'd pained him that he hadn't been right alongside Ewan, fighting for their lives. Yet, he knew what Ewan had asked of him had been the correct choice. Declan was a Teal. He was faster than those attackers, and Emry had been unable to fend for herself. Ewan saw the need to protect her above himself.

But Emry being Princess Emerald wasn't what Declan had signed up for. Ewan had been more a brother than a friend to him, which made Emry practically family. Could he knowingly lead her to her potential demise? He wasn't so certain he could.

The Princess Emerald he'd anticipated encountering should have been nothing more than a random renowned beauty, rivaled only by her sister. Both sisters were famous for their good looks throughout all of Enlennd, even stretching so far as Heerth. The infamy, however, had misled Declan into believing that Princess Emerald was merely a conceited, spoiled, overly pampered pretty peacock with the personality of a bland cracker. He'd feared his hours spent in her company would have been painful. Turns out, it was much worse than that. Instead of finding her boring, he'd discovered her to be the older version of that tenacious and energetic girl he'd secretly been mourning since his father had told him she'd died. As soon as he returned to Anexia, he and his father would have a serious chat.

Emry's abilities were another topic that made Declan's head spin. She could evaporate through cracks, materializing on the other side, and run as fast as most Teals. He didn't know much about the capabilities of a silver-eyed. When he'd seen her around the manor with Ewan, she'd never used her abilities in front of him, which wasn't unusual. Most people didn't develop to their full potential until they reached adulthood – sixteen for women and eighteen for men. He'd tried to research what Silvers could do, but hadn't found much from the books in the palace library.

One of the books Declan had selected was on all known eye colors and their respective recorded abilities. However, it was a very dry read with more emphasis on how patterns are formed over time in the veining and speckling of eyes. Apparently, six or so generations back, at the time of the book's publication, it was common for people to have more than two colors in their eyes. Emry would have fit in nicely with them. All this time he thought her mixed colors unique, when really, she was simply traditional.

Releasing a moan, Declan slowly pushed himself onto his feet. He'd been snacking at the small circular table off to one side of his room. It sat only one, and barely comfortably. He didn't think it was supposed to be used for every meal, as he'd been doing. If not for all the rain, Declan would have been sent out to the training yards with the palace guards so as to practice whichever skill he wished in preparation for The Trials. He would've made some new friends and taken his meals in the barracks between his sparring sessions. Too bad the storm shut everyone up inside, even the guards. No one ventured out.

A knock sounded on Declan's chamber's door. It was most likely Peffun again, coming to check on him. No one else came to his door. Pulling a face, Declan sank back into his chair. "Come in."

Peffun strode inside. After a short bow, he addressed the Challenger, "Sir, your attendance is requested this evening by the royal family to attend a banquet honoring Princess Emerald's Challenger of the Midlands."

"The Mid arrived today?" Declan blurted. "In this weather?"

"Yes, sir," Peffun practically scoffed at Declan's outburst. The man probably found him boorish and frowned upon on all Anexians.

Declan blew his breath out in a rush, taking in this new information. He'd get to see Emry, but from a distance. She'd be seated next to her father and the Mid, while he'd be placed somewhere amid the courtiers. At this point, after three days of having only Peffun as a companion, he'd take any outing that included people. He turned to Peffun. "What color will I be wearing tonight?"

:  :  :  :  :

He was watching her again. Emry could practically feel it. Declan's eyes had scarcely left her all evening. Curse this infernal rain! She would've liked nothing more than to tear off out of the palace with him on a wild ride, but not even she was foolish enough to go out in this. It didn't make sense that the man seated to her right had traveled through it. And he called himself a Mid! He should've known better.

Residents of the Midlands were merchants and lake fisherman, inhabiting an expanse of land that was mostly covered in water. Mids were hard working, steady folk. They lived with the land and water, studied its seasons. The vicious storms of Enn often traveled eastward over the Midlands before shifting North and mellowing over the Kruth Mountains. Mids knew the intensity of the storms well. The rain would swell their lakes and ponds, turning their green lands into swamps. Emry wasn't sure there was a Mid alive who would traverse an Enn storm when there was time to wait it out. That included the man beside her.

Cadoc Ernst was a giant of a man. Emry counted herself of average female height, and she didn't even come up to Cadoc's shoulder. His shaggy, pale blond hair went just past his sharp jaw, with strands hanging over his forehead, hooding his oval eyes. He was a base vibrant green – the color of new leaves – with thick veins of black threaded throughout, which meant he dealt with nature and had immense strength. Cadoc's arms and chest gave Emry no doubt of his strength. The validity of him being a Mid, however, was a different story.

For one thing, Cadoc's accent and sentence structure sounded nothing like the guttural tones of a Mid. Even the Mids who had relocated there spoke differently. Then, there was the sheer size of him. Mids were very average, neither tall nor short – having a great many citizens with mixed-blood from all the regions. Finally, there was the way he acted and carried himself. From the moment Cadoc swaggered into the hall, he demanded attention. Yes, he was attractive, but he seemed aware of it. He was confident and a little brash. This was not the behavior of a Mid. Residents of the Midlands were known to be unpretentious and reserved. Cadoc was neither, at least, not during the last hour.

"It looks to be me competition only has eyes for you this evening, dearest princess," Cadoc casually commented as he took a deep swig from his chalice.

Emry glanced up from her plate and caught Declan's gaze once more. It wasn't hard to pick him out of the sea of courtiers. He was the only one, other than Emry and Cadoc, dressed in coral and mint. She broke eye contact first, though, forcing her gaze to Cadoc. "Are you certain I'm the one he watches? Perhaps it is you he scrutinizes."

Cadoc snorted. "No, dearest princess, that be not the look a man gives his competitor."

"Then what look would you say he's giving us?" Emry asked.

"Just trust me, dearest princess." Cadoc winked at her. "He be not staring at me."

The wink was the final straw. This man was *not* a Mid. Emry had spent nearly five months in the Midlands. Not once had she seen a single Mid wink. They were too proper for that. Now, as for Emry's time in Kruth...

"I believe congratulations are in order," Emry said, deliberately changing the subject.

"For being yer Challenger, dearest princess?" He raised an eyebrow.

"Precisely." She leaned closer to him so that they wouldn't be overheard. "My only question is where did you accost my former Challenger to steal his letter of authenticity?"

Cadoc sat back in his chair, a smile tugging at his mouth. He was amused. "What you be insinuating, dearest princess?"

"Oh, I'm not insinuating," she countered. "It's an absolute statement of fact. You are no a Mid – you're a Kruth."

"You be mistaken. As you can read for yerself, in me papers, I'm yer Midlands Challenger." He swallowed the rest of his half-full chalice in one gulp. A maid quickly refilled it.

Emry frowned. The past three days of being in the same building as Declan but unable to speak with him had been tedious. Her confinement to the indoors had not helped her mood, either. Cadoc was obviously a Kruth. She was finding her patience with his charade thinning.

Challenger papers didn't have names on them, only the region from which they'd come. It made stealing them even more enticing. Cadoc had claimed the papers on his own and made it to the palace during an immense tempest. No one would eject him from The Trials at this point, not even if he'd killed the former Challenger. It was an old law that Enlennd adhered to strictly – if the contestant was robbed of his papers then he was unfit to be Knight, or so went the logic of Emry's ancestors.

"Why do you hide where you're from?" Emry spoke her thoughts out loud. "Do you not wish to give your region credit, should you succeed at The Trials? Have they wronged you?"

Cadoc regarded her with a frown of his own. "You be quite perceptive for one so pretty, dearest princess."

She grunted. "Then, are you suggesting you were surrounded by dimwits in Kruth? I don't think there has ever been a child born to your region without great beauty. Ugliness is not something with which Kruths are burdened."

"We be not short on charm, either." He winked again.

"Nor pride," she shot back. "So, why do you refuse to be acknowledged as the clever Kruth who stole the Mid's spot?"

"Me kind mother was a Mid," he said softly. "I be not wanting her people put down."

Honorable of him. Surprising and a little impressive. "But," she prodded, "you did take the Mid's papers?"

"What choice did I have?" He shrugged. "Me own region denied me."

Emry furrowed her brow. "Why would they do such a thing? You seem very ... capable." She inclined her head toward one of his biceps that looked as though it could burst the seams of his waistcoat at any given moment.

Whoever the maid was that measured the Challengers had to be either terrible at her job or brilliant. The extra snug fit was well worth admiring. Emry couldn't help but gawk a little herself. Cadoc's pectorals were enormous.

"They feared I be too impetuous, comparatively," he replied a little bitterly. "Assumed I'd do something rash."

"You? Do something rash?" Emry flashed him a grin. "Never."

# CHAPTER FIVE

Two more days passed without much change. The rain and wind bullied the roof and walls of the palace, while lightning and thunder joined the mix every so often. Emry had had her fill of it all. This storm was one of the longest Emry could remember. She was about ready to curse the elements. She wasn't meant to be kept indoors for so long – she craved the opportunity to be under the open sky again. Being cooped up with Citrine, Freddick, and, occasionally, her father for nearly a week, was starting to wear on her nerves. She loved her family. Their company wasn't what bothered her – it was being a prisoner to her home because of the weather.

After taking her evening meal with her family and Freddick in the palace's smallest dining room, she'd decided to not go straight to bed as she let Fanny assume when the girl came to help her undress and plait her hair. Once Fanny had left her alone in her shift, she donned her favorite robe again and snuck off to the library, which was located in the opposite wing from her family's rooms. She made it there without anyone noticing, barefoot of course. Shoes – slippers included – only made for noisy steps.

Once inside with the library door shut firmly behind her, Emry made her way to her favorite spot – the settee in front of the immense floor-to-ceiling window that looked out over the palace gardens. It was at the back of the hexagon-shaped room and was the obvious focal point. The ceiling was twenty or so feet above with built-in shelves going the full span of each wall. Five wooden ladders on rails, allowing them to slide back and forth easily, were attached one per wall.

Within the confines of the room itself were eleven freestanding shelves, which created aisles. These shelves were barely shorter than those of the walls, each having ladders of their own. Couches, benches, and chairs were placed sporadically throughout the space for the comfort of readers. The whole effect was relatively inviting, yet, Emry rarely had any company whenever she visited. Her father was never much for reading, and Citrine thought the room stifling with only the one window. Since the library was only for her family and the infrequent special guest, Emry generally had the library to herself, which was also a reason why she was drawn to it.

Because of the way the aisles were situated, anyone who sat in front of the window was shielded from the door. Emry had privacy here. The library was her retreat. During storms, she'd escape at night to sit in front of the window, in attempt to catch any stray beams of moonlight that managed to sneak through the cloud cover. When she was forced to remain indoors, this was her consolation. Over the past five nights, this was her third visit. If the storm didn't pass soon, she'd be coming every night to keep her sanity.

As she rounded the last bookshelf, the window appeared, finally unobstructed. She released a sigh and plopped onto the settee in a most unladylike fashion. She raised her feet off the floor, tucking them inside her robe, and hugged her knees. There were no moonbeams tonight, but the room was dark enough that outside still seemed brighter than inside. Emry smiled to herself as the rain splattered across the thick glass.

"Emry?"

She whirled, gaping. There was no mistaking his voice. "Declan?"

"I'm honestly not trying to startle you on purpose," he said, joining her, "and this time I wasn't following you."

From what Emry could see of him in the light from the window, he looked a little rumpled. His tunic was open and the top three buttons of his shirt beneath were unbuttoned, revealing his neck. He must have been lounging somewhere in the library when she'd arrived. "How long have you been in here?"

"Since just after dinner," he replied. "I sent Peffun to do some laundry and managed to slip out while he carried off my clothes."

"Peffun?" Emry frowned, unsure why Declan had to sneak into the library.

"My valet, your servant?" Declan prompted. "Or do you have too many to know them all?"

Was he mocking her? Or was he honestly asking? She wasn't sure. "We do have many, but I recognize most of them," she answered. "This Peffun must be one of the recent temporary hires for the Challengers. Why are you trying to avoid him?"

Declan grunted. "He's taken it upon himself to be my chaperone wherever I go, making sure I steer clear of you and your family."

Emry chuckled softy. "That's why I haven't seen you? Because of this Peffun fellow?"

"What do you mean?" He gave her a confused look. "I was at the banquet."

"Yes, Cadoc and I both observed you watching me," she smirked, unable to keep the teasing out of her voice. "Did you think we wouldn't notice?"

"No, I meant for you to catch me," he admitted. "I'm wondering what you meant about not seeing me."

"Oh." Emry quelled the small part of her that liked he'd wanted to draw her attention. "I only meant that I haven't seen you around the palace all week, and I run into Cadoc at practically every corner."

He stared at her for a long moment. "Are you saying that I could have gone where I pleased during this entire storm if I hadn't allowed Peffun to follow me around?"

"Well, not into our personal chambers, but other than that, yes." She paused. "Your valet really has been following you around the palace?"

"Like a baby duck to its mother." He sat back, leaning his head against the top of the settee, and groaned. "There went five worthless days of my life that I can never get back."

Emry watched him. "Why did you want me to notice you at the banquet?"

"Maybe I just can't keep my eyes off of you," he grinned up at the ceiling.

Her response was a roll of her eyes. "I meant other than the obvious."

Declan looked at her then. His grin had shifted into something like surprised delight. But he said, "I wanted to see if you'd give me an inkling of what my competition is like."

"What would you like to know about Challenger Cadoc, the supposed Mid?" She asked with a smile.

He rested a hand at the back of his neck, leaning against it. "You don't think he's a Mid, either?"

She grunted. "No. That man is a Kruth."

"He's enormous," Declan added. "If I were you, I'd have my hopes set on him to win."

"But he's not the one I've already set my hopes on," she said quietly.

He blinked at her. "Who have you picked? Me?"

"Surprised?"

"I think you might need to adjust your expectations, now that I've seen Cadoc." He winced.

"Afraid you won't be able to best him?" She tilted her head to the side.

"It's more like acceptance at this point. Unless the man is useless with any form of weapon, which I highly doubt as he is a Kruth, I haven't the slightest chance." Declan sighed. "In fact, I'm starting to worry what the actual Kruth Challenger will look like if Cadoc the Giant was the reject."

She raised her eyebrows. "Cadoc the Giant? Is that what I should tell my father to introduce him as at The Trials?"

"Cadoc is the sort of creature children fear will eat them."

Startled laughter ruptured out of her. "Cadoc, a child-eating creature? That's pretty awful of you."

Declan shrugged. "I accept what I am."

"Ewan would say that." Emry realized with a slight pain in her chest that he was the last one to have used the phrase with her.

"I remember." His voice was distant.

It was odd, really. The two people in the world Ewan had been closest with were once again together. If only Ewan were here to enjoy it. Emry's smile faded to a frown, and she spoke the words that had been bothering her for hours. "Today my father told me he's going to begin arranging my betrothal."

Declan stared at her for a moment. "With whom?"

"Trezim Azure Niroz, third prince of Heerth," she told him. She gazed out the tall window in front of them. "My father's advisors have convinced him that Trezim will make a fine husband and an advantageous, strategic match."

He frowned. "Have you even met him?"

"I've spent many months in Heerth." She nodded, still not looking at him.

"And do you find the prince favorable?" Declan asked slowly.

"Honestly," she grumbled, "Trez is spoiled and egotistical and infuriating ... and an incredibly great man." She paused. "Trez is a very good friend of mine. My father, knowing this, has agreed to the demands of his advisors because he doesn't think a match with Trez would upset me."

"Would it?"

"No." Emry turned to him and shook her head once. "But Trez and I will never be married."

"Because-"

"Because," she said, interrupting him, "no one can force me to marry anyone. Not even the king of En-lennd."

"You told your father no." His brow furrowed.

"I told him no." she nodded. "And he said he doesn't think I have a choice in the matter."

Declan was frowning. "But you said..."

"My father and his advisors assume my only options in life are the ones they've presented me with," she explained with a sigh. "Which is not true. I've learned how to not be helpless."

He nodded and leaned forward with his elbows on

his knees. His hands were interlaced at the back of his head. Without looking up he asked, "Emry, do you want me for your Knight just because I'm familiar to you?"

"Yes and no," she replied. "I trust you."

Silence. Then, "I think that boy you knew might be gone."

"I hardly knew you then," she glanced down at her hands. "Before the night Ewan died, I think I saw you a total of maybe six times. Maybe spoke to you twice."

He sat up. His face held a mix of emotions that Emry couldn't quite read. Confusion. Guilt. Distress. Or was that dejection? Finally, he spoke, "If you don't even know me then how can you say you trust me?"

It was the question she'd been asking herself for months. Sure, her acquaintance with his father let her know that he came from good stock, but she hadn't spent much time with Declan alone. She felt like she had – thanks to those dreams. But the persona her mind had created for Declan while she slept could very well be nothing like how he actually was. So far, it hadn't seemed that way. He'd acted just as she'd imagined. Only time would tell, though. So, how did she tell him that she saw him as a friend without divulging her pact with the Rioters? It was a secret that affected the safety of more than just herself. She couldn't speak of it within the palace. Hadn't even fully told Cit.

But she saw the turmoil within him. He was torn. Torn between loyalty to his people, the Rioters, and a distant memory of a lost friend. She suddenly felt sad for him. As she'd guessed, the situation wasn't an easy one for him.

Emry angled her body towards him on the settee. With one hand, she gently placed her hand on his cheek and turned his head toward her. "Declan, you were the brother Ewan never had. He loved you. He trusted you. The man you are today is no different than the boy he knew."

"And what if you're wrong?" He breathed.

She shrugged, dropping her hand. "Then, I'm wrong, and I'll just have to deal with the difference once you're sworn to me."

They fell quiet for a moment, and Emry stifled a yawn with the back of her hand. Declan noticed. "We should call it a night."

"Alright." Emry nodded as Declan pushed himself up with his hands on his knees. He then offered both of his hands for her to take. She slipped her hands into his, and let him pull her to her feet. There wasn't much space between them. Their faces were close. Her eyes landed on his mouth. It would have been so easy to just tip her head upward and... With a sharp intake of breath, she quickly took a step backwards. "Until the next, Declan."

He nodded once, a slight crease between his eyebrows. "Until the next, princess."

:  :  :  :  :

By the following morning, the clouds had disappeared, leaving crystal clear blue skies. By breakfast, the remaining three Challengers arrived. Apparently, Declan hadn't been the only one biding his time during the storm.

The first was the Glav – a wiry, dark-skinned man with long, black hair twined into a thick braid at the nape of his neck. His name was Hedron Neige. His bronze eyes were veined with teal. The teal didn't worry

Declan, though. He doubted the man posed much competition when it came to speed. The veins were thin and not his base color.

Not thirty minutes after Hedron trotted through the palace gates, Aife Sugned practically erupted into the courtyard. The actual Kruth, as Declan had feared, put Cadoc to shame. His height was like a young oak tree. Aife had a good three inches on Cadoc, who had at least five on Declan. Like Cadoc, Aife's hair was white blond and a little shaggy. His square jawline was shadowed with a fair colored beard. To the surprise of none, Aife's eyes were a base black, sprinkled with ice blue. It meant that he was mostly muscle mixed with a little ice manipulation. Coming from Kruth – the coldest region in the country – the pale blue was fairly common.

About six hours after Aife's thundering steps were heard within the palace walls, the Challenger for Enn slipped in somewhat quietly. Apparently, Piran Bricke lived somewhere in the capital and had been to the palace many times. Piran was of medium size, much like Declan and wore his wavy hair to his shoulders, as was the custom of men in Enn and Quirl. His chestnut hair had more red in it than brown. Unlike any of the other Challengers, his eyes were base purple with spots of pink. Purple dealt with the elements of autumn – usually death – and pink with spring – birth and rebirth. To have a Challenger with such a mix was odd. Generally, those with purple and pink in their eyes had similar professions to those with base ruby, which dealt with blood and healing.

With base purple, bronze, green, black, and teal, no one could claim the Challengers weren't diverse. When they were to be presented all together at The Trials, they would make an interesting group. Declan simply hoped his speed would best the other contestants enough to make up for the areas where he lacked.

The arrival of the three Challengers, though, meant that the next three nights would be filled with banquets for each of them. Then, the morning following the last one would begin The Trials. Even though the official start date had been set for a few days after that, with all the Challengers now present there was no reason to wait. The date was only there to give the contestants time to arrive. If one region's Challenger hadn't shown up by the given day, then his region would have been eliminated from The Trials, and they would have commenced without him. Since all five regions were now accounted for, it was time to begin.

This meant that Declan's next three days would be spent training. Excluding his required presence at the banquets, he'd be devoting his every waking moment to his bow, sword, and agility. Now that he'd had a glimpse of his opponents, he realized there could be some room for growth, especially where Aife and Cadoc were concerned. He needed all the practice time he could squeeze in before The Trials. There'd be no rendezvous with Emry, if he were to win as she wished. Hopefully all his extra preparation wouldn't be a waste.

# CHAPTER SIX

The morning of The Trials, Emry rose slowly. Well, slower than usual. She knew she should have been excited for The Trials to begin – its completion was the beginning she'd been anticipating for years. Yet, all she felt was apprehension and exhaustion. If Declan failed, she could wind up attached to an arrogant braggart like Hedron, or that blundering imbecile, Aife. Yes, the man was gargantuan and could kill his enemies by simply sitting on them, but if Emry was forced to live with that Kruth as her Knight, she was in danger of wrenching his light out of him. It was impossible to have a normal conversation with him. The entire evening she was trapped at his side, he'd only discussed his horse, if the great beast he'd barged in on could be characterized as such – it was more like a moose without antlers.

It'd been days since she'd spoken with Declan. She'd seen him at the banquets. That first one he'd been placed beside Cadoc and was then joined by the others one by one on the nights following their coming-out feasts. She'd also caught a few glances of Declan while he practiced outside the palace guards' barracks. Any sightings were always at a distance, however. Aside from the banquets, her stolen glimpses of him were all while she'd snuck away from the palace. As it was usually members of her Royal Guard that sought her out during her disappearances, to join Declan outside the barracks would have ended her escapades immediately. Besides, Declan needed to focus. She'd only be a distraction. Or so she vainly told herself.

From what she did observe of his practice sessions, though, she couldn't help but feel like he was holding back some of his skill. He'd moved slower than she'd remembered. She doubted it was due to her memory. It was more likely that he wanted to appear less of a threat to his competition. Very strategic of him. If this really was the case, Emry was pleased he'd thought to do so. Today would prove if his subterfuge had been worth it.

As Fanny helped her into her dress for The First Trial, Emry struggled to keep herself calm. The more she thought about The Trial, the more nervous she became. Aside from The Third Trial, the Knight's Ball, this first one was the only one she had an inkling of what it would entail. Her father and Vardin had shown her, Citrine, and Freddick the course the day before. Up until the point she'd laid her eyes on it, she'd had full confidence in Declan's abilities. Now, she truly feared for his well-being, let alone him coming out in the lead. Little wonder so many Challengers historically were injured during The Trials. After what she'd seen, it would be impossible to avoid some sort of mutilation to at least one of her Challengers.

"You seem tense this morning, dearest princess," Fanny commented as she deftly buttoned up the back of Emry's gown.

Emry had to mentally stop herself from snorting. "I am tense."

"Do not fret," Fanny comforted, "it will be over quickly."

"Hopefully not too soon," Emry replied softly, worried that her Trials would fail if all her Challengers were maimed during the first event.

She watched herself in the long, ornate mirror propped up opposite of her. They were in her dressing room, off of her main chambers. The mirror was a bit too gaudy and out of fashion for Emry's taste, but as it had belonged to her great-grandmother – the last princess to have had a Knight before Emry and Citrine – she'd kept it for sentimental reasons. Mostly as a reminder to never allow herself to be forced into marriage with such a sour man as her great-grandfather. The man, Cobalt Randor, second prince of Quirl, had not treated his wife, Sapphire Nylles, well at all and had raised his only child, Topaz Nylles, to be just as arrogant as himself. It was common for the children of two royal families to take the last name of the parent with the highest title. As Sapphire was queen of her country, and Cobalt only second in line for the throne in his, their child claimed Nylles.

Sighing, she returned her attention to her reflection. Fanny had chosen cream as the color for today's activities. As was currently popular, the floor-length gown fell straight from a high waistline, situated just below her bust on her ribs. The neckline swooped to form a deep U, and her long sleeves came to a point with a small ring stitched in for her middle fingers to slip into. The dress was a thick muslin to keep her warm throughout the early autumn day. A single, wide ribbon – the color of rich chocolate – wrapped around her waistline and tied into a bow at her back. It was simple, as was expected for her First Trial, but the cut of it practically screamed elegance.

In less than three hours, her five Challengers would be presented to her as one group for the first time. They, too, would be wearing cream. Fanny had chosen wisely. Should one of them begin to bleed, it would be easy to spot, so as to offer assistance quickly. No one wished a Challenger to perish from a Trial – it would only bring anger from his region. Thanks to the night before, Emry now knew exactly how easily one of her five could be hurt. Cream was an excellent choice.

The First Trial was really a large obstacle course, made up of four parts: The Pond, The Plummet, The Crossings, and The Greens. Each was unique in the set of skills necessary to complete them. Yet, they had one constant – they were all designed with the intent to inflict damage.

"I need to braid your hair, dearest princess," Fanny's voice yanked Emry from her thoughts.

"Of course." Emry nodded once as she moved to her vanity and took a seat, facing herself in a much smaller mirror placed above her pale blue vanity.

As Fanny's nimble fingers worked through Emry's thick, dark hair, her mind wandered back to The First Trial. It would take an hour to travel to the site. Vardin made certain it was built far from any prying eyes.

It began with The Pond, which was really nothing more than a man-made pit filled with water and an assortment of dangerous fish. There were fresh water eels, piranhas, and grizzits. There were others, but those three had made Emry the most nervous, especially the grizzit fish. Grizzits had long, flat bodies and were generally varying shades of gray. Being somewhat related to piranhas, they had mouths filled with tiny sharp teeth. They weren't all that fond of human flesh. However, they were known to swarm humans with bites to draw their distant cousins – piranhas – to the site. Grizzits liked to snack on the scales of other fish of prey, having an odd preference for piranhas.

During The First Trial, the Challengers would begin by swimming through The Pond. It was the only way across to progress to the next stage. On the opposite side of the water from the starting line, there was a platform with only one small staircase leading up to it. The Challengers would be required to brave the murky water by stroking up to the staircase in order to exit. If swimming were the only factor, Emry wouldn't have been very worried about Declan. How he would do within water filled to the brim with fish of prey was another matter.

If Declan and his competition somehow managed to cross The Pond to the location of the staircase, they would move into The Plummet. As its name suggested, The Plummet risked a possible fall off a precipice into a chasm that Emry assumed was also man-made. From the platform at the end of The Pond to the grounds of The Crossings, her Challengers would be relying entirely on their upper body strength. A thirty-foot deep ditch, spanning the length of nearly sixty feet, sat directly beneath several sets of hanging metal rings. The rings were about ten inches in diameter and hung from strands of rope, which were attached to a large wooden frame bridging the expanse of the trench. In order to not plunge to the bottom, Declan would have to swing ring to ring across the ditch. Emry sincerely hoped he was strong enough. If he wasn't, he'd never make it to The Crossings.

If the first two sections hadn't claimed at least one Challenger, Emry was certain the third would. It was basically four layers of oscillating half-moon shaped blades. Each was the size of a small pony, spread apart by no more than a few steps. Two guards on either side of each of the four wooden structures that the blades hung from would use levers to rock them back and forth. From what Emry could tell, there was little to no space between the ground and the steel. She hadn't witnessed them in action, though, since no operators had joined her family's inspection of the course. The blades were staggered with such a short distance in between that she wasn't sure how any of her Challengers would fair.

Then, the final leg of The Trial was The Greens. It was a two-hundred-yard dash through a meadow that was under fire by five separate archer towers along the finish line. There would be no cover, and the closer her contestants came to the towers, the better the archers' aim became. Yet, of all the four stages to The First Trial, this concerned Emry the least. Declan was a Teal. The Greens would be a stroll in the park for him.

"All done, dearest princess," Fanny said, stepping back.

Emry took in her maid's work. Fanny had twined a simple rose gold tiara into her ornate braid. Emry smiled. "Thank you, Fanny. It looks lovely."

"Not to be too contrary, dearest princess, but you look quite a bit better than just lovely," she retorted. "Striking is the word that comes to mind."

"Thank you for your flattery." Emry laughed. She was accustomed to Fanny's abounding compliments.

"Flattery has nothing to do with it," the woman huffed. "You look every bit the beautiful princess, ready to strike courage into the hearts of your men."

"I suppose that *is* the idea," Emry commented. If she was being honest with herself, there really was only one man she'd ever wished to inspire. It was unfortunate he was one of her Challengers.

: : : : :

Declan was sweating. Already. Before The First Trial had even begun. It wasn't hot out, either. He was anxious – no use lying to himself. This was beginning to feel like he was heading toward one of those duels back in Quirl. But this wasn't one of those. This was Enlennd. Not Quirl. He wasn't in that camp. He got out. Deep breaths. He was here by his own choice. He was free.

It was his choice that had him currently inside a large carriage, second in line to a very long procession. His carriage was right behind the Royal Coach. A second Challenger carriage followed the one Declan sat inside of. Usually there was only one, but Aife and Cadoc were such large men, the other three contestants hadn't been able to fit inside with them. Behind the Jewels and the Challengers, hundreds, if not thousands, of villagers, courtiers, soldiers, palace guards, merchants, and even foreigners made their way toward The Trial. Some rode on horses or mules, others in carriages of their own, but most walked.

For nearly an hour, Declan listened to the uproar of voices, animals, and some amateur musicians who hoped to gain some coin by their merry-making. Even though he was with the Glav and Enn inside the carriage, none of them had spoken a word the entire journey.

Piran sat at Declan's right and had been peering out his window since they'd departed. On the stuffed bench opposite of Declan, Hedron was sitting with his legs spread wide and his head tipped back against the top of the bench. He looked like he was sleeping, but Declan doubted he actually was. Hedron had entered the cramped carriage first and sat directly in the middle of the bench that faced their destination, purposely forcing

Declan and Piran to make the journey feeling as though they were going backwards with very limited space. It had annoyed Declan, but it wasn't the place for a scene. He'd save his irritation at the Glav for fuel in The Trials.

The carriage slowed its pace and then came to a stop. Piran was out the door before the vehicle had completely ceased moving. Hedron sat up, suddenly alert. Declan felt like rolling his eyes as Hedron followed Piran a heartbeat later. He did release a sigh as he eased himself off the bench and out the door to his left – the one across of Piran and Hedron's exit.

Despite the cool morning air, the bright sun made it mild out. Declan squinted as he stepped down onto the gravel road. The two Challenger carriages had parked side-by-side directly behind the black Royal Coach – the kingdom's emblem emblazed along its doors in silver. Beyond that, the road dead-ended at a forest of tall trees with leaves already wearing their autumn coats of purple, orange, and red. He guessed the trees hid The First Trial from view. He tried to spot Emry, to see if she'd emerged from her coach, but the procession was swarming the area.

To Declan's surprise, Hedron and Aife were both wrapped in an embrace of some kind with two different women. After thoroughly kissing their partners, they moved on to new ones. Declan knew it was an unofficial tradition for the young women of the regions to kiss the Challengers for good luck, but the way those men were tearing through the crowd was a little startling, even for Declan. He searched for his other two Challengers and discovered Cadoc was also enveloping a woman. Yet, the way he held her looked like he wouldn't be releasing her anytime soon.

"Are you looking for me?"

Declan whirled to find a Ruby, dressed in a simple dark blue gown. "Brielle?" He gaped, unbelieving. "What are you doing here?"

She grinned. "I couldn't miss your First Trial."

He felt his brow draw together. "You came by yourself?"

"Of course not," she laughed lightly, tossing her shoulder length hair slightly as she did. Had her voice always sounded so high to him? A couple of weeks shouldn't have made him forget that she sounded so much younger than her actual age. "Bran and my parents are here, too."

"Did my parents come?" Declan scanned the crowd over her head. She barely came up to his chin.

"No, your mother said she refused to come watch you be injured," Brielle replied, quickly dashing his hopes. "She swears you're going to your own demise."

"She may be right." He frowned. "I haven't seen The First Trial yet."

"You will end up just fine," she said, shaking her head. "Your uncle came, though."

"He did?" Declan blinked. "Where?"

"I'm not sure…" her voice trailed off. Then, "Are you not happy to see me?"

He finally looked her in the eye. Sparkling ruby and pink greeted him. Pretty eyes. But, nothing special. At least not to him. Had Brielle always been so plain? Yet, she'd traveled a long way to see him. He was grateful to have some support in the crowd today. He smiled. "Of course I am," he assured her. "I'm really glad you and the others have come to see me. I assumed I'd be going it alone."

"Good." She laid both hands on his vest, gripping

its edges, and tipped her head upward. That familiar blush tainted her cheeks pink. "I traveled a very long way for this."

Declan understood what she wanted of him. He'd barely have to dip his head for their lips to meet. But the idea of kissing her again seemed off.

Having Brielle so close to him made him feel like the whole procession was suddenly watching him. Impulsively, Declan lifted his gaze over the top of her head again. About sixty or so feet away from him, Emry stood beside her sister and father. She was actually the only one watching him. His eyes locked with her piercing silver ones, and he realized with a start why Brielle's ruby ones no longer drew him.

: : : : :

When Emry stepped out of her family's coach, it took all of her focus and years of etiquette training to stop herself from fidgeting. She knew she needed to give the outward appearance of tranquility, but it was a near impossible feat when internally she was a fretful wreck. How could she be expected to look calm when she could barely keep herself from trembling?

She joined her sister at the front of the convoy – where the gravel road they'd taken met the forest – and faced the throng. Her Challengers had already begun to work their way through the young women. Emry couldn't spot Declan, but three of her contestants were carrying on the pre-Trial tradition. The only one she was mildly surprised by was Cadoc. He hadn't seemed the type of man to participate. Yet, he wasn't really moving on from the pale blonde in his arms. Emry frowned. She had a suspicion that this woman was more than just a Trial kiss.

"Who's the girl with your Knight?" Citrine asked, her voice low so only Emry and Freddick could hear. Since Emry didn't officially have a Knight, it was a taunt on Cit's part. "It looks like he may know her."

Emry scanned the crowd, finding Declan still beside the carriage he'd ridden in. The petite redhead was obviously Anexian with her wavy hair cropped at her shoulders. Emry watched as the girl slid her hands over Declan's chest.

"Freddick," she tossed at her sister's Knight, "why don't you go have them blow the trumpets?" It was an entirely jealous demand on her part. The trumpets began The First Trial and immediately ceased all kissing.

Cit's Knight merely bowed with a knowing smile. "Yes, dear princess."

As the redhead pushed herself against Declan, her head tipped upward expectantly. Emry's eyes stayed glued on Declan's face. She braced herself for the inevitable pain that would splinter through her chest. It was only a matter of seconds until she'd see him offer up his affection to the redhead. Emry waited, her breath catching in her throat. Somewhere in the back of her head she knew she was being a little ridiculous. She'd only just been reintroduced to his life. She had no claim to him. Yet, still her heart beat faster.

But it never happened. Instead, he looked up, directly into Emry's eyes. It was as if he sensed her watching him. Then, the trumpets blared. It was time. Declan stepped back.

# CHAPTER SEVEN

The sound of the trumpets made Declan jump. To the obvious dismay of Brielle, he fell back a step out of her grasp. He offered a small apologetic smile as something similar to relief filled him. "Duty calls."

"So it does." She frowned. "Succeed in your endeavors."

"Or die trying," he finished the quote automatically. It was an Anexian phrase that meant she wished him luck, and he'd promised to try his hardest.

He made his way around her toward the front of the crowd. She slid her hand down his arm as he passed, but he didn't glance back at her. His gaze had locked with Emry's once more. He noticed the other Challengers had heeded their cue as well. Piran and Cadoc had already taken their places on their knees with their heads bowed and hands clasped behind their backs – about ten steps from the Jewels. Declan knelt beside Piran as Hedron did the same beside Cadoc. Aife dropped at Declan's left, and he swore he heard a small thud from that monster of a man hitting the ground.

There was movement from the line of the royalty, but Declan couldn't tell who had moved with his face down toward the gravel. However, he knew Captain Vardin of the King's Guard would be presenting the Challengers to Emry and assumed it was he who had shifted.

As the din from the procession died down, Vardin's voice shouted, "Dear princess, Emerald, are you ready to greet your Challengers?"

"I am, Captain," Emry rang out clearly.

Presentations were done in order of arrival. Declan knew he'd be called first. When Vardin yelled out his alias and region, Declan rose and lifted his eyes to the Jewels. Well, to Emry. She held his gaze until Cadoc was presented before transferring her attention to her other contestants. Declan's eyes didn't move, though. He took her in openly.

Like her Challengers, she was dressed all in cream, except for the ribbon situated over her ribs. The brown of the ribbon matched the plain vests each contestant wore over their simple shirts and the boots they'd all tucked their pants into. Emry's long, midnight black hair had been done in an elaborate braid that somehow incorporated her tiara into it. She was absolutely stunning. Even beside her sister of professed equal beauty, Emry seemed to have surpassed her greatly today. Declan suspected Citrine's simpler braid and gray gown were meant to fade into the background. It was Emry's Trials after all.

"Welcome, my men," Emry said, pulling Declan from his thoughts. "I am pleased you have traveled from our five regions to honor your home in claiming the position as my sworn Knight. I wish you all the best," her eyes slid over the five men, ending on Declan, "and may one of you win."

With that small speech, the trumpets pealed out again. Emry dropped her hands to her sides from where she'd had them clasped in front of her. Declan frowned. Was she shaking? The king turned to begin down a small path behind him, and Emry followed.

Princess Citrine and her Knight were at their backs. Vardin went next and then the Challengers trailed after.

The path through the tall evergreens was short – really only going through one line of trees. It opened almost immediately to a small valley below, surrounded by forest and hills on all sides. Declan hadn't seen which direction the carriage took him from the palace, but judging by the terrain, he assumed he was closer to the Kruth border than before. He was the fourth Challenger in line, making him almost the last to lay eyes on The First Trial. When he did, he nearly swore.

From Declan's vantage point on top of the hill, he could see it perfectly. He was high enough up that he could make out four different stages, but it wasn't so far beneath him that it'd be a trek down the hill. The Trial was an obstacle course in the center of the valley. Makeshift observation stands, which appeared to have been constructed quickly, flanked the opposite side of the course from where Declan stood. He had his doubts that there would be enough space for everyone in the mass behind him. To the right of the course, situated towards the middle of it, was what Declan guessed was the King's Pavilion. It was much smaller than the stands, and a little more carefully constructed. It would be where Emry and her family sat with select members of their Court.

Before he had the chance to really take in the course, he was urged forward by Aife's enormous form. Declan descended the hill at a leisurely pace, keeping his eyes on Emry's back ahead of him. Her thick braid dropped all the way to her lower back. He found himself wondering how long her hair was when it was loose. Not even the matrons of Anexia had their hair as long as hers. When was the last time she'd had it cut?

"Pick it up, Anexian," Aife grumbled from behind Declan, surprising him. Declan wasn't trailing Piran by more than six steps.

"There's no rush," he replied over his shoulder. There really wasn't. The Jewels had to make it down the hill and then be seated before the Challengers were even permitted to approach the course. Then, the rest of the procession had to be ushered into the stands before the actual First Trial could begin. Declan wasn't really a patient person, but he knew that today it was something he'd need to implement.

Aife muttered some retort under his breath that Declan couldn't catch, but that was all he said the rest of the way down to level ground. He must have realized that Declan was right.

At the base of the hill, Vardin came to a halt, causing the Challengers to do the same, as the Jewels continued on to the King's Pavilion. Declan and his competition waited with their hands clasped behind their backs. A few minutes later, Emry and her family settled into their seats. Princess Citrine's Knight stood directly behind her – his feet spread shoulder width apart and his hands behind his back. With a nod from King Onyx, Vardin began forward again, leading the Challengers to stand in front of the King's Pavilion. Once they reached it, each contestant turned to The First Trial, their backs to their sovereigns.

Taking a stance similar to that of Knight Freddick, Declan scanned the course and tried not to wince. The Trial wasn't going to be a breeze, not that he'd expected it to be. His mother might have been right after all for not wanting to come watch him be hurt.

On the other side of The Trial, the procession was shuffling into the stands. Declan ignored them. His attention was focused on figuring out how to cross the course. The small lake at the front looked easy enough, but he didn't assume it would just be a test of his swimming. He worried what lay beneath the surface. The crescent-shaped blades looked ominous as well. Declan really wasn't sure what the best path through would be. He decided that he'd hang back for a moment at the start. It would allow him to see how his competition fared as well as let him know what he'd be facing in the water. He wasn't concerned about having to make up the distance later. Thanks to his teal eyes, he could easily close the gap if he was a little hesitant at the beginning.

It took about thirty minutes to fill the stands and another ten for the rest of the crowd to mill in. Those who couldn't find a seat were forced to stand on the opposite side of The Trial from the King's Pavilion. When the last person had descended, Vardin rejoined the Challengers. He'd been overseeing crowd control with the palace guards.

Without a word, the Challengers faced the Jewels and bowed. Then, they made their way to the starting line of The First Trial. Aife led them, which made Declan second in line instead of fourth this time. The starting line was really nothing more than a strand of rope laid over the ground a few steps from the water's edge. Declan stopped behind it and resumed his position of hands clasped at his back and legs spread apart. The other contestants did the same.

Captain Vardin moved between them and the water. "Your First Trial is divided into four stages," he told the Challengers. His voice was only loud enough for them to hear. "The Pond is first, followed by The Plummet, The Crossings, and The Greens. You must complete them in order of succession to finish The Trial. Those who skip a stage or do not complete the course will be disqualified and removed from The Trials. The last man to cross the finish line will be eliminated." He paused, letting the rules sink in. "Honor your regions," he said, wishing them luck.

With that, he returned to the King's Pavilion. Once Vardin had positioned himself behind King Onyx, Emry stood. A hush fell over the stands and those standing. Someone had given Emry a small white flag. When she waved it, it would signal the start of The First Trial. Declan's heart quickened. This was it.

Emry lifted the flag above her head. With the distance between them, Declan couldn't be sure, but he felt like her eyes were on him. With a swift flick of her wrist, Emry brought the flag down.

Aife, Hedron, and Piran ran to the water's edge and leaped in. The crowd erupted into encouraging cheers. Declan was surprised to see that Cadoc had hung back as well, assessing the other contestants before beginning himself. Declan watched Hedron and Aife swim side by side. Aife's long arms were matching Hedron's swift strokes. They were almost to the middle of The Pond. Declan stepped to the water. The men seemed to be doing fine. Perhaps he could get in now, too.

Just as Declan was about to jump in, though, Aife let out a startled cry, reaching for his right leg. Hedron grinned at him from a few feet away, a dagger gripped in his left hand. Piran swam up ahead, oblivious to the men behind him. Declan stared as he realized what Hedron had done to Aife's leg. As Hedron sheathed his knife and continued forward, splashing from Aife brought back Declan's gaze. Aife was flailing in the water, gurgling under the surface. A gash shouldn't have caused him to react that way. Then, Declan saw the bite marks up and down Aife's massive arms. One fish still clung to his wrist. A grizzit fish.

Declan swore. He hated grizzits. They were nasty creatures that would make as many holes as possible on a person just to attract other fish for their own food. Declan glanced around. No guard was close enough to yank out the big man. Swearing again, Declan dove for Aife.

The moment he hit the water, he was moving. It was frigid. He had to force his muscles to keep stroking through the stinging water. Within seconds, he was to Aife. Reaching an arm under Aife's shoulder, Declan began to drag him to the side of The Pond. But Aife was practically twice his size. Declan strained to keep both of their heads above water. It only took a moment for the grizzits to turn on him, assuming him to be an extension of Aife. Declan grit his teeth as the fish began to sink into his legs and arms. He worried his rescue attempt would only bring him the same fate as Aife's.

But then Cadoc was there on the other side of Aife, helping Declan. Almost instantly, the job of carrying the big man became easier. Declan nearly let out a sigh of relief. They reached the shoreline a minute later. Both Cadoc and Declan pulled Aife out of the water to three waiting guards. Cadoc yanked a grizzit fish off his shoulder and tossed it to the ground. Without a second glance back at Aife, both men returned to The Pond.

Not wanting to deal with any more bites, Declan tapped into his speed. He raced through the water, outpacing any fish. The stairs appeared in front of him, leading to the next stage. Declan climbed out and ran his hands through his hair, shaking out the icy water. He gritted his teeth to keep them from chattering.

Hedron was already to The Crossings with Piran not far behind on The Plummet. Releasing a sigh, Declan eyed the closest hanging ring. In order for him to grab it, he'd have to jump off the platform, relying on his stiff, wet, slippery fingers to catch himself from falling into the pit below. To get to the ring after that, he'd swing his body back and forth to reach it. Then, he'd have to repeat the process all the way down to the end. But first, he needed to dry off his hands.

A quick scan of the area told him the best option was to wipe his chilled hands on the platform. Not a great solution, but better than nothing. Taking a deep breath, Declan dried his hands the best he could on the gritty wood and straightened. He planted his feet and jumped for the nearest ring. He nearly overshot it. Only one hand managed to grasp it.

Grimacing, Declan swayed his body – his free hand stretched out for the next ring. When he felt steel, he released the first ring and swung for the third. His progress was slower than he would have liked. His still slick hands made him cautious. Cadoc was soon passing him by with ease. Declan briefly envied the black in Cadoc's eyes. This was where excessive strength would come in handy. The cold water down his back was replaced by sweat as he grunted his way across.

When he finally landed back onto solid ground, Declan moaned. He'd managed to not fall in a ditch only to be chopped up by The Crossings. It wasn't a nice sentiment. Hedron had only made it past the first three rows during all that time. He was currently facing the fourth row. Piran was working on the third, and Cadoc the second, leaving Declan alone to hiss at the first. He noticed that Hedron had gained a gash down his back from somewhere – most likely one of the crescent blades.

Declan watched as Piran bobbed through the third row, narrowly missing a blade that would have claimed his right arm. When Cadoc went to slide through the second row, Declan stepped to the left side to catch a better glimpse of the man. Cadoc ended up not moving, which gave Declan a diagonal shot of The Crossings. Each row moved in the opposite direction of the next. But an opening emerged, creating a path through each row if he were to run at an angle. There was a pattern to the swinging blades. He would never have seen it if he hadn't moved off to the side. The opening was only there for a few seconds. He'd have to sprint through the blades.

Sucking in another breath, Declan waited for the opening again. Then, he bolted, dodging metal. Declan passed the last row at the same time as Hedron. The two men tore off across The Greens. Declan made sure to put some distance between him and the Glav, not wanting to become another victim to Hedron's knife. As Declan had expected, arrows began to rain down onto The Greens. Hedron sped up and Declan did the same, keeping pace with him. Declan didn't really need to come in first to move onto The Second Trial. There was no need to outrun Hedron, who clearly was trying his hardest to take the lead.

Neither Hedron nor Declan ran in a straight line. They both zigzagged their way across to disrupt the accuracy of the archers. As they neared the finish line, Hedron pulled ahead and Declan eased up. Hedron crossed to thunderous applause with Declan a couple seconds later. Hedron bent over, his hands on his knees, panting heavily. Deciding that it didn't hurt to give the appearance of being winded, Declan dropped into the same position. In actuality, though, Declan could have tripled his speed and still breathed easy.

Vardin was suddenly at Hedron's side. He grabbed Hedron's wrist and raised both of their arms above his head. "Our winner to Princess Emerald's First Trial!" He shouted.

The crowd roared their approval as Vardin released Hedron's wrist. Declan straightened. Piran joined them, followed closely by Cadoc. Declan noticed a bloodied tear in Cadoc's sleeve where it looked like an arrow had grazed his arm. Vardin watched the contestants with his oddly bland blue eyes.

"Good work today, men," Vardin congratulated. "The four of you have won a spot in The Second Trial." He nodded toward two women and a man standing near the base of one of the archer towers. "Be sure to see a medic before we head back to the palace."

Declan frowned at the group until he caught a glimpse of their eyes. Medic. Right. In Enn, Rubys were called medics.

Piran was the first to move toward the Rubys. He had a few bites to be taken care of. Declan was next. As one of the women – a Ruby base with lavender flecks – tended to Declan's own bites and scrapes, his eyes drifted toward Emry. She was smiling at her sister, laughing. He was glad to see her more relaxed.

"You survived."

Declan turned to the familiar voice as Marsdon clapped a rough hand on his shoulder. "You did well, Thane."

"Thanks for coming, uncle," Declan replied, acknowledging Marsdon's use of his alias and ignoring that strange twang of disappointment again. "I appreciate it."

"Your parents would be proud of you," Marsdon told him, releasing Declan's shoulder. "You helped save a man's life today."

The medic on Declan's arm nodded. "The gash in the Kruth's calf was deep. He wasn't a strong enough swimmer with the grizzits. He would have drowned."

Declan shrugged. "I couldn't have it done it without Cadoc."

Hedron's actions did drop Declan's somewhat already low opinion of him even further, though. Despite the fact that it wasn't against Trial rules to injure one's competition during a Trial, it was an unscrupulous venture. He'd be wary of the Glav for the duration of The Trials.

"I look forward to watching you again," Marsdon said.

"How long will you be in Breccan?" Declan asked, tilting his head to one side as instructed by the medic.

"Throughout The Trials," Marsdon answered with a small smile. "I want to see my nephew become the Princess Emerald's Knight with my own eyes."

His uncle's confidence touched Declan. "Thank you, uncle."

"Until the next, Thane."

Declan nodded. "Until the next."

# CHAPTER EIGHT

Emry collapsed onto her sister's bed and buried her face into its array of orange and red pillows and blankets. Even though the footprint of her sister's rooms were a mirrored image of her own, Cit's looked almost nothing like hers. Cit fancied shades that matched her eyes, which meant everything was the color of fire.

Citrine's maid, Sadie, was finishing braiding her hair for the night at the vanity by her closet door, while Freddick stretched out on his Knight's cot just outside the bedroom's door. "Where have you been?" Citrine's voice filtrated to her through the pillows.

Releasing a groan, Emry pushed herself out of the fluff. "With Father and Vardin," she replied, "discussing my Second Trial."

That piqued Freddick's attention. Through the doorway, he asked, "Have they decided what it will be?"

"They have." Emry nodded.

"Sadie, that will be all," Citrine told her maid with the wave of one hand. "I can do the rest myself."

"Yes, Citrine." Sadie curtsied and turned.

Emry watched her exit. "How do you get her to use your name?"

Citrine shrugged, picking up on the braid where Sadie had left off. "She doesn't care about formalities as much as Fanny. Anyway, what's your Second Trial?"

"It will be a find Princess Emerald hunt," she told

them. Just as Freddick had joked.

"A what?" Citrine blinked.

Emry sighed, rubbing her eyes with her fingertips. She shouldn't be as tired as she was. The First Trial had taken too much out of her, and she'd only been worrying. She wondered how Declan was managing. "Basically, The Trial will be to see if any of my Challengers can find me before the palace guards."

Freddick stood and leaned against the threshold into Cit's room. "It won't be a public Trial?"

"No," Emry shook her head. "It will just be Father, Vardin, my Challengers, and us."

"That's strange." Citrine had finished her braid and was wrapping the end of it with a thin strap of leather. "I've never heard of a private Trial."

"I know. Father and Vardin say that I'm not a usual princess – in that I tend to disappear too much." Emry tried to look sheepish, but knew she was failing, unable to contain a smile.

Citrine rolled her eyes. "So, they think your Challengers would do a better job of catching you than the palace guards?"

"I think they hope so," she said.

Her sister grunted. "They won't. You'll hide in the shadows, and your Challengers will do no better than the guards. Not to mention, once you're sworn to the Knight you physically can't go anywhere without him."

"Yes, but Father doesn't know that little effect of your bond," Emry pointed out. Freddick and Cit couldn't be more than thirty feet from each other. If they tried, it caused them pain.

"Well, enjoy evading them for now," Cit retorted.

"Unless…" Freddick's voice trailed off as he eyed Emry.

She grinned. He'd realized the opportunity her father had handed her. "Exactly."

"Exactly what?" Citrine frowned.

"What if I were to allow *certain* Challengers to find me?"

Citrine's mouth dropped. "You can choose who wins The Trial."

Emry nodded again. Citrine and Freddick were the only two living people who knew of her ability to disappear into the shadows. Of becoming the very shadows themselves. Her father had no idea how she always managed to slip through his guards' fingers. "I could hide until Declan finds me."

"It's like you've been handed The Trial on a silver platter," Cit blurted.

"It's exciting, isn't it?" Emry smirked.

Having the opportunity to help Declan win The Second Trial really did relieve some stress for Emry. The Third Trial was the Knight's Ball. No one was eliminated from that one. In fact, the two previously disqualified Challengers were invited to participate. It was a public display of polite unity from the five regions. Emry would be required to step to a native dance from each Challenger's region with said Challenger. The Fourth Trial would be the next competitive Trial. It would be some sort of hand-to-hand combat test. If Declan managed to best at least one of his opponents, he'd be one of the remaining two for the final Fifth Trial. Emry would choose him, and her worries would wash away.

"When is The Second Trial to take place?" Freddick asked.

"Tomorrow afternoon," she replied. "I need your help to think of where Declan could find me without it seeming too obvious."

: : : : :

The next day, Emry was dressed more like an Anexian woman than an Enn. She wore a long-sleeved, charcoal gray tunic that came to the middle of her thighs, over tight black pants, called *leggings* by Anexians. On her feet, she wore a pair of simple, flat canvas shoes — the color of her tunic. It was the style most female Anexians wore day-to-day. Gowns in Anexia were meant for special occasions. Or those wealthy enough to not have the need to work. There had been many times that Emry wished all the women of Enlennd would adopt such practical clothing, especially for riding. Sidesaddle was so tedious.

Fanny had braided her hair on top of her head — wrapping the braid around to form a sort of crown. With her hair up and in Anexian garb, Emry would move easily through the palace. It had taken some convincing on her father's part to permit her to don the tunic and leggings for her Second Trial. Yet, when she insisted that in order for The Trial to be authentic, she would need to either wear her stable hand outfit or dress like an Anexian, he agreed to the latter.

Her Challengers had been summoned that morning to join the royal family in the banquet hall just before the midday meal. No other information had been given. They wouldn't be expecting to begin The Second Trial, since it wouldn't be a public meeting with her family. They'd most likely assume it'd be the time they would be told what The Trial would entail. The element of surprise was ideal, according to Onyx. Emry didn't ever announce her escapades, so she'd supposedly be startling her Knight regularly. Onyx wanted to see who would be able to keep up with her.

A messenger boy had been sent to Emry's rooms, letting her know that her Challengers were assembled with her father and sister. It was the signal for her to disappear. Emry grabbed a small, brown leather satchel from the back of her expansive closet, hidden by her shoes. The satchel was what she brought with her on her trips out – what she lovingly referred to as her adventure bag. It held a small amount of coin, a book or two, and often a stolen snack from the kitchen.

Slipping the bag over her head, across one shoulder, Emry shut the door to her chambers behind her. The hallway of her family's quarters was bright. The white paneled walls and polished wood floor shone from the many skylights above. The rooms of the royal family sat on the top floor of the palace. There weren't many shadows up here. Emry would have to either go downstairs to the floors below or up to the roof to find any dark corners to hide in.

As planned, she'd take the servants' stairs at the end of the hallway up to the roof. It was the closest exit to the palace. From there, she'd climb down the wall facing the gardens, at the palace's rear.

Emry walked quickly across the soft, sage-colored rugs that ran down the middle of the hallway, over the wood, and slipped into the staircase without anyone noticing. The simple wooden stairwell wrapped downward for three flights and then upward for one. Emry went up. She could hear the voices of servants below her on the stairs – several maids gabbing about who would be staffing the Knight's Ball. Emry stepped as quietly as she could up to the door that ended the stairwell and slid out onto the metal roof.

Squinting in the sunshine, Emry padded to the edge of the roof she'd be pulling herself over and glanced down. Along the entire length of the rooftop, a short, four-foot wall with slits at its base for water to seep through acted as a guardrail. The palace was four stories high. Its exterior was mostly smooth gray rock with a green copper roof. The walls were incredibly slippery – meant to allow the water from the massive storms to simply slide right off. This also made it practically impossible to climb up or down, except for one section of wall that faced the gardens.

This particular section was covered with thick, navy colored ivy, called Weeping Veins. It was a breed of ivy that only grew in Enn. This was why the groundskeeper of the palace had it showcased on the wall. Pale white flowers would bud from it in the spring, lasting until the end of summer. They were poisonous to the touch, causing a rash to form for a week or so. The first time Emry had scaled the wall, she'd made the mistake of not wearing gloves. Her rash had lasted for more than two weeks.

Even though it was already autumn, Emry didn't want to take any chances with the ivy's flowers. In case there were some late blooms, she'd brought a pair of gloves in her satchel. She dug into the bag and pulled them out. As she slipped her fingers into the soft leather, she watched the gardens below for any unwanted witnesses. The gardens appeared to be empty – a positive of going out during a mealtime.

Emry gripped onto the edge of the short wall and swung one foot over, securing it inside the nearest ivy branch. Then, she did the same with the other. Tossing one last glance over her shoulder to the ground, she began the climb down – once again grateful she'd never been frightened by heights.

: : : : :

Declan was wandering. Even though he maintained a somewhat determined look on his face, he couldn't lie to himself. After Vardin explained the task of The Second Trial to him and the other unsuspecting Challengers, the five men separated, dispersing into the palace. His first idea had been the stables, but it'd taken him longer to get there than Piran. He'd arrived in to time to catch the end of a conversation between Piran and a groom. The princess hadn't been there today. Unsure of where to go from there, Declan returned to the palace, where he'd been meandering about for the past twenty minutes.

He doubted Emry would be anywhere inside, since she favored the outdoors. Yet, he couldn't bring himself to go out searching for her when he had no inkling of where to start. If only she could've left him some sort of clue. Then again, how could she give him a hint without having any of his competition stumble upon it as well?

Without fully realizing it, his feet brought him to the door of the palace's library. As if pulled there by some invisible rope. It was highly unlikely that she'd hide in such an obvious spot. Yet, Declan entered the library anyway. The familiar musty scent of books hit him. Making his way through the aisles to the enormous window at the back, he found the small sofa he had shared with Emry and sat down. In daylight without the cover of rain, the view from the window of the palace gardens was expansive and beautiful.

Directly beneath the window were graveled paths

leading out of the palace into elaborate flower patches – all directing admirers toward a large, ornate fountain. The fountain was carved stone, depicting three over-sized wilted roses with their long stems twined together, drooped and dripping water into the basin below. Beyond that was a grove of what appeared to be fruit trees. To the left was a short maze of shrubs, taking up a good fifty square yards of garden space. If the shrubs had been more than three feet tall, they would have made an excellent hiding place. However, the current sovereign clearly preferred the ancient maze to be kept below shoulder height. To the right of the fountain, there were more walking paths and flowers with the addition of sporadically placed trees, shading most of the walkways. From his spot on the settee, he couldn't quite see what lay beyond that.

Easing himself up and closing the distance between him and the window, Declan peered further into the right side of the gardens. There was some sort of glass building that Declan could barely make out amid the trees. As he watched it, a gray-clad figure erupted across the gardens only to evaporate into the shade of the very trees Declan had been watching. Declan stared for only a moment. The person had been dressed like an Anexian woman. And the way she'd ran… Declan whirled back the way he'd come, finally having an idea of where Emry was.

: : : : :

When Emry's feet were back on the ground, she allowed herself a few breaths within the safety of the palace's shadows, pulling the darkness around her as camouflage. If someone were to walk right by her, she wouldn't really be hidden. She'd look like black swirling mist if a person looked too closely. Daylight shadows weren't as strong as nighttime ones, but good enough that for someone ten or so steps away she'd fade into the shade.

The climb down the ivy took longer than she would've liked, but it hadn't been unpleasant. Not like that first time. Because she'd moved slower, though, she'd given her contestants more time to find her. To get to the greenhouse, she'd have to run through the open flower paths to find cover under the myrtle trees. With a sigh and one last scan of the gardens, Emry bolted out into the sunshine.

Sticking to the paths, the gravel crunched under her feet as she moved. If only it was night and a full moon, then she would have been able to sprint like a Teal. As she'd done with Declan. Sadly, it was midday. Her father's idea. So Emry ran as fast as she could. If her former governess saw her now – running like a boy instead of floating about like a princess – she'd probably feign a fainting spell. Fortunately, no one saw her. She made it to the shade of the myrtles without being stopped by one of her Challengers. Immediately pulling the shadows around her once more, Emry decreased her speed.

She was panting, which only made her wish she could run more often. A distance like that wouldn't have winded one of her contestants. Her required activities as a princess at the palace really didn't push her physical exertion enough. She'd grown soft since coming home from Heerth and her trips around her kingdom. The greenhouse was about twenty more steps away. There was no reason to run now that she was able to conceal herself in the shade.

As she drew closer to the greenhouse, a hazy figure inside caused her to halt in place. Emry pressed her back against the nearest tree and dropped into a crouch, trying to make herself as small as possible. Hedron swung open the door to the outside and slammed it behind him so hard that Emry feared its paned glass would shatter. Emry sucked in a breath, urging the darkness to enfold her as best as it could. Hedron would *not* find her if she had anything to do about it.

The Glav whistled and an oversized crow appeared above his head, landing at his feet with a squawk. He glared at the bird. "You said she was in the gardens. I've searched them all. There's not a trace of her."

The crow cawed, and Hedron grunted. His bronze based eyes meant he could communicate with animals. "Search again," he ordered the bird. "I'll follow you."

In reply, the crow leapt upward, returning to the sky. Hedron sighed, as if tired of the inconvenience in having to pursue the princess. He turned toward her, and Emry held her breath. His eyes only rolled over where she squatted on the balls of her feet – to her relief. When Hedron departed into the rest of the gardens after his bird, Emry slowly rose to her feet, glad to be rid of him. Making sure she really was alone, she snuck into the greenhouse.

The square structure was made almost entirely of fogged glass. It was the citrus garden of the palace. Emry breathed in the tangy aroma with pleasure. She usually didn't need to escape here. Since it was on palace grounds, it wasn't really running off. And she could usually convince Citrine to join her in the greenhouse. Cit loved the citrus trees almost as much as Emry did.

At the back end of the greenhouse, there was a wrought iron bench covered with coral colored pillows for comfort. Near that, a similar iron table and two chairs stood invitingly. Emry had shared many midday meals with her sister and Freddick at that same table, enjoying the warmth of the greenhouse. Even though the Kruth Mountains were by far the most frigid portion of Enlennd, Enn was plenty cold. Even in summer, it wasn't unusual for the ground to frost sometimes. The greenhouse provided a comfortable respite from the chill outside, while still being out of the palace.

Emry moved to the bench and sank down. It was set between two of the larger potted orange trees, which offered Emry just enough shade to hide within. Once again drawing the shadows around her, Emry tucked her legs under her, letting just her feet hang off the bench, and rummaged through her satchel for the book she'd brought along. She wasn't sure how long it would take for Declan to happen by.

She – along with the input of Citrine and Freddick – had picked the greenhouse because it could be seen from the library window. Declan wasn't familiar with all of her favorite haunts, but he did know that she liked the library. Maybe if she were lucky, he would have ventured to the library, seen the gardens, and explored them from there. It was the best idea that the three of them had come up with, anyway. Hopefully, it would work. She would stay concealed as best as she could until Declan stumbled upon her. She'd already avoided Hedron – she could do the same with the rest.

Apparently, Emry didn't have to wait long. She'd barely settled in with her book when the greenhouse door cracked open. She froze, shrouded in her shade disguise. When Declan's head appeared, Emry grinned and immediately dispersed the darkness. Declan visibly startled. Emry could only imagine what she looked like suddenly materializing on the bench. The black shadows wafted away from her into nothing. "Hello, Challenger Dexx," she said, emphasizing the *deck* sound again.

Declan stepped inside, shutting the door at his back. "How did you do that?"

She tapped one finger at the side of her eye, as she'd seen him do. "I'm a Silver. I'll tell you more about it sometime."

"Does this mean I'm the first to find you?" He joined her on the other side of her bench.

"It does." Emry reached into her satchel again. She yanked out three ribbon strips the length of her hand, and handed him the blue one. "Congratulations, you've won The Second Trial."

He took the ribbon from her, rubbing his thumb over it, and frowned. "You let me find you."

"Would you have preferred not to find me at all?" She asked. "Because no one would find me if I didn't allow it."

"Are any of your abilities normal?" He eyed her warily.

"You sound like Cit." Emry closed her book. There would be no reading with Declan nearby.

"So, that's a no?"

Fortunately, she wasn't forced to respond. Piran strolled into the greenhouse. As soon as he saw them, he rolled his eyes. "I should have come here first."

"I'm surprised you weren't here sooner," Emry admitted as Piran dropped into one of the chairs at the table. "Where have you been?"

"The stables," he replied, rubbing his eyes with his palms. "I was thinking too big. Of course, you wouldn't go far from the palace for your Trial."

Emry offered him the gray ribbon from her lap. "An honest mistake. You barely came in second."

"Trying to make me feel better?" Piran stood again, taking the ribbon before returning to the chair.

She shrugged. "You're able to move on to the next Trial. I wouldn't be too upset about it."

Piran nodded, taking a glance around. "Nothing looks singed. When was the last time your sister was here, Emry?"

At Piran's use of Emry, Declan turned to her, an eyebrow raised. "Piran's an old friend," she explained to him. "When we were barely more than children, he'd escape the boring banquets and balls with Cit and me. We'd come here a lot. Also, his mother helped train Cit with her abilities. They both are orange-eyed." She shifted her gaze to Piran. "If Cit heard you mentioning her practice sessions to someone other than me, she'd scald you. She hasn't accidentally burned anything in months."

"That long?" Piran chuckled. "She's become so accomplished."

Emry grinned. "Don't let her hear you talking like that."

"No, no," he shook his head, "I know better than that. I think I still have a scar from the last time I teased her." He paused, reflecting on some private memory. Then, "What are you wearing, by the way?"

"Anexian clothes," she answered. "Much more practical than my Enn gowns."

"You mean more liberating," Piran drawled. He personally wore fawn colored pants, tucked into black boots, with a navy waistcoat over a crisp cream shirt. A neckcloth, matching his shirt, was tied around his neck in the latest fashion. His combed hair and sideburns were trimmed and plastered exactly in the right places. He was dressed to the pinnacle of fashion for the modern day Enn male – as usual.

Declan, on the other hand, contrasted somewhat in his pale blue shirt and brown vest. His clothing was new, most likely made especially for The Trials. His sleeves were rolled to his elbows and the top two buttons of his shirt were undone. He wore dark brown pants without boots. His simple leather shoes were the same color as his pants. He looked so Anexian. The current Enn fashion was not as relaxed as that of Anexia. Piran looked very formal, where Declan looked more rugged – hewn from something harsher. Between the two men ... Emry favored the look of the Anexian. There was just something about the way Declan's clothes fit that made her warm all over. He noticed her watching him. His brow furrowed, but he didn't say anything. Emry only smiled.

Piran, oblivious to the exchange, asked, "So, how long will we be in here?"

As if in response, the greenhouse's door opened again. All three turned as Cadoc walked inside. Emry pushed herself to her feet, holding up the green ribbon – her last one. "We're done."

# CHAPTER NINE

The Knight's Ball was rumored to be the actual reason why so many traveled to Breccan for The Trials. Emry's father had spared no expense on the food and decor for her Ball. In honor of her eyes, the theme was a silver, starry night sky. Citrine's had been inferno. Themes were generally based on the princess's base color.

Inside the palace's ballroom, three hundred floating flames created by a team of orange-eyed would light it, giving the appearance of stars in a moonless firmament. Gray-eyed specialists would keep the ballroom cool, pulling in a breeze from outside, while also creating a few sporadic clouds to give the illusion of cloud cover above head. Blue-eyed servants would be close at hand to keep every guest's water glass from ever becoming empty.

Strong spirits had not been served at formal Enn events since Emry's grandfather had been surprise attacked by Perth during a large festival. He'd been so intoxicated that night, it was nothing short of a miracle the palace managed to fend off the assault without their king. Since then, alcohol had been banned from all public royal events.

Even though the vast majority of those attending the Knight's Ball would miss the beauty of the ballroom, they wouldn't be heard complaining. Outside, on the meadows between the palace and the woods that led into the city proper, would be the party that was deemed as the *real* Knight's Ball – or the People's Ball. There, wine would flow freely, and vendors of all regions would be peddling their delicious eats. Instead of one large dance floor, several would emerge, usually one per region playing the rhythms and steps of said region from the fingertips of countless musicians. Young adults generally did the dancing, but at the beginning of the night, families with children also took part in the fun.

The uproar of their music and laughter a year and a half before had drawn Emry away from her sister's Knight's Ball within the palace to watch the celebrating from a balcony. She'd watched the glorified chaos longingly. The variety of people and the combined joy they'd shared had made her sister's extravagant palace dance look stuffy. Emry only wished to one day experience the sort of careless freedom the guests of the People's Ball had. Even though both her indoor and outdoor parties would carry on well into the early hours of the morning, she'd be envious of those on the outside.

At the Knight's Ball, Emry would be required to whirl through a traditional dance from each of her five regions. Depending on the origin of the song, she'd pair with its corresponding Challenger. Once she'd danced with each one, they would be free to escape out to the People's Ball, while Emry would be trapped under the watchful eyes of her father, Vardin, and the palace guards. There'd be no escape for her.

At least Emry would be wearing the prettiest, softest gown Fanny had ever brought to her. It was a floor length, high-waist satin dress with slightly puffed capped sleeves and a low, heart-shaped neckline. Unlike most gowns, it clung to her. The satin shifted only when she shifted. It was the shade of her namesake jewel with silver embroidery along its hem and waist-line. And it was spectacular. Not even Citrine's gowns from her Trials had been so fine. The seamstress Fanny had employed was by far the best in Breccan.

To match the theme of her Ball, Emry's hair had once again been piled on top of her head – braided, curled, and pinned – with small silver-plated diamond and emerald hair pins sporadically placed throughout. A few strategically arranged ringlets escaped the coiffeur to frame her pale face. The tiny, shimmering studs throughout her black hair gave the illusion of wearing stars on her head. The tiara placed at the front of her hair looked like a braid of silver with five emeralds spread across it. A pair of dangling, tear-drop emerald earrings finished the ensemble. Fanny had outdone herself. Emry would be unequaled.

Despite all the reasons she kept telling herself why she shouldn't care, she still found herself hoping Declan would notice how she looked. The girl he'd almost kissed at The First Trial had bothered her more than she wanted to admit. Realistically, Emry had no claim on Declan. Yet, no matter what she did, she kept feeling tugged toward him. When she'd round a corner in a palace hallway, she'd find herself searching for him and would feel disappointed when he wouldn't be there. Emry was going insane. It was the only logical explanation.

As Fanny worked her finishing touches on Emry's hair, Emry tossed a glance towards the blue stained-glass window in her dressing room. From her seat at the vanity, she didn't have to turn her head to look out it. Even though the varying shades of blue glass blocked her view of any objects on the outside, she could see that the sunlight was fading. The first dance of the Knight's Ball took place at sunset. It was nearly time for Emry to make her way to the ballroom.

"All done, dearest princess," Fanny said warmly. "Your Challengers won't be able to keep their eyes off of you."

Emry smiled. "You have superb taste."

Fanny ducked into a curtsy, her cheeks a little flushed. "Thank you, dearest princess."

The door to Emry's chambers clicked open, and Citrine called out, "Emry? We're all waiting on you."

"Well, it is your Ball after all," Fanny grumbled, her voice only loud enough that Emry could hear her.

Emry chuckled and rose to her feet. "Thank you, Fanny."

"A pleasure."

She turned as Cit strolled into the closet. When she saw Emry, she grinned. "Don't you look nice?"

"I think the word you meant to say was exquisite," Emry smirked, leaning one hand on her vanity as she bent to slide on her silver slippers.

"Is that how you wish your Knight to think of you?" Cit teased with a roll of her eyes. She only ever referred to Declan as Emry's Knight now. "What if he thinks of you as merely beautiful?"

Emry glared at her sister. "My Challengers may think of me how they wish."

For as elegant and inspiring as Emry's dress was, Citrine's wasn't that far behind. Fashioned in the same style as Emry's, the cayenne color of Cit's dress had been an excellent choice. It pulled out the deeper orange hues of her eyes. Tied in with the simple gold circlet that had been weaved into her hair, Cit looked every bit the enchanting princess.

"Father sent me to get you," Cit told her. "Your Challengers and the Court have assembled."

"Very well." Emry cast a last look at herself in her heirloom mirror before following Citrine out of the closet, into her rooms beyond, and on to the ballroom.

: : : : :

Declan adjusted the sleeves of his silver jacket again. He felt overdressed. The jacket, which was more shirt than coat, buttoned up one side of his torso and then diagonally up to his throat. It had been embroidered with emerald green thread that matched the color of his pants and the buttons on its front. His black shoes that Peffun called "dancing shoes" had a slight heel to them, which made them click every time he took a step. His short hair had been slicked back so that no piece could possibly fall over his forehead. It was all so formal.

The other Challengers didn't seem like they minded the matching attire. Even Aife who was barely able to walk with his injured calf looked more comfortable than Declan. How was that even possible? The man was practically bursting out of his seams.

Restraining himself from fidgeting anymore, Declan clasped his hands behind his back. He and the other four contestants were standing in the center of the extravagant ballroom, surrounded by courtiers, all waiting for the arrival of the Jewels. As was required, Declan was facing the doors to the ballroom. A troupe of musicians were behind him, playing soothing music soft enough to encourage conversation but not lively enough to begin any dancing. That wouldn't start until Emry was there for it.

To distract himself from his growing impatience, Declan surveyed the ballroom once more. Situated on the second floor of the palace, it was paved in white marble that was veined with gray. Its walls were supposedly whitewashed wood paneling, but at the moment they were shrouded in long swathes of shimmering black cloth from floor to ceiling. The ceiling was a mural of the kingdom's emblem. Yet, Declan couldn't remark on the magnificence of its artist because a thousand tiny floating flames filled the space below it. With the ceiling a good twenty feet above his head, not even Aife could worry about being burnt.

Directly beneath the flames, wispy clouds crafted by Grays drifted back and forth, slowly moving across the whole room. At the back of the musician stand, three sets of double doors opened onto one expansive balcony overseeing the front of the palace. To the left and the right of the dance floor were tables lined with appetizers, sweets, and a variety of lemonades and juices.

This was by far the most lavish affair he'd ever attended. Every detail was executed to perfection, including the attire of the guests. Each person was dressed to the height of Enn fashion. The men had their hair coiffed just so, and the women had theirs up on top of their heads in intricate braids and curls. Declan had never seen so many people looking so fine. Yet, there was something bland about it all. Even though everyone was dressed remarkably well, they all looked the same. No one really stood out.

Just then, the music halted. The doors from the hallway into the ballroom were opening. It was the signal that the Jewels had arrived. Declan straightened slightly. He was ready for the Knight's Ball to begin, because the sooner it did, the sooner it would end and he could get out of his Enn clothes.

The entire room dipped into curtsies and bows, except for the five Challengers at its center. As the king strode in, the most beautiful woman Declan had ever laid eyes on floated in as well – her hand on her father's arm.

Declan knew he was gaping, but he couldn't help it. Emry was spectacular. He dared anyone to look better than she did. From the way the rich, green satin hung on her slight frame to the diamonds and emeralds sparkling in her dark hair, she captivated him. She stood out. He couldn't turn away. As she approached her Challengers, he realized he was grinning foolishly.

Before Onyx and Emry came to a stop, the five Challengers dropped onto their knees. The king called out, "Rise," and the room obeyed.

Declan rose to find his gaze greeted by Emry's. She was smiling politely. "Welcome, my men." She released her father's arm and extended a hand toward Declan. "Shall we?"

The musicians immediately began again. This time, loudly and playing an old Anexian ballad. Since Declan was the first to arrive to The Trials, his region's dance was first. Onyx stepped back, offering the dance to his other daughter who had been standing behind him and Emry. Declan hadn't even noticed her there. He took Emry's hand, planting a kiss on her fingertips as he bowed to her again. Then, in one fluid movement, he pulled her into position in front of him and began to twirl her around the dance floor.

He was vaguely aware of other couples joining in around them, but his eyes couldn't leave her. She bit the tip of her tongue. "You're staring. You haven't looked away from me since I came in."

"Trust me," he chuckled. "I'm not the only one."

Emry tossed a quick glance over her shoulder. "What do you mean?"

"You're gorgeous, Emry," he replied softly.

Her face broke into a grin – the polite smile dissolving into the real thing. "You promise you're not teasing me?"

"Has the palace thrown out all its mirrors, stopping you from seeing for yourself?" He asked.

She dropped her eyes to his shoulder. "You're too kind." Her voice sounded strained, distant even.

He blinked. "It's true, Emry. Why does that upset you?"

She opened her mouth, but then immediately pressed her lips back together. They spun a few turns and still she didn't answer. The dance was coming to a close. Declan felt like cursing the troupe for picking such a short song. He couldn't have her leave him without giving him some sort of reply.

"Emry," he prodded.

"I'm not upset." The words felt like a lie. She still wouldn't look at him. "You are an old friend, and I appreciate your compliment. That's all there is to it."

"I don't believe you." The words were out before he could stop them.

"About what?" Her eyes snapped up.

"That that's all there is to it," he said with a frown.

"Dec," she breathed, "that's all it can be."

He nearly stumbled. She'd called him *Dec*. Had she ever done that in real life to him before? He knew he wasn't dreaming. She'd stunned him with the intimacy of the name no one else ever used, except in his…

"Say it again," he whispered.

"What?" She looked startled.

He leaned in closer, putting his mouth to her ear. She smelled as lovely as she looked – like jasmine and moonlight. "What did you call me?"

Her grip tightened on his hand. "Dec."

"You should use it more often." He meant it. Coming from her, it felt natural. Declan eased back so he could see her eyes again. She was staring at him with a strange look on her face. One he couldn't quite decipher.

But before she could reply to his request, the song ended. It was time for Emry to move on. Declan nodded and released her, dropping into another bow. He brushed his lips over her hand again and to his surprise found himself wishing he was grazing her lips instead. "Thank you for the dance, dearest princess."

"Enjoy your night, Challenger," she responded.

As he stepped back, she turned toward the waiting Cadoc. The next song began – some Midland jig. Declan moved further away from the newly formed rows of dancers. He watched as Emry twined through the rows with Cadoc opposite her. She was wearing that polite smile again.

Declan suddenly felt hot. He spun around, putting his back to Emry and the other dancers. The thought of having a glass of that mint lemonade sounded great. Where were those refreshment tables?

: : : : :

The next thirty minutes, consisting of four different tunes from four different regions, went by slowly for Emry. Her Mid song with Cadoc had limited her communication time due to the required steps of the cotillion. She'd silently acknowledged his lack of passion in the dance. Yet, she couldn't say she thoroughly enjoyed it either, having never been truly fond of Mid contra dances. Then again, her time with Cadoc had been far more enjoyable than the dance with Hedron.

Not a minute into their shared steps, the Glav pointed out how odd it was that she was found in the greenhouse during her Second Trial when he'd already searched the area. By the last note, after arguing through the entire thing, Hedron left sneering and seething, while Emry held no remorse for losing him as one of her contestants. When he whirled off, his long braid nearly hit her in the face.

Her dance with Aife had been her mostly twirling around him while he stood in one place. His inability to move without limping was a real shame – especially since Kruth steps were some of her favorites. They were so lively. Aife's limited mobility had made dancing with him difficult, but even if he hadn't been injured, his height and mass would have not been pleasant for Emry, either. It wasn't easy being partnered with a man who was probably three times her size.

When it was finally Piran's turn, Emry was practically relieved. She welcomed his arm as they began an Enn waltz, somewhat similar to the one she'd shared with Declan. As something of a lifelong friend, Piran was easy company. He was also closer matched to her own height. Dancing with Piran was comfortable. For the first half of their song, neither said much. It wasn't until Citrine floated by in the arms of Vardin that Emry noticed Piran begin to stiffen.

"He's not actually her suitor, you know," Emry assured Piran gently. "That's just a Court rumor."

He glanced down at her, his face flushing. He'd still been watching Cit. "The princess may rest her feelings wherever she wishes."

Emry frowned. "I told her to take your suit more seriously last year."

"You did?" Piran raised an eyebrow.

"You're a good man." She nodded.

He spun her around twice, as the dance required, giving them a break in the conversation. When she returned to his arms, he asked with hopeful eyes, "Emry, would it be worth pursuing her again? Would she one day accept me?"

"I-" Emry didn't know what to say – what Cit would want her to tell him. She didn't want to crush him, either. Taking a deep gulp of air, she said truthfully, "I don't know what the future will hold."

Piran wasn't quite crestfallen, but he obviously wasn't ecstatic about her answer. "I see."

"I've always liked that you never cared about claiming the throne," Emry added thoughtfully.

"Of course not," he laughed lightly, sounding a little more like his usual self. "Why would I when I'm the heir to a dukedom? That has always been more than enough for me."

She smiled. "Which is the reason why I've always liked you."

Their song finished its last few notes. Piran bowed over her hand, kissing the air above her knuckles – as was proper. Declan actually touching his lips to her skin could produce a scandal in Enn if he made a habit out of it.

"Until the next, dearest princess," Piran smirked. He knew her opinion of the title.

"Away with you," she shooed him off with the wave of her hand. "I know there's someone else you'd rather annoy with that dreadful phrase."

As soon as they parted, Piran headed for her sister, and Emry dashed for the doors to the balcony at the most sedate pace she could manage. She'd done her duty and had partnered with each of her Challengers. It was time for a break from them and her Court. Taking a glimpse at the People's Ball from the balcony wouldn't hurt, either.

The moment she stepped into the cool night air, Emry slowed and breathed in deeply. Even with the Grays keeping the ballroom cool, there was no substitute for the real breeze outside. The moon above sent its soothing rays down onto her bare arms, tingling her skin. She tipped her head upward for a moment – pulling in what light it offered her.

The balcony was mostly empty since there were no seating arrangements outdoors. Several clusters of guests scattered the expanse, but none seemed to mind Emry. She didn't even need to use her ability to hide as she leaned up against the stone ledge of the balcony. No one wished to bother her.

Beyond the palace's front courtyard, out on the meadow, at least a dozen bonfires were lit with hundreds surrounding them. She saw five distinct areas of dancers, all twirling and hopping about to different rhythms. From the balcony, the chaotic ruckus of that ball mingled with the lilting music from her own. Despite the beauty of the palace's ballroom, Emry still wished she could escape down to the forbidden party.

"I know what you're thinking." Declan's voice made her jump as he joined her at the railing. He didn't even apologize for startling her this time. "But it's too risky."

Emry twisted her head around toward him. "What do you assume I'm thinking?"

"You want to experience some fun with some commoners."

She grunted. "I'm afraid you'll need to be more specific."

"Don't sneak out to the People's Ball alone," he requested, his voice low so only she could hear him.

"I wasn't going to," she admitted sadly, longingly gazing out at it once more. "I was only wishing."

Declan propped his elbow on the balcony's ledge, leaning back onto it. "I'm a little surprised you'd rather be there than here."

Emry threw a glance at the pretty figures dancing behind her. They moved so stiffly to her. "Are you, though?"

He chuckled. "I guess not. Why do you want to go?"

"To see it at least once in my life." Emry sighed. "Who knows the next time there will be another Trials?"

"You have a point," he nodded. "I was about to go see it for myself."

Emry tried to hold her smile in place but feared it ended up looking more like a grimace. "You'll have to let me know what it's like."

"Or…" he let his voice trail off.

She blinked. "Or what?"

# CHAPTER TEN

This was a bad idea. No, a terrible idea. Yet, Emry didn't turn back. She dashed through the palace halls to her chambers, grasping onto the shadows for her cover. She'd yanked off her tiara and slipped out of the gown Declan had praised her in as swiftly as her suddenly stiff fingers permitted, before donning the Anexian garb from her Second Trial. If anyone noticed her missing at the Ball, her room would be the first place they'd search. She had to be quick.

After grabbing her adventure bag, leaving the books behind this time, Emry bolted up to the roof. It was where she would meet Declan. Just as she'd changed, he'd gone to his room to do the same. She just hoped he'd found his way up to the roof as she practically burst out onto it. Outside was dark except for the little light the moon had to offer. Emry widened her eyes, adjusting them into her night vision, as if she were some nocturnal beast.

He wasn't there. Emry's already quickened heartbeat from her recent run through the palace began to pound against her chest. Had he changed his mind? She walked to the edge of the roof to lean against the stone railing.

Part of being a Silver was being able to see in the dark. The world didn't look exactly like seeing when it was bright out, but she could see the world well enough. Her night vision didn't offer much variety when it came to colors – everything had a blue sheen to it. Also, outlines of objects and buildings were much more muted, having little detail to them. It was still fairly useful, though.

The door from the stairs snicked open. Emry readied herself to fade into the darkness if necessary, but Declan emerged. "Dec?" she whispered, using the name he apparently preferred.

He turned toward her voice. A crooked smile split his face as he walked to her. "You ready?"

She bit the tip of her tongue. "Are we being too reckless?"

"Yes. Have you changed your mind?" His smile slipped.

The logical portion of Emry's mind was screaming against leaving, but the impulsive side of her silenced that part of her brain. She ended up shaking her head. "As long as you don't mind us possibly being caught."

"Us?" He lifted an eyebrow. "Between the two of us, I'm actually allowed to go to the People's Ball. No one will question *my* presence." His gaze shifted from her eyes to the top of her head. "Your hair gems are going to make you stand out."

"Oh, I forgot I had them on." She grazed a hand over her hair. "Could you help me take them out? I can't see them all without a mirror."

Declan made a face as she turned her back to him. "What am I supposed to do?"

"Just pull them out."

Emry heard a slight moan from him before his fingers began working through her hair. She held out a hand for him to place the hairpins in once he'd removed them. He tentatively yanked on her hair as he went. Emry kept in any grunts from whatever jabs to her skull he gave her. He was clearly struggling with rifling through her hair for the jewels. A couple minutes later he said, "I think that's all of them."

"Thank you." Emry faced him again. She slipped the hairpins into her satchel. "Do I look forgettable now?"

"Hardly," he replied dryly, causing her to look up in surprise. "Stay close to me tonight so I won't have to fight anyone off."

She blinked. "I can take care of myself, you know."

He grunted. "Then, why am I currently enrolled in your Trials?"

"I'm assuming for your own amusement," she smirked.

"If that's what you think, our views of fun differ greatly," he retorted. Emry laughed, and he smiled down at her. "So, how do we get to the party from here?"

"We climb down the wall, of course."

"Of course?" He repeated incredulously.

"Why else would I suggest the roof as the best exit to the palace?"

"I thought there would be a ladder or stairs or something." He grimaced.

"There is of sorts." She tossed a glance over her shoulder toward the palace gardens. "Come on."

Declan watched as Emry pulled herself up onto the railing before swinging one leg over its edge. Seeing her straddling the wall made him suddenly nervous. She dug into her bag and pulled out a pair of gloves. She frowned. "I only have one pair, and I doubt these would fit you. I don't think you'll need any, though. I didn't see any flowers last time, but even if there were any, they'd be closed up now that it's night."

"Last time?" He blurted, not sure why he'd need gloves for flowers. "How often do you descend walls?"

"Not that often," she answered, sliding on her gloves. "The ivy should hold both of our weight."

"Ivy?" His uneasiness was increasing. The idea of climbing down a four-story wall while only clinging to ivy vines sounded ludicrous. He'd never been fond of heights. The First Trial had been a struggle, and this was more of a drop than that. "I don't know if this is a good idea."

"Why not?" Emry had been about to swing her other leg over the wall. Declan opened his mouth to tell her his doubts about the ivy's stability, but she cut him off. "You're afraid of heights, aren't you?"

"A little," he admitted. "But I'm more concerned with- Emry!"

She'd dropped out of sight without a word. He gripped onto the wall and leaned his head over the side. She was barely out of arm's reach. "Come on," she said with a smile. "Just focus on one foot at a time."

"Emry," he hissed, running a hand through his hair – freeing some of it from the oils used to slick it back.

"I'll see you at the bottom," she called up.

He swore under his breath and eased himself over the railing. It only took him a moment to catch up with her. "I don't like this," he hissed as he passed by.

"You're clearly better at this than I am," she noted.

"No, I'm just faster."

Three minutes later he was on the ground. Taking a deep breath, he looked up to see how far Emry still had to go. She was barely halfway. He rubbed his eyes with his hands. "Emry, jump off the vine."

"What?"

"This is taking too long," he grumbled. "Jump, and I'll catch you."

"Are you being serious?"

"You're going too slow. Someone is going to spot you."

"So, you think me jumping is the answer?"

He smiled. "Now who's the one afraid?"

"Fine." It sounded like she was speaking with her jaw clenched. "You better catch me."

"Jump," he commanded.

She did. Declan moved beneath her. When she landed on top of him, they both were knocked to the ground. Emry moaned, her face in his chest. "Are you alright?" He asked, pushing himself up onto one elbow, while his other arm was still wrapped around her middle.

"You're not exactly a pillow," she muttered, shoving herself off of him.

"Anything broken?"

"No, I'll survive," she retorted, easing up onto her feet.

"Serves you right for choosing the palace wall as your exit." He stood as well. "Now, get on my back."

She stared at him. "What kind of Knight are you planning on being? You should be showering me with apologies for probably bruising me, not ordering me about."

He bowed deeply. "I'm sorry I wasn't soft enough for you, *dearest princess*. Now, if you would like to make it to the Ball before sun up, I beg you to humbly allow me the great honor of carrying you through the palace grounds on my quick teal-eyed legs."

"That's more like it." Emry grinned, revealing her straight, white teeth. "I will take pity on your impatience and permit you to transport me." She mockingly extended her hand for him to kiss.

With a smirk of his own, Declan grabbed her hand, dragged her to him, and picked her up onto his back. He slipped his hands beneath the back of her knees. Her arms instinctively wrapped around his neck. "Try not to choke me," he drawled.

Declan didn't give Emry the chance to respond. He tapped into his speed and tore off. Four steps later, he set down a very startled princess on the outskirts of the party. Those sitting on blankets and barrels nearby fortunately didn't give them a second glance as they enjoyed their ales and food. Not wanting to draw too much more attention, Declan took the gawking Emry's hand, twining his warm fingers through her cold ones, and headed into the crowd.

"You-" Emry gripped onto his arm with her free hand. "That- that should've taken you longer."

He shrugged. "I told you I was fast."

"At that rate, you could get to Anexia in an hour!"

That was an enormous exaggeration. Declan laughed loudly, realizing he liked her holding onto him more than he should. This was not appropriate conduct of a Challenger to his princess. But he couldn't bring himself to release her, especially not now that they were moving deeper into the crush of people. He could end up losing her if he let go of her. At least, that was what he told himself. She didn't seem to mind, anyway.

Sweet and savory scents filled the air, mixing with the smell of sweat from the throng. Music thrummed around them, vibrating the ground. Declan continued to push his way through the clustered cackling and chatting groups. They were mostly adults – the families with children having already begun the short trek back to Breccan, to their lodgings for the night.

A large bonfire appeared ahead of him. That was where he'd find merchants and dancing. Emry held tight to him as he maneuvered them out into a clearing.

At least thirty musicians were clamoring away beside maybe fifty dancing couples – all Kruths. Declan guided Emry up beside him so she could view the spectacle. He moved his hand to the small of her back without releasing hers, making her bend her arm behind her. He leaned in so that his mouth was next to her ear. "Would you like to stay here or find another region?" He shouted.

She shook her head, brushing her hair against his face. Glancing up at him, she yelled, "I want to dance!"

He nodded and pointed to her bag. "Give me that!" Kruth rhythms required more twirling and jumping from its female participants than its males. Her bag wouldn't get in the way if he wore it instead of her.

Understanding what he meant, Emry slipped her satchel over her head and handed it to him. He then yanked it over his head and one shoulder, letting it strap across his chest as she had done. Once that was settled, Declan took her hand again and pulled her out to join the other dancers.

The dance floor was really nothing more than long planks of wood strewn and nailed together over the meadow. It was temporary and rough, but it did the job. Declan stepped onto the planks just as the song shifted into a new one. It was one he recognized. With Emry still in tow, he swung her around opposite of himself. The grin she sported was contagious. The corners of his mouth turned upward as he moved his right hand to her left side. She, in turn, moved into her first position – both arms stretched behind her back with her head tipped upward. Around them, the other couples did the same. All waited for the signal to begin.

When the musicians hit the note, the couples roared and began to spin. After the third rotation, Declan gripped onto Emry's waist with both hands. She covered his hands with her own, and Declan lifted her up in the air. When he brought her back down, her hands slid onto his shoulders before he caught her right in his left. Then, together, they circled and spun their way around the dance floor with the other couples.

Three more songs breezed by, leaving Declan sweating, but not winded – thanks to his Teal eyes. His sweating was more from the crush of bodies than exertion. Beside him, Emry was panting between laughs, but after each dance ended she asked for another. He carried her through them happily. She was an easy partner and was quick on her feet. As for himself, Kruth steps weren't terribly different than Anexian ones – just much faster with fewer breaks. In truth, Declan preferred Kruth dances to Anexian, but it was something he'd never admit to anyone back home.

As the fourth song gave way for a fifth, Emry jumped up and down – the loose strands of her hair sticking to her face – and gripped onto his upper arm. "This is my favorite!" She shouted.

Declan stared at her. "You know it?"

This particular dance, called the Mountain Thunder by Kruths, was done in rows with partners side by side, grasping one hand. It was footwork heavy and very Kruth. As the dancers stepped, their heels produced a noise like thunder, thus giving it its name. Few people outside of the region ever learned it. As if to prove his point, some of the couples exited the dance floor, leaving closer to thirty pairs.

Emry bit the tip of her tongue. "Do you not?"

No, Declan knew it. Part of being a Teal meant that he was a very swift learner. Taking her hand once more, he pulled her into the nearest row. "Come on."

As the dancers began the kicking and stomping of Kruth's regional gem, the crowd turned their attention to them and began to cheer. To learn the treasured steps of the Mountain Thunder was a sort of coming of age tradition in Kruth. Young adults stamped for their elders and juniors as entertainment.

Emry's forehead beaded with sweat. She was no longer grinning since she was now gasping, but the determination in her eyes made Declan smile. She didn't miss a single step. He had a suspicion this was her favorite because she'd mastered the infamous footwork.

Most of the musicians quieted, leaving only the fast-paced drums to accompany the pounding feet in unison. The rows then shifted positions – couples grouping into circles rather than straight lines. It was some of the more complicated choreography. Yet, Emry continued to hold her own. The circles split into distinctive couples, faced every which way, and the rest of the musicians picked back up again – this time louder than before. The crowd erupted again. The Mountain Thunder was almost done. When the final steps were made, Emry threw up her hand that was joined with Declan's and cheered.

Declan glanced down at her through the uproar. Emry's chest was heaving and her face red, but she was beaming and vibrant. She caught his eyes and laughed up at him. It really was her favorite.

The music began once more. Emry didn't seem interested, though. She put one hand up to her mouth, like she was holding a cup. Declan nodded, realizing she was thirsty. He led her off the wood planks toward the merchant wagons at the other side of the bonfire. They found one that offered water, and Declan purchased two mugs full of it, ignoring Emry's protests about him spending his money on her.

She practically drank the whole thing in one swig. Declan raised an eyebrow. "Would you like another?"

"No," she said sheepishly, "I'm replenished now."

"Where did you learn the Mountain Thunder?" He asked, unable to hold back his curiosity any longer.

"In Kruth," she answered. "It took me a month, practicing every day for a good three hours, but I finally got it. I love it so much. Kruth dances are my favorite."

"Mine, too." The words were out before he realized it.

She didn't seem to care. Instead, she nodded. "You have excellent taste."

A hand on Declan's shoulder made him bristle. Before he spun to see who had gripped onto him, he grabbed Emry's hand again. He didn't want to take any chances of losing her while his back was turned. When he did face his accoster, he allowed himself to relax a little. It was Marsdon.

"Uncle," he inclined his head in greeting.

"Good to see you," Marsdon said kindly. "I was hoping you'd join us common folk tonight. Although, I expected to find you amid Anexians not Kruths."

Declan chuckled. "I could say the same for you. What brings you here?"

"Kruth sticky rolls," he replied, releasing his grasp on Declan.

Of course, it was the rolls. Declan knew all about his uncle's near obsession with the Kruth pastry. "Well, don't let me keep you from indulging yourself."

"Brielle is over by the Anexian fire waiting for you," Marsdon commented, jerking his chin in the direction that must have been where the Anexians were situated.

Was it Declan's imagination or had Emry stiffened behind him? Declan couldn't stop his slow grin as he tugged an unsuspecting Emry forward to join him and his uncle. Marsdon blinked in surprise before dropping his gaze to their entwined fingers. Emry was eyeing Declan warily.

"This is Emry," Declan introduced. "Emry, this is my uncle, Marsdon."

"A pleasure to meet you, sir," she said in a perfect Anexian accent, startling Declan momentarily. She offered her hand. "Your nephew is sure to make our region proud."

*Our region?* Declan frowned but then remembered that her mother had been Anexian. By blood, Anexia was about as much her region as Enn was. Marsdon's smile was warm as he clasped her wrist while she did the same to his. "A pleasure," he intoned. He tossed a glance at Declan. "You need to let the Wynpreg girl know she no longer holds your fancy."

"Next time I see her," Declan assured. It was fairly common in Anexia for young couples to form and then separate only a brief time later.

Emry was watching him again. Marsdon said his goodbyes with them and moved on. Declan led Emry back out to the edge of the party. She didn't say anything until he stopped just beyond anyone's hearing range. "You think it's time we return to the palace." She didn't say it as a question.

"I do," he replied. "I don't want to risk anyone else recognizing one of us."

She nodded. "You're right. We have been out for a

while."

Her eyes lingered on their hands. He still hadn't released her. Emry's elation from earlier had disappeared, leaving her looking unhappy. Declan furrowed his brow. "Is something wrong?"

"Thank you, Dec." She lifted her eyes to meet his, and Declan once again found himself savoring the sound of his shortened name on her lips. It felt so right coming from her. Ignoring his question, she went on, "No one else would have taken me here. I appreciate it more than you know."

"Why are you sad, Emry?" He knew he was prying, but he couldn't stop himself.

"I-" She stopped, shaking her head. "I'm alright. It's just a little depressing to think that I'll probably never get to experience this again."

Declan chuckled and kissed the top of her head – compromising with the sudden urge to kiss more than her forehead. "Maybe you or your sister will have a daughter for another Trials. Then, you can sneak out to the People's Ball again."

She was giving him an odd look. "That wasn't what I meant."

Before he could ask her to explain, she forced a smile. "But you're right. We should be getting back to the palace wall."

He grunted. "Never again. I'll take you to the stables, where it's safe."

"I guess that works." She sighed dramatically. "Will you help me onto your back?"

# CHAPTER ELEVEN

Emry shut the door to her rooms and leaned her head against it, releasing a groan. "Why did I do that?"

"What exactly did you do?"

She yelped as Cit opened up her balled fist, filling her palm with fire and the room with some light. "Don't scare me like that!" Emry ordered.

Citrine was on a settee, still in her ball gown. Freddick was lounging in the chair beside her, also in his formal attire. With a glare at Emry, Cit tossed the orb of fire in her hand into Emry's nearby fireplace. The wood inside it immediately caught flame, brightening the room. Citrine stood up with her hands on her hips. "Where were you?"

"Relax. I didn't run off alone." Emry slipped off her canvas shoes, leaving them by the door.

"Who were you with?" Cit demanded.

"The man you keep referring to as my Knight," she grunted, dropping onto the couch across from Citrine. "He took me out to the People's Ball."

Her sister gaped at her. Even Freddick showed surprise on his usually serene face. "Why?" Cit blurted.

"Did you not just hear me asking myself the same question?" Emry moaned, rubbing her eyes.

Citrine cleared her throat as if searching to find her voice again. "You do realize you're confusing his loyalties to the Rioters when you encourage his attention."

"No, he needs to feel like I trust him completely, which I already do, before he steals me off to Anexia," Emry replied. "Spending time with him only shows that I'm comfortable with him. It still fits with my plan."

"Oh, forgive me, I must have used the wrong word – I meant his *affection*, not attention," Cit shot back. She was still standing but had moved over by the fire.

"His affection?" Emry blinked.

"Emry," Freddick pulled her gaze to him, "you're already walking a fine line with having him supposedly kidnap you. If you wish him to continue to hold his duty to the Rioters higher than any loyalty he has to you, you must put your feelings for him aside."

"My feelings," Emry repeated softly. "Am I so transparent?"

"You've been obsessed with him for years. It's hard not to pick up on it," her sister retorted, twirling a small flame between her fingers like a street magician would do with a coin. "After spending an evening alone with him, I'm sure even he's aware of how you feel now."

"And you don't think me telling him Father wishes to marry me to Trez would throw him off?" Emry asked, pretending to have something beneath her nails that needed to be removed. She knew that information hadn't changed anything between her and Dec, but she wanted to distract her sister. She didn't feel up to discussing her ever deepening attachment to the Anexian.

The room fell silent, except for the crackling of the fire. It took another moment to pass before Citrine managed to choke out, "You told him what?"

"Well, it's true."

"It's also never going to happen. Did you tell him that, too?" Citrine was bouncing her flame between her hands. "What other secrets about yourself have you given the man?"

Emry refused to take her sister's bait. Instead, because she knew it would rile Cit up even more, she said, "Don't worry. I haven't mentioned your undisclosed marriage."

Citrine's jaw dropped. Before she could form a response, Freddick broke in, "We just want you to be careful, Emry. The future of our country could be in jeopardy if Declan doesn't fulfill his promise to the Rioters."

"I know." Emry sighed, suddenly exhausted. "But there's no need to worry. He's a man of his word. After he becomes my Knight, he'll take me to Anexia. He won't fail his people. Even if that means betraying me."

"Only to find out you've been deceiving him all along," Citrine quipped. "He may never forgive you for that."

Emry let out a short, bitter laugh. "Isn't it fun to be the future queen?"

: : : : :

The Fourth Trial was the last public Trial. The fifth was always private. Since the fourth was the final Trial to be witnessed by the masses, its attendance rivaled that of the People's Ball. It would take place inside Breccan, at a local arena. The arena had been the designated location for The Fourth Trial for over a century – since The Trials for Emry's great-something grandmother. It was designed to hold a large capacity of spectators, making it perfect for The Fourth Trial.

Since the Knight's Ball, three nights ago, Declan had spent almost every waking moment sparring off with palace guards – one after the other. Even while still holding back most of his speed, Declan hadn't been bested.

According to Trial law, Declan couldn't fight a fellow contestant until The Fourth Trial, but that didn't stop him from viewing his competition take on others. Both Piran and Cadoc were well trained. What Cadoc lacked in speed, he more than compensated with brute force. Piran, on the other hand, was exceptionally light on his feet.

With all of Declan's practice time, he hadn't spoken with or even seen Emry since they'd parted in the stables after the People's Ball. He told himself it was because he needed to focus on his next Trial, not because he regretted his actions toward her that night. He'd been such a fool. The entire evening he'd treated her as a woman he was pursuing – even letting her know he held no other attachments – rather than the princess he was to serve as her Knight. He was an idiot. What she'd said at the Knight's Ball was true – it was all there could ever be. But he couldn't stop wanting to be near her. Couldn't stop himself from looking for her around every corner. Couldn't stop the disappointment when she wasn't there.

The problem was the way she'd looked at the Knight's Ball. One glance at her had sent all rational thought he might have possessed running. She'd entranced him. That was not to say she wasn't usually pretty, because she was. Very much so. It was just that at the Ball, she'd really outdone herself.

It was sad, really. From now on, he would compare every woman he came into contact with to Emry, and they would all be found lacking. He knew he'd never be content with another woman, knowing that Emry graced the world somewhere else. These were not comforting thoughts. So, for the past three days, Declan had buried them beneath hours and hours spent punching at palace guards.

Today, though, Declan would see Emry. She'd be there at her Fourth Trial, watching and hopeful. Declan really didn't want to disappoint her … or his region. Practically all of Anexia was relying on him. If he failed, he'd be injuring the future of the Rioters. And Emry. He'd dash her hopes to shreds. No, he couldn't lose. He wouldn't. It'd be better for him to die than be eliminated. That sounded a bit dramatic, but if he didn't become Emry's Knight, Anexia would most likely disown him. He'd be left homeless and alone. His mother might accept him back, but he had his doubts about his father. The man's loyalty to the Rioters and The Mistress ran deep. Declan's only real option was to succeed.

Now, as he stood waiting in one of the five ancient hallways at the base of the enormous arena, anxiety was welling up inside of him. This upcoming scenario was all too similar to his duels in Quirl, because he would be dueling just as he had then – without any weapons, ability versus ability. It was making him sweat. He forced himself to take deep breaths. This wasn't going to be like those. And he'd chosen to do this. No one was forcing him to face Cadoc and Piran. This was his choice. His.

Redirecting his attention elsewhere, he noticed the end of the arched, stone-paved passage was filled with bright light. Out there was The Fourth Trial. Behind him, somewhere out the opposite side, was the carriage he'd shared with Cadoc and Piran. As soon as they'd arrived, they were separated into different hallways. It was why Declan was alone in his.

The shouts and applause from the anticipating audience clamored down into Declan's somewhat dreary hall. Wiping his palms on the legs of his pale gray pants, the color he assumed Emry wore today, Declan gulped in a deep breath to try to calm himself. It was almost time. He'd already been informed that he and Cadoc would face each other first. Piran would watch from the sidelines until one of the two men lost. Then, Piran would battle the winner while the loser saw a Ruby before his next match. Declan hoped that wouldn't be him.

Suddenly, the uproar of the crowd was silenced to barely more than a murmur. It was Declan's signal to exit the passage and enter the arena. Taking another deep breath, he made his way out into the light.

: : : :

Emry was going for a countenance of serenity, but from the sideway glances Citrine kept shooting her way, she suspected she was failing miserably. Terrified wasn't quite strong enough of a word to describe the way she felt. When her Challengers had emerged into the sunlight, Emry's eyes had snapped immediately to Declan. He moved toward the center of the arena with far more confidence than Emry had.

She sat between her father and sister in the royal box. It was situated as the front row of the middle of the oval-shaped arena, and like everything else, it was built of mortared stone blocks. The only real difference between the box and the other seats was that a wooden pergola shaded it so that the sun never touched the royals. The seats, though, were still just as uncomfortable as any other stone chair would be.

Declan's eyes rolled upward to catch her gaze, as if sensing her watching him. Emry forced a smile, which felt more like a grimace. The corners of his mouth turned up.

"You should blow your Knight a kiss," Citrine smirked, leaning in so that only Emry could hear her.

Keeping her eyes on Declan, Emry retorted, "Wouldn't that be encouraging his affections?"

"He needs some sort of encouragement if he's to beat Cadoc the Giant," Cit muttered, straightening.

At her sister's use of Declan's title for the Kruth, Emry's grimace shifted to a grin. "Perhaps you're right."

As slowly and subtly as she could manage, Emry brushed her thumb down her lips before tapping it to her heart. It was an Anexian sign of endearment generally used at a parting, but sometimes it meant good luck ... for one's sweetheart. It was a bold move on Emry's part. Yet, it was all she could think of to let him know she was cheering for him without shouting it into the arena.

The sign caught Declan off guard. He nearly stumbled as he came to a halt at the reddish-brown clay round he would be fighting Cadoc on. He stared at her – his expression a strange mix Emry couldn't read.

"What did you do to him?" Citrine whispered.

Emry shrugged innocently. "I just wished him good luck."

From their two other tunnels, Cadoc and Piran joined Declan beside the clay round, which had been set directly in front of the royal box. The round was raised off the stone floor by about half a foot. Emry's Challengers would have to step up to get onto it. It was a little more than twenty feet in diameter, giving the

Challengers plenty of space to duel. There were only two rules they would need to abide by – no weapons were permitted on the round, and if a contestant stepped off after the duel had begun then that man forfeited. The purpose of The Fourth Trial was for Challengers to fight relying on their skills and natural abilities alone.

Vardin appeared in the base of the arena dressed in his usual black, grey, and white attire, complete with cape. He stepped onto the clay round, stopping at its center. Cadoc and Declan did the same, staying at its edge. Piran backed away, giving himself a wide berth of the upcoming conflict. Cadoc and Declan stood on opposite ends of the round. They eyed each other silently.

"You know the regulations," Vardin called out, his smooth voice clear and loud. The two contestants nodded once to each other. Vardin lifted his hands into the air before dropping them. "Begin!"

The moment Vardin backed off the clay, Declan collided with Cadoc in an enormous boom. Emry stared. The blow should have sent the big man to the ground. Declan had obviously tapped into his speed with how fast he'd bolted. Yet, Cadoc held his ground. It was Declan who bounced backwards, landing on his rear. Emry noticed a look of admiration on Declan's face as he jumped back up onto his feet. She had to admit she was impressed, too. Cadoc had been strong enough to stop a man faster than a stampeding horse.

Declan took off again, shifting into a blur of color around Cadoc. The sound of Declan's fists meeting Cadoc reverberated into the stands. Cadoc didn't even flinch. Instead, he walked into the middle of the round with Declan still whirling around him. Emry could feel herself openly gaping now. The Kruth was making Declan look more like a pest than an opponent.

Realizing his method was clearly not working, Declan stopped just outside of Cadoc's reach. Parts of his shirt clung to his skin from where the sweat trickled down his body. He was panting, watching Cadoc somewhat in awe. He wasn't alone, though. Emry and at least half of the arena were doing the same thing. The only sign Cadoc had received any sort of beating was the beginning of a bruise around his left eye. His stance was relaxed and not a bead of sweat had formed. The man was essentially made of stone.

With a shake of his head, Declan dove for Cadoc once more. Cadoc didn't budge. Oddly enough, he closed his eyes and reached one arm out in front of him. Emry frowned. She had a feeling Cadoc was doing something significant but wasn't sure what that was.

A moment later Cadoc's fist closed over Declan's shoulder, yanking him to a stop. Emry blinked. How had he managed to do that? Before she could give that question much thought, Cadoc slammed Declan down onto the ground.

Emry gasped and gripped the arms of her chair. Declan's skull hitting the floor had a sickening thud that echoed inside her head. Cadoc swung a fist at Declan's face but stopped it less than an inch away. He glanced up at Vardin, who was still at the edge of the round. "Call it!"

Vardin raised an eyebrow. "Finish him."

"I do that, and he dies." Cadoc shook his head. "Call it."

"Very well." Vardin practically sighed in resignation. He turned to Emry and her family. "Challenger Cadoc is the winner."

The stands erupted into applause. They most likely

had been cheering the whole time, but Emry hadn't heard them until now. She'd been too distracted. Two medics rushed onto the round lifting Declan up. They lifted one of his arms over each of their shoulders before dragging him off into one of the tunnels, removing him from Emry's sight. Another medic hovered around Cadoc, running her hands just above his skin as she healed his bruises.

Emry took a deep breath and then slowly released it. Cadoc had behaved honorably. She'd remember that. As for Declan, she told herself that he would be fine – that the medics would fix his injuries. Her real concern should have been about Declan possibly losing The Fourth Trial. Yet, after watching Cadoc destroy him in just a few minutes, she doubted Piran could do better. Even though Piran had the ability to quickly self-heal, she still didn't believe him strong enough to knock out the great wall of Cadoc. This meant that Piran would lose, making Cadoc the champion of The Fourth Trial. Piran would then face Declan for the spot of runner up. Emry just hoped Declan would be well enough to win that fight.

: : : : :

Declan came to with a slap to the back of his head. His eyes flew open to the face of a blond Ruby. The man cracked a smile, revealing crooked teeth. Strange for a Ruby. Usually they'd straighten their own teeth out. The Ruby backed up a little. "Good. You woke up."

"Was I not expected to?" Declan croaked out. His brain felt like someone was hitting it with a mallet.

Another Ruby appeared in front of Declan. This

one had dark hair and scruff covering his jaw. "Other than your head, what hurts?" He asked.

Declan grunted. The pounding in his skull was making it hard for him to remember he had any other body parts to worry about. "I don't think anything else does."

"Here, let's take care of your headache," the blond said, placing his hands on the back of Declan's head.

The pain began to fade, leaving Declan lightheaded. It was a vast improvement, though. He sighed in relief. "Thank you."

"Of course." The blond removed his hands, and the other man offered him a rag to clean them.

Declan stared at the Ruby's red-stained fingers. "Is that my blood?"

"Yes," the dark one nodded, "but it's not fresh. We've already taken care of that."

"Think you're able to stand up?" The blond straightened above Declan, extending a hand to him.

"One way to find out." Declan clasped the man's wrist, accepting the help up to his feet. He teetered for a moment, but the Ruby still had his wrist and had gripped onto Declan's shoulder with his free hand, steadying him. Declan took a few deep breaths before nodding for the Ruby to slowly release him.

"Can he fight?"

Declan turned to the voice behind him. Vardin stood at the exit to the tunnel Declan and the Rubys were in. He frowned at the captain as the two Rubys ran their hands up and down his body, barely above his skin and clothes. When they stepped back, the blond answered, "He's healthy enough."

"Good. He has two minutes to be out on the round." With that, Vardin spun around and left them, his cape snapping behind him.

Piran must have lost to Cadoc as well. Not surprising. The last thing Declan remembered was being yanked as if by an unseen rope into Cadoc's hand. The green in Cadoc's eyes had allowed him to create a "path" between himself and Declan. It was how he'd been able to get a hold of Declan even while tapping his teal-eyed speed. Declan knew of others with the same ability, but it was a rare enough trick that he hadn't expected Cadoc to have it in his arsenal. Obviously, it was a mistake on Declan's part that he'd paid for.

"You need to go," the dark-haired Ruby pointed out.

"Right." Declan nodded once. "Thank you again."

He walked out into the sunlight and squinted. This time, he didn't look at Emry. He wasn't sure how he looked, and her reaction to his appearance might have told him things he didn't want to know. He made his way to the round again where Cadoc and Piran stood beside it with a couple Rubys. Piran's Ruby was finishing up with what Declan guessed had been a broken nose. Cadoc inclined his head to Declan as he headed towards them, and Declan returned the gesture. Declan held no ill will to the man.

Vardin climbed onto the round. Declan joined him, and Piran left his Ruby to do the same. Vardin glanced between them then raised both arms above his head. "Begin!" He shouted, flinging his arms downward.

The captain's feet hadn't even left the clay before Declan crashed into a startled Piran. He'd aimed his shoulder into Piran's chest. The poor Enn didn't stand a chance. He was pitched backwards off the round, landing a good fifty feet away. Declan stopped at the edge of the round and watched as the two Rubys ran for Piran. He knew that Piran would be fine – he hadn't hit his head.

"Your majesty and dear princesses!" Vardin materialized with Cadoc at Declan's side. He was facing the royal box. "I give you the champions to Princess Emerald's Fourth Trial!"

Declan was vaguely aware of the crowd's roaring around him as he looked up at Emry. She was grinning widely. Even though he knew he still had one more Trial ahead of him, competing against Cadoc the Giant, Declan couldn't help but smile, too. It felt good to advance from another Trial. He'd worry about The Fifth Trial later.

# CHAPTER TWELVE

It was really happening. After years of careful scheming, it was finally all coming together. Emry felt like squealing as she collapsed onto a sofa in her front sitting room. She stretched her legs out in front of her in a most unladylike manner.

Following the last Trial, she'd retired early for the night, stripping down to just her shift and favorite black robe. She'd had her dinner sent up to her rooms a couple hours ago. A small fire crackled happily in its hearth near her. Emry watched its light flicker above her on the ceiling. For the first time in months, she was relaxed. An enormous burden had been lifted from her shoulders.

A soft rapping on her door competed with the noise from the fire for a moment before Citrine and Freddick slipped unceremoniously into her chambers. They had also dressed down for the night and were in soft robes of their own. Freddick sank onto the settee opposite of Emry, and Citrine flopped down beside him.

"I thought you'd be twirling around the room, not lying there," her sister teased.

Emry smiled. "I was waiting for you to join me before I began the celebrating."

Cit laughed. "I'm happy for you, Emry."

"As am I," Freddick added in his low voice. "Congratulations."

"If anyone should be congratulated, it really should be Declan." She straightened, letting her feet drop to the floor. "I mean, he was the one to do all the work."

"But you're the mastermind behind this whole ruse." Citrine rolled her eyes.

"No, that would be Declan's father, remember?" Emry stood, unable to sit still any longer.

"You asked for Declan specifically, though," Citrine pointed out.

"I think begged is a better word for it," Emry grumbled, stepping closer to the fire to warm her endlessly cold hands.

"So, how long now until he carries you off?" Her sister asked quietly.

Emry shrugged, her back to them. "Levric refused to give me a date. He said it would depend on Declan."

"Are you nervous?"

She turned. "About what?"

Cit's face had turned sad. "About how Declan will react when he finds out."

A sharp knock on her door stopped Emry from having to respond. She exchanged a quick glance with her sister. Who would venture to her rooms at this late of an hour? "Come in," she called out.

The door cracked open and in strode Onyx. Upon seeing him, Citrine cast tiny flames from her palm to light the lanterns scattered around Emry's front room. Emry frowned. "Father, what brings you here?"

Onyx didn't answer her question. Instead, he said, "Citrine, Knight Freddick, would you leave us alone?"

"Yes, Father." Citrine jumped up to obey. Freddick trailed behind her. As Cit passed Emry, she flashed a quick encouraging smile.

Once her sister was gone, Onyx gestured to the settee Cit had just vacated. "Please, take a seat."

Emry lowered herself onto it while Onyx positioned himself on the sofa across from her. She eyed him warily. "What is this about?"

"Your Fifth Trial," Onyx told her.

"What?" Emry blinked. Sudden panic shot through her. What if her father had an actual event planned for her Fifth Trial? She'd been so trusting in the notion that Cit's experience would mirror her own. She'd completely ignored the possibility that she might not be given the option to choose her Knight. The thought made her stomach churn.

Her father scratched at the top of his knees with his hands. He looked uncomfortable. "Do you know what your Fifth Trial will be?"

"No," she said slowly, struggling to keep her voice even.

Her father smiled slightly. "For your Fifth Trial, you must decide which man you would have as your Knight."

"Oh." The word came out as a sigh. Emry nodded, instantly relieved. "I am to choose."

"Yes, and I would like you to make your decision now," Onyx replied tentatively. "I wish him to be sworn to you tonight."

"Tonight?" Emry blurted. She'd thought it would have been at least another day.

Onyx's brow drew together at her reaction. "It would ease my heart if I knew you were finally properly protected."

Emry bit the tip of her tongue, holding in the urge to scoff. She could protect herself just fine, and there was no imminent danger to merit an immediate ceremony. Yet, what did it really matter if it was earlier than anticipated? He would be sworn to her either way. She nodded. "Alright."

"Do you have a preference already?" Onyx asked, running a hand over his graying beard.

"I-" Emry hesitated. She needed to be careful with what she revealed. "I believe I do."

"Good. Good." Onyx nodded. "Which man would you have as your Knight?"

:  :  :  :  :

Declan was practically dragging his feet as he followed Peffun through the palace's dark hallways. He'd been shaken from his sleep barely more than ten minutes prior. The only hurried explanation Peffun had tossed at him along with some clothes had been something about The Fifth Trial.

If Declan was really on his way to the last Trial, he was in no condition to compete. He was taking the effects of The Fourth Trial from earlier that day hard. Every inch of him was sore. It didn't help, either, that he'd slept less than two hours before Peffun had hauled him out of bed.

Not even bothering to hide his yawn, Declan rubbed the corners of his eyes with one hand. In his current state, Cadoc was sure to best him in whatever it was that they had to do. If Declan was being honest with himself, he was too exhausted to care. When Peffun halted in front of a door, Declan glanced up at it blearily. It took him a few seconds to recognize where they were.

He raised an eyebrow at Peffun. "The library?"

"This is where you have been summoned," the

small man replied loudly with a bow. "I will leave you here."

Declan watched the man go. He had no doubt that whoever was inside the library had heard Peffun's booming voice, announcing Declan's arrival to them. Yawning again, he reached for the doorknob. The massive room was dark and seemingly empty, except for the dancing of candlelight at the far end – over by the only window. Figuring that was his destination, Declan trudged through the book-laden shelves. As he rounded the last corner, he pulled up short.

Emry, wrapped in that slinky black robe of hers, was standing in front of the window beside an elderly ruby-eyed man Declan had never seen before. Seated on the settee that faced the window was the king. Both men wore simple garb of muted colors – nothing formal. It made Declan feel slightly better about his undeniably disheveled appearance. However, the way all three of them were staring at him made him feel more than a little awkward. Declan dipped into a hasty bow. When he straightened, Emry's voice drew his attention to her.

"Challenger," she said, "would you do me the great honor of becoming my Knight?"

It took a moment for her question to register. "Your Knight?" He blurted. What about The Fifth Trial? Had Cadoc somehow dropped out?

She smiled, but it didn't touch her eyes. She was tense. "Yes, would that please you?"

"Of course, dearest princess," he stammered. A part of him worried he'd fallen back asleep somewhere along his way through the library. Or, perhaps, Peffun had never actually woken him up, and this was just some dream. This wouldn't be the first time he'd dreamt of Emry.

"Excellent!" The old man exclaimed. He gestured for Declan to join Emry at her side. "Let us begin."

As Declan moved to stand at Emry's right, she was sure everyone in the room could hear her heart pounding against her ribs. It was all she could hear. Her excitement was competing with her fear that someone would come barging in, thwarting everything. Darius – the Keeper of the Old Tomes – needed to hurry up with the ceremony. As there was only one Ruby in Enn ever alive at a time who could properly read the Old Tomes, who knew the ways of swearing Knights to Princesses, Darius was the sole option to complete the ritual. Unfortunately for Emry, he was a slow mover.

Darius exchanged long, silent – bordering on uncomfortable – looks with both Emry and Declan. His eyes flitted between them for a good five minutes. If he didn't get on with it soon, Emry was going to scream. Her hands were beginning to sweat. She discreetly wiped them on the slick fabric of her robe, which really did nothing to get rid of the moisture. Finally, Darius offered them all a wide grin.

"Well, then. Face each other, please." He motioned for them to obey. "Yes, just like that. Now, join hands."

Declan's left hand reached for Emry's right, but Darius stopped him. "My mistake. I didn't explain that very well. Take her right hand with your right, and then her left with your left. You both need your wrists crossed, but unable to pull your hands apart."

There wasn't much space between them. Declan lifted his bent arms to Emry's at chest level, crossing them at his wrists. Emry did the same, slipping her clammy fingers around his warm, dry ones as she cupped his hands. She hated that her palms probably felt wet against his, but he politely didn't seem to notice. His eyes were glued to her face – his gaze intense. She would have liked to look away, but dared not. She'd just asked him to be her Knight. She couldn't act uneasy with her choice.

Not even the pressure of Darius's calloused and wrinkled hands covering their own had them break eye contact. The light from the candelabras flickered over Declan's eyes as Darius's hands warmed to a temperature above that of a natural body. They grew hot but not to the point where his touch burned. Emry felt the warmth spread outward into her limbs – up to her chest, down to her toes. Then came a gut-wrenching yank from inside of her.

Emry gasped. It was as if a rope had been secured around her heart and was now being tugged through her body into her arms toward Darius. Her limbs felt as if they were on fire. She wanted to cry out in pain, but she couldn't find her voice. She tried to pull her hands out of Declan's grasp, but her body wouldn't respond. She was frozen in place. It was torture. Outright torture.

Across from her, Declan was clearly concerned. His face was strained, tight. Was he feeling it, too? Emry began to shake. Sweat beaded on her forehead and silent tears slid down her cheeks. It was becoming too much. Tiny bright lights twinkled across her vision. She was going to faint. Emry squinted from the strain and her eyes accidently adjusted into that ability she rarely touched. She realized with a start why she was in agony.

She could see it. Two small cords of light were being pulled from both Declan and herself. The cords were drawn from their hearts and were moving toward one another at a glacial pace. Emry had never seen her own light – her own life force.

To see Darius bring it out of her was fascinating but overwhelmingly excruciating. For every inch the two ropes crept across the space between her and Declan, it felt like an hour had passed. Emry was having a hard time breathing. But it was almost to Declan's. Just a little more…

When the two ropes joined into one, Darius removed his hands, and Emry collapsed. Declan caught her before she went far. She slumped into him, panting. Her sight went black. She was so incredibly dizzy she was sure she was about to pass out. From somewhere far away, she heard Declan say her name.

Darius's confused voice was muffled, as if she were under water. "I don't understand. Her sister didn't react this way."

There was a steady roaring in Emry's ears – like wave upon wave was crashing inside her head. Slowly, her eyesight picked out something in the darkness. It was the rope of light, connecting her with Declan. She released a sigh. The rope meant that it was over – Declan was her Knight.

Her Knight's blurry face came into view, followed by Darius's, who was waving his hands barely an inch above her head. She blinked up at them as her vision continued to clear and her eyes adjusted back to normal. Darius smiled, his ancient face crinkling up. "There now, she has returned to us."

"Are you alright?" Her father's head popped in between Declan and Darius's.

Emry found her voice. "Yes," she managed.

"I am sorry. I was not expecting that to happen," Darius apologized. He glanced at Declan. "She needs to rest here for a few more minutes before you take her back to her rooms. That's all it should take for her to feel herself again."

"Be sure to carry her back," Onyx ordered. "Do not let her walk."

"Yes, sire." Declan nodded, his face pale.

Darius disappeared from Emry's line of sight as her father bent over, kissing her forehead. "Rest well, Emry. No adventures tomorrow."

Her father hadn't called her *Emry* in years. She forced on a smile in an attempt to be reassuring. "Yes, Father."

Onyx gave Declan a stern look before taking his leave as well. Once the door to the library clicked shut after the exit of the two men, Declan groaned and rubbed his eyes with his palms. "Well, that was awful."

Emry grunted. "You weren't even the one to faint. That was incredibly painful."

"I swear, that Ruby was trying to catch us on fire," he retorted. "Please don't make me go through that ever again."

"You couldn't move, either?"

"Not at all."

She frowned at him. "Why didn't it affect you as much as it did me?"

He flinched. "I have a higher pain tolerance than most."

"If I'd known Darius was going to blend our light, I would have been better prepared for it," she grumbled, pushing herself up to sit. They were on the settee across from the giant window.

"Easy," Declan warned, steadying her with one hand on her elbow. "What do you mean he blended our light? What light?"

Now that Declan was her Knight and unable to run

away, she was willing to let him in on some of her more unusual abilities. "There's light in everyone. It's life – the material our souls are constructed of. And I can see it. To swear us to each other, Darius took out light from each of us. He blended it together to form a rope of it between us. It's how we're now bonded."

"You can see light inside of people," he repeated slowly.

She nodded before placing her elbow on the back of the settee and leaning her head into her open palm. There was a throbbing behind her eyes. Her heart was still struggling to settle down in her chest … And she could feel him. There, on the other end of their new tether. Declan was there. It was an odd sensation. It was as if she could reach out her hand and use the rope as a guide to him – like they literally had been tied together.

"I can feel you." The words slipped from her mouth. She winced, realizing she probably should have kept that information to herself.

"I know." He rubbed at his eyes with one hand. "I can feel you, too. And the chain that links us."

"You can?" She figured her being able to sense it was an effect of her abilities. Declan noticing it as well was surprising.

"It's like I could find you anywhere with my eyes shut." He grunted. "Feels weird."

Emry bit the tip of her tongue. If he thought that was weird… "There's something else you should know. We can't be more than thirty feet apart. As in, we're now physically incapable of it."

"What?" He blurted, whirling back around to face her.

"My sister had to discover this on her own," Emry

told him. "If we're too far from each other, we both feel it. Cit says it's sort of like being stabbed in the stomach."

Declan was staring. "Is that all?"

"No," she shook her head, "neither of us can cause the other any harm. We'd just bounce off each other."

He sucked in a breath, running a hand through his hair. "I wasn't planning to be on a leash."

"Neither were Cit and Freddick," she retorted. "But enough of this for tonight." She stood, slowly, so she wouldn't feel dizzy from the motion. "I'm tired, and you look like you haven't slept in days."

"I'm exhausted," he admitted.

"Then, you may take me as quickly as you can muster to my rooms. I couldn't possibly walk myself as that would be disobeying my king's demands."

Declan moaned and turned his back to her. "Fine. Get on."

Using the settee as a stool, Emry climbed up onto his back and wrapped her arms around his shoulders. "Would you like some directions?"

"I know where your chambers are."

"You do?" Emry blinked.

She gasped as Declan tapped his speed without warning. A few seconds later she found herself in her very own sitting room. Emry slid off of Declan, stunned from more than his extraordinary swiftness. "Have you been to my rooms before?"

He didn't wait for an invitation to sit beside the still glowing fire, the room's only light source at the moment. "Not inside, but just outside the door plenty of times."

"I'm fairly certain I mentioned avoiding my family's quarters."

"No one stopped me." He shrugged.

"You mean no one saw you," she retorted.

A mischievous, crooked grin split his lips. "My abilities might have given me an advantage."

She rolled her eyes and began for the door leading to her bed. "Come on, then. I'll show you where you're to sleep from now on."

Declan caught up to her just as she dropped onto the edge of a bed that could have accommodated at least three people. He gawked a little at the thick four posters and white linen sprawled over the top, creating a filmy canopy. At the sight of the soft white comforter and stack of fluffy pastel colored pillows on top of the mattress, he felt his eyes droop. His body ached to collapse anywhere at this point.

Emry must have noticed his expression because she smiled. "Your cot is by the door."

The plain, brown cot was in stark contrast with the opulent comfort of Emry's bed, but Declan saved dwelling on that thought for another time. He sank down onto his cot – barely remembering to shuck off his shoes and shirt before his head hit the gray, somewhat flat, pillow. He was vaguely aware of Emry closing her room's door as he pulled on the gray flannel blanket. When she blew out the only lamp in the room and settled into her own bed, sleep finally allowed him to succumb to it.

The last thing he remembered before slipping away completely was Emry whispering, "You did it, Dec. You won."

# CHAPTER THIRTEEN

Desolation. Anger. Fear. So much fear. Everywhere. Enveloping. Constricting. Suffocating.

Emry bolted upright in her bed. Swirling, ethereal clouds of intangible black surrounded her, filling the entire room. She stared at the fog blearily in the limited moonlight that snuck through her windows. The sight of it felt off. Wrong even. She wasn't having a nightmare, and it had been months since she'd simply lost control in her sleep. No, this mist shouldn't be happening. Yet, there it was. She had the unsettling sensation that it wasn't coming from her. But that didn't make sense. No one else in the palace could call out the darkness.

"No more."

Declan's moan reminded Emry with a start that she wasn't alone in her room. She frowned. Was he asleep? Was he the one having the nightmare? Even if he were, that didn't solve the question of why the room was encased in tendrils of shadow. He was a Teal.

"Please, please, no more." His voice cracked. He was begging. "I can't."

The desperation and absolute anguish in his voice sent Emry shoving back her comforter and dropping her bare feet to the floor. She didn't even bother with her robe when she saw the twisting wall of murky smoke obscuring Declan from her view. He was entrenched within the darkness – victim to his dream.

With the wave of one hand, Emry pushed through the torrent, creating a path. She slid into the vortex, and the gap she'd created closed behind her. As she'd suspected, the mist was oozing out of him. She laid a hand on his shoulder, and her fingers were instantly drenched – his body soaked in his own sweat. "Declan, wake up!" She shook his shoulder.

His eyes flew open, but he didn't seem aware of the motion. He was still asleep – blind to the conscious world. "Declan," she repeated.

Instead of responding, his face contorted in some sort of unseen pain. He clenched onto his blanket and cried out, arching his back as if he were fighting against invisible restraints. The clouds grew thicker and seeped outward, choking out what little light there was in the room.

Emry had had enough. With a grunt, she climbed onto Declan's cot and straddled him. Ignoring the sticky feeling of her now sweat-soaked shift, she placed one hand on Declan's wet chest and extended the other toward the shadows. Declan groaned beneath her, silent tears streaming out the corners of his eyes. What sort of horrors were haunting him?

Knowing what had to be done, she sucked in a breath and then drew in the darkness. Slowly, Emry channeled in the swirling shadows from the room – drinking in his pain and sorrow. Emry gasped as the emotions momentarily overwhelmed her. She gulped in air, forcing back the sheer panic and the instinct to block out the fog immediately. Relying on her years of practice, Emry pushed through the onslaught of emotions and grasped onto the underlying power that supported them – to the raw energy of the anguish. As that power filled her, consuming the space where the misery had been moments before, Emry exhaled.

The depth of Declan's pain had to have been great. The strength of what now flowed through Emry was substantial, and it wasn't ending. Declan was still asleep, discharging his nightmare into the room. To make matters worse, his breathing was so shallow that Emry wasn't sure his lungs were taking in air anymore.

"Breathe, Declan," she pleaded.

Applying more pressure to the hand she already had on his chest, Emry did the only thing she could think of to wake him. Utilizing some of the energy she'd taken from the room, she tipped her head back and urged a flash of bright light out of her body. If the light hadn't been coming from herself, then she would have been momentarily blinded. As for Declan, whose unseeing eyes had been open, he released a startled cry and jerked up. Emry was flung from his chest onto the floor. She landed on her side with a grunt, surrounded by the last of the mist.

While Declan tried to rub some sight back into his eyes, Emry noticed a scar the width of her pinky and the length of her forearm that ran along the entire right side of his ribs. It was shaped like a crescent moon, going from the front of his ribs to his back. She'd seen that before. In her dreams. Strange her mind recalled a scar she'd probably glimpsed ages ago while he'd sparred with Ewan outside in the estate's gardens.

This was the first time she'd seen him with his shirt off – close up in real life – in years. The lean, bulging muscles she'd admired previously beneath his tunic were now displayed before her, and she couldn't help but stare. His body was beautiful. His shirts had not done him justice. She decided this was how she preferred him – muscles out in the open for her eyes to devour. They were just as she'd dreamed. Her imagination had been shockingly accurate on that account.

His moon scar wasn't the only mar she found on him, though. More than a handful of others of varying widths and lengths were strewn across random places along his middle. Scars her dreams had missed. Most were thin and short things. None nearly as big as the moon one. But the fact that he had so many … It confused Emry. He couldn't possibly had gotten these all from his time on the Anexian border. What had he been doing? Emry wanted to reach out and trace her fingers over each one.

"What is that?"

Declan must have regained his vision. Emry looked up from his middle to his face, but his eyes weren't on her. His gaze was locked on the remaining wisps of darkness flitting about in the moonlight. She winced before lifting a hand and sucking the rest of it into her fingers.

Emry clenched down onto the power his nightmare had given her. Focusing her attention inward, she compressed it before burying it into that place deep inside of herself where she stowed her power – the vast reserve no one knew about, not even Cit. Where the pain and sorrow she stole from others laid dormant until called upon.

Now, she had Declan's attention. He was gaping at her.

"You had a nightmare," she said, pushing herself up to lean back on her hands. One of them still felt moist from when it'd been on his chest.

"With smoke?" He blurted.

"It was a really bad nightmare."

"What?"

She bit the tip of her tongue. This was not a conversation she was expecting to have on their first night. With a groan, she pushed some strands of loose hair out of her eyes. "You being sworn to me now might mean that you have some side-effects of my abilities. I do the same thing."

"You create smoke while you sleep, like an orange-eyed," he grunted incredulously.

"No, that wasn't real smoke. Those were shadows." She frowned. "When I have nightmares, I unwittingly call out the darkness."

Emry watched as he processed that revelation. She wasn't in a mood to answer questions, though. Not with those sculpted pectorals out distracting her. So, before he could form a response, she switched the topic. "What were you dreaming about?"

His eyes shuttered almost instantly. He wiped his damp face on his blanket. "Something that happened years ago."

Well, it appeared that Emry wasn't the only one avoiding explaining herself tonight. Fine by her. She needed to change out of her sticky shift anyway. But that didn't mean she wouldn't be bringing this back up at a future date. She stood. "I'm sorry that it still haunts you, and I emphasize haunt. Because what I heard of that dream sounded like pure torment."

He grimaced. "Nicely put."

"We can revisit this topic later."

"Sure," he nodded, "same with your shadow calling."

"I'm sure you won't forget," she muttered before heading to her closet.

By the time she returned, Declan was laying on his

side with his face to the wall. She guessed he wanted her to assume he was asleep again, but his breathing was still too ragged. Once in bed, she stared up at the thin linen canopy above her head, listening to Declan breathe. It took a long time for her to fall back asleep.

: : : : :

Declan woke to sunshine streaming into the room. At dawn. After a night of tossing and turning with little sleep, following a very physically taxing day, seeing those two large open windows, on either side of Emry's bed, filled with light brought Declan into an immediate bad mood.

Thick, white drapes sat on either side of the panes. But, for some reason, they weren't being utilized. Now that he thought about it, they weren't drawn in the middle of the night, either. Moonlight had filtered into the room. Why have curtains if you never used them? Declan glared at the windows before tossing an arm across his eyes.

Maybe an hour later, the rustling of sheets roused him from his flimsy dozing. Emry was waking up. How she'd stayed asleep until now with the room so bright was beyond him. The soft thud of her feet hitting the floor followed by her even quieter footsteps irrationally set him on edge. He blamed it on jealousy from her getting more sleep than he had. She was moving away from him. Worried that she'd pull on his new thirty-foot leash, he half moaned and in a voice that came out a pitch deeper than usual, he asked, "Where are you going?"

She froze in place, her footsteps ceasing, but didn't respond.

"I know you heard me," he grumbled without removing his arm from his face. "Where are you going?"

"To my washroom. Did I wake you?"

"No, the sun did," he grunted. "That's what happens when you leave the windows open."

"Oh. Right. I forgot people don't usually do that at night."

"You forgot?" He blurted, finally dropping his arm and opening his eyes. The genuine tone to her voice startled him. She was standing in the middle of her room, wrapped in that black robe she favored.

"I've been sleeping with them open since I was a child and haven't had to share a room with anyone since I was in a nursery with my sister," she replied.

He sat up and stared at her. "What sort of deranged person sleeps with the windows open?"

Emry folded her arms across her chest and leaned a shoulder against one of the thick squared posts surrounding her bed. She smirked. "Well, aren't you cranky in the morning? Would my precious Knight prefer that I keep the drapes pulled so as not to affect his slumber?"

Declan winced. His absolute exhaustion was robbing him of both his manners and memory. Emry was a princess, and he was now her sworn servant. "Sorry." He hung his head. "You can smite me if you like."

"Oh, I see. *You* give me permission to smite you. I didn't realize you held the higher position here."

He'd dug himself a hole. Working on limited intellectual power from his lack of rest, and seeing no other option, he shoved back his rather scratchy blanket and dropped the short distance to the floor from his cot to his knees. He placed his hands over his heart and lowered his gaze to her bare feet. "Forgive me, dearest princess. I have had a rough day and night. That is my feeble excuse. For my offensive words, I know I now must die."

She padded to him, but he didn't lift his eyes from her slender feet. "Call me 'dearest princess' one more time and I might just have to smite you after all."

"You would sully these lovely fingers?" Declan reached out and took one of her hands between his. He rubbed his thumb over her callouses. He had yet to discover where they'd come from.

"With pleasure." She sneered wickedly.

"Then, the words will never grace my lips again." He glanced up at her before planting a kiss on her hand.

Emry rolled her eyes. "Is every morning going to be like this?"

Declan rocked off of his knees to sit on the floor. "I really am sorry. I shouldn't have snapped at you."

She sank down across from him. "I wasn't expecting you to be sworn to me last night. It was so late that I didn't even think about the windows."

"Why do you sleep with them open?" Declan rubbed at his eyes with his palms.

"I like the moonlight to hit me while I sleep," she replied, as if that wasn't an odd desire. "The morning light doesn't usually bother me because I'm up at daybreak anyway."

"Why?"

She frowned. "Why what?"

"Why do you get up so early? Don't princesses usually sleep in late and have their servants bring them breakfast at lunchtime?"

"Have you spent much time with princesses?" She rested a hand on the floor to the side of her and leaned into it, tilting her head. "I didn't realize you were such an expert."

"I may have overheard some maids discussing how the princess was ready for her breakfast in the afternoon," he said.

Emry grunted. "That would be Cit. She and Freddick often wake up late."

"But you don't." He stifled a yawn behind his hand. "Why do you get up earlier?"

"To run amuck through the woods and slide down palace walls, of course," she retorted.

"I'm putting a stop to going down that wall."

"I have Heerth lessons in the morning. My tutor is a busy woman and likes to dedicate her mornings to me and her afternoons to her other affairs," Emry explained. "Works for me, because then I'm free by lunch for any exploring."

"How fortunate." Declan said blearily. It was becoming a real chore to stay focused. His body ached to lay down.

"You look very tired."

"I feel very tired," he mumbled, his palms on his eyes again.

"Then, go back to sleep. I don't have Heerth lessons today, since it was supposed to be the day of my last Trial and all." Emry pushed herself up to her feet.

Declan tossed a glance at his rather uncomfortable, sad excuse for a bed. After being spoiled with the finery of his room in the palace, the cot was really a letdown. Taking a deep breath, he slowly grunted his way to his feet. Once upright, he found himself yawning again.

Emry was frowning. "You really didn't sleep well last night."

He shrugged. "It is what it is."

"Take my bed."

"What?" He blinked.

"If you're ever going to fully recover from your fights, you need some rest, and that stretched bit of canvas isn't going to give it to you." She waved a hand toward her soft, fluffy tower of pillows and blankets. "Go get some sleep in my bed. You'll feel much better afterwards."

Somewhere in the back of his head a warning bell was going off, but Declan was too drained to listen to it. Emry's bed was inviting. His feet began moving toward it without him even realizing it. A moment later he was slipping between her bed's silken sheets, unaware of how he'd gotten there so fast. He managed to murmur out his thanks before drifting off.

Emry watched him walk as if he were in a trance toward her bed. She let out a short laugh before turning her attention to the drapes beside her windows. Once they both were shut, and the room was cast into darkness once more, she stepped to her attached washroom.

Twenty or so minutes later, she was dressed in a simple burgundy gown with a navy blue ribbon wrapped around her ribs, tying at her back. Some time that morning, a servant had rekindled the fire so that her front room was nice and warm in the early autumn chill. With a sigh, she sank into one of the sofas beside her fireplace. She'd already rung for breakfast and Fanny to do her hair. Emry had brushed it out and was waiting for Fanny's magnificent agile fingers to work her mass of hair up into a tight braid.

She'd been sitting for barely a minute when the doorknob to her chambers turned and in strode her sister, followed closely by Freddick. Seeing them burst in didn't surprise her, but seeing them up at this hour did. Emry stared. "It must be later than I thought it was."

"Funny," Cit retorted, dropping down opposite her sister. Freddick chose to stand beside the fire, his hands clasped behind his back. "It should please you to know that Cadoc has already been sent on his way. I think he was given the news shortly after sunrise. When will you be sworn to your precious Knight?"

"I have a little remorse about Cadoc's departure," Emry said. "I was fond of him."

"But not as fond of him as you are of Declan," Cit snickered.

"Did you remove your Knight's bed?" Freddick asked, his eyes on the spot beside the door into Emry's bedroom.

"No, I just moved it into my room," Emry shook her head. "I kept bumping into it every time I'd go through the door. I put the thing inside along the far wall so that I'd stop hitting my shins on it. Last night went by so quickly, I forgot to move it back. After dealing with his nightmare, though, I think it turned out for the best. Which reminds me, why didn't you ever mention how awful that ceremony is?"

"Wait. You're already sworn to him?" Cit blurted, gawking.

She nodded. "Father wanted it done immediately."

"Why?"

"Something about my safety." She waved a hand in dismissal.

Cit frowned. "Then, where's Declan?"

"In my bed."

Freddick broke into a hoarse cough. Cit's mouth dropped open. "He's where?"

"Relax. It's not what you think." Emry rolled her eyes. "I told him to get in it."

They stared at her. After a moment, Cit said, "You're not explaining yourself proficiently."

With a sigh, Emry relayed her encounter with Declan the night before, followed by his fatigue this morning. "So, I told him to rest in my bed," Emry finished. "That's all. Hopefully it helps."

"Just to be clear," Cit replied slowly, "Declan used *your* ability while he slept."

"Yes. Has that ever happened to the two of you?" Emry asked.

"No." Cit shook her head. "Never. We've never used each other's abilities."

"In what way was the ceremony difficult for you?" Freddick frowned.

Emry grunted. "Declan and I both were frozen in place while feeling like we were on fire. Sound familiar?"

Cit and Freddick exchanged glances. It was Cit who spoke. "We didn't experience anything like that. It was over fast and was, honestly, forgettable."

A knock sounded on Emry's door, halting her next question in her throat. "Yes?" She called out.

"Are you ready for me, dearest princess?" Fanny's high-pitched voice mumbled through the door.

There would be no more discussion with Fanny in the room. She sighed. "Come in, Fanny."

# CHAPTER FOURTEEN

It'd been six days since Declan became Emry's Knight. Six long, drawn-out days of waking up too early and going to bed too late. Emry's Heerth lessons were far more hands-on than anything he'd ever learned in a classroom. Declan had spent more time on his feet trailing Emry as she met with her teacher during the past six days than he had since arriving at the palace, and that included training with the guards for The Trials. Emry spent her lesson with her language tutor out wandering the palace grounds, speaking only in Heerth. Declan didn't speak Heerth. So, every morning Declan trudged along behind Emry for hours, bored out of his mind.

The afternoons were spent entertaining foreign dignitaries and courtiers over tea. Extravagantly dressed peacocks who offered the princess lots of pretty smiles. Their words, though … those felt more like sparring matches with Emry. Meant to condescend or test her intelligence. She'd merely endured their offhanded comments politely, always ending the conversations with how grateful her father was to have them here at the palace.

Afterwards, though, back in the safety of her own rooms, she'd complained for another hour to him about how much she'd love to speak her mind. She'd done so once, Declan discovered, and her father had lectured her on her responsibilities to please the people they ruled. How his advisors had needed her to simply be kind and courteous, not contrary. Clearly it was a sore spot for Emry because after each long ordeal, she vented to Declan about how helpless they expected her to be.

Evenings with Emry were spent dining with her family in a private room and then lounging with Cit and Freddick for an hour or so before retiring. Emry to her lavish bed, and Declan to his sad little cot. She'd fall asleep fast, leaving Declan to listen to her breathe for a while after. At least he hadn't had another nightmare. That was positive.

As the days passed, Declan began to discover all sorts of things about Emry. Like no matter how tightly her maid braided her hair in the morning, by midafternoon, dozens of tiny wisps of hair somehow managed to escape, floating around her head as she moved. Also, she was fairly successful at mimicking accents. Her Heerth tutor was constantly praising her pronunciation of various words and phrases. One surprising habit Declan had observed about Emry was even though she was for the most part graceful, she'd sometimes bang her hip or elbow or foot on stationary objects. She was too involved in her own thoughts to notice the obstacles.

Then, there were her appetite quirks. She liked gravy on her meat, but not her potatoes. Instead of honey on her breakfast biscuits, she soaked them in syrup and butter. She preferred all her beverages to be at room temperature. And she despised onions, mushrooms, turnips, and beets. Her servants made certain that none of these offensive vegetables every graced her plate, but if one piece did happen to meander its way into her dish, she would pick it off to the side without any complaint. Unlike his previous assumptions about the Princess Emerald being spoiled and selfish, Emry was not easily upset.

The past six days really had been educational. That odd twang of disappointment he'd get when running into someone was gone. It'd disappeared literally overnight. Somehow swearing himself to Emry had fixed whatever piece inside of him had been broken for the past two years. He no longer felt like he'd been expecting someone other than the face he was greeted with. It was a relief. Normal people didn't feel disappointed every single time they saw one of their friends or family.

Declan had even learned some new things about himself. Keeping an eye on Emry might have been part of his job description, but outright staring at her definitely was not. Several times a day he caught himself openly ogling the princess. Sometimes he couldn't help it.

When she'd laugh, her nostrils would endearingly flare out a little. Or if she drifted off in thought while someone was talking to her, she'd unconsciously twirl the freed tendrils of her hair around her middle finger – all etiquette completely forgotten. Her polite smile would slip into a real one at whatever she was pondering or slowly disappear into a frown. Her reaction either way left him wondering where her mind had traveled.

The truth was, he had fallen for Emry – in real life – despite the obvious fact that doing so would only lead to future heartache. Declan was a Rioter, and she was a Royal. She was good-natured, kind, and trusting. Declan was sent to betray her – to pluck her from her home and cast her into captivity. She would never forgive him for it. He was supposed to be her big brother's loyal best friend — someone who would never hurt her. Emry's innocent confidence in his character and Declan's knowledge that it was severely misplaced made him sick to his stomach.

Declan wanted to say that he regretted becoming Anexia's Challenger, but he'd by lying to himself. If he hadn't, he would never have become reacquainted with Emry. He would have missed out on being near her every moment of every day. Also, if it hadn't been him, the Rioters would have chosen some other lesser man who could have failed in The Trials. Or the man could have won and been put within Emry's life without caring about her safety at all. Or worse, the man could have fallen in love with Emry as Declan had, because who wouldn't love her?

She was exactly as he'd imagined her to be, back in Quirl. She was exhausting and breathtaking. She was determined and clever. To spend the rest of his life at her side was more than he could ever hope for, though. He would eventually fulfill his duty to the Rioters, and she would hate him forever. It was incredibly depressing.

He moaned and rubbed his eyes. Emry was currently changing for bed in her very spacious closet. Her maid, Fanny, had barely left from braiding Emry's hair for the night. Declan was currently stretched out on one of the stuffed sofas in Emry's front room, waiting for his princess to finish so he could sleep.

A knock sounded on the door to Emry's chambers, but before Declan was able to react, Princess Citrine strode in with her Knight. Citrine's long, loose braid fell over one shoulder, and she wore a thick burgundy robe tied at her waist by a black cord. When her eyes landed on Declan, she laughed. "Emry's still not done in there?

She takes forever."

Freddick offered Declan a nod in greeting as he lowered himself onto the sofa. Citrine, apparently unsatisfied with the amount of light the scattered lanterns in the room gave off, tossed a ball of fire from her palm into the empty fireplace. She then joined Freddick.

"She shouldn't be much longer," Declan replied. Visiting with Cit and her Knight was usually done in Emry's rooms. Although, the night before, Emry had dragged him to Citrine's rooms for a change of scenery.

"So, how was afternoon tea with the Perth ambassador?" Citrine asked him. The smirk on her face meant she knew exactly how it went.

Declan shrugged, trying for nonchalance. "It went fine."

Citrine chuckled. "How thinly veiled was her contempt for the man today? Did he egg her on until she sat there, silently seething? Trying with all her might to refrain from saying something she'd later regret?"

That was a good summary of his and Emry's experience with the Perth man. Since the king had been tied up in another meeting earlier that day, the chore of entertaining the newly arrived ambassador had fallen on Emry's shoulders. The man had shown up two weeks early, yet felt entitled to an audience with at least one of the Jewels. So, for three hours, the entire very one-sided conversation had been about how inferior Enlennd food and customs were to those of Perth. He'd droned on about how grateful he was to his newly appointed queen that his required visit to Enlennd would be short.

"When it gets really bad," Citrine went on, "beyond the point of merely irritating, Emry's eyes will gloss over and she'll take on a blank look. If she ever comes to that, then you know it's time to intervene before she does something drastic."

"Drastic?" Declan raised an eyebrow.

"Once, she tossed a full goblet of punch over the head of the prince of Quirl." Citrine grinned. "Father was furious."

"And yet I still don't feel any remorse for doing it," Emry said, joining them. She took a seat on the opposite side of Declan's couch, facing her sister.

"Do you ever?" Citrine rolled her eyes.

Emry wasn't able to reply. The door to her chambers burst open. Both Freddick and Declan leaped to their feet while the sisters whirled in their seats. Captain Vardin, dressed in full uniform, cape included, barged in, followed closely by the king and several guards. Emry and Cit exchanged a quick glance before rising as well.

Vardin pointed to Declan. "There he is. Seize him!"

Declan gaped. "What? Why?"

The guards hurried to obey, but Emry jumped in front of Declan, blocking their path. She lifted one hand to stop them. "You will not touch my Knight," she snapped.

The men hesitated, awkwardly shifting their gazes between Vardin and their princess. Emry turned to Onyx. "Father, what is going on?"

Onyx was frowning. However, it was Vardin who answered her. "I received news from my scouts that your Knight plans to kidnap you for the Rioters," he spat out.

Declan's heart skipped a beat – his insides suddenly cold. He was dumbfounded. How could Vardin have discovered this? Only a handful of people outside of The Mistress's Committee knew his intentions. Declan could list them all and knew none of them would have given him up. He stood there gawking at Vardin, unable to find his voice.

Emry, on the other hand, took the accusation much better than he did. She merely rolled her eyes. "And where would your scouts for the palace guards have heard this? Some sketchy tavern in the wrong side of Breccan, perhaps?"

"In the heart of Anexia," Vardin shot back through clenched teeth.

"What are scouts for the Royal Palace Guard doing in Anexia?" She asked slowly, her voice low.

"Emerald." Her father's voice pulled her attention from Vardin. "This is not the issue at hand."

"Father, you don't actually believe my Knight would be able to kidnap me against my will, do you?" Emry demanded. "He is sworn to me. He cannot harm me."

"Just because he can't doesn't mean that other Rioters couldn't," Vardin butted in. "I was also informed of an impending attack on the palace by them."

This was news to Declan. Emry's head whipped back around to Vardin. "An attack on the palace? By the Rioters?"

"Before the next full moon," he told her.

She let her breath out in a rush and looked at her sister warily. "One week," she hissed.

Vardin sneered, his flat blue eyes flashing. "Now that you see the gravity of the situation, please step aside so my men can remove the Rioter."

"No." Emry glared at the man.

"Emerald," Onyx said.

"Father," Emry ground out through clenched teeth. She was on the brink of seething. "He is *my* Knight. As I said before, he can't hurt me, and he will never betray me."

If Declan could have melted into the floor he would have. Emry could have kicked him in the groin and that pain would have still been preferable to the shame that now filled him. She was blindly standing up for him. Declan almost wanted Vardin to arrest him. It might have helped diminish his guilt.

"We will get you another Knight," Onyx tried to soothe.

"Oh, no." Emry let out a short laugh. "I will never go through that ceremony again."

"Stop being childish." Vardin snorted. "Step aside."

Emry twisted to the captain with such malice in her eyes that Declan was momentarily startled. "There is only one person in this world who is permitted to give me a command, and it is *not* you. Do not forget your place, Vardin." She pointed to the door. "It's time for you to leave. You entered my personal rooms unannounced and uninvited. Kindly take *my* guards and get out."

No one moved for a moment – all waiting for Vardin's reaction. Even Onyx stood frozen in place. Vardin didn't respond, though. He simply spun toward the still open door, his thick, black cape snapping behind him. The palace guards went to follow him, but pulled up short when Vardin turned back for his last word. "Don't say that I didn't warn you when the Rioters carry you off, dear princess," he sneered and stormed out.

Once the guards had dispersed as well, Onyx sighed. "Emry, Vardin is only trying to protect you. He fears your Knight-"

"Do you know who my Knight is?" Emry interrupted, still angry. "This is Declan Sharpe."

At the mention of his real name, Declan stiffened.

The king stared at him in surprise. "This is the boy who saved you in Anexia?"

Of course, her father should have known about what he'd done all those years ago. Yet, it still alarmed Declan that the king knew his identity. It gave Emry's father a name to hunt once he took her away to Anexia – to The Mistress.

Emry nodded. "The same."

"Why the alias?" Onyx frowned.

"He's the son of Levric Sharpe." Emry shrugged. "He didn't want his close family ties with the Rioters to harm his chances at The Trials."

How very astute of her. Declan had never mentioned his reason for using an alias. Come to think of it, though, she'd never even asked. He also hadn't been aware of her knowledge on Rioter leaders. She'd mentioned her father never involved her in political affairs. How had she learned of his father's station? She'd never met his parents in Anexia. Declan had only ever encountered the younger Emry on the estate she'd lived at with Ewan.

Onyx rubbed his beard with one hand. "You really think you are safe under his care?"

"I trust him more than I do my own guards," she retorted, almost bitterly.

"Very well." Onyx frowned at Declan. "Take care of my daughter."

"With my life," he promised truthfully. Even though he had obligations to uphold with the Rioters, there was no way he'd let anyone lay a hand on Emry. Ever. Not even The Mistress herself.

Satisfied, Onyx nodded. "Until the next."

When her father was gone with the door shut behind him, Emry sank onto her sofa with a groan. "Why is Vardin spying on Anexia? He's not over the military – he has no business sending people there."

Declan had to stop himself from staring. *That* was what concerned her the most out of that entire conversation? Not the allegations against him and the Rioters?

Citrine must have thought about him, though. She tossed a worried look his way. "We only have one week?" She was asking him like he knew the answer to that.

Emry grunted. "He doesn't know anything about that because it's not true. The Rioters aren't planning any attack." He frowned. How could she possibly know that? Emry went on, "But Vardin brought it up for a reason. An attack is coming, but don't believe that it'll be a full week."

Citrine sat as well, twirling a ball of fire between her fingers – a nervous habit Declan had discovered. "What do we do?"

Emry dug her fingers into hair, loosening her braid a little. "I don't know. I need to think. I need to go out."

"Now?" Her sister blurted.

Emry merely shrugged as she stood again. "I'll be fine. Declan will be with me."

Citrine didn't look convinced. "Where exactly are you wanting to go?"

"Just up to the roof," she replied, making her way back towards her closet. "I'm going to change."

A minutes later she was back, frowning. She was clearly preoccupied. As she walked past the large window of her front room, a strange sensation overcame Declan. It was like that invisible chain he felt inside his chest – the one connecting him to Emry – suddenly shrank to nothing. Like he was standing beside her. Or rather, like he was seeing through her. Seeing out the window through her eyes. And he saw a glowing orb of fire flying straight for him – for her.

He flung himself forward before his mind fully registered the movement. Within a heartbeat, he crashed into Emry, landing on top of her on the floor. Just as they hit the wood planks, glass shattered behind them – some of it raining onto his back. Emry gasped, ducking her head into his shoulder.

The scent of smoke filled the room. Declan jumped to his feet, pulling Emry up with him, and spun to the window. A red-hot ball of flames sputtered on top of Emry's floor. The ball he'd seen – Emry had seen. Declan stared as Citrine leapt to it, sucking away the fire into her open outstretched palms. She didn't look at all concerned by the mass of heat she was consuming. To be honest, she was practically smirking as the ball cooled into a lump of ash.

From behind Declan, Emry swore. "One week my-" she was cut off by the breaking of more glass. This time, it came from her actual bedroom. Citrine rushed off with Freddick after the noise – most likely to defuse another fireball. Emry followed, while releasing another curse. Declan couldn't help but grin at her very unprincesslike choice of words.

"The palace is under attack," Freddick told them, while Cit drew in more flames. He was frowning at Declan.

Guessing at what Freddick was thinking, Declan blurted, "It's not the Rioters. I knew nothing of this."

"Of course this isn't the Rioters," Emry snapped, surprising Declan again. She risked a glance out the new hole in her wall, between the remaining shards of her window and wood. "We need to find Father."

"You find him," Citrine ordered. "I'll keep the fires to a minimum."

Emry nodded. "Go up to the roof. You'll have a better vantage point."

"Good idea," Citrine agreed. "You stick to the shadows."

"Obviously." Emry grabbed Declan's wrist and took off, hauling him along.

"Be safe!" Citrine shouted at their backs.

"Right. Because I'd do anything different," Emry muttered as they darted into the hallway outside her chambers.

Declan was confused. How could Emry have been so certain this attack wasn't the Rioters? Did she have some other culprit in mind?

"Do you know where the menagerie is?" Emry asked over her shoulder.

He did. "I do," he answered. "Why? Are you wanting me to take you there?"

"It would be faster," she said somewhat sheepishly. "That's my father's usual retreat."

Coming to a halt, Declan pulled Emry behind him and crouched down a little. "Fine, climb on."

Once she was situated, Declan tapped into his true speed – the pace he'd acquired in Quirl – and sprinted down the hallway. For the millionth time, the world around him blurred as he ran. He dashed past palace guards and panicked servants seemingly rooted in place. He and Emry were invisible to their eyes. They'd only be aware of the breeze he created as he passed. He exited the palace and entered the gardens, making his way to the menagerie. Countless balls of fire streaked through the sky towards the palace. At least twenty windows within Declan's view were broken with smoke seeping out of them into the night.

At the door of the menagerie, Declan pulled to a stop and released his grip around the back of Emry's knees, depositing her on her feet. Before he even reached for the door, it swung open, revealing the king. Onyx stared at them for a moment in surprise before shifting his gaze upward. The lines on his face hardened. "You must take Emry away."

"Father," Emry stepped around Declan, "I'm not going anywhere. We're under attack!"

The king ignored his daughter. He let out a high-pitched whistle. The clip-clopping of hooves on a hard surface thumped behind him. An enormous white steed poked its head through the doorway, resting its chin on Onyx's shoulder. "This is Aggron," Onyx told Declan. "He will carry both of you. Are you practiced in projecting your speed into your mount?"

"I am."

"I'm not leaving!" Emry barked.

"Your majesty, at last we've found you."

Declan turned to his left. Six palace guards were approaching. Both of Emry's hands wrapped around Declan's right arm so tightly that he could feel her nails digging into his skin through the cloth of his shirt. When the lead guard – a light-haired man with ridiculously long sideburns – saw Emry, a huge smile split his lips.

"Dearest princess," he said.

Those two words cast such a sick feeling into his gut that Declan fell back a step. But he the emotion hadn't been his own – it'd come from Emry. Somehow, he'd felt what she had. That couldn't be right...

Onyx moved slightly to the side, permitting Aggron through the wide door. "Go now," he hissed to Declan.

"No matter what, do *not* turn back."

Before Declan could respond, Onyx released another whistle and faced his guards with a somewhat serene look. Several large animals emerged from the menagerie. Declan recognized a small black bear, an ocelot, and what looked like an abnormally large dog. He didn't wait to see why the king had summoned them. He jumped onto Aggron's white back and reached down to Emry in one fluid movement. The guards, upon seeing Declan mount, rushed forward. Onyx's animals did the same – towards the guards.

"No!" Emry screamed as Declan settled her in front of him.

"Ride!" Onyx shouted.

Declan obeyed. Emry struggled against him, spinning around in the saddle to see her father. Declan didn't release his grip around her middle, though. Instead, he urged his speed into the beast he rode. Aggron accepted it almost greedily. The utter lack of resistance startled Declan. He dug his hands into Aggron's long mane, enveloping Emry with his arms, and kicked his heels into the horse's flanks. Aggron galloped off at a pace Declan had never witnessed before in a horse – not even from those Declan had projected into in the past. Aggron was magnificent.

"No!" Emry shrieked into Declan's ear. She'd managed to switch directions so that she now straddled the horse, facing Declan. "*Daddy!*"

The absolute desperation in Emry's voice shocked Declan. He glanced at her, but she was focused on the scene behind him. He snuck a quick glance over his shoulder and glimpsed in the distance the small figures of the guards encircling the king with their swords drawn. The bear and the overgrown dog lay limp near a couple of the guards they'd managed to take down, and there was no sign of the ocelot. A cold dread washed over Declan as he realized what the sight meant.

"Take me back! Take me back!" Emry pleaded, her fingers clawing at his shirt. "I have to help him!"

Declan risked another look. The group was now unrecognizable. They were nearly off palace grounds. "It's too late, Emry. I'm sorry."

If the king had just been murdered by his own guards, as Declan assumed, Emry certainly wasn't safe there. At least, not tonight. They needed to go somewhere to rest and think before deciding what to do next. Somewhere far enough from the capital that they wouldn't be disturbed or chased. The Kruth border could work.

"You did it again. You did it again to me," Emry whimpered.

"What?" Declan blinked down at her and realized she was sobbing against him. Guilt filled his chest. He was only thinking about getting as far away from the palace as possible. Loosening one hand's hold on the mane, he wrapped it around her back. "I'm so sorry, Emry."

"You did it again," she repeated into his shoulder. "You did it again."

# CHAPTER FIFTEEN

By the time Emry caught the first hint of pine in the air, her tears had dried, leaving a seeping cold throughout her. Pine only grew on the Kruth Mountains. Declan must had taken her beyond the Kruth border. For the first time since leaving the palace, Emry lifted her head from Declan's shoulder. She'd spent nearly the past two hours dampening it. Even without the moon in the sky, she could sense that it was almost midnight.

"We'll stop at the next village," Declan told her, his voice soft. He still had one hand on her back – had had it there the whole journey.

Emry didn't trust her voice to reply. She merely nodded in response.

"I think we should spend the night at an inn and decide what to do next in the morning," Declan went on. "Did you happen to bring any coin in that bag of yours?"

Again, Emry nodded. Cit always made fun of Emry's adventure satchel, but it really did pay to be prepared.

"Good," he said. "We should be there in a few minutes."

True to his estimate, several minutes later lights appeared around a bend in the highway. A small village stood in the midst of the dark, rugged Kruth pine forest. Naturally, there were a smattering of other trees mixed in, but Emry couldn't name them. She was momentarily startled to find so many buildings lit at such an hour before remembering that they were on a major highway. Travelers were bound to stop here at all hours of the day and night.

As they reached the first building, Declan slowed the horse to a normal trot. Her father's animal wasn't even panting. At the speed it had been going, the beast should have been near death. Aggron was remarkable. Her father had trained him well. That thought sent the corners of Emry's eyes burning afresh.

When Declan seemed inclined to stop at the first inn they reached, Emry stopped him. "Wait. The ones on the outskirts are always the most rundown with the worst cooks. Go to one in the middle of town."

"Travel much?" Declan grunted, continuing on down the road.

"I've lived in Kruth before, remember?"

A couple of minutes later, they arrived at the center of the town. There were three inns, all with their windows on the ground floor lit. Declan headed to the nearest one. A wooden sign with crisp black letters swung above its front door, declaring itself as *The Painted Pony*.

Declan dismounted first before lifting Emry down by her waist. There was a post to tether horses, but they had been riding Aggron barebacked. Without any rope, there was no way to keep him put. Emry rubbed the animal's nose with one hand. He'd helped them escape, fulfilling his purpose. It was time to set him free.

"Thank you, Aggron," she whispered, stepping back.

"Ride home," Declan told the beast, slapping him on the rump.

Aggron didn't need any further encouragement. With a neigh, he trotted off back the way they'd come, as if he'd understood Declan's command. Emry turned to the inn. Light from the inside filtered through the windows onto its front porch. The laughter of a few travelers drifted out to her.

Beside Emry, Declan watched Aggron retreat into the darkness with a great deal of appreciation. That was the most impressive mount he'd ever had the pleasure of riding, and he doubted he'd ever find another to top it. The thought made him a little sad to see the horse go.

"Dec, could I use your dagger for a minute?"

"My dagger?" He repeated, glancing back to Emry.

"Yes, the one you keep in your boot," she replied, her gaze still fixed on the inn. "Could I use it?"

"Is there some sort of danger that I don't see?" He asked as he bent to retrieve it. He hadn't known she knew about the blade.

"Not at the moment," she said, taking the extended weapon.

"Then why-" He didn't finish his sentence out of pure surprise.

With one hand, Emry grabbed onto her long, thick braid, and with the other she swiped Declan's blade through it just below her neck. He stared as she shook out her hair. The locks that had once fallen below her hips were now chopped to her shoulders. It would take years for her hair to regain that length.

She offered him the dagger back with a smile that didn't quite reach her eyes. "Thank you."

"You didn't have to do that." He returned the dagger to his boot.

Apparently Emry wasn't done yet. Inhaling deeply,

she shut her eyes, and Declan audibly gasped. Her black hair transformed in front of his eyes. Beginning at her roots and sliding down to her ends, silvery streaks appeared throughout her whole head. Some thin strands remained dark, woven between the altered ones, but most had faded as if the color had been sucked out. When she was finished a moment later, her overall hair color was now blonde. It was more of a pale gray, though, than golden. And it was the exact color he remembered her having years ago.

Declan knew he was gawking. "I didn't know anyone could change the color of their hair."

"I can only go light or dark." She shrugged, slipping her now shorn rope of black hair into her satchel.

He blinked, suddenly realizing Emry's hair had darkened from the blonde simply because she'd willed it to do so. "You've been able to do this for years, haven't you?"

She nodded and gestured to the inn's door. "Shall we? It's chilly out here."

Was it cold? Declan hadn't noticed. Then again, he usually was warmer than most people. "Just wait."

"For what?"

"If you think it necessary to change your appearance, then I probably should too." With a grimace, Declan drew from his own ability, pushing it out the top of his head, the lower portion of his face, and his throat. He forced his hands to stay still at his sides when the telltale itch erupted. He reminded himself that the itchiness wouldn't last long. The hair he was growing only needed to look like he'd missed a couple weeks of shaving and hadn't just freshly cut his hair, as he had done three days ago.

Emry watched him with raised eyebrows. "I didn't

know you could grow hair in thirty seconds."

"It's not a particularly useful talent." He rubbed his now whiskered chin. "Not a whole lot of demand for it."

"Seems useful right now." She extended her hand to him. As he slid his fingers between hers, he wondered when doing so had become second nature to him.

"Be my husband."

"What?" He blurted, his eyes darting up from their joined hands.

"Inside the inn," she explained, "be my husband. It'll just be easier that way."

"Oh. Right."

They walked up the front steps onto the wide porch, and Declan pushed open the door, holding it for Emry before entering himself. The first floor of the inn was, in Kruth fashion, a tavern. Round tables of dark wood with circular benches to match filled most of the space. A basic, straight staircase sat at the back, which led to the guest rooms upstairs. Next to the bottom of the staircase was the door to the kitchen and Innkeeper's quarters. Then, along the right wall was the bar that, in Kruth, also acted as a front desk.

Declan wasn't surprised to find most of the tables occupied. Kruths were known for their usual late nights. Declan suspected the majority of the current patrons were locals. Upon his and Emry's entrance, the light haired bartender gave them a nod in greeting. The burly, heavily bearded Kruth wouldn't say more until they approached him. Kruths were a lively group, but they weren't ones to pester.

Making his way to the bar with Emry beside him, Declan returned the man's nod. "Evening, good keeper.

Do you have an available room for the night?"

The man set down the rag he'd been wiping the wooden counter with and stepped closer to them. He leaned his hands onto the bar that separated him from Declan and Emry. "Aye," he said. "You be needing one?"

Declan nodded. "For my wife and I."

He raised an eyebrow at Emry. "Newlyweds?"

Of course he'd assume that. Declan had an Anexian accent, and Emry's hair was now only to her shoulders – the length of unmarried girls. If she was recently wed, her hair wouldn't have grown much yet.

Emry didn't skip a beat. Flashing him a smile, she answered in an Anexian accent, "Do we look it?"

The man chuckled, scratching his scraggly salt and pepper beard. "Welcome to *The Painted Pony*. I'm Coit Fannon, the unfortunate owner of this stinking shack."

"Pleased to meet you," Declan replied. "I find your shack fairly clean. How much for the night?"

"Sixty for the both of you," Coit answered.

Not a bad price to Declan, considering that was what he'd paid at one of the inns on his way through Kruth to The Trials. And that had been just for himself. So when Emry sounded like she was choking from the price, he turned to her in surprise.

"Sixty?" She blurted.

"Aye, you heard me," Coit said, now gruff. "Sixty."

Declan was ready to pay the man, just to get it over with, but Emry was clearly not. Suddenly sounding like a Kruth native – another talent revelation to Declan – Emry called out loudly, "Looky here, Dec, we made a wrong turn and ended up at the palace because this piti-ful little excuse for an inn be not possibly charging us sixty for only one night."

Coit snarled. "Why not insult me wife next?"

"I hope she be prettier than this place," Emry grunted, maintaining her Kruth accent.

Declan's jaw dropped. What was she doing? Coit was enormous and was now glaring at them. "The price be sixty."

"Then we be making our way to the inn across the street," Emry shot back, her voice still louder than necessary. She was drawing more and more attention to them. "Perhaps we be finding honest folk there."

"You compare me pride and joy to that rickety old hovel?" Coit exclaimed. "You could feel the wind through the holes in their walls!"

Emry rolled her eyes. "Oh, and there n'er be a draft in yer humble abode, I be sure."

"Fine," Coit grumbled. "Fifty."

"You better be feeding us both along with the room for that much," she retorted. "We be willing to stay for forty."

"Are you trying to rob me blind?" Coit blustered. "Forty-five."

"I heard the food across the street be excellent," Emry told Declan, still mimicking a Kruth. "Should we give it a try?"

Coit's voice dropped slightly. "There be no better cook than me wife."

"Care to prove that?" Emry smiled mischievously. "Throw in a couple meals for us along with that room, and we can pay the *outrageous* forty-five."

"You be making me poor wife starve for so low a fee," Coit sighed.

"So, we have a deal then?"

"Deal." Coit stuck out a beefy hand. When Emry clasped his wrist, her hand looked like a child's compared to his.

"Thank you, Coit," she said.

He snorted. "I would've done it for forty."

"I would've done it for sixty," she smirked.

Coit tossed back his head and laughed, changing his entire demeanor. "Oy, that be fun. What be yer name?"

She grinned, transitioning back to her Anexian accent. "Emry Sharpe." At the sound of her using his surname as her own, Declan was momentarily startled.

"Who taught you to barter like a Kruth?" Coit asked, picking up his rag again and returning to his wiping of the bar.

"A good friend," she told him.

"Well, Mrs. Sharpe, grab yerself a table and I be having some of that food you be practically stealing from me sent over," Coit winked.

"Thank you," she repeated, leading Declan away by the hand towards an open table near the back.

Once they were both seated, Declan regarded her with raised eyebrows. "That was unexpected. You haggle like a Kruth." He shook his head. "I didn't even realize that was an option. I paid the price I was given when I traveled through Kruth on my way to The Trials."

"Well, that's unfortunate." She kept up her Anexian accent. "Your mother never mentioned Kruth bartering?"

"My mother?"

A round woman in her mid-thirties with bright red hair and pale blue eyes appeared at their table. She dropped two mugs of some sort of sweet-smelling, steaming beverage in front of them along with a basket of warm bread. Both Declan and Emry thanked her before she left assuring them she'd be back with more food.

Emry snatched one of the slices of bread and tore off a piece of it, popping it into her mouth. "Yes, your mother. She's half Kruth, isn't she? She could have warned you about what to do."

Declan stared at her. Not once had he ever referenced his mother's lineage. Not even with her brother. Only a few people in his own village knew that particular detail. His mother's father, the Kruth, had died not long after she'd turned ten. Her mother had remarried an Anexian, the man Declan counted as his grandfather, only a year later and moved to Anexia. Everyone had assumed her step-father was her biological father. He was Marsdon's actual father, and Llydia never corrected anyone who mistook him as her own. For Emry to know that his mother had Kruth blood shocked him. "How do you know she's part Kruth?"

"Were you not the one who told me?" She frowned.

"Who else would have told you? I never told Ewan."

The front doors to the inn banged open behind him. Emry's eyes drifted past him to the new travelers. She stiffened. "Palace guards," she hissed.

"Here?" Declan tossed a quick glance over his shoulder. Sure enough, three of them fully garbed in their uniforms stood conversing with Coit. He grimaced, turning back to Emry. "They must be Teals. No one else would have caught up with us already."

Emry sucked in a breath. "They've spotted us. They're coming this way."

He winced. "Let me do the-"

She didn't let him finish. Without giving him any notice, she slid her hands behind his neck and leaned in

– her mouth meeting his. Declan should have been stunned. Instead, his instincts took over. Time slowed, and he found himself kissing her back firmly. Her lips were even softer than they looked. She drew him in closer, and he didn't put up a fight.

Kissing her was familiar – as if he'd done so countless times before. But he hadn't – not in real life. This was their first, and he couldn't remember the last time he'd tasted someone so lovely.

When a strong hand on his shoulder yanked him away from Emry, Declan was legitimately startled. He'd forgotten about the guards. Taking on a Kruth accent of his own, he blurted, "You better be dying to be pulling me from me wife's embrace."

The brown-haired guard did in fact have teal eyes, as did the other two standing behind him. One of them looked fairly familiar. Declan might have sparred with him before. If it weren't for Declan's new beard, the man probably would have recognized him right off.

The brunet released his grip on Declan with a slight shove. "We're searching for a young couple much like yourselves. What's your name, Kruth?"

"Declan Sharpe," he answered truthfully, grateful he'd gone by an alias in the capital.

"And hers?" His eyes shifted past Declan, narrowing on Emry.

She stood, placing her hands on her hips. "I don't have to tell you," she retorted in her Anexian accent. "You have no power outside the palace. Those aren't the uniforms of a soldier."

Declan guessed Emry was being difficult on purpose. She was playing the part of the distrusting Anexian. Declan's shaggy hair and beard looked Kruth enough, but Emry's short hair was purely Anexian. She was committed to her new look.

Naturally, the guards were offended by her lack of cooperation. The brunet glared at her and snapped, "The king has been murdered by one of your kind not two hours ago. Don't provoke me."

"One of my kind?" She blurted. Her surprise was genuine. Even Declan was a little alarmed. It wasn't the lie that he'd killed the king – he'd suspected that was Vardin's intention after he tried to arrest him – it was that they'd already begun its circulation.

"Princess Emerald's Knight," the guard spat out. "He slew our king and kidnapped the very princess he was sworn to protect. They are whom we chase. So, I ask you one more time, what is your name?"

"What be happening here?" Coit's deep voice brought the guards' attention around. Two of the men had the wisdom to take a step back from the Kruth's bulky form. The brunet held his ground, though.

"This doesn't concern you, keeper," the brunet spat out – upward into Coit's face.

"This be me inn and you be harassing some of me guests," Coit replied evenly. "They be not the ones you search for. I think it be time for you to move along."

The guard looked like he was about to argue further when several of the other Kruth men at the surrounding tables stood, backing Coit. He prudently shut his mouth and nodded at his companions. "Let's go."

Declan watched them exit. Once the guards were gone, he turned to Coit. "Thank you," he said, returning to his normal accent.

Coit scratched his chin. "You know there be more guards on the way if what they say be true."

"I know." Declan grimaced.

"Would you be faster on horse or foot?"

"On foot." Declan frowned.

"Kruth be not safe for a pair of young Anexians while they be roaming around," the big man told them. "I suggest getting as close to Anexia as yer feet be able tonight."

He nodded, tossing a quick glance at Emry. "We'll just pay you for our meal and be on our way."

Coit grunted. "You be not eating anything. Just leave, but best go through me kitchen."

"Thank you, Coit." Emry adjusted her bag's strap across her front. "I won't forget your kindness."

"Bah," Coit smiled, "you be making me blush, lass."

Taking Emry's hand in his own again, Declan followed Coit through the back of the inn and into the large, warm kitchen. Coit veered right, toward another door. When he pulled it open, he poked his head out for a moment before holding it open for Declan and Emry to pass through.

"Good luck," Coit said.

"We appreciate your help," Declan replied.

Coit offered them a nod in farewell and shut his door. Declan took a deep breath and turned to Emry. "Time to climb onto my back again."

She hesitated. "Where are we going?"

He winced, realizing the destination in his head would validate the very same accusation Vardin had confronted him with earlier. He needed to deliver his idea gently. "I can't hide you very well in Kruth. I'm not all that familiar with the terrain."

"I know." She frowned. "You want to go to Anexia."

"Yes, to my parents. They can help us hide."

"Alright, but I don't think the main roads will be safe."

"I wasn't planning on using them," he admitted.

She hesitated. "I think I'm going to project one of my abilities into you."

"What?"

"I can see in the dark," she told him. "I'm going to transfer it to you, much like how you did with your speed and Aggron."

"Thanks, that would be useful."

She nodded and motioned for him to turn around. A minute later she was situated on his back. "Ready?" He asked.

"Just don't overexert yourself," she said, her voice soft. "If I become too heavy, or you tire out, just stop. I can hide us in the shadows while you rest until you can run again."

He placed a hand over hers around his neck. "I'll keep that in mind."

Declan took off. Almost instantly the shadows of the dark became illuminated as Emry pushed her ability into him, trickling through that chain that bound them. The world took on a bluish hue. He could see a good twenty feet ahead, which was an immense improvement. Usually in the dark, he'd have to rein in his speed due to his lack of vision. With Emry's ability, though, that problem was eliminated. He ran at his true, full potential.

Adjusting his grip on the back of Emry's knees, Declan doubled his speed. He heard Emry gasp into his ear as he veered off the road into the surrounding forest. To her, she wouldn't even be able to make out the shapes of the trees and underbrush. Everything would be one dizzying mess. For Declan, straight in front of him appeared like everything around him was frozen in place, while at his sides, it was a blur.

Declan knew that when he ran time was hard to measure. He usually just focused on the terrain to gauge the distance he'd traveled, but having Emry on his back was making even that difficult. For the first little while, he hardly noticed her weight. As he kept going, she grew heavier with each step he took until his heart raced uncontrollably and his lungs felt scorched. Something as basic as breathing became a struggle. His muscles ached, then contracted, and finally were on fire.

Hours or minutes passed. Declan didn't know. All he knew was that every inch of his body was screaming for relief – for him to collapse into a heap. But he couldn't stop. He wouldn't stop. No matter what Emry had told him, he refused to leave her unprotected just so he could rest. He'd rather suffer than have her left vulnerable. So, he just focused on putting one foot in front of the other. Everything else faded.

Sound disappeared from the world, melting into the very ground he no longer felt beneath him. His vision from Emry's ability shrunk, caving in on itself, abandoning him to the darkness. He was wheezing, but even that seemed to recede as his breathing became more and more shallow. All that existed was his movement and Emry. He had to get her to safety.

The night went on … or was it frozen just as the world around him was? It didn't matter. Declan's feet knew the way. His blindness wasn't hindering – the green veins in his eyes were leading him home.

When his feet at last slowed, he knew he was there. He'd reached Anexia. He was home. His parents would shelter Emry, even though she was a Royal. He knew his mother wouldn't send them away. He just needed to tell her that they were in trouble … but he was so very tired. He hadn't the strength to open his mouth. Really, he no longer had the strength to move. His feet halted, and his legs finally gave out beneath him. He tried to warn Emry as he fell, but nothing came out. Darkness was everywhere – enveloping him. It claimed him easily.

# CHAPTER SIXTEEN

Declan had completely ignored her request. At first, Emry was furious. She could tell that he was weakening – his pace decreasing slightly and his arms supporting her trembling. But then she *felt* it. On the other side of that rope of light between them, she could feel him pushing himself too far. Offering too much of himself. Emry called into his ear for him to stop, to rest. He stubbornly continued, without even giving her the courtesy of a reply. He probably didn't think she could take care of them both while he slept. It was utterly infuriating.

When his shaking intensified, her anger shifted to terror. Declan was more than just over-exerting himself – he was dying! His refusal to take a break was costing him dearly – it was draining him of his life! He was pushing himself far beyond his physical capacity.

Emry pleaded with him to stop – shouting until her voice was hoarse, tugging on their bond with all her strength. Still, he wouldn't respond. She took away her ability, in hopes that he'd slow down if he couldn't see, but still he trekked on. Declan was now running blind on the last burst of his strength.

She would've let go, compelling him to halt when he reached their thirty-foot limit, but she feared what her landing would be like at the speed they were travelling. Not to mention, his grip around the back of her knees was like an iron vice, basically trapping her. She was forced to watch him deteriorate.

"Declan, you're killing yourself!" Emry was trying not to panic, but the feeling of being helpless again was gnawing at her insides. She had no idea what to do to interfere. So, when he actually did stop with a sudden jolt, Emry was momentarily stunned.

That emotion didn't last long, though. Almost immediately, Declan collapsed backwards on top of her. Emry landed in a murky puddle. She braced herself with one hand behind her, the frigid mud oozing between her fingers, while the other wrapped around his chest to keep him from flattening her. Large drops of rain splattered across both of them. Emry wasn't sure how long it had been raining, but from her thoroughly soaked backside, she guessed it'd been a while.

"Declan," she managed to grunt out beneath his weight. He didn't reply. Emry adjusted her eyes briefly, switching her sight to that part of her – that ability – she barely ever touched. If anyone saw her, her eyes would be glowing. Shimmering silver, like moonlight on water. She dropped her eyes to Declan and forced back a sob.

His inner light – the life force only a Silver could find within someone – was terrifyingly faint. Emry bit the tip of her tongue and glanced around desperately for any sign of life. The rain in her eyes made it impossible to see more than a few feet away, not to mention it was still dark out.

Releasing something between a growl and a groan, Emry adjusted her eyes again, returning the world to that blue tint. The night took shape, even through the rain.

There. On the other side of some trees. It was a

lone house in a clearing. Emry hoped someone was home. She doubted they were awake, and there was no way she could drag Declan to the house. Nor could she leave him – the distance was further than thirty feet. She'd have to wake them and lead them to her. She winced, knowing that she'd be begging aid from strangers. But Declan was dying. She had no other choice.

Before she lost her nerve, Emry reached out toward the house with her hand that supported Declan's chest. A wispy thread of silvery light shot out from her hand toward the house, growing longer and longer as it traveled. When it slipped through the glass of one of the house's windows, Emry flooded the whole interior with a brilliance so bright it could be confused for daylight. That ought to get their attention. Emry silently pleaded for someone, *anyone*, to follow the light path she'd created back to her. If no one came then Declan would die, right here in her arms.

Shaking water from her eyes, Emry struggled to keep back the hysteria. Even if the strangers brought Declan and her inside, Emry had a growing fear that nothing could be done for him. Rubys could do amazing things, but she'd never known one to bring back a life force this weak. She wouldn't think that way, though. She couldn't. Declan needed her to keep a clear head.

The strangers had to be awake by now. Why wasn't anyone coming out? Was the house empty? Declan couldn't … No. Someone had to be there. They just needed an extra shove out the door. Emry grimaced, unsure of how else to draw them to her.

Then, suddenly, a blur erupted out of the house and to her side. Emry jumped. The person had to be a Teal.

Emry shook her head to try to clear the water in them. She blinked and gasped.

"Llydia?" She blurted in her Anexian accent – the accent she'd had since birth.

Declan's mother, dressed in a long, cream night-gown beneath a dark robe, crouched beside her in the mud. She laid a hand on his chest. "Is he…?"

"No." Emry shook her head. "Not yet. But he's fading."

"We need to get him inside." Llydia stood slowly, shouldering herself against his left side while Emry shifted under his right.

Together they began to drag him toward the house, but it was slow going. They struggled with his weight through the muck. Emry kept up her silvery rope to light their way. After about ten steps, Levric appeared between the trees, obviously looking like he was yanked from sleep in his loose shirt over his brown pants. Without a word, he hefted up Declan's legs, walking backwards as Llydia and Emry went forward. Levric made a significant difference. They were able to shuffle much more swiftly.

It took Emry a minute to realize that the presence of Declan's parents meant that they were in Anexia. The heart of Anexia. Declan wasn't from a border town. The fact that she was at his home was surreal.

Declan had brought her across the country in one night. One night! She had never heard of anyone ever being so fast. It was impossible. That was why he was now so close to death. Emry's heart raced as the panic returned. It was getting harder to push it away.

They were almost to the house now. Levric rotated them so that Llydia and Emry were now walking back-wards. This way, he would take most of Declan's weight as they hobbled up the front steps, out of the rain. The front door had been left ajar. They slid inside without having to hesitate.

"Through here," Llydia said, inclining her head to the left.

Emry allowed herself to be led through a main room, a kitchen, and down a small hallway. She felt guilty for the messy trail of mud and water they left in their wake. Declan's parents didn't even notice.

They paused momentarily at a closed door, just long enough for Llydia to open it, before shuffling into the simple bedroom. Emry, assuming Declan's parents wished to deposit him on the bed, made her way towards it. Somehow the three of them managed to lower him onto it a moment later. Emry released his weight with a grunt, only now realizing she was panting.

"I'll go for the Ruby," Levric said, his voice gruff.

Emry adjusted her eyes to gauge Declan's light, and a sickening emptiness spread through Emry's chest. "It won't help." Her voice cracked as she switched her vision to normal. She shoved her shaking hands behind her back and took a deep breath. "His light's almost gone. He's going to die."

Her last words had come out as barely more than a whisper. She stared down at Declan, avoiding his parents' eyes. It was horrible news to deliver, especially after the fight Llydia had given about Declan entering The Trials. Emry could only imagine what the depth of their sorrow would be at losing their only son…

But it couldn't be more than her own. With each one of Declan's shallow, labored breaths, she felt her heart shattering into smaller fragments.

Even though Declan had never been meant for her, she'd secretly dreamed that eventually he could have been. That maybe one day, when all the political turmoil and war-mongering in her country had settled, he'd be willing to give her a chance to win him over. To prove that whatever darkness was inside her was worth overlooking. Worth dealing with.

The past couple weeks of being near him had brought her hope. He'd seemed to genuinely care for her, and not simply because she was his late best friend's little sister. Then, their kiss in the tavern … it had felt like a good idea in the moment, but it had only left her aching for more. Now, it would torment her for the rest of her life.

She bit down hard on her tongue to stop her chin from trembling. Declan's arms lay at his sides. Arms that had never truly been wrapped around her – had never held her tightly against him. And now they never would. Tears welled up in her eyes, blurring her vision.

Emry sank onto the side of the bed beside him, grasping his cold fingers in her own. For once his hand was colder than hers. A single sob escaped. She desperately reined in the others that sought to consume her. What right did she have to mourn him? She had no real claim to him. His parents should be the ones holding his hand. But she couldn't release him. She couldn't move – didn't want to.

"Oh, Declan," she whimpered. She brushed back the hair that was plastered to his forehead with her hand. Traced his eyebrow with her fingertips. She loved him, and he wouldn't live to ever find out. She loved him with all her heart. Her mind. Her soul.

The sobs broke free. Emry bent over his hand, bringing her lips to his skin. He was so cold. Tears dripped onto his fingers as her body shook again and again. Declan. The wonderful man she'd dreamt of for years. Her Declan. He would die. And a part of her would die with him.

"Emry," Llydia said softly from somewhere behind her. "Heal him."

"What?" She glanced over her shoulder. Both of his parents stood at the foot of the bed, their attention on their son.

"Take my light."

"No!" Emry jumped to her feet, still grasping Declan's hand – still not willing to let go. "You don't understand what you ask. He needs too much."

"Then, take mine as well," Levric told her.

"No." She shook her head. "Last time was a disaster. I may not be able to stop again."

"I would rather die myself than watch my child die in front of me, knowing there was something else I could have done." Llydia's voice was low, determined. "Heal him."

"He'd never forgive me," Emry breathed. "I really could kill you."

Levric frowned, strands of his wet shoulder-length hair dangling around his face and dripping water. "Let Declan live and make that decision for himself."

Emry knew she shouldn't. The one and only time she'd ever transferred light from one person to another had been nothing short of a nightmare. It was unlikely her second attempt would be any better. Yet … she wanted to do it. She wanted to save him. It was downright selfish of her. Sacrificing his parents so that he could live – to maybe give her the chance at one day convincing him to return her love. It was devious, greedy, and dreadful.

But she would do it. Perhaps it was some of that darkness deep within her that influenced her choice.

Some of that anger and twisted fear she'd stolen and stored that made up her mind. Right now, though, she didn't care. Declan was dying. She'd contemplate her selfishness later.

"Alright." She glanced down at Declan. "I'll try my best to take as little as necessary."

Tears lined Llydia's eyes – eyes so similar to her son's. "Thank you."

"You both need to sit down." Emry grimaced. She doubted they'd be thanking her afterwards.

Levric disappeared through the room's door, while Llydia worked on slipping off Declan's mud-caked boots. Emry probably should have helped, but she was rooted in place, vaguely aware of the sludgy puddle she'd dripped onto the floor and quilt.

She wasn't sure how to mentally prepare for the feat ahead of her. She would be delving into one of her most taxing abilities – tapping into that part of her she didn't use. And she'd be literally tinkering with the lives of three people she cared very much about. Something could easily go wrong, as it had with her sister and mother – the one other time she'd done this. Her past experience was not very encouraging.

A moment later, Levric returned with two wooden, crisscross-backed chairs that had been painted a dark green clearly many years before with how many scuffs and nicks were worn into them. He bumped his way through the door frame and set the chairs down beside Llydia. She silently lowered herself into one of them, and Levric took the other. Both turned to Emry expectantly.

She took a deep breath. "I apologize now for anything I do that may end up harming you."

"We asked for this," Llydia said. Levric only nodded, his face grim.

"Very well."

Emry adjusted her eyes. It was easy to find the light inside of Declan's parents. Theirs was thriving – swirling within them. Life. They were so full of life. Blinding compared to Declan's sad little flicker. Extending her free hand, Emry beckoned first Llydia's light then Levric's. A trickle flowed out of both, slowly strengthening into a steady stream by the time it reached Emry's fingers. From somewhere far away, she heard a sharp intake of breath. They could feel it – could sense the essence of their lives were in her hands.

The sheer power of them infused her core, tingling through her. She could feel their fear for their son. Their love for him. Their hope for his future. Their trust in her to help him. Emry bit the tip of her tongue. She didn't want to disappoint them. They believed she could save Declan while sparing them as well. She wished it to be true.

Their combined light was welling up inside of her. It was time to begin the transfer – just as her mother had taught her ages ago. The challenge still lay ahead. The darkness inside of her – the power she kept hidden and subdued – was heightening her own senses. It ached to be called upon – to help her replenish the void within Declan. With a grunt, Emry quieted it, shrunk it back down. She would *not* fill Declan with power stolen from darkness.

The temptation to keep Llydia and Levric's life force as her own came next. It was a weak want – vastly overshadowed by her selfish wish to have Declan alive. The light would go to him. But for one more heartbeat, Emry savored the power of their lives before urging it outward into the cold hand she still held.

Llydia gasped, and Emry wasn't surprised. Her mother had never told her if it had hurt giving her light to Cit all those years before, but Emry had seen the paling of her skin and the shaking in her hands. She'd held in whatever pain Emry had caused to save Emry from concern – to make sure that Emry saved Cit's life. And just as Cit had gulped down her mother's light, Declan was doing the same to that of his parents.

Slowly, his short, shallow breaths lengthened and deepened. Some color came back to his face. He was healing!

It was almost time for Emry to release his parents. Declan was nearly his old self. Yet, still she drained them. She could hear their ragged pants. Emry was taking too much. She needed to stop the flow. Declan had reached his former capacity. Her mother had told her it was best to break all the connections at once, but it was complicated. The flow of light wasn't easy to plug up all at once. That had been her problem with Cit. She'd given her sister too much of her mother, and it had cost them both.

Panic rose up in Emry's throat. Last time, she'd thought of a dam drying up the light, but that had taken her mind too long to build. She required something quick, swift. Something to slice through the streams of light. A knife. She needed a knife. She mentally picturing a long blade. It was more sword than knife. Emry imagined it dangling just above the light from Declan's parents. Then, at once, she swung it downward as she released her grasp on Declan's hand.

Llydia and Levric's light retracted, and they slumped in their chairs. Emry's eyes returned to normal. Her hands braced her up over the side of the bed. She was gasping for air. If she felt like this, then Declan's parents…

She glanced up at them. They both were pale, but breathing. At least they were breathing. Her gaze then shifted to Declan. He was still unconscious, but he was inhaling in and out easily. Relief. Such blissful relief washed over her.

He was alive. Alive.

Emry sank to her knees, burying her head onto the edge of the bed. It was over. She'd managed to save Declan without killing his parents. It was a small victory.

"You need to change out of those clothes before getting some rest." Llydia's voice was strained, weak.

"I didn't bring anything else." Emry lifted her head from the bed.

Llydia eased herself out of her seat, leaving behind a wet mark from her own rain drenched clothes. "Come. I'll find you something."

Emry obediently followed her to the straight, narrow staircase. No longer reluctant to leave Declan's side. She was about to trudge up the stairs after Llydia, when on the fourth step she could go no further. It was as if that rope connecting her with Declan had wrapped itself around her chest and was dragging her backwards every time she attempted to move forward. Holding back a curse, Emry gritted her teeth. After such a long night, she'd forgotten about her Knight-induced limitations.

"I can't go up there," Emry said, her jaw clenched.

Llydia turned around. She raised an eyebrow, but said, "Wait here."

A couple minutes later, Llydia returned with a stack of fresh clothes and a washcloth. She extended them to Emry, who took them from her. "Thank you."

"For tonight, you can just rub off what mud that you can with water from the sink and the washcloth," Llydia told her.

"Thank you," Emry repeated. She really wasn't wanting to go to bed with the mud caked on beneath her fingernails and up her calves.

Llydia frowned. "You'll have to sleep in the room with Declan tonight. When he wakes we can make other arrangements if you prefer."

"I think that's actually the best option," she replied. "It's less confining if we're close to each other."

"Alright," his mother said slowly. She clearly didn't understand what Emry meant. "Take all the time you need to rest. We'll discuss what happened later."

What had happened. Fresh tears filled the corners of Emry's eyes. "My father's dead." Her voice cracked on the last word.

Llydia gasped and sank onto the bottom stair as Emry's tears spilled over. Whatever leash she'd once had over her emotions had been fractured sometime during the night. Emry took a breath before she went on, "By our own guards. I was there. They would have come after me, but- but Declan took me away before I had the chance to do anything."

"Oh, Emry," Llydia breathed. "I'm terribly sorry. He loved you very much."

All she could do was nod her thanks. She would have wiped her cheeks if her hands had been empty … or clean.

"Your sister?" Llydia inquired tightly.

"I don't know."

Llydia pulled the flaps of her robe closer around herself. "We've heard nothing of it. I had no idea."

Emry let out a half-sob, half-laugh. "I don't expect

you to have heard anything. It happened less than six hours ago."

"Then-" Llydia stared at her. "Then, how are you here?"

"How do you think Declan almost died?" She asked quietly. "He ran so fast. I think faster than anyone who's ever lived."

Footsteps sounded behind Emry. She turned to find Levric. At the sight of their faces, he frowned. But all he said was, "If you've been up all night, you should sleep."

"Just lay your wet things over a chair." Llydia stood. "I can get them later."

"That won't be necessary." Emry shook her head. "I'm sorry about the way I woke you. I didn't know what else to do."

"Think nothing of it," Levric assured.

Emry thanked them again before heading toward the kitchen, as Declan's parents climbed the wooden staircase. It wasn't until she pumped water into the basin to wet the cloth Llydia had given her that she realized the house was still fully lit because of herself. She quickly drew the light back into her palm, casting the house into darkness once more. Then, forming a small ball of light in the same hand, she tossed it above her head to illuminate just where she stood. The little orb floated above her head, like her own personal star.

She scrubbed herself off the best that she could with the rag and some nearby soap on the counter. It made her feel a little better, but not really clean. Whenever she would wake up, she'd take care of that. For now, this would have to do.

Picking up the bundle of clothes again from where she'd set them beside the sink, she made her way back into the room with Declan. She shut the door behind her. Levric must had changed Declan, because he was now beneath a new quilt in a clean, dry shirt, breathing softly. He was breathing. He was alive. He didn't die.

And they were in Anexia.

Exhaustion hit Emry. It had been too many hours since she'd last slept, and too much had occurred. She was suddenly too tired to think. All she wanted was sleep.

Not caring that Declan was within sight, Emry sucked the floating star into her outstretched palm, dimming the room, and began to undress.

Declan was still unconscious, still recovering. It was unlikely that he'd wake anytime soon. Or, at least, that was what she told herself as she peeled off her sopping tunic, leggings, and shoes. Llydia had given her a short-sleeved linen nightgown. In Anexian fashion, the gray fabric only fell to her knees.

Once that was on, Emry threw a quick glance around the room. It wasn't big. The only pieces of furniture were an armoire in one corner, a chair in another, and the bed Declan was on in the center. It was fortunate the bed was wide enough for two because she would have to share it with him. In her thin, drafty nightgown with her wet hair, the floor was not an option.

With a groan, Emry slid beneath the quilt, pleased that the sheets weren't chilly. She rolled onto her side, putting her back to Declan, and shifted over to the bed's edge. She didn't know how he'd react when he woke to find her next to him. It'd be better to give him as much space as possible.

Releasing a sigh, Emry shut her eyes. The images from the past few hours came flooding back then. The long ride on Declan's back, the Kruth inn, her father's death … He'd died. Her father was dead. Just like her mother. Just like Ewan. Maybe even like Cit. She had no idea what had become of her sister.

Sobs overtook Emry again, rocking her entire body. Had she ever cried this much in one day before? She covered her mouth with one hand to silence herself. Grief consumed her. She'd never felt so alone before. Declan might as well have been a world away and not just on the other side of the bed. Her tears continued, coming one after the other. Completely out of her control.

This was her life, she had to remind herself. This was the path she'd chosen, years before. The possibility of losing loved ones along the way had always been there. Her father's death was just another name on an ever-lengthening list. Deep breaths. She needed to take deep breaths. She could do this. She was in Anexia. Declan had fulfilled his purpose as her Knight. She could do this.

Deep breaths. Air. In and out.

Slowly, almost pathetically so, Emry's sobs subsided. Her trembling lessened. And eventually, her heart calmed. Then, once again, she drifted off to sleep listening to Declan breathe.

# CHAPTER SEVENTEEN

It was the chirping of birds that woke Declan. The warm, yellow sunlight filtering through the gaps in the curtains helped keep him from drifting off back to sleep. He opened his eyes to an unfamiliar ceiling. Well, no, not entirely unfamiliar. It was just one he hadn't seen in over a month.

He was in his room. For a second, he thought he was dreaming. He had no memory of coming home.

But then, hazy images from the night before returned to him. He'd run off with Emry to Anexia. They must had made it. He was in his room.

Where was Emry?

Declan pushed himself up. As his hand shifted on the quilt, his fingers brushed a cool hand. He glanced left.

His princess was on her side, facing him. Her even breathing was barely more than a whisper. It was strange to see her with blonde hair again. It was how he'd seen her in his dreams.

As if she felt his gaze, her eyes fluttered open. Those deep, silver orbs, veined with black and gray, shimmered up at him. "Dec," she breathed, her voice hoarse.

"Hi, Emry." He smiled.

She laid there watching him for a moment, as if her eyes were hungry for just the sight of him. Then, she cleared her throat and in that Anexian accent, she asked, "How are you feeling?"

"Fine." He shrugged. "I slept well enough. How about you?"

Once again, she just looked at him — not responding right away. When she finally did, it wasn't to answer his question. "What do you remember from last night?"

He frowned down at her. "I'm sorry about your father."

Her expression didn't change. Her eyes held that same careful trace in them. Like she was gauging his every action. "Is that all you remember?"

"I know I brought us here," he replied. "I know I carried you."

"What about when we got here?"

Declan shook his head. "That's where it gets fuzzy."

She nodded once and rolled onto her back, gazing upward. "We arrived early in the morning, just before dawn."

"Did we wake my parents?"

A beat. "Yes."

"What happened to me?" Declan winced. "Why can't I remember?"

"You passed out," she said to the ceiling. "Your parents and I had to carry you inside."

Guilt. Emry was suffering from guilt.

Declan nearly jumped at the emotion. It had come down that invisible chain that tethered him to her. *He* felt what *she* was feeling. How was that even possible?

Wait. Emry had met his parents. And he hadn't been awake to help explain why they were there. His parents had to have been shocked to be yanked from sleep by a stranger and their inanimate son. But they'd let Emry stay … in Declan's room.

His father was an intelligent man. He would have discerned the identity of Emry on his own. Why else would Declan – the sworn Knight to Princess Emerald – show up with a random female when he was supposed to be bringing his princess to Anexia? No, Levric would have figured out who she was immediately. That meant The Mistress and her Committee probably already knew of her presence. No wonder his father had let Emry spend the night with Declan. Levric didn't want her out of his sight.

Declan moaned and dropped back onto his pillow. He pressed his palms into his eyes – as if that could stop the headache forming behind them.

Emry turned her head. "What's wrong?"

Who did he care for more? His people or his princess? He snorted. He already knew the answer to that. It was Emry.

At The Trials, he'd endured Cadoc's fists for her. He'd carried her across the country in one night just to avoid being pursued by the men who had killed her father. He'd taken her here, to his father, because he knew she'd be safe.

Even if The Mistress herself ordered Emry into harm, Levric would push back. Declan's father didn't hurt the innocent. No matter if Rioter or Royal. It was a quality in him that Declan had always admired. Here, Emry would be alright.

But should Declan warn Emry? Admit to what he'd done? Show her the truth in Vardin's words? Shame filled Declan. Pure shame. At what he had not only agreed to, but had volunteered for. To lead a young, unaware, trusting girl and deliver her to her enemy for devouring. What sort of monster was he? He was no better than those that had held him captive. The burden of his mistake crushed into his chest, flattening his lungs. Air … he couldn't take in enough air.

Beside him, Emry pushed up onto her elbows. "Declan?"

His hands tore at the collar of his shirt. The fabric around his neck was suddenly too tight. What had he done? He'd promised himself years ago he'd never cause another innocent harm. To never experience imprisonment as he had. Yet, he'd done just that for the greater good of his country. For the Rioters. For The Mistress. A nameless face he'd never even met before!

It wasn't supposed to have been this way. The princess was supposed to have been cold, selfish, spoiled … a Royal. Not Emry.

He'd told himself the Jewels deserved to be knocked down a notch – to suffer as Anexia and other commoners had. As *he* had.

But that was before he'd known the Jewels – who they were. Ewan. Cit. Even the king hadn't been the arrogant pig Declan had made him out to be in his mind. And Emry.

Why was his room so stifling? Declan sat up, yanking off his shirt. He was panting.

"Dec," Emry's hand slid over his back – her fingers cold and stinging. But for once, it was refreshing. Better than the heat of the room. She was kneeling next to him. "Dec," she repeated, "it's alright. Whatever it is, we're alright."

The concern she was experiencing for him seeped into his chest. He nearly swore as her emotion filled him. So, he could feel her mood now. Perfect. When she discovered what he'd done, he'd get to know just how deep his betrayal would hurt her.

He was disgusted with himself. He glanced down at his hands in his lap and wasn't surprised to see them trembling.

"Look at me."

At the command in her voice, Declan's eyes flew to her. Her silver eyes. Eyes that were like a night sky. Dark depth mixed with starlight and moonbeams. Eyes that sparkled. Eyes that were endless.

And below those eyes ... Declan's gaze dropped to her mouth. The lips he'd tasted just the night before. Soft and sweet and luring. He'd wanted more. Hadn't liked being snatched away from them.

As if Emry's own thoughts had drifted in the same direction, she tilted her chin upward, giving him better access to her mouth. It wouldn't take much for him to close the distance between them. She'd kissed him last night, perhaps he should return the favor.

But he was about to betray her. How could he possibly be thinking of kissing her again? Declan was going insane. He had to be.

Her lips, though. They were so close. Right there. Waiting for him.

Declan swore. And pressed his mouth to hers. He slipped a hand behind her head, his fingers twining into her hair. She didn't balk. No, she parted her lips, willing him to deepen their kiss. He greedily obliged her silent request. He wrapped his other arm around her waist, yanking her against him.

Some small part of him, in the back of his mind, was humiliated at his life choices. Declan blocked that part of himself out. Emry was engulfed in his arms. And he would kiss her like there was no tomorrow. Like this was the last moment they had before she discovered what he had done. Before she despised him forever. He was hungry for her, and she seemed just as eager.

In the years to come, this would be all he'd have to remember her by. So, he selfishly went on. Savoring the taste of her lips. The warmth of her body. The sweet scent of her skin. Every heartbeat of it.

Until Emry suddenly broke free. She tore out of his grip with a strength he hadn't known she possessed. He stared at her, his eyes wide. His breathing came out in ragged gusts.

"Why?" He managed to choke out. Why had she stopped? Why did she let him kiss her for as long as she had? Why had she kissed him *like that?*

The door to his room swung open, revealing his mother. Declan's gaze whipped towards her. Emry had heard her coming. How? He sure hadn't.

Llydia took in him and Emry on the bed with her own mild surprise. He wasn't sure what exactly he'd been expecting her to say, but it certainly wasn't, "Sorry, if I'd known you were awake, I would have knocked."

His mother? Knock?

"I told you not to worry about my clothes." Emry slid off the edge of the bed to her feet.

"I was already washing some of my own," was his mother's reply.

"Thank you." Emry smiled as she met Llydia halfway into the room, taking a small folded pile of linen Declan hadn't realized his mother had been carrying. "You really didn't have to."

"It was nothing." Llydia shrugged it off, in her usual manner. "How long have you been up?"

"I don't know," Emry threw a quick look his way, "maybe fifteen minutes?"

Sure, if she wasn't counting the time they'd spent devouring each other's mouths. Declan merely shrugged noncommittally. It was all he could do. He wasn't exactly sure what was happening. Emry was acting as if nothing had been going on mere seconds before his mother swept in.

"How are you feeling, Declan?" Llydia asked him warily.

Did it show how unsettled Emry had left him? He forced a smile on. "I'm fine."

It hit him then that he hadn't seen her in over a month. The last time had been before The Trials. She'd been worried over his safety. To the point of tears.

With a grunt, Declan shoved himself out of bed and pulled her into a hug. "It's good to be back, Mom. Sorry we barged in on you last night."

She kissed his cheek. "You know you're always welcome at home. We're very proud of you becoming the princess's Knight."

Declan stilled. How much had Emry shared with his parents?

"They know who I am, Dec," Emry said softly.

"Oh?"

"We can discuss everything later," Llydia told him. "Right now, you and Emry need to wash before the hot water ends."

"Emry," Declan repeated.

"That is the name I go by in Anexia," Emry replied, her gaze not quite meeting his. To Llydia, she said, "I'll go get cleaned first."

Llydia nodded. "It's just next door."

Emry thanked her and went out the door – her bundle of clothes pressed against her chest. Declan watched her exit. When his attention returned to his mother, she was observing him with an amused gleam in her eyes.

"Hungry?" She asked.

: : : : :

Emry shut the door to the washroom and leaned back against it, tipping her head upwards. She was a fool. An utter fool.

Intelligent women didn't kiss the men they were deceiving. Not when they loved them, anyway. Or, so she told herself. What had possessed her to think Declan was the right choice to be her Knight, to take her here? What sort of demented masochist was she?

With a groan, Emry hoisted herself from the whitewashed door. Maybe a shower would improve her state of mind. She took in the small space.

The floor had been tiled in a mosaic of small hexagons. In such a modest village, especially in Anexia, to have any tile at all expressed an affluent household. Outside of major cities, tile was difficult to come by. It had to be purchased elsewhere. For Anexians, usually their tile was bought in the Midlands.

These particular tiles of sea green, teal, and navy were imported all the way from Heerth. Emry knew because she'd sent them to Levric. As both a gift and payment. She doubted Declan knew their true origin.

To have a washroom inside his parents' house at all signified some amount of wealth. More than just a simple village blacksmith could manage. Most homes didn't have one. Families tended to bathe in the community bathing house – run by the local Orange and Blue. That was, if the village was even big enough to have people of both base colors. Often, there was just one or the other – a Blue to fill the tanks of water used for washing, or an Orange to heat the water to a comfortable temperature.

Declan's village did have both, fortunately. It had just cost a small fortune to run pipes underground from the community bathing house to his home. Again, Emry knew just how much because she'd paid for it, a little more than two years ago.

Her eyes drifted to the large, oval porcelain tub. A copper faucet hung just above its lip with three levers above it. The middle lever was to turn on the water – a request to the Blue. The lever on the left signaled the Orange to make the water hotter, and the one on the right to make it cooler. Above the levers was a large window of fogged glass, brightening the whole room.

To the left of the tub, in a corner, was the shower. Its copper faucet was set into the ceiling, but unlike the tub, it didn't just pour out water. This faucet was square with many small holes for the water to stream from. The shower's levers were stacked just outside of it. The hot being on top and cold on the bottom, with the middle one to turn it off and on. In order to minimize the amount of water spraying everywhere, two tiled half walls had been constructed. But where the short walls would have connected there was a space open for someone to get in and out of the shower.

A toilet, slim vanity, and mirror completed the washroom. It was nothing lavish – not like the ones Emry had enjoyed in Heerth. But it was still a luxury. One Emry was especially grateful she'd forced on Levric because a shower sounded delightful.

: : : :

It turned out the group who had traveled to Brec-can to watch him in The Trials wasn't back yet. His mother had given him the news while Emry bathed and he ate. When Emry emerged all clean with damp hair, Declan went to take a shower of his own and shave. He wasn't fond of sporting a beard. It reminded him too much of a former life.

By the time he was clean and dressed, Emry was finished eating. He was about to sit next to her at the kitchen table, across from his mother, when Levric strode in. One look at his father's face, and Declan was instantly nervous. He knew that face. It was the one he wore with The Mistress's Committee.

Emry glanced up at him and smiled. "Hello, Levric."

Levric nodded his head in greeting before glancing at Declan. "I'd like for the two of you to come with me."

Declan's mouth went dry. He tried to swallow. "Where are we going?"

"To my shop," Levric replied, shifting his gaze to Emry.

"Alright," Emry said, pushing herself up with her hands on the table. To Llydia, she smiled. "Thank you for dinner. It was delicious."

Llydia waved a hand. "Of course."

Outside, the sun was setting, casting the sky in or-ange and pink hues. Declan trailed behind his father and Emry. All three of them were silent as they trudged along the worn dirt path from his house to the nearby village square.

He tipped his head upward. His heart was pound-ing. This was it. This was when Emry discovered just what a horrible person he truly was. He clasped his hands behind his neck. A trickle of fear spread through him. Not from himself, but from Emry. She was anxious as well. Why? Did she suspect something?

They headed under a copse of trees, and Emry crafted a ball of silvery light in her palm. He blinked. He hadn't known she could do that.

As she tossed it above their heads, suspending it in the air, she glimpsed his face. "When you live in a palace, you have servants to light a room for you," she told him.

No one spoke for the rest of their short journey.

Levric's shop was the front room of his smithy. It was where he sold the metal goods he'd shaped. Between the shop and the adjoining forge was a single room with a rough-hewn table and chairs. It was where Levric usually took his meals during the day and where he often met with Committee members.

Once they were inside the shop, Emry drew her ball of light back into her hand. His father paused, casting a look at him. Like he wasn't sure if Declan should continue on. Declan frowned. "I go where Emry goes."

She nodded. "From now on, Declan hears everything."

That was an odd way to put it. But Levric merely dipped his head once. As Emry extinguished the light on her palm, Declan's father opened the door into that middle room.

The room was lit and six of the eight chairs were already filled. Declan recognized them all to be Committee members. He sucked in a breath – the beat of his heart blaring in his ears. Levric moved to take a seat. Declan tossed a glance at Emry, trying to gauge her reaction to the people now staring at her.

Emry didn't even hesitate at the threshold. Without

waiting for an invitation, she sank into the remaining chair.

Declan froze at the door.

With one hand, she pushed back her hair out of her face, and asked, "What news from Breccan, my friends?"

# CHAPTER EIGHTEEN

There was a roaring in Declan's ears. He didn't hear the response to Emry's question. Something about where the palace had been burnt. He didn't care. Emry had called some of The Mistress's Committee members her *friends*. She knew them!

"What of my sister?" Emry's voice drifted to him. "She was supposed to have stopped that from happening."

"She did salvage most of the palace," came the response. Declan didn't see who'd said it. His eyes were on Emry.

"Is she alive?" Her tone was even, but Declan could feel the fear within her – through their tether.

Someone else answered her. "As far as we know. But her Knight…"

"Out with it, Warks," Emry demanded.

Levric cleared his throat. "Freddick is dead, my Mistress."

That one word bowled Declan over – hands on his knees, breath ragged. It was as if he'd been punched in the stomach. An onslaught of emotions swept through him. All from Emry. Anger. Sorrow. More anxiety. But it was his own outright betrayal that coated his tongue.

*MISTRESS!*

Emry's head whipped around to him, her eyes wide. Declan glared at her. The way she looked made him wonder if she'd heard him screaming inside his head. Good. Maybe she could feel some of his emotions as he could hers. Then, she might feel even just a portion of what her deception had cost him. The disbelief and rage that ripped and twisted his insides.

He'd thought he'd be the one betraying her. But all along Emry had been duping him. She was The Mistress. The Mistress! Leader of the Rioters ... and princess of the Royals. Declan was going to be sick.

"Your sister has been confined to her room," Warks said from somewhere far away. He drew Emry's gaze away from Declan. "Vardin is the only one permitted to see her. The rumor is that she's too distraught to leave her quarters."

"Oh, held prisoner to them more likely," Emry muttered. "How did her husband die?"

Husband? Cit had a *husband*? Who, Freddick? Declan's jaw dropped.

"He was drowned by Vardin himself," Warks replied.

Declan was gaping. Outright gaping. They knew. They all knew that Emry was both the princess *and* The Mistress. But no one had thought to warn him.

His own disgust overwhelmed him. He had to get out of this room. The people he'd risked his life for in The Trials – they'd lied to him. Deceived him. All of them. The Committee. His parents. Emry.

Without a word, he whirled out the door. He stormed through his father's shop and into the night air until he could go no further. Until that leash he'd inflicted upon himself – out of duty to the Rioters – snapped him back. He stopped in his tracks, looked up at the stars, and roared.

: : : : :

Emry could *feel* his disgust. Ever since she'd heard his voice shout inside her head. It was the reaction she'd been dreading – had been anticipating. But she hadn't expected to experience his emotions right alongside him. It made it infinitely worse. How was it even possible? It was all she could focus on. She fought to stop herself from wincing. From letting the few members present from her Committee see her so affected.

Not once had Cit or Freddick ever mentioned feeling each other's moods. They hadn't even given her the impression that they could read the other that well. In fact, it seemed more like they rarely knew what the other was thinking.

Another wave of hurt and betrayal … and rage. His emotions were overpowering her. He'd never forgive her. Just as she'd thought. Emry concentrated on keeping her breathing even. Now was not the time for self-pity. She needed answers from her Committee. She needed to form a plan of action after being so blindsided by her own palace guards. By Vardin. That pig.

Emry shoved out Declan's fury with that of her own. "Drowned?" She hissed.

"Your sister could only protect herself from Vardin," Eddvert Warks – the leader of her Eyes, her spies – said grimly. "He filled the lungs of Freddick with water right in front of her."

"Oh, Cit." Emry grasped onto the edge of the table to steady herself. She forced her air in and out slowly. It was not the time to grieve. To panic.

Cit was alone. Alone and suffering. But at least alive. She was alive. She needed to have someone with her, though. Moira would be Emry's first choice – Piran's mother and Cit's mentor. But for the woman to be drawn away from Court to the protection of Cit would make a statement. Emry required subtlety, and from someone Cit trusted.

Piran. He could disappear for a little while, and no one would notice. He'd done it many times before. Emry bit the tip of her tongue. "How long will it take to send a message to Piran Bricke?"

"The Duke's son?" Warks blinked. "A day. Tomorrow evening at the soonest. Depends on how fast our harriers can fly."

"Good." Emry nodded. "Send one immediately. Petition Piran to take care of Cit – to sneak into the palace."

"From you, my Mistress?" Levric inquired from beside her. He meant which persona would she be using.

Emry shook her head once. "No. From the princess. Let him know I'm alive, but in hiding. That Vardin compromised us. Barest details. Use my code. He and Cit know it. He could show her."

"Yes, my Mistress." Warks inclined his head.

She frowned. "Anything else?"

"There is the question of why…" Levric trailed off.

It was what she'd been asking herself. She leaned back in her seat. "I think whoever called the attack wanted us to be distracted with Vardin and his pets. We may have to wait for more reports to come in before we can discover why. And who."

A few voices rumbled in agreement around the table. Emry took another steadying breath. She didn't want to wait. She wanted answers now. She wanted to go slit Vardin's throat. But he was too far, and she might still have need of him for information. It was infuriating. "We can reconvene when we hear more."

"Will you be going to the estate?" Warks asked. If he were to pass on news as it came in, he'd need to know her location.

The estate he referred to was the one she'd stayed at with Ewan. The one she'd lived in until she was eleven. It had belonged to her mother's family. Now it belonged to Emry. "No. I would be expected to hide there. I'll stay with the Sharpes."

"It would be our honor, my Mistress," Levric added. So formal. Emry nearly rolled her eyes. He only said it for the benefit of her Committee members. As her unofficial second in command, he was always boosting her up with his respect.

Emry pushed herself to her feet, using the table as support. Her companions rose as well. "Until the next, my friends."

"Until the next," they intoned.

She nodded once at Levric to join her and headed out of the room … to Declan.

: : : : :

He'd noticed the chain between them had slackened. By the time Emry and his father were outside, Declan was already thirty feet ahead – as far as he could possibly get. From Emry.

But she wasn't walking nearly fast enough. His body was crying out to run. Begging for him to tap into his speed and disappear. And there wasn't a thing he could do about it. He'd willingly tied himself to Emry. To *The Mistress*!

Declan swore. Could she and Levric pick up the pace? They were meandering along as if they had all the time in the world. As if Declan wasn't fuming up ahead of them. Stomping around in the dark – letting his feet guide him home.

His father had to be wondering why Declan hadn't taken off already. Why he was still close enough to hear them chatting about the birds that would carry Emry's messages. Harriers. He'd heard his father mention them before.

Even though Emry sounded interested, Declan could feel her sorrow and fear muddling her concentration. It didn't help his mood – sensing Emry's behind him. This new thing between them irritated him. He didn't want to experience her emotions. To empathize. He was infuriated.

And she was going *so* slow!

He didn't want to be left with his thoughts. He wanted to sprint so that the only thing inside his head was the sound of his feet hitting the ground. This sedate stride wasn't distracting enough. He didn't want to understand why her being The Mistress wounded him. Didn't want to know why it even mattered when he'd been planning on handing Emry over to The Mistress all along. Didn't want to own up to the fact that him feeling betrayed was hypocritical. She hadn't trusted him with her secret identity any more than he'd done with his plans to kidnap her. The plans *she* had given him, as The Mistress. She'd known what he was going to do all along.

That was really what it came down to. He felt like a fool. He'd been duped – by people he cared about. It was what outraged him the most. He'd been used as a tool. As he once had been, years before. The circumstances were drastically different, but when he got down to it, he'd played the puppet. Again. And he hadn't seen it coming because it'd been Emry. Of all people, it had to be Emry.

His light in the dark. The girl from his dreams. The

woman who danced the Mountain Thunder. Emry. Princess and Mistress. Declan felt ill.

Finally, his house came into view. The bottom floor was lit. His mother was inside. He realized he wasn't ready to face her.

Declan climbed the porch steps and opened the door to an empty floor. A little relieved, he made his way to his room. He slipped inside and flung the door shut harder than he'd intended. He heard Emry and his father enter the house and then part ways for the evening. Levric wasn't one to poke into the affairs of others. He evidently believed whatever was bothering Declan could be cleared up by Emry because he merely bid her goodnight.

As Emry stepped towards Declan's room, she grimaced. She'd felt his anger the whole walk back from their meeting. His mood hadn't changed since coming inside. She paused at the threshold of the door he'd just slammed – her hand on the doorknob.

This was it. The conversation she'd been anticipating for months. She'd known he'd never see her the same way once he found out who she was. The revelation of her being the princess was insignificant compared to being The Mistress. At least to a Rioter, like himself. It was why she'd selfishly let herself kiss him earlier. Like it was the last time ... because it most likely was.

Emry gulped in a breath and twisted the knob. The room was dark. Instead of adjusting her eyes, she formed a dim orb of light in her palm and tossed it above her head.

Declan was sitting on the floor below the room's one window. His head was tipped back, and his eyes were closed. Before Emry finished shutting the door behind her, he asked one word, "Why?"

She knew what he was asking. *Why didn't you tell me who you are?* She could practically hear the words inside her head. Holding in a sigh, Emry slipped off her shoes and leaned back against the door. She pressed her palms into the wood behind her to keep them from trembling.

"Because the only people who knew were sitting in that room, minus your mother." She winced. "I- I haven't even told Cit. She only knows I've communicated with the Rioters. She doesn't know I lead them."

The mention of who she was made his disgust return. But he still didn't open his eyes. "My parents know," he said, his voice low.

She swallowed. "I told them not to tell you. Not until you brought me here."

"Why?" He demanded again.

"You weren't my Knight yet," she explained, keeping her voice as level as she could. "What if you had failed? Had lost my Trials? The fewer who know my identity the better. I have to keep it a secret, so I can save our country."

"Save our country?" He snorted. "From what? You're both a Royal and Rioter."

"Exactly," she replied evenly. "Our country's divided. As the leader of the Rioters, and now the Royals, I can reunite our people. I wanted you to take me here as seemingly against my will so as to finally stimulate negotiations with my father. So his ancient counselors could no longer ignore The Feud." She dug her nails into the door's wood. "Do you think that our neighbors have neglected our weakness? Uniting us was the only way to protect us from invasion. But I was too late. Look what happened at the palace. Things obviously went wrong."

That resonated inside of Declan. He turned over her words inside his head as he experienced a flash of guilt and grief through him. Emotions from Emry.

When he didn't respond, though, she went on, "I want to know who told Vardin that The Mistress wanted the princess."

No wonder Emry had acted the way she did the night before – her lack of surprise overall. Was it really only one night ago? He frowned. It seemed much longer. Wait. His eyes flew open as his mind registered what she'd just admitted.

"You're the heir," he blurted.

Emry let out a short laugh and slid down onto the floor, her back still against the door. "Everyone assumes it's Cit because she's taller and had her Trials first. But Trial order doesn't signify birth order. And that stupid Enlennd tradition of keeping the birthdates of its princesses secret doesn't help either. I've always hated that. It's only done so that princesses can be married off without the elder one needing to be taken care of first. No one even remembered Cit and I existed until Ewan was killed."

He blinked. "You're the queen."

"Now, I am."

It was a lot to process. Emry. The Mistress. And now queen. All this time he'd been battering himself with guilt, but it'd been what she'd wanted all along. As The Mistress, she'd picked him as her contestant for Anexia, for the Rioters. Then, as the princess, she'd needed him to play the role of an abductor.

"You used me," he hissed through clenched teeth.

"No, Dec," she said softly. Sadness. There was so much sadness in her. "I requested you because you were the only man I trusted for the job."

Her despair swept through him. For what, he wasn't sure. Either way, he didn't want to feel it. He wasn't ready to sympathize – to forgive. He was still livid. Loosing something like a growl, he shoved himself to his feet and glared at Emry. She was probably purposely blocking the exit. He spun to the window and pushed it open.

Declan hefted himself up through it. First one leg, followed by the other. He dropped the few feet to the ground and welcomed the cold night air. It cooled his rage. He leaned his back to the wall and stared upward at the flickering stars.

He heard Emry shuffling around the room, followed by the creak of his bed from her weight as she climbed into it. Declan's leash was as much his as it was hers. She couldn't go anywhere else.

That ball of light extinguished, and Emry whispered, "I'm sorry, Declan."

There was so much sorrow attached to those words, seeping through that invisible chain into his chest, that Declan couldn't stop the twin tears from escaping the corners of his eyes.

He stayed out against the wall for a long time.

# CHAPTER NINETEEN

Declan wasn't there when Emry woke the next morning. He'd come to bed some time during the night, after she'd fallen asleep. There was an indent in the bed beside her, but no Declan. He'd already risen. Through the closed door of his room, she could hear the muffled voices of him and Llydia in the kitchen, but she couldn't quite make out the words.

Emry sighed. Last night had gone about as well as she could have hoped. At least Declan had let her explain herself. That was further than she'd gotten in some of the scenarios she'd played out in her head. So there was that. It still didn't make his fury with her any easier to swallow.

It was going to be a rough day. Emry burrowed beneath the quilt, purposely ignoring the fact that it smelled like Declan. This morning felt like those she'd endured right after her mother's death, and then again after Ewan's. Dark days. Filled with tears. All Emry had wanted to do then was lay in bed with her curtains drawn – bedridden by her despair. She hadn't really done that … but she'd wanted to.

Maybe for a few hours each morning she'd succumb to the desire. After their mother died, though, she'd spent every other hour comforting Cit. They'd only had each other those first couple weeks in the estate – until their father and Ewan joined them in Anexia.

Ewan's death had been harder. She hadn't had a reason to rise in the mornings. Cit had gone to their father for her comfort. And Cit hadn't known Ewan as Emry had. Especially not in those last few years. With his death being after her mother's, Emry knew exactly what she'd miss. All his teasing. All his easy smiles. The strength she'd relied on. Gone. It'd taken her much longer to feel like herself again. She'd forced herself to get out of bed each day. If Trez hadn't drawn her to Heerth, giving her a goal that motivated her to keep living, she wasn't sure how she would have survived at all.

The death of Onyx, though, was different. Not only had she lost her father, she'd inherited a crown. Of a nation that was divided and had been betrayed. There was now a whole slew of responsibilities and problems piled on top of her, and Emry didn't want to face any of them.

Her throat began to burn. Tears welled up and spilled over. Emry pressed her forehead into her pillow. Even with him in the other room, she could still feel Declan's anger sizzling. Anger at her. His trust in her injured.

Once again, loneliness dug its icy talons into her chest. She'd done this to herself. Had isolated herself as The Mistress from those she loved. She'd told herself it was for the greater good. For her people. Now, it just seemed like she'd been deceiving herself.

Emry's tears shifted into silent sobs. She squeezed her eyes shut and curled into a ball, her body shaking. For now, she'd let the despair take her. There was no one to watch her break. She'd deal with everything else in a few hours – whenever she would finally decide to get up.

:  :  :  :  :

There was sobbing inside Declan's head. It'd been going on for a few minutes now. From his actual ears, he couldn't hear anything, and by the way his mother acted, he assumed she couldn't either. It made the noise that much more frustrating. The sobs belonged to Emry.

He no longer owed her anything. He'd brought her here just as she'd plotted. He'd fulfilled his purpose to her. She had no other need of him. Or so he told himself.

That other part of him, though ... That part that had become attached to her – had fallen in love with her – that part felt shame. Shame at sitting still while her heart ached in the other room. While she broke apart. She felt overwhelmed and alone. With no one to turn to.

Declan swore out loud, startling his mother. He pushed himself to his feet. He'd been sitting at the kitchen table. "Sorry," he murmured and headed to his room.

The curtains were still drawn when he slipped inside. Through the dim light, he made his way to the edge of the bed and sat down. Emry was beneath the quilt, trembling. Slowly, he peeled it back. Emry didn't move. With one hand on her back, Declan gripped his other around her wrist and lifted her up. She wouldn't meet his eyes as he guided her to him. He pressed her into his chest and wrapped his arms around her. She grasped onto his shirt, burying her face into it. He sighed and rested his chin on top of her head.

"I'm still upset with you," he said softly into her hair, "but you don't deserve to suffer alone."

She nodded against him as she cried. One sob after another. He just sat there, quietly rubbing circles on her back.

After a while, her shaking subsided and her tears dried. He still held her. It wasn't until her hiccups grew far apart that he gently eased her back to look at her. Her face was red and splotchy, and she wouldn't raise her gaze from her hands in her lap. She'd released her grip on his shirt.

"Thank you," she whispered, her voice hoarse. "How- how did you know I was crying?"

Declan winced. She didn't know what he could feel. That her emotions somehow transferred to him. It was an incredible invasion of her privacy that he had absolutely no control over. "I-"

He stopped. Maybe he was a coward, but he didn't want to tell her. Not yet. Not after she'd just bawled her eyes out into his chest. He took a breath and changed course. "I need to go into town. To see my father. Would you be able to get ready so I can go?"

It was rude of him to completely sidestep her question and request she go out in the condition she was. But Emry only nodded, her eyes still glued to her hands. "Give me twenty minutes."

: : : : :

It looked like it might rain. Emry glanced up at the varying shades of the dense, gray clouds high above her head. The gloom didn't help her mood much. At least she wasn't crying anymore.

To her mortification, Declan had come to comfort

her. Stopped her insides from being ripped apart. How and why, she wasn't sure. But she was almost as ashamed about how much she'd enjoyed his arms around her as she was at him finding her in that state. She'd only let herself cry in the first place because he hadn't been there. No one was supposed to have witnessed her like that. It was why she hadn't made a sound.

And yet, Declan had known. He'd known she was breaking, and despite how angry he was with her, he'd come. How did he know? Emry had the suspicion that he could sense her emotions, just as she could with his.

The thought was unsettling. How much could he discern? Did he learn how she felt for him…

Emry's cheeks burned. She was sitting on a barrel that flanked the door into Levric's shop. Declan had gone inside about fifteen minutes before, in search of Levric. The idea that Declan was inside, listening to every sentiment roiling inside of her made her want to disappear. There were parts of her she didn't want anyone to know about.

Suddenly antsy, Emry slid off the barrel. She couldn't go far, but she didn't have to sit still.

Keeping close to the perimeter of Levric's shop, she followed its walls around toward the back. To the forge.

As she rounded the corner, she was startled to find a hardened clay round. Just like the one at the arena during her Fourth Trial, like the ones she'd seen in Heerth. On this side of the smithy, it was hidden from the road and village.

Standing on the round, was a decent looking redhead – not extraordinarily handsome, but striking in his own way. He was gripping onto a thick, round staff that came up to his shoulders. The staff was about the width of her fist and was flat on both the top and bottom, like an elongated cylinder. The young man was leaning his weight on the staff, while he spoke with a cluster of three girls, all in Anexian garb, who looked to be a few years younger than Emry.

The girls weren't what drew Emry's attention. The redhead on the round with that particular staff looked like a lovely distraction. Impulsively, Emry approached the round, and called out, "Do you actually know how to use that thing, or do you need it to keep you on your feet?"

The redhead turned in surprise. A Ruby. His eyes matched his hair. They swept her up and down as a grin formed on his thin lips. Emry merely watched him evenly. He'd clearly forgotten the girls behind him. "Of course, I can use it."

"Good." Emry walked over to one side of the round. There were three staffs on the ground in the grass. One was the same length as the redhead's, but the other two were shorter. Not as short as Emry preferred, but for today these could work. She picked up one of the shorter staffs and stepped onto the round. With one hand, she pulled the hem of her dark blue tunic up her thigh a little, permitting herself more flexibility. Llydia had gratefully lent her some of Declan's sisters' old clothes. The tunic was a touch tighter than she preferred, and the gray leggings were a little loose. They still beat wearing dirty clothes, though.

Across from her on the round, the redhead chuckled. "I'll try to go easy."

"Don't." Emry balanced the staff between both hands in front of her. "I've had a rough couple of days. I need a good workout."

He smirked. "If you say so."

Inside the forge, back by the flames, Declan stood with his father. He'd stopped by to hear Levric explain his reasons for keeping him in the dark about Emry. While they'd talked, he'd noticed Bran flirting with the Drummond twins and Katrina Nimkle out on the round Levric had built for Declan over a year ago. They hadn't spotted Declan. It wouldn't have been terrible if they had, but he wasn't ready to explain yet why he was back already instead of still in Breccan. Then, Emry appeared, and she grabbed a staff.

Declan stopped mid-sentence. He couldn't even remember what he'd been saying to Levric. He could only stare as Bran dropped into his opening stance – too narrow as usual. Emry, by contrast, widened her footing. She was grasping her staff about a forearm's length in on either side.

Bran made the first move – a quick twist of his body to bring one end of his staff upwards in an attempt to pop hers out of her hands. A cocky cheap shot. Except it didn't work. She swung hers downwards at the same time. He yielded a step towards her, and the other side of his staff that she hadn't hit rocked up. Instead of blocking the oncoming blow to her head, Emry angled herself sideways and slid her staff down the length of his body until she was squatting down by his knees.

Then, with a flick of her right wrist, she flung her staff out in an arc, while still gripping onto it with her left hand. The staff swung wide, coming up behind Bran as Emry replaced her left hand with her right. Just before her staff knocked into him, Emry caught the free end with her left hand and tugged it to her – through Bran. He ended up flat on his back as Emry rose out of her crouch.

Declan gaped. The way she'd moved – fluid, silken, smooth, and *fast*. Bran hadn't seen it coming. Of course, he hadn't. Because the last time Declan had seen someone make a move like that…

Emry knew the Turanga.

"Your stance is too narrow, and your staff is too long," Emry told Bran as she offered him her hand. Bran, never one to pass up an opportunity to touch a woman, accepted her help up. "It's making your movements sluggish. You should use one more like this length." She tapped her staff into the round.

Bran blushed. "That's what the Kruth women use."

No wonder he'd come at her like that. Those moves were meant for brute strength. He must have trained with a Kruth.

Declan flinched, realizing with a jolt that those thoughts hadn't come from himself. They were from Emry. He'd already known which style Bran favored. Declan had somehow, unwittingly moved on from experiencing Emry's emotions to thoughts?

"Well, Kruth men are oxen," Emry told Bran. "Someone your size should really be using one like this. You need to go for speed rather than strength. Let's try again."

Bran exchanged his staff for a shorter one and faced her again. It was still a similar outcome. Bran finished on his back. Before he was back up to his feet, though, Declan was already moving toward them. Emry's back was to him as he exited the forge.

*Disappointing, really.* Emry's voice grumbled unknowingly inside Declan's head. He nearly stumbled. That was her voice *inside* his head.

Out loud, Emry asked Bran, "Are you the best at this in the village?"

Bran shook his head and glanced past Emry. His eyes landed on Declan and widened in surprise. He pointed. "No, he is."

Somehow Emry knew it was him before she even turned. She'd told him once that she could feel him. He didn't doubt she felt him behind her now. Declan watched her shoulders tense up as she slowly spun around. She was biting the tip of her tongue.

"Where did you learn the Turanga?" He asked, his voice low.

"In Heerth," she replied. "Trez taught me. I could almost hold my own against him."

"What are you doing here, Declan?" Bran's stunned question brought Declan's head around. He'd stepped up next to Emry.

"My Mistress." Levric joined Declan's side. Bran's eyes bulged as Levric inclined his head to Emry. "We have received more reports."

Had they? Declan was just with his father. He hadn't mentioned anything to him.

Emry nodded. To Bran, she said, "Excuse me."

As she followed Levric into the forge, Declan merely shrugged at all the unasked questions in Bran's eyes and fell into step with his father.

# CHAPTER TWENTY

Warks was waiting for them in that middle room between the shop and the forge. He didn't rise from his chair at the table as Emry took a seat across from him. She loved that her Committee never made a big fuss over her. She was The Mistress, their leader, but she didn't need to be hailed like some divine object. She received more than enough of that at the palace.

Levric dropped into the chair at Emry's left, and Declan hesitantly took the one to her right. Warks rapped the knuckles of his right hand on the table, waiting for them to be settled. Emry leaned back and tilted her head. "What news, Warks?"

The middle-aged, lavender-eyed Mid ducked his head slightly, a few strands of his chestnut hair falling across his forehead. He was bedecked in the colors of The Mistress – black. "Your friend Piran has agreed to watch after your sister."

Emry blinked. "You heard back from him? Already?"

"Your Eyes have been working tirelessly since the attack," Warks replied. "They were able to make it happen. Although, their harriers should have a day or two to rest. If you need any more messages relayed, keep that in mind."

From anyone else, it might have sounded like it was an order. But from Warks, Emry knew he was merely suggesting she wait. He was a gruff, blunt man. Direct and to the point. She liked that about him. It was why he oversaw her Eyes throughout the country. Her spymaster couldn't be one to dance around a subject.

"Noted." Emry nodded once. "Thank you for pushing the message across for me."

The man only inclined his head again. Emry licked her lips. "Do we know how long until the guards trailing Dec and I will get to Anexia?"

"Four, maybe three days," Declan answered her.

She turned to him, surprised. "Seriously? You're *that* fast?"

He shrugged, and Emry could have sworn she felt a little smugness emanating from him down that strange bond between them. "I am what I am."

"Any speculations on who might have aided Vardin in the attack?" Emry asked Warks, peeling her eyes away from Declan.

Warks frowned. "As of right now, it still looks like he was the leader."

"The man wears a cape at all hours of the day," Emry retorted. "There's no way he was the mastermind. He's always been egotistical and a little power hungry, but stratagem isn't his forte."

Vardin could have been manipulating Emry or Cit since childhood for their hands in marriage. Onyx would have trusted Vardin with the kingdom. Their Court even spoke of how he would have been a lovely consort for Cit, not knowing that she was the younger sister. Yet, the man had mostly ignored them, focusing his attention on climbing the ladder to become Captain of the Guard. The man was ambitious, but not towards the throne.

No, something about this was off. It was as if this

desire to overthrow the Jewels was a recent one for Vardin. Or maybe he'd just suddenly come into the means to finally act upon the urge.

"I'll see what I can find," Warks told her.

"Thank you."

Levric cleared his throat. "We need to discuss what Declan is going to be for you."

Emry stiffened. The wording – he hadn't meant … had he? Her heart sputtered.

"The two of you are connected, are you not?" Levric continued. "Until our Ruby friend returns to release you, Declan will often be by your side. It will seem odd that he is always with you, unless he is given a position that makes his presence appropriate."

She relaxed slightly, and was that amusement she felt from Declan? Had he noticed her tension, and found it funny? "Right. What did you have in mind?"

"Bodyguard to The Mistress."

They'd discussed this many times before. She didn't need a personal guard. Levric kept bringing it up, and for once, Emry couldn't refuse him. It was a win for Levric. Declan needed an excuse for his constant presence at her side and his father knew he'd be capable of watching Emry's back. She clenched her jaw. "Fine."

"What about the princess I was just barely sworn to protect?" Declan asked evenly. There was that disgust seeping into her again.

Warks answered this one for her. "She's in our custody, brought here by you, as promised."

"So, am I to call you 'my Mistress?'" His voice was low, bordering on bitter. The question was meant for Emry alone.

She swallowed and faced him. "Call me Emry, just as you've always done."

"Is that what your Committee calls you?"

"No. They never use my name," she replied, ignoring his budding resentment sizzling through her. "I couldn't risk anyone discovering who I am."

"Of course not," he retorted.

Emry opened her mouth to respond, but Levric cut in, "The two of you should go get some lunch. Since we must wait once more for information, you should try to enjoy the rest of the day."

She twisted around to him, eyebrows raised. But he was already on his feet. Warks stood as well. Silently cursing inside her head, Emry shoved herself up. "Thank you, Warks. Let me know of any changes."

"Yes, my Mistress."

They bid their farewells, and Emry led Declan outside. By now, she was comfortable with the walk back to his house. She kept ahead of him the entire way back, and he seemed content to let her.

:  :  :  :  :

Declan was growing to despise the silence between him and Emry. They were sitting on the large, wraparound porch of his house, in twin wooden chairs with a small round table between them. They'd eaten out here at his mother's insistence, but they'd both finished nearly twenty minutes ago. Neither one had moved to get up, so still they sat. In silence.

Emry was glaring out into the woods. Her finger was twirling a chunk of her loose hair. Blonde hair. Because she was back to being a blonde again. He honestly wasn't sure whether he preferred her like this or with dark hair.

He was getting snippets of her thoughts. A couple

words strewn together now and then. Mostly nonsense. But they were actual thoughts. It was enough to frighten him. Their bond was strengthening – despite the tension between them.

It surprised him that her thoughts came out in that Anexian accent of hers. He'd assumed she preferred the inflections of her Enn region and was only keeping up the Anexian since they were in Anexia. But inside her own head, she apparently thought like an Anexian.

Her moods now were a steady stream. One after the other – like waves crashing over him. And he had no idea how to stop it. She felt so much all the time. A constant barrage of emotion flitting about inside of her. A constant influence in his head and heart.

He was still too much of a coward to ask her if she felt him the way he did her. From the glances she'd sometimes tossed his way, he thought she might.

Levric had mentioned a Ruby releasing them. From this thing between them? The idea of no longer being on a leash sounded nice, but no longer sharing this connection with Emry felt … wrong. His very soul had attached itself to her. The notion of separating from her nearly sent him into a panic.

*I can't just sit here.*

Hearing Emry spew a full sentence inside his head made him jump. Emry twisted in surprise, eyebrows raised.

"Is something wrong?" She asked out loud.

Yes and no. He wasn't sure what to say. Her mood was a mix of frustration and fear, sorrow and shame. Having a combination of emotions was common for her. It was confusing and exhausting keeping up with her.

At least this current mix pointed in the same direction. She was feeling helpless and useless. For her sister, her country, her people. She needed a distraction. One that maybe they both could benefit from.

"You don't want to just sit here," he said at last, pushing himself to his feet.

"What?" Now she was startled.

He ignored the questions forming in her eyes. "You know the Turanga."

"Yes…" Her voice trailed off.

"I know it, too."

She blinked. "Congratulations?"

Declan snorted. "We both could use a workout to blow off some steam."

"A workout," she repeated incredulously.

"Climb onto my back." He spat out the words before he could change his mind. "I'm going to take you somewhere we won't be interrupted."

Emry frowned up at him. Her mood shifted between uncertainty and curiosity. And trust. She trusted him. Even though she knew he didn't trust her, she still believed he'd never harm her or put her into danger. It was true but still unsettling she felt that way after how he'd reacted towards her.

She slipped that bag of hers she'd brought from the palace – the one she'd had with her all day – across her body and stood. "Is it far?"

"Just on the border of Kruth, Anexia, and Quirl."

"So, it'll take you, what, twenty minutes to get there?" She grunted.

He spun around, hefting her onto his back. "Fifteen tops," he smirked and took off.

: : : : :

The woods had a mild chill to them. Emry dropped to her feet and glanced around at where Declan had taken them. The leaves here were already falling. It meant they were close to the Kruth Mountains but not quite in them as there were few pines. Declan had stopped in a clearing of sorts. The underbrush was a combination of dried leaves, twigs, loose gravel, and soil. No vines or other growth.

Up ahead of them was a cottage made of thick, stacked logs with a thatched roof on top. There was a small porch out front with two wooden, square pillars holding it up. The door had been painted a dark, hunter green. Four windows framed the porch – one on the left and three on the right. A chimney of stacked stone poked out of the roof, and a neat pile of chopped wood was leaning against the right side of the cottage, waiting to feed future fires.

Then, in between Emry and the cottage was a massive swath of canvas. It was held down on the four corners by four miniature boulders, and then one was set in the middle. She guessed the canvas was protecting something underneath.

She turned to Declan. He was watching her, his hands in his pockets. He was feeling uncertain. His anger was gone, for the first time that day. She furrowed her brow. "Who lives here? What is this?"

"This is my home," he replied quietly.

"You live here?" She blurted.

"Sometimes." He nodded. "After my time in Quirl, I needed a place to call my own. To be alone."

Emry blinked. "You lived in Quirl?"

"About a year and a half ago." His eyes took on that shuttered look again, and she could sense his growing unease.

"No one told me." She frowned. Neither one of his parents had breathed a word of it to her.

"I was there a little more than a year." He glanced away toward the cottage.

There was more she wanted to ask, but he walked to the canvas. He bent down and rotated one of the rocks to the side, off the heavy fabric. He moved on the next one, and Emry shoved off the little boulder across from him. A couple minutes later, the rocks were out of the way. Declan began to roll up the canvas. Emry joined him and together they revealed a clay round beneath.

It was identical to the one by Levric's forge and at the arena in Breccan, except for the hue of the clay. This one was a dark, chocolate brown, rather than the reddish tint of the others. Emry crouched on top of it and brushed her fingers over its smooth surface. It was meticulously level, more so than the one at the forge. Someone had to have spent a great deal of time crafting it.

She could feel his eyes watching her again. She turned. Declan was standing at the edge of the round, grasping two staffs. One in each hand, resting on the ground. Where he'd grabbed them from, Emry had no idea.

One staff was a size Bran would have deemed suitable for a woman – the size he should have been using. The other she was sure he'd think was meant for a child. It was the perfect length for Emry. She glanced from the staff to Declan. He'd known her preference.

"I have other sizes, but I figured one of these would work for you." He extended his hands toward her, the staffs tilting forward.

Emry went for the smaller of the two. Even though

she could wield the other one, the smaller was far more comfortable and allowed her the freedom to be lighter on her feet. "Where'd these come from?"

"Inside," he answered as he sat down on the edge of the round.

"You went inside?"

He tapped the corner of his eye with one finger. "I'm fairly quick."

As Declan began to peel off his boots, Emry shucked off her flat canvas shoes and placed her bare feet onto the cool clay. The hem of Declan's pants fell loosely around his ankles as he stood again, staff in hand. She didn't miss the fact he'd selected the size of staff she'd told Bran to use.

"How well do you know the Turanga?" He stepped to the opposite side of the round from Emry. "As well as you know the Mountain Thunder?"

She shook her head. "Better."

"Is that so?" He quirked a brow.

"I've spent more time in Heerth than I have Kruth." She shrugged. "How well do *you* know the Turanga?"

He smiled and hefted his staff into the air. Before it could touch the ground, he grabbed it with one hand, flicking his wrist so that the other end of it swung in an arc around to be snatched by his free hand. "Care to find out?"

# CHAPTER TWENTY-ONE

This was better than him not talking to her, she told herself. Sparring with him and his quick teal-eyed feet would most likely knock her on her back, but it'd give her a workout as he'd said.

Emry weighed her staff between her hands, gauging if it was fully straight – searching for any bends in the wood. She was pleased to find no flaws. "Are you so sure we can even fight each other?" She was stalling as she ground her fingertips over the wood. "With us being sworn and all."

"The Turanga isn't just about fighting," he retorted.

"It's a dance." She smiled to herself as she repeated Trezim's words from years ago.

Declan prowled in front of her, dropped down onto one knee, and angled his staff over his head toward her. It was a common opening position for beginners. Emry stood above him, tilting her own staff so that it crossed his. Their eyes locked.

"Try to keep up," he smirked.

Then it began. Emry shifted one hand upward and the other downward while dipping into a crouch, just as Declan rose to his feet. They'd basically swapped positions – Declan's staff now on top. From there, Emry tapped her staff against Declan's twice, pushing herself back up to standing with every thrust, before bringing her arms in front of her to shoulder height. Declan mirrored her actions, tapping her staff twice in the middle, just as she'd done to his. These were all usual first steps, meant to gauge one's opponent respectfully.

The Turanga always began slow. It was designed to build – in sequence of attacks, footwork, and speed – until the partners moved out of pure instinct. Fluid and precise. A dance – a performance to behold.

Emry stepped left, and Declan twisted his body so that his staff could once again make contact with her own. She circled around him and struck again. He was there in a blur – his staff below hers. They fell into a rhythm. Their hits filled the clearing with the rich *thwack thwack* of their shafts.

It felt good to use her muscles again. It'd been a couple weeks since she'd been able to slip away for any sort of real exercise. Her body had missed the exertion. She began to feel hot in her long-sleeved tunic.

He picked up the pace a little – his arms moving quicker. Emry matched him easily. He did it again, and she followed. After a few more strikes, though, Declan took a step back, frowning. "You're holding back. Why?"

"I'm just following your lead," she replied, surprised.

Declan grunted. "Do you want to continue on hacking away like Kruths, or do you want to do the Turanga?"

Heerths scorned the rough swings Kruths dared to call fighting. They thought of Kruths as little more than heathens.

"Fine." Emry yanked her tunic over her head, revealing her sleeveless shirt beneath. It was the same color as her tunic with a swooping neckline. It clung to her and fell to just above her thighs. She tossed her tunic off the round to where she'd left her shoes. "Let's do the Turanga."

He grinned and pulled off his own shirt, throwing it by hers. "It's about time."

Before Declan had the chance to make the first move, Emry flung herself at him – swinging her staff with one hand down towards his head. Ever the Teal, Declan was there to block her blow. But by the time their staffs touched, Emry had already flicked her wrist so that it bounced off into her outstretched hand.

"That's a little more like it," he scoffed.

Emry no longer followed Declan. No longer cared if his staff would be there to stop hers. Again, with only one hand, she swung her staff. This time for his hip. His staff appeared before hers, ready to thwart her attack. She'd expected as much. Before she'd even heard the thwack, she twisted her body to catch the rebounding tip of her staff. She then plunged to one knee at his side – shoving her staff, gripped in both hands, at his shins.

His vertical staff connected with her horizontal one. Just as she'd planned. She tilted her staff diagonal and slid it in a half circle to the right, putting her directly under him so that as she straightened she'd break his grip. Not that that worked.

No matter how fast she was, he was still quicker. He'd processed her next move and adjusted for it before Emry could finish executing it. He was more than just an average Teal after all. He was only sparring with her – refusing to attack. Knowing he'd always have the upper hand. He was content in giving her some exercise.

Well, he was underestimating her. Annoying of him. She'd made herself into The Mistress after all. It hadn't been simply because she was already an important political figure. She'd had to earn her position. It had taken work and a great many trials of her own.

As Declan blocked another strike, Emry couldn't stop her sneer. Declan had been right about one thing. She *was* holding back.

Emry became shadow. Even though she was beneath the cover of the trees surrounding the clearing and could have simply drawn the shadows cast by their shade to her as a sort of cover, she wanted to thoroughly unsettle Declan. To show him she was stronger than she looked. More talented than he'd thought. So, she became swirls of darkness before his eyes.

She went to take a step to the left, intending to solidify there so as to cast a blow for his thigh, when she darted a glance over his shoulder to a spot behind his back. Not a heartbeat later, she was there. She found herself standing in the spot she'd been looking at. Just like that. She'd moved like a Teal, while as shadow. She'd never done that before.

Declan was, of course, already facing her, having spun with his unnatural speed. She could feel his surprise. His eyes were wide as their staffs smacked together. Emry was startled, too. How had she done it? She bit at the tip of her tongue. She wanted to do it again.

Becoming shadow once more, Emry glanced over Declan's shoulder and urged her body forward. She felt herself slip through the world. Almost immediately she was there on the other side of Declan. This time she watched him make the turn to face her. He was still a little blurred, but she caught his movement.

He just stared at her – the staff in his hands forgotten. Well, she'd wanted to unsettle him. Emry grinned.

She'd just leveled the playing field. "Try to keep up," she smirked.

: : : : :

Declan was sweating. Emry kept popping in and out around him, transforming into smoke to reappear at some random location around him just long enough for her to take a swing at him. Then she did it again and again. Had Emry always been able to move like this? From the surprise that had coursed through her the first time, he had the impression that this was something new.

And Emry was becoming faster and faster, as if with each move she took she gained confidence. So that her next move was more complicated than her last. This had to be a new skill, but one she'd picked up real quick.

She was misting herself about faster than most Teals could travel. As he whirled to stop a strike for his knees, he had to admit her pace was closer to his own.

Round and round they went. Continually picking up speed until Emry was more smoke than flesh. Until Declan was panting and his heart racing. Until his muscles protested. Until it was pushing him to his limit, like those duels in Quirl had.

Finally, Emry misted to the edge of the clay round, away from Declan, and dropped her staff in front of her. She bent forward, her hands planted on her knees. Her chest was heaving, gasping in for air. Declan tossed his own staff to the side and mirrored Emry's position.

How was he so out of breath? Emry shouldn't have been able to do this to him. He hung his head, wishing his lungs could take in more air. *How?* He demanded silently.

Across from him, Emry straightened, her hands on her hips, still panting. "I don't know."

His head snapped up. She'd just answered his unvoiced question. That meant … she could hear him like he could hear her.

"I could become shadow before, but only move as fast as I normally can," she managed to get out between breaths. "Not this – this Teal speed stuff." She waved a hand between them.

Declan heaved himself upright. "It's unnatural how fast you were."

"I know."

"No, I meant even for a Teal," he said.

"I know what you meant."

He blinked. "How?"

"I- I can hear you." She frowned. "Inside my head, sometimes."

So, it was the same for her. "Since when?"

"I don't know, a couple days." She winced. "Shouldn't you be more concerned that I'm hearing you at all?"

"You've been in my head, too." He ran a hand through his hair. "I think it's getting stronger. This bond between us."

"It is."

"Did Cit ever mention…"

"No. Not once." She shook her head. "I don't think this happened to them. She never showed any sign of having Freddick's abilities, either."

"Why are we different?"

She yanked at the hair on the back of her head, digging her fingers along her scalp. "I don't know."

His breath rushed out of him. "You were able to

tap into my speed. Not just Teal speed, but *my* Teal speed. I've never heard of anyone taking on the abilities of another person. This can't be normal for a princess and her Knight."

Emry went very still. Shock. That was shock, shooting from her into him. Followed by a quick flash of terror. He stared. "What? What is it?"

"I think I've heard of this before," she breathed. "Or something similar."

"And that scares you?"

"It means the Ruby did the wrong ceremony." She fell back a step. "I don't think we'll be able to break off our bond. Not if it's what I think it might be."

"We might be sworn together forever?" A portion of him, somewhere deep inside, sighed in relief at the thought. "What do you think we are?"

She didn't answer. Instead, she retrieved her staff. "Care to go again?"

"Emry-"

He wasn't able to finish. She was to him, swinging her staff, forcing him to spin out of her reach. "Emry," he began again, but she turned to mist before solidifying at his side, striking again.

Declan swore and tapped into his speed. He shoved his staff inside the space between hers and her body and yanked it to him, dragging her forward a step. She would've collided with him if she hadn't transformed into smoke again.

She reappeared less than a blink of an eye later at the opposite edge of the round. She was nervous, and Declan was getting annoyed. Her eyes darted past him to his cottage. It was her next move. Her escape route. He knew it, could feel her thinking about it. He was tired of chasing her.

Going for the element of surprise, Declan shot forward to Emry. He went to wrap his arms around her, but instead of flesh they were swirls of black mist. Like what Emry became. Stunned, he pulled to a stop and toppled on top of Emry, solid once more. She landed on her back – her stomach pressed to his own.

Emry was gaping. Somehow during their fall, he'd managed to pin her down – their arms above their heads, Declan clasping her wrists.

*How?* She demanded inside his head.

*I don't know,* he answered honestly.

Her eyes were searching his. *You became shadow. You…* She gasped. *You have silver veins in your eyes.*

"What?" He blurted.

*It's true.* Disbelief, shame, and fear twisted together, flowing between them. From Emry.

He frowned. *What are we, Emry?*

"We're a Pair," she whispered, her breath mingling with his own.

# CHAPTER TWENTY-TWO

"What is that?" The term Pair sounded vaguely familiar, but Declan couldn't remember where he'd heard it.

"It's ancient," she replied. "People aren't really sworn together like that anymore. The Old Tomes hold the ceremony, and there aren't many alive who can still read them."

The Ruby who had sworn them together could read the Old Tomes. *You think the Ruby did the wrong ceremony.*

Emry shut her eyes, her shame returning. "Yes."

*What's a Pair?*

She didn't answer or look at him. He slid his hands from her wrists up to her hands, threading his fingers with hers. "Emry?" He prodded gently.

It took her another moment to open her eyes. When she did, he was startled to find Teal flecks encircling her pupils – blending in with the silver, gray, and black veins in her own. The Teal hadn't been there a moment ago.

He was so focused on the flecks that he nearly missed her explain, "Pairs are equals in the might of their usually differing abilities. Their strengths and weaknesses complement each other, so that they bring out the best in one another. Each Pair is a unique match."

Her face had gone pale. Declan furrowed his brow. "That doesn't sound so bad."

She stared at him like he hadn't heard her. "Five hundred years ago, people became a Pair because that was how they married."

The words hit his face before he internalized them. He and Emry being a Pair meant – married. They were married? His jaw dropped. Is that what this was? It seemed deeper, longer, undying ... unique. Married? To Emry. He'd been married to Emry for more than a week and hadn't even known it.

This revelation felt like a missed opportunity. Not because he'd been married without his knowledge, prohibiting him from choosing his bride. No, he would have picked Emry a thousand times over. Despite the title she'd kept hidden, he still would have chosen Emry. She had no parallel. He loved her. All of her. The Mistress and Jewel.

As much as he hated to admit it, he understood why she'd withheld information from him. She walked a fine line as two different people. And all his anger aside, he loved her – loved her with a ferocity that had kept him alive in Quirl. His reoccurring dreams had led him to that fact, and he'd discovered over the past couple weeks that the person he'd concocted in his mind was the very same woman beneath him. It was as if he'd imagined her into life. How could he not love her?

No, the missed opportunity was that they'd been married and he hadn't known.

*Please say something,* her mind begged him.

He gazed down at her. She was frightened. Why? He didn't want to believe it was because she was bonded to him rather than someone else. Was it that she hadn't expected to be tied to him forever? Did it ruin her plans as the leader of Enlennd?

Emry shut her eyes again. "I'm sorry, Dec."

*For what?* He asked, genuinely surprised.

*For bringing this on you,* she responded. *I should have guessed it was wrong when the Ruby started to blend our light. Cit and Freddick never had a tether of light. I knew it felt off. No wonder it felt like our souls were being ripped from our bodies. They were being joined together.*

Was she rambling? He blinked. She was worried that he was upset at being her Pair. Not at how this would affect her own future. Not at being unwittingly married to a common Rioter. Declan couldn't help but smile at the absurdity of it.

Releasing a low chuckle, Declan bent his head and pressed his mouth to hers. Softly, gently kissing her – as if anything more would spook her away. After a moment, he pulled back and rolled off of her, onto his side, facing her. He leaned on one elbow and rested his other arm across her middle, his hand on her hip. She watched him silently.

"I don't blame you, Emry."

She winced. "I don't know if it can ever be broken. We could be tied together forever."

*You mean married.*

"Yes, if it's still a valid form of marriage." She groaned and raked her scalp with her hands. She raised her knees, planting her feet on the clay beneath them. "This wasn't how it was supposed to go."

"Have you heard of anyone else being a Pair recently?"

"They're only rumored to be a Pair," she replied. "I can ask them if the bond can ever be broken, so you won't have to be stuck with me forever."

There was a question in her voice, giving him a choice. She wanted to know how he felt about it – how he felt about her. Her words were an offering of herself, with more than just a hint of her vulnerabilities in the background. It was an honest question.

They'd kissed more times than any proper Knight would deem appropriate. He couldn't stop himself, though. She was so easy to kiss, to hold … to love.

He no longer cared that she was both Mistress and princess – queen. It didn't matter. To him, she was just Emry. The woman he'd been attached to for years. His Emry. Forever. The thought made him grin. Why would he ever want to break their bond and let her leave him?

Declan sat up and crossed his legs in front of him. Emry mirrored him, their knees touching, hands in their laps. *Do you want to be free of me, Emry?*

A quick flash of fear from her was smothered by a blanket of calm determination. Her eyes pierced his own. "No, I don't. Why would I push you away when I finally have you close?"

: : : : :

If Declan couldn't hear her heart thundering inside her chest, she'd be shocked. She was sure it could be heard all the way to the palace. Yet, Declan was just sitting there, watching her. He hadn't made a sound. How long had it been? A minute? Five? An hour?

His emotions were not helpful either in deciphering his thoughts. He was happy, but about the same as he'd been before her declaration of wanting him. There was another emotion, but Emry couldn't interpret what it was. He'd felt it a couple times before that day, and Emry hadn't been able to puzzle it out then either. It was warm and calm – like being content only much more intense.

She was so focused on figuring out the name for his emotion that she almost didn't hear him whisper, "I think I love you, Emry."

*Love.* Emry nearly repeated the word out loud. That's what it was! It was love. He loved ... her. The words finally sank in. He loved her. Emry stared at him in disbelief. He loved her? When had this happened? Just this morning, he'd told her he was still upset with her. But, he did take her here to his secluded cottage in the mountains to help her relax ... and then discovered they were a Pair.

"You know I can feel your surprise." He flinched. "I realize I don't exactly fit into your extended schemes. I doubt The Mistress intended on being attached forever to her Knight, but I- I'd like to stay your Pair."

His stumbling confession warmed Emry, spreading outward from her chest to her toes. It just seemed so surreal. How had they gotten to this point so quickly? She'd been sure it would take months to convince him to return her feelings. It was almost comical how he didn't think he was a part of her extended schemes. He'd been in her thoughts, schemes, and dreams for years.

*Please say something,* he repeated her own words inside her head.

Emry didn't respond. Instead, she leaned forward, slipping her hands behind his neck, and pressed her lips to his. Firmly. Deliberately. His mouth parted, a silent plea to continue, as he placed a hand on her back, steadying her. She kissed him a moment or two longer before pulling back enough to rest her forehead against his.

"Oh, Dec," she breathed, "I *know* I love you."

The air rushed out of him, as if he'd been holding

his breath, waiting for her reaction. His arms wrapped around her, pulling her against him. He buried his face in her hair as his love filled her.

"How long?" He asked into her hair.

She let out a short laugh. "It's been years."

"You were barely more than a child five years ago."

That wasn't when she fell in love with him, but she was almost an adult when they'd first met. Emry leaned back, her eyebrows raised. "How old do you think I am?"

"Seventeen?" He offered.

"I'm twenty," she retorted.

Declan gawked. "You were fifteen? Were you small for your age?"

"I'm maybe an inch taller now than I was then."

He blinked. "Why do I remember you being younger?"

She shrugged. "I was your friend's younger sister. You probably didn't think much about me."

"That's not true," he said quietly. "I thought about you every day when I was in Quirl."

"What?" She blurted. "Why?"

"Because you were my light in the dark," he breathed.

Emry rocked slowly backwards onto the clay, out of his grasp. She was stunned. "Why would you ever think that?"

"You were the one person I'd ever saved," he answered, his voice both soft and low. "I told myself my life wasn't all a waste if I'd managed to help you."

"But you thought I was dead."

He shook his head. "My father didn't tell me that until after I came back from Quirl."

"It was Levric who told you I'd died?" Emry exclaimed. "Why? He knew I hadn't."

"I asked him about it this morning." Declan tipped his head upwards to the trees. "It was because I had wanted to go find you after I returned. You being both The Mistress and a princess at that point complicated me seeking you out. Although, to be fair, all he'd told me was that the girl I'd known, the one I'd saved that night, had died. I'd been too depressed to push to learn how. If I had, he probably would have clarified."

That statement brought several new questions to Emry's mind, but all that came out was, "Why were you in Quirl?"

Declan tossed a quick glance over his shoulder at his cottage. Emry could feel his unease. "Would you like to see the inside before we head back?"

"Yes, but that doesn't answer my question." She frowned.

He pushed himself to his feet and extended a hand to help her up as well. Once she was standing, he moved to the edge of the round and bent to pick up the shirts they'd thrown there carelessly. Emry stepped to her shoes and slipped them on. Declan handed her her tunic.

"Inside is much more comfortable," he replied without meeting her eyes. "I can tell you about my Quirl experience in there."

Emry followed him off the round to the small front porch of his cottage. It was two steps off the ground and barely big enough for them both to stand on. He pushed open the door, holding it back for Emry to pass inside.

She wasn't sure what she'd been expecting, but the bright, open space hadn't been it. The entire cottage was only one room. Large windows lined the front and back walls. Wide planks of whitewashed wood floors ran the full length of the cottage.

Off to the left of the door was a small kitchen – just half a wall of upper and lower cabinets that had been painted a light gray. The countertop was butcher block, stained a rich, dark brown, and had a square portion cut out of it for a metal basin, complete with water pump. Emry wasn't surprised he was on well water up here in the mountains.

Straight ahead was a table for two, the same color as the cabinets. To the right of her was a cast iron stove across from an inviting, dark blue stuffed couch. An oval, low-lying table that also matched the cabinets sat between the stove and the couch. Then, along the far right wall was a bed about the same size as the one they'd been using in his parents' house. It, too, was light gray. Its quilt was surprisingly the same dark blue as the couch. He must have upholstered it himself with whatever fabric was left over from the quilt.

*Do you like it?* Declan asked hesitantly.

"I do," she said, "It suits you. Did you make the couch?"

Declan yanked his shirt over his head. Emry was a little sad to watch those muscles of his be put away. "I did. I built basically everything you see."

"You built this place?" She stared at him.

He nodded, taking a step into the kitchen. "Are you thirsty?"

"I could use some water."

"Make yourself comfortable," he told her, gesturing toward the sofa that he'd apparently created.

Emry sat, tucking her legs underneath her, and a moment later Declan returned with a cool glass of freshly pumped water. He handed it to her before lowering himself down next to her, his leg brushing against her knees. She took a deep sip of it as he did the same from his own glass.

When she'd had her fill of water, she set her cup down on the low table and said, "I'm ready to hear why you were in Quirl."

His unease returned. His gaze was glued to the glass in his hand that was now resting on his thigh. "Are you sure you want to know? It's what gave me that nightmare."

She pulled a face. "From all your hesitation, I've already come to the conclusion that it was horrible. Why were you there?"

"It wasn't by choice," he said bleakly. "I was captured one night while I was out on border patrol."

"Captured?" Emry repeated. That didn't make sense. Enlennd and Quirl had been on friendly terms now for almost three decades. Unless ... She sucked in a breath. *You were one of The Stolen.*

"Yes."

The Stolen were a tragedy her father had neglected. Due to the carelessness of his worthless advisors, they were overlooked innocent citizens who had been taken from their regions and enslaved by a radical king-sanctioned group in Quirl. The former king. Ryde Randor was now the king, after he'd killed his father, the previous one. He'd dissolved The Stolen immediately.

"You were one of The Stolen, and no one told me!" Emry slid off the couch to her feet, tugging at the hair on the back of her head. "Why did no one tell me? Who all knows about this?"

His gaze drifted away from his glass to the stove across from him. "My parents. I think they told my sisters. Although, they've never mentioned it to me. Much of my village suspects I went through some sort of torment while I was away. They don't know exactly what, though. A few members on your Committee might know a little more."

"So, not many," she said softly, dropping her hands to her sides. "Levric never told me. No one ever told me."

He wouldn't raise his eyes to meet hers. But she could feel his pain building. Past memories surfacing. "What happened to you in Quirl, Dec?" She breathed. "What did they do to you?"

"They forced me to become faster," he replied darkly. "Every day. For over a year. Until I escaped."

That fear she'd felt their first night together – from his nightmare – was filling him again. A thick, viscous sludge seeping through him. Then, just as he had that night, tendrils of black smoke emanated from his chest. He jumped at the sight of it before turning to Emry, his eyes pleading. She offered him a sad smile and stepped into his rapidly forming wisps of dark clouds.

Kneeling in front of him with his legs on either side of her, she extended one hand and placed it over the source of his stream. Then, she pulled his pain into herself, just as she had done before for him. "It takes time to learn how to control it," she told him gently. "I'm going to have to start giving you lessons or you'll end up shrouding the world in darkness unintentionally."

Emry forced a chuckle. She was trying to lighten his mood a little – help diminish the flow emitting from him. She didn't quite have the desired outcome. Instead, those beautiful green-flecked Teal eyes, now veined with silver, stared deeply into her own. "What all can you do, Emry?"

The question was bound to have been brought up

again sooner or later. Still, she frowned as the clouds evaporated into her. She pushed the power from his pain down inside of her, and then sat back, gazing down at her hands.

"That depends on whether or not there's a Full Moon out," she began, "If there is, I can do more. During a Full Moon, I can run on light as fast a regular Teal, as you witnessed. Although apparently, now as your Pair, I can move as fast as you whenever I please. So, that particular ability is less exciting. I can see in the dark. Find a person's life force inside of them. Absorb the pain of others – shifting it into power for myself. Become shadow, or smoke as you've called it. I can take cover in shadows, calling them to shield me from sight. I can change my hair color. I can light a house, and I can suck a person's life out of them."

The cottage was silent for a long few minutes as Emry let Declan process what she'd said. His emotions shifted one after the other. Surprise, awe, more surprise, unease, fear, confusion, and then, finally, surprisingly, admiration. Emry glanced up from her hands at that one, catching his gaze.

After another moment, he raised an eyebrow and asked, "Is that all?"

She let out a short laugh, "Do I need more?"

"I look forward to discovering which other abilities of yours transfer to me," he gave her a small smile. "I'm hoping for sucking the life from someone. That sounds useful."

Emry gawked. He accepted her. That last ability always made Cit, her father, and even Ewan uncomfortable. They'd go out of their way to make sure she never had to use it. Sacrificing themselves, when Emry could have saved them. She frowned. If they had only let her help them...

"If they knew what you could do, why did they have me take you away?"

*You heard my thoughts?* Emry blinked. She didn't hear that from him. Just when he spoke to her directly.

"I can sometimes," he confessed.

She frowned. "They had you 'save' me because as a Silver, if I were to steal a life, then the darkness that filled that person would seep into me – becoming a part of me. Supposedly. But what they didn't know, is that I have been sucking in the darkness of others for years."

"Like what you did with me."

She nodded. "I take in the raw energy supplying the darkness within someone, and store it up inside of me, should I ever need to use it."

He raised an eyebrow. "And you've been doing this for years?" When she nodded, he asked, "How much power are you hoarding inside of you?"

"I'm not sure. I haven't used much of it. So, probably a lot," she admitted. "But just to be clear, with Ewan, you did save me. I was young and unable to protect myself then."

Declan grunted and leaned forward, resting his elbows on his thighs. He dug his hands into his hair, yanking at the strands. The motion made his hair stand on end, in that way she'd admired on him before. There was just something so attractive about seeing him all disheveled. It made her want to run her own fingers through his hair. Him being so clearly stressed only added to the urge. He needed comforting. Perhaps she should wrap her arms around him. She was willing...

His gaze slowly tilted upwards from the floor. He was grinning crookedly, cockily even. It took Emry longer than it should have to realize why. She groaned and rolled her eyes. "This connection between us is going to be more trouble than it's worth."

"I don't know," he smirked. "It's nice to know you'd like to embrace me."

"Embrace you?" She let out a short laugh. "I think you're just hearing what you want to hear."

He blurred in front of her on the rug. Some small part of Emry's mind took note of how she could now make out his movements rather than him just appearing in places. That was a very small part of her, though. Her main focus was on Declan, whose face was currently inches away from her own.

"It's getting dark out," he said.

"I know." Her eyes drifted to his lips.

"We should head back."

"We should," she agreed, still focused on his mouth.

He noticed where her attention was held. He chuckled. "In a minute."

Declan closed the gap between them and kissed her firmly.

# CHAPTER TWENTY-THREE

Declan and Emry had returned to the edge of the village a little before sunset. Emry had insisted they stop by the bakery so she could bring his mother a cake. Now, they were making their way back to his parents' house through the woods. Declan was carrying the cake box, despite his comment that being her Pair didn't make him her own personal pack mule.

The sound of their feet crunching over leaves was interrupted by a shout, "Declan!"

Both he and Emry turned. Declan stiffened. Brielle was heading towards them. Somehow, Emry recognized her face. He felt it. Had they met before? He tossed a surprised look at Emry.

*I saw her at The First Trial. You almost kissed her,* Emry told him.

Declan remembered. Emry had been watching him that day. Their eyes had locked. She'd been the reason why he hadn't.

Brielle was eyeing Emry as she reached them. "Bran said that you were back, but I had to see it for myself. You returned faster than I did."

"It was unexpected," Declan replied.

"He also told me you were in the company of someone..." Her voice trailed off, her eyes not leaving Emry.

*Would you like me to introduce you?* Declan silently

asked.

*Who was this girl to you?* Her brow drew together.

*We've kissed,* he answered. That really was all it had been.

*She's pretty.*

Declan nearly snorted. Yes, Brielle was pretty. However, next to Emry, she was incredibly plain. More so even than when he'd last seen her at The Trials. If that was possible. The disparity between them had grown over the past weeks.

Brielle cleared her throat, as if she'd been waiting a while for a response, "Are you going to introduce me to your friend?"

*Oh, right.* Declan couldn't help but smile. He and Emry would have to work on having outward conversations with people while they communicated internally. He turned to Emry. "My Mistress, this is Brielle Wynpreg, a resident of my village."

*That was cold. No old fling wants to be called a mere resident,* Emry shot at him down that chain. Out loud she said with a nod of her head, "A pleasure."

Brielle's smile slipped a little. "The pleasure is mine, my Mistress."

"Wynpreg," Emry repeated thoughtfully. "Are you by chance Aaron Wynpreg's daughter?"

"I am." Brielle nodded.

"I'm told he's the best Ruby in the region," Emry remarked. "Are your talents similar to your father's?"

"Mine differ slightly," Brielle admitted, "but he tells me that I'm just as strong as he was at my age."

"That's good to hear. Perhaps I will be calling upon you soon." Emry shifted her gaze to Declan. "Come. Others are waiting." She smiled at Brielle – polite and somewhat forced. "Until the next, Miss Wynpreg."

Brielle dipped her head – the same gesture Emry had used in greeting. On Brielle, though, it looked hurried, eager, childish even. "Until the next, my Mistress."

As Emry turned away, Brielle caught Declan's eyes. "Will I be seeing you later?"

Declan frowned and tossed a glance at Emry's now retreating back. She wasn't so far, though, as to miss Brielle's question. He returned his gaze to the Ruby. "I'm sorry, Brielle. My attention is required elsewhere."

Brielle's eyes drifted to Emry, who had hesitated at a polite distance away. "I suspected as much. Take care of our Mistress."

"Of course. Until the next, Brielle." Declan offered her a smile before heading after Emry.

Once he and Emry were out of Brielle's sight, Declan noticed Emry was watching him. "What?"

*I didn't realize you liked such fresh-faced women. No wonder you were so startled when you heard my age,* Emry quipped. *It must be real rough for you to be the Pair of someone so old.*

Declan rolled his eyes. "You're not as funny as you think you are."

*I wasn't trying to be funny.*

He slid an arm around her middle, pulling her against him, and kissed the side of her head. *For what it's worth, you handled that well.*

She grunted. "I am the Mistress, you know. I wasn't just born with that title. Now, the lessons I received for some other title I possess, could have helped me in dealing with poor, gullible, little girls who mistakenly adore you. But who's to say?"

*Mistakenly adore me?* He grumbled. *Women flock to me.*

Emry laughed and slid her own arm around his back. "I think you mean young, inexperienced girls."

"Then what's your excuse?" He shot back. "You

clearly adore me. How did that happen?"

She grinned. "I was once a young, inexperienced girl."

: : : : :

The remains of dinner were strewn across the table in front of Emry. Empty cups, bowls, and plates. They were in Declan's parents' kitchen. Declan was leaning back in his chair beside her, his head tipped up toward the ceiling, legs stretched out in front of him beneath the table. She could feel his oncoming exhaustion and couldn't blame him. She was feeling a bit of the same herself.

His mother had graciously cooked them a tasty Anexian dinner – roasted potatoes and carrots, lamb, and thick slices of warm bread and butter. They'd finished with a slice of the cake Emry had purchased from the bakery.

Llydia hadn't joined them for the meal, though. After setting out their food, she'd left with a basket full of it for Declan's father, leaving them alone to eat.

"So, what now, Emry?" Declan asked the ceiling. "Are we really to just wait for news from your sister, or do you have some other scheme in mind?"

"As my Pair, you're supposedly my equal, so I could ask you the same question," she retorted, popping a piece of bread into her mouth. "What schemes might you have?"

"I'd like to find out if we actually are a Pair. If we really are married," he replied. "Who is this other rumored Pair?"

Emry winced. "One of them may not be too pleased to see me again."

Declan glanced at her with a raised eyebrow. "Why not?"

She bit the tip of her tongue. "I once tossed my drink in his face. In a ballroom full of people."

"The Quirl prince? He's a Pair?"

"He was the prince," she corrected. "Now, Ryde Randor is king, since he killed his father."

*No.* The name sent a jolt through Declan. Like lightning. He'd only heard that name once before, from the lips of… "Rand. King Rand."

"You've heard of him," she tore off another piece of bread. "I think he does go by Rand now, but he'll always be the snarky Ryde to me."

Declan gawked. He tugged at the collar of his shirt as the memory of the last time he'd seen Rand hit him. Of their last conversation. Before they'd both escaped that camp of death and misery. Rand had finally told him what his real name was. Declan hadn't known. He hadn't recognized the name – had never studied the royalty of other nations. He'd barely known the names of the Jewels.

But Rand had told him that one day the people who put him in that camp would pay. That they would regret their actions as they knelt before him. That their last words would be spent begging their new king for mercy, and he'd deliver them justice instead. Declan had no idea Rand already held a position of royalty. He'd mistaken Rand's rant for mere vengeance, thinking that Rand would try to take over some kingdom with his incomparable abilities.

And since Declan had left Quirl, he'd paid little attention to it. Had tried to avoid any mention of it even. If not for his infrequent visits from Fiona, he wouldn't have even known that Rand was still alive. She was the one who…

Cool anger filled him, not raging but there – icy. Tendrils of dark mist began to swirl behind him. Emry grabbed onto his arm, stopping any more from escaping him. "Dec?" She sounded alarmed.

"Who is his Pair?" He blurted.

Emry stared at him, startled.

*What's her name?* He asked darkly.

"Fiona. His queen."

He let out an almost bitter laugh. "Not consort? Isn't that what royalty usually make their spouses?"

"Apparently, Ryde's unorthodox," she replied. Declan could feel her confusion at the way he was acting. "It was her title of queen that first began the Pair rumors."

"Have you met her?"

She shook her head. "No, I haven't seen Ryde since the night I humiliated him. He disappeared from the public eye for a few years, and when he came back, he murdered his father. And then became king."

Declan's ice crept into Emry's veins. She released her hold on his arm to rub her own arms with her hands – suddenly cold. She waited for his next response. She knew Declan felt her confusion. He would explain himself. But if he didn't hurry up with it, she'd have to start prodding him.

It took him another minute before she heard in her head, *Rand and Fiona were with me. There, in Quirl. We were all Stolen.*

"Ryde was Stolen?" Emry couldn't hide the disgust from her voice as she realized what that meant. "His father sent him there?"

*I didn't know he was the prince.* Declan leaned his elbows on the table and rubbed his eyes with his palms. *I don't think any of us did.*

"And Fiona?" Emry's voice was barely more than a whisper. She couldn't believe the former Quirl king had made his own son a prisoner. She'd met the man more than once. Ryde had his eyes – Gray. The man had been civil enough. Not the demented villain he had to have been. What sort of person sent their own son into a pit of despair?

*Fiona was my friend,* Declan replied. *She taught me the Turanga.*

"She's Heerth?" Emry frowned. "I didn't know that."

He grunted, the corners of his mouth almost pulling up into a smile. *She always did prefer to keep herself a mystery.*

That feeling of love filled him again. Given, it was a much more subdued version than what he'd experienced in regards to her. This was closer to what he felt around his parents, but it was still there. Was Fiona one of his past interests as well? Emry bit the tip of her tongue. *You care for her.*

Declan turned to her. He was amused. Emry nearly cursed. Of course, he'd felt her unease. This stupid connection between them meant she'd never have another silent emotion again.

He began to chuckle and slipped one hand behind her neck drawing her closer to him. He pressed his lips to hers for a moment before leaning his forehead against her own. "I've never come close to what I feel for you, Emry, with anyone."

Warmth spread through her, and he kissed her again. Slowly, softly. "Fiona was always Rand's. But she is my friend. She was the one who told Rand and me to start holding back, as she had done from the beginning."

"I've been told many times that Heerths are quite clever," Emry intoned Trezim's favorite phrase.

"She helped save my life. Her advice was the second most significant thing that happened to me in that camp," he said, his eyes going distant.

Emry frowned. "What was the first?"

Just then, the front door burst open. Declan whirled, his form slightly blurred to Emry as he moved at Teal speed. In strode Levric and two other men behind him. Sentries and spies. Her Eyes. Black handkerchiefs were tied around their necks.

Emry laid a hand on Declan's shoulder and rose, urging him silently to stay where he was. From the look on Levric's face, whatever he had to say was too important to wait.

"My Mistress," Levric inclined his head in greeting when he saw her. "Vern and Carl discovered another Silver."

# CHAPTER TWENTY-FOUR

Declan watched as Emry's whole demeanor trans-formed. The smile in her eyes vanished – her gaze twisting into something icy and foreign. Her posture contorting to sharp angles as she dropped one shoulder and stuck out one hip, while tilting her head slightly to the side. It was a pose Emry as a princess would never had been caught in, but as Mistress ... the effect was astonishing.

The completely casual way she held herself made her actually appear more confident, commanding even. Her eyes showed that the men before her had her undi-vided attention, but her body told them that she was in control and could handle what they threw at her. De-clan couldn't help but stare.

"Where?" She demanded of his father – the word unhurried. It was more a curious command for infor-mation.

Levric, never one to curtail the attention of another, gestured for the gangly young man several years De-clan's senior to speak. Declan had met him once. Carl.

Carl bobbed his head at Emry once, out of respect, before saying, "Mistress, we found the wisp of him near Small Falls – just black mist like we were told to keep an eye out for. When Vern sent a warning bolt at him, he materialized and said he had a message for The Mis-tress of Rioters."

Declan frowned as he tried to make sense of what he'd heard. His father's village sentries had found a silver-eyed and Vern, being a Gray, had shot a lightning bolt near the black mist that had been a hiding Silver? Was that right? If these men had discovered a Silver in the woods near the collection of short waterfalls stacked on top of each other, where there was shade a plenty, the man had either wished to be found, or he wasn't nearly as good as Declan's Pair. He couldn't help but smile at the thought of Emry as *his* Pair.

Emry dropped her hand from his shoulder and waved it once towards herself in a beckoning motion. "What was his message?"

Before Carl could respond, Levric said casually, "He's outside, Mistress."

Her brow raised. "You brought him here? Who is keeping him contained, if not you, Vern?"

The dark-haired, tanned Gray had as deep a voice as the thunder he created. "He's out with Marta."

Emry offered a small amused smile. "I should have known." Declan had never heard of this Marta. Emry's gaze shifted to Levric. "You're alright with doing this in here?"

He inclined his head again. "I'm sure you'll keep the messenger under control."

She grunted but nodded. "Very well. Bring him in."

As the men went out the door to retrieve the Silver, Declan stood, figuring this was not a time for him to be sitting. He caught Emry's gaze. She was frowning. *Worried?* He asked.

*Yes, about you.*

That startled him. "Why?"

*Your opinion of me might change,* she replied. *You may not like what you see.*

Carl and Vern returned, flanked by a woman Declan guessed to be Marta, and a slight figure all in black. The man was barely more than a boy. He couldn't have been more than eighteen. And he was short, shorter than even Emry, who was not a tall woman. He had a wiry, almost malnourished frame. No muscles at all on him. His face was oval with a rather wide nose and thin lips. His eyes were silver, but not Emry's silver. Emry's were an intricate mix of several shades combining into a shimmering silver. This boy's — Declan really couldn't call him a man — were base silver with thick bands of black trailing outward from his pupils to the whites of his eyes. They didn't shimmer, in fact they did the opposite — they sucked in the light around him, making him appear as if he were still partially in shadow.

Vern's fingertips sizzled as he ordered the boy to his knees. A threat of what would happen if he didn't listen. With a curl of his lip in a silent snarl, the boy did as he was told. In that moment, calm filled Declan. From Emry.

She stepped around the table, her eyes locked on the boy with her head tilted in an almost challenging way. Declan didn't like her approaching a potentially dangerous subject without him, so he followed her, halting a few steps behind her when she pulled to a stop.

"He was armed only with this, my Mistress." Carl stepped forward, extending the black hilt of what should have been a knife on his open palm. The hilt was missing its blade.

"Like the others," Emry mused, taking it from him. She turned back to the boy at her feet and sighed. Declan had to stop himself from raising an eyebrow. She had sighed as if dealing with a frustrating young child. It was not a reaction he'd been expecting from her.

Emry gripped onto the shadow blade in her palm. It was of decent weight. Not as elaborate as the ones Trezim had had her train with in Heerth, but it would respond easily enough to her touch. She returned her attention to the young Silver. He was the fourth one her Eyes had discovered sneaking along the borders of Anexia, but he was the first to stay alive long enough for her to chat with. The others had stabbed themselves with their own shadow blades before her Eyes had managed to question them. Emry frowned. This was going to be unpleasant at best. At least now she'd discover where all these young Silvers were coming from. Hopefully.

She dropped into a crouch in front him, putting them eye to eye and pointed the hilt under his nose. If she were to activate the blade, the tip of it would have been somewhere inside his forehead. She grunted at his blank stare. "Hard to come by, these blades. Not many know what they are. Most assume their steel has simply shattered off." Emry pulled back slightly on the hilt so that if activated, the blade would now poke into his nose. "For those of us who know how to wield them, however..." She tilted her hand and urged a miniscule amount of power outward into the hilt. A black curve of shadow solidified into thin, black steel, barely grazing the Silver's cheek. He didn't even blink.

The curve of the blade momentarily startled Emry. There was only one place with blades shaped like that – Perth. It was Perth made. Did that mean he hailed from Perth as well? She scowled and stood, adjusting the hilt in her palm. "Speak," she ordered. "Deliver this momentous message."

The Silver opened his mouth, and the room grew

darker – the lights Emry had floating up at the ceiling dimmed momentarily. Shadow swirled around the man, disintegrating his image, contorting his body into something else. Her mind registered that it was no more than an instant, yet that portion of her that had come from Declan slowed the transformation down for her. Levric and her Eyes weren't even given time to react, but behind her, she could feel Declan's unease growing. He saw what she did.

Just like with the blade in her hand, the black mist began to solidify, forming a human once more, but not the one who had been kneeling there. This figure was standing and was definitely a woman. Unlike with the blade, though, the figure remained mostly in shadow. Her tight gown and curves were somewhat translucent, but her arms and head were compacted darkness. The woman looked like a living statue.

As her face took shape, Emry noticed the black crown of entwined thorned vines atop her head – and recognized it. She'd seen it on the former sovereign of Perth – the one before the current queen slaughtered him and his family. This figure was Varamtha Roqaene, the current self-made queen of Perth.

In that instant, Emry decided to look like her Jewel self. With a tug on that bond she shared with Declan, she urged some of his speed into her and reverted the color of her hair to her own raven black just as the queen of shimmering smoke came completely into focus.

"Greetings, Mistress of Rioters," the voice was like smooth velvet, sultry. Deeper for a woman but not at all masculine. Emry stared at the figure, waiting for the rest of the message. It took a moment for her to continue with, "You are the Mistress, are you not?"

The queen could see Emry. This wasn't a message – this was a meeting. One she was not prepared for. Stifling a groan, Emry dropped into her stance of choice – right hip jutting out, left shoulder elevated above the other, head tilted to the right with her chin lifted ever so slightly. "I am whom you seek. I just thought you would keep going. Didn't realize you needed an affirmation."

*She's not really seeing us, is she?* Declan's voice blurted inside her head.

*I really don't know,* she admitted. *I didn't know this was a possibility.*

"It is a pleasure to meet another female of influence," the queen said.

"I would return the compliment, but I'm not really sure who you are," Emry replied. She was almost positive who the woman was, but she'd let her confirm her own identity.

"Did my messenger not introduce me?" A frown dragged down the corners of her shadow lips.

"He did not."

"That's infuriating." Her brow pulled together momentarily before smoothing out again. "My name is Varamtha Roqaene, Queen of Perth."

Emry paused before dipping her head once in acknowledgement of the title. She purposely made no move to bow. "What brings your majesty here?"

Varamtha lifted one corner of her mouth in a smile that promised both trouble and reward. It was a smile of seduction and stratagem. Emry knew it well, because she'd worn one similar on occasion over the years as Mistress. She did not return the gesture as Varamtha said, "I seek a bargain before I lay waste to your country's capital."

: : : : :

Rage. That was blinding, undulating rage coursing through Emry and into Declan. He felt it welling up inside of her – overtaking her body, causing her to shake. Tiny tendrils of smoke began to seep out of her back, right between her shoulder blades.

*Easy, Emry,* Declan soothed down that chain between them. *Find out what she wants before lashing out. Play the game.*

*Game?* Emry hissed back. *Is that what this is to her? A game?*

*It's a play for power, and she wants something of you, The Mistress,* he said gently. He urged his calm outward, to quench some of that wrath. *Reel it in, Emry. Discover what she wants so you can explode on her later, when she'd actually be present for it.*

He watched Emry take a deep breath, drawing in the black mist as she drew in air. Then, she took another, and her body returned to that angled stance. "Bargain?" She repeated, her voice low, dark. "You seek a bargain, now that the Jewels are the weakest and my Rioters may finally have the upper hand?"

*Nice direction,* Declan said to Emry, lacing the thought with approval.

"But that is precisely why I wish to strike an accord with you," Varamtha crooned. "I'm told that the mass of the Royals who oppose you live within the region of Enn, whereas you reign the majority of the other four, with practically complete control of Anexia. I hear that this includes even the military, since the former two kings had their armies stationed along Enlennd's borders for years."

Emry wasn't as surprised as Declan was that

301

Varamtha knew this information. *News of The Mistress was bound to travel to other nations,* she told him.

Out loud, she asked, "So, what is it you wish of me? Since you so clearly know everything about me and my people, I imagine you've already guessed my answer."

Varamtha inspected the nails on one of her slender, smoke hands. "I admit to my own assumptions. However, my terms, I believe, you would find most agreeable."

Declan's Pair placed her own hand on her dipped hip. "I'm growing impatient, Varamtha."

At Emry's bored tone and her lack of formal address, Varamtha's eyes slowly lifted, catching Emry in a steely gaze. "This is my offer, *Mistress,*" she said evenly, emphasizing Emry's title. "In less than a week, my troops will lay siege to the capital of your Jewels. With one princess in hiding and the other in captivity, my victory will be swift. However, I do not desire to remain in Enlennd, as there are other countries on your continent in need of my attention. I wish to move on to my future ventures quickly. You control the strength of Enlennd's military, and here is where you must decide. You may try to fight me out of your lands, or you can let my troops pass by. If you accept my claim over Enlennd, we can avoid bloodshed."

"You want my people to succumb to you – to trade out one sovereign for another," Emry hissed in disgust.

"No, I want you to be my steward over Enlennd."

"What?" The word came out clipped.

Varamtha grinned wickedly. "As I said, you are a female of influence. I've already promised the capital to someone, but the rest of Enlennd is in need of guidance during this complicated transition."

"And I suppose you'll be wanting to have the use of

my soldiers as well," Emry retorted.

"In a year or two," she replied casually, "once Enlennd has accepted its new position as a province of Perth."

Emry snorted. "And my alternative is war, sending aid to those Royals in Enn."

"Not really a scenario of which you approve," Varamtha's smile was bordering on smug.

"If I am to agree to this, will my people be harmed?" Emry inquired slowly, her voice cautious.

"Not if they allow my troops to march unhindered through their lands," she responded. Not really a promise. The wording unsettled Declan. Emry, too.

*What do you think?* She asked him.

*Agree to it,* he replied immediately. *We can discuss this more once she's gone.*

She nodded her head once, ever so slightly. *I think so, too.*

"Alright, Varamtha," Emry said, her voice even. "You have yourself a bargain."

"Excellent." Varamtha grinned. "Now let us seal our deal in blood. Force the death of my messenger by his own hand, and I will accept your allegiance."

And with that, the black smoke that formed Varamtha dissipated into the boy still kneeling on the floor complete with that blank-eyed stare. Declan felt like gawking. That Perth queen had just ordered them to make her own servant stab himself.

He turned to Emry, but before he had the chance to speak, she flung that blade made from smoke into the boy's chest. He loosed a gurgled gasp and fell backwards, but his body never touched the floor – he disintegrated into swirling black mist that disappeared altogether a second later. Declan was openly gaping now.

Emry pointed at the spot he'd been just a heartbeat before. "Who else saw her?"

Vern, Carl, and Marta blinked at her for half a second before Levric said quietly, "I did, Mistress."

That seemed to wake up the others. "I did," Marta said in a higher pitched voice than Declan had expected.

"So, did I," Vern said. Carl only nodded.

"Good." Emry dropped her hand. "Then, she was connected to his mind, not mine."

She placed her hands on her hips and blew out a rush of air. There was no emotion attached to her for the first time in over a week. The lack of it disturbed Declan. It was as if an icy black mist encased the tether between them, blocking that constant flow.

*I can't feel your mood,* he sent into the dark, just to see if the thought would even reach her.

*I know,* came the reply – her voice quiet in his head. *I didn't want you to, and I didn't want to feel yours.*

*Why not?* Declan blinked at her admission. How had she even managed to shield herself from him? Was it simply by shooting some of the darkness within her between them?

Her voice was strained, pained, *Because you watched me kill him.*

At that tone, Declan turned to her. She was worried about what he'd think of her? He nearly snorted. If she only knew all of what he'd done. Declan reached out into that chain, as if he were reaching out his own warm hand, and brushed it through that cold smoke of midnight darkness.

*Emry,* he said, his voice soft, *you don't ever have to hide from me. I'm one of The Stolen. I breathe the life of a tormented soul daily. Let me in.*

She only shook her head slightly, just enough that he could see, and refused to meet his eyes. *Not yet.*

He tried to push back the hurt at being rejected. Once she calmed down enough, he'd push her to evaporate the mist between them. For now, he'd be patient. So, all he said in reply was, *Your hair is still dark.*

*My Eyes already know I can change its color,* she told him as her gaze shifted to her three spies. "Have our bronze-eyed send out the harriers to my generals in each region. Tell them to alert my Eyes there to search for any lurking Silver Perths and to subtly prepare their troops for any last minute movement."

"Yes, my Mistress." Carl inclined his head and then the three Eyes began to exit.

"Thank you," Emry said to their backs before turning to Levric. She threw her arms out wide. "I made a bargain."

She sounded as if Levric hadn't witnessed it for himself. He scratched his chin. "Did you?"

"Did I not? He's dead like she asked. I sealed it in blood," she spat out in disgust, returning her hands to her hips.

Declan watched his father as he replayed Varamtha's terms in his head, and found the mistake – or in this case, saving grace. "The knife. You didn't force him to kill himself."

Her eyes widened slightly, the understanding brightening them. "She'll think I did, though."

"For now, we should let her assume you did," Levric recommended. "It could help us avoid unwanted attention."

Emry nodded and rubbed the corners of her eyes with her fingers. "We can discuss this more with my

Committee in the morning. If we're lucky, we'll have some new information."

"Yes, my Mistress."

She let out a sharp bark of laughter. "It's just us, Levric. No need for titles." She paused. "Could you draft those letters to the generals? You know the code the best. I don't want any miscommunications."

He inclined his head. "I was just about to head that way."

"Thank you."

Levric hesitated. "There was no way out of that boy's death, Emry. If you hadn't, she would have killed him herself. For some reason, she doesn't permit her spies returning to her alive once they've been cornered."

"I know," Emry said quietly. "Her Silvers always end up dead. Still doesn't make it any easier."

"I hope it stays that way," Levric commented thoughtfully and then headed outside.

Once they were alone again, Emry finally met Declan's gaze. Exhaustion lined her eyes, along with a wild vulnerability he had never seen there before. She still had that smoke between them. "I need sleep," she told him, a brittle edge to her voice.

He nodded and ran a hand through his hair. It reminded him of all the sweating he'd done at his cottage. It'd been a long day. "I'll join you after I take a shower."

"Alright." She moved to pass him, but Declan stopped her with a hand on her wrist. She wouldn't look at him. Shame managed drift to him through the mist. Declan frowned and placed a kiss to her forehead. When he was done bathing, they would talk. "I won't be long."

# CHAPTER TWENTY-FIVE

Declan took a near scalding shower. It was early enough that the Krizinks – the local Orange and Blue – were still working their shop, permitting Declan plenty of hot water. As he let the water roll down his face and back, he slid an invisible hand into the darkness between him and Emry. He'd already realized he hated it.

It felt so unnatural to no longer feel her emotions. He saw the irony in that, but it was true. Emry was a part of him. And she was not about to sleep through the whole night with this mist shielding him from her.

He twisted off the water lever and wiped his eyes before stepping out of the shower enclosure onto a braided rug. As he grabbed his towel, his gaze slid over his reflection, catching on his eyes. It was the first time he'd seen the change in them that Emry had mentioned. The thin, silver veins branching out from his pupils only strengthened his resolve to speak with Emry. He quickly dried off and dressed.

Emry was already in bed when he slipped inside his dark room. Declan blinked a few times and suddenly he could see. The room took on a blue tint, startling him. It was one of Emry's abilities. He let out a short laugh. What else would transfer to him from Emry?

He glanced over at the bed. Emry was beneath the covers in its center, breathing deeply. Declan grunted. Of course she was in the middle – she was too used to sleeping alone in that giant bed of hers at the palace. Her position didn't matter, though. He was about to wake her.

He padded to the edge of the bed and crawled beneath the blankets, facing Emry. Then, with one hand, he reached out and brushed his thumb along her jaw, cupping her face with his hand. When her eyes stayed shut, he leaned in and nipped her top lip between his own. That stirred her. Her eyes fluttered open, and she pulled back slightly when she saw Declan right in front of her.

"Can I help you?" She mused.

"It's later," he replied. "I'm ready for you to let me in again."

"Oh, *you're* ready," she retorted. "Didn't realize I was waiting on you."

"What are you trying to hide?" He asked. "We're a Pair. I'm not going to judge you for your fear, or anger, or remorse."

She released a short laugh and rolled onto her back, staring up at the ceiling. "That's just it, Dec," she breathed. "I feel nothing."

"Nothing?" He repeated, raising an eyebrow.

"I feel no remorse. Any that I had at first is already gone." She grunted. "If I had to do it all again, I would choose the same outcome. I'd do it a thousand times over if it meant that it protected my people, or, as in this case, someone else from doing the killing. Save them the pain of having their soul fractured. Mine already has. Why waste someone else?"

Declan stared at her as she went on darkly, "That's why I blocked you, I didn't want you to feel my absence of regret and discover just how dark and disgusting I am to be able to murder a youth just for a bargain with a psycho that may or may not shield the innocent lives of Enlennd. Her response was no promise." She rubbed at her eyes. "But this bargain might buy us some time for the next few days. Then again, who's to say. Vardin said we had days, but he attacked that night."

Emry was getting off topic, but Declan kept silent. She'd at least answered his question, even though her answer had not been what he'd expected. A very small part of him did feel a little disgusted with the way she'd detached herself from killing that boy, but it was the tiny portion of him that still remained from before his days in The Stolen's camp. Those months he'd been forced to fight other Stolen experiments day after day – until they sobbed and begged for him to stop the beating, the pain. Until finally his scum Quirl masters allowed him to back off.

Declan understood what it meant to emotionally remove himself – to smother the guilt and rage and fear that threatened to overwhelm him just so he could face another day. So that he wouldn't entirely shatter. If Emry claimed her soul already was, then did that mean... "You've killed before," he voiced the thought – his words quiet.

She continued her study of the ceiling. "Yes."

"More than once."

The same response. "Yes."

"When?"

He'd meant the first time, and she seemed to understand when she responded with, "The night Ewan died. That Teal who tracked us, who I'm sure you thought you'd outrun, got too close. You were busy. We were desperate. I ripped out his light just as you stumbled, throwing me into a tree. If I hadn't, he would have sliced through us both," she said each word flatly, monotone. Each sentence was a staccato fact, separate but all a part of a larger story.

Declan ached for her. For what that night had cost her. Had cost him. A line was crossed that night for both of them. Before he'd taken off running with Emry, he downed two attackers himself. Even though he'd been on border control for over a year at that point, he'd never had to draw blood until then – until his life had depended on it. All this time he thought he'd been the one to sacrifice so that another could live. He'd never guessed at her own. He frowned. "I'm sorry, Emry."

Her head whipped towards him. "*You're* sorry? For what?"

"For the anguish that has led you to this point," he said softly. "I'm sorry you had to endure it."

She stared at him for a long moment, and Declan felt that invisible black mass between them shift. He didn't wait for her to realize she'd loosened her grip nor for an invitation. His consciousness barreled through the mist, connecting with her on the other side. As her sorrow filled him, he loosed a sigh of relief. Not feeling her had worn on him more than he wanted to admit. Even her sadness was better than the void that'd been there.

*The first person whose life I stole was my own mother,* Emry's voice in his head held such pain and was so quiet that Declan almost flinched.

"What?" He breathed.

"I killed her to save Cit." Her voice cracked as she turned her head back to the ceiling. She squeezed her eyes shut, and Declan watched tears fall out the corners of them, slithering down her face. "I was twelve, my abilities had just barely manifested that year. Cit was so sick for too long. It took my mother two months to figure out that Cit's own abilities were manifesting – that she was burning herself from the inside out, slowly and unwittingly. By the time she realized what was going on, Cit was near death. No Ruby could heal her fast enough to reverse her scorched insides."

Emry opened her eyes as more tears trickled out. "So, my mother, not able to just sit there and watch her daughter die, taught me a new trick. I transferred her light – her life force – to my little sister. But I was too young, too inexperienced, and my teacher was the subject, unable to guide me. I took too much." Again, Emry's voice broke. "I took too many years off her life. I severed the connection too late," she whispered. "Because of me, just a few months later, she was gone."

Sorrow and shame washed over him, surging into him from Emry. There was so much of it that tears of his own pricked his eyes. *Who else knows?* He couldn't find his voice to form the words.

"For years, I thought only my other did. I never spoke of it to a soul." She swallowed. "But it turns out your mother knows about my unwanted ability."

He blinked. "She does?"

She gulped down a deep breath as her shame renewed. "She had me do the same for you."

Declan went very still. "When?"

"You ran across an entire country in one night with me on your back," she retorted. "I begged you to stop, but you kept going. You were dying! And there wasn't a Ruby alive who could bring you back." His horror rose with each word. He knew she felt it, but still she went on, "Your parents asked me to give you their light, and I selfishly agreed to it. You're still alive because of them."

"How much did you take from them?" Declan couldn't hide his outright revulsion now and anger. Both roiled inside of him. He would never had asked that of his parents. He'd sooner die than have them offer themselves up.

Emry grimaced. "I was better this time. I think I only took about a decade from each."

Declan swore, "*A decade?*" He ran both hands along his scalp, yanking his hair. "A decade!"

"And they would've given more if necessary," she shot back. "They wanted you to live. This was the only way we knew how."

"And you just let them give their lives for me?"

"Yes."

"Why?" He demanded.

"Because they weren't the only ones in the room who loved you," she snapped.

Declan swore again and pressed his palms into his eyes. "They sacrificed years of their lives for me."

"They're your parents," she replied. "They would have given you their every breath."

Silence fell between them as Declan continued to massage the front of his eyelids. Eventually, Emry rolled onto her side, facing away from him. His own guilt engulfed him. Guilt at causing his parents to make such a difficult choice. Guilt at not recognizing earlier that some sort of sacrifice had had to have been made for him recover. Guilt at his own folly in nearly killing himself.

"You shouldn't feel guilty," Emry said softly. "It's done, and they thought you worthy of their sacrifice."

"Worthy of their sacrifice," Declan repeated darkly. He released a short, bitter laugh. "I am many things, Emry, but worthy of someone sacrificing their life for me is something I am not. Not even close."

Emry slowly rotated from one side to the other. She was staring at him. Disbelief oozed out of her. "Why would you ever think that?"

He twisted onto his side, putting their heads on the same pillow as he held her gaze. "You think you're some sort of monster? So filled with darkness that I would push you away?"

She frowned but didn't respond as he grasped onto her hand with one of his own. "Trust me, whatever evil you survived, I can top it."

Using all the mental strength he possessed, Declan yanked on that chain connecting them and hauled Emry into him. Dragged her consciousness into his own. Into a memory – one of many just like it. He brought her into his mind to show her exactly what he'd done. Of the monster he was himself...

*Heloise had had enough. I could see it in her black and blue eyes. She was exhausted and bleeding. Her head had to be throbbing with the long gash I'd given her down the right side of her pale, freckled face.*

*I stepped back, panting, and lowered my bloodied fists to my side. I wasn't sure how much of the blood on them was hers or my own. The wound she'd managed to land on my forearm had been trickling down for who knew how long. These duels always made me lose track of time.*

*"What are you waiting for?"*

*I turned to Kearns and pointed at the curled up, shaking Heloise on the clay round. The girl's golden hair was plastered to one side of her head from her own blood. "She's done."*

*Kearns' upper lip crooked into a sneer I'd come to recognize too well – the scar through it scrunching into a sort of zigzag. "She's done when I say she's done. Hit her again."*

*My choice was to either inflict pain or be the one on the receiving end of it. Kearns was the most ruthless of the Back Rubes - our name for the Backward Rubys – in the camp, which was saying something. The one in front of me had to have been pulled from some sick, disturbed cesspool to have become the way that she was. She never showed mercy. I'd say she even delighted in watching the anguish of others.*

*"Get on with it," Kearns hissed.*

*I gritted my teeth and prowled forward. "Get up," I ordered the girl at my feet. She couldn't have been more than sixteen – barely an adult. Stolen from her family in South Quirl.*

*"Please," she sobbed, her dirty fingers digging into the clay as she struggled to rise. "No more. I can't."*

*I knew what she begged of me – how she felt. I'd been just like her at the beginning. Broken inside and out. Until I grew stronger. Until I was finally able to hold my own. Until I became the tormentor instead of the tormented. Until the only parts of me that were still shattered were within my soul – hidden from the barbarians who enslaved me.*

*I wanted to stop. I wanted to rip Kearns apart. I wanted to roar at the unfairness of the world – at the events that had led me here. But I didn't.*

*No, instead I blocked out my horror and disgust at my own actions – burying my emotions deep within me – and tapped into my Stolen-made, abnormal speed. Heloise didn't have time to scream before my fist connected with her face again...*

Emry jerked her consciousness backward so hard that she physically jumped back to the edge of the bed. She gaped at Declan, her breath ragged. He'd pulled her into his mind. Into his mind! She'd witnessed a scene from his past. A horrid, sad, terrible memory.

Tears filled Emry's eyes again. Hot and searing. "Oh, Dec," she breathed. Her words were laced with sorrow. Her heart ached for him. For the girl he'd fought. For all who had suffered in that camp.

"I'd try to make it easier for them," his low voice was barely more than a whisper. "I'd hit where it'd make them look worse than they were. To stop it sooner."

How had he come back from that? How had Declan managed to stay good in the midst of such evil? A relentless cold seeped through Emry, causing her to tremble. She wasn't sure if it came from her Pair or herself.

*I hated what I was,* Declan told her. *I hated who I was. At times I wished for death.*

Emry couldn't help but cry. There was so much pain within him. Remorse and shame and sorrow. He doubted his own importance – an old wound brought on by the true monsters who had held him captive. Using the quilt as a handkerchief, Emry dried her eyes. *Did you not understand what I said earlier? I wanted you alive. I transferred your parents' light because I didn't want you dead.*

Declan frowned at her. "I didn't deserve it." *I deserved to die.*

"Well, too bad," Emry retorted. "You're alive, and I'm infinitely grateful."

"Why?" He breathed – the corners of his eyes wet. *Why do you love me? What can I possibly offer you?*

Emry nearly laughed at the absurdity of his question. Instead, she simply closed the distance between them and nuzzled her face into his chest, inhaling in his scent. *Even if the only thing you had to offer me was your arms around me, that would be more than enough.* You *are more than enough.* She felt his arms slide around her middle, holding her tight against him. She could hear his heart racing as she went on, *You are strong, compassionate, and brave.*

*You've survived horrors in your life without losing who you are. And there's not a man alive or has ever lived that I'd rather have as my Pair. I love you, Declan, because of who you are.*

He didn't say anything for a few moments, but he didn't loosen his grip on her. Emry was content to just stay as they were. She could feel his love for her through their bond – warm and caressing. Finally, he said two words into her hair, "Thank you."

"For what?" She smiled against his chest.

*For accepting me as I am.*

Her heart ached within her for what he'd had to endure – for the events that had caused him to question his own worth. "Of course, I do. You're exactly what I've always wanted."

Declan squeezed her at that before kissing the top of her head. "I love you."

*Good.* She grinned and burrowed further into his grasp, staying that way while her breathing steadied and slowed. Until she drifted off to sleep.

# CHAPTER TWENTY-SIX

Emry was up, bathed, dressed, and fed before Declan emerged from his room. She'd once again risen with the sun, despite the long day she'd had yesterday. Despite spending the night wrapped in Declan's arms off and on. She was sitting at the kitchen table when Declan walked out – hair mussed, in the same clothes he'd slept in. His eyes landed on his mother at the stove first. Without a glance at Emry, he marched right to Llydia and wrapped his arms around her, squeezing her tightly. In a hoarse voice, he said, "Thank you, Mom."

Llydia turned wide eyes on Emry. She stared at her for a moment, then, "You told him."

"I told him." Emry nodded and took a sip of her tea.

Declan stepped back. "I'm sorry it came to that, but thank you."

"Of course." Llydia rubbed his upper arms with her hands, looking up at him. "I'd do it again if I had to. I love you."

"I love you, too," he replied.

His mother smiled and gestured to the seat beside Emry, as if telling him there was no further need to discuss it. "Sit. I kept a plate warm for you."

"Thank you," he said as she set the food in front of him.

Emry watched as he dug into his breakfast. *Your*

*mother is a lovely cook,* she ventured tentatively. She was still trying to gauge his mood this morning. After last night, she wasn't sure how he felt.

*She is.* His gaze flicked up at her, amused, before returning to his plate. *Do you cook?* A question out of curiosity.

She took another sip from her mug. *I can, actually. My months in the Midlands made me a friend with a baker. She and her husband taught me some tricks of their trade.*

Surprise leaked out of him. *I half expected you to say no.*

*Just half?*

*Well, you know other things that I wouldn't have guessed – like the Turanga and the Mountain Thunder. I guess you being able to cook, too, really isn't that unbelievable,* he replied, his attention still on his plate.

*I can't tell if that was a backhanded compliment or just a sad attempt at flattery.*

He shrugged. *Take it as you'd like.*

She winced. *Are you still upset from last night?*

*No, just hungry.*

Emry watched him shovel in a few more bites. Then, she asked too innocently, *Hungry for what exactly?*

His eyes snapped up to her, and he offered her a crooked grin. *You're looking pretty this morning.*

*Just pretty?* She took another drink. *I thought I looked quite a bit better than just pretty when I glanced in the mirror earlier. But then, I do recall someone mentioning once that I'm gorgeous.*

Declan laughed, startling his mother who had been whistling to herself as she washed the dishes she'd refused to let Emry help clean. She raised an eyebrow at him, and he shook his head, "It's nothing. Sorry."

To Emry, he linked a hand around the back of her

knee and pressed a kiss to the soft skin beside her eye. *Was this someone ruggedly handsome?*

*He's a bit full of himself actually,* she quipped. *Thinks he's the fastest man alive.*

*Sounds like someone who can finally keep up with you.* He smirked – his hand still cradling her leg.

*Only time will tell,* she retorted.

Declan brushed circles on the side of her knee with his thumb in response. Emry watched the motion absently. His touch felt right – had always felt right, like he'd been made just for her. In a way, she supposed he had. Pairs were equals in abilities after all – a perfect match. That was what he was for her. Perhaps a small part of her had suspected what he'd one day become, so she'd clung to the idea of him for years until he reappeared in her life. Until she fully fell in love with him.

*I felt a tug towards you for years, too,* he told her as he took his last bite. *Even that day in the forest when I first arrived at the palace. It was why I didn't tell your guards which direction you went.*

Of course, he'd felt her thoughts. Emry wasn't sure if she should be embarrassed he'd heard her admission or happy that he'd experienced what she had. That he understood.

"You're a quiet pair this morning," Llydia commented.

The wording had Declan exchanging an amused look with Emry. *Lucky guess?*

"Just lost in our thoughts, I suppose," Emry said out loud.

Declan stared at her. *Was that a joke?*

Emry rolled her eyes and stood, bringing her now empty mug with her. She set it on the counter beside the sink, which Llydia immediately began to wash.

Emry thanked her before turning back to Declan. She leaned up against the table beside him, her arms folded. "I'm assuming you wish to bathe this morning?"

His hands moved to her hips as he looked up at her. It was as if he couldn't resist a need to touch her. Emry suppressed a smile, but knew that he was fully aware of the giddy warmth that now fluttered through her. "I'd like to," he told her.

She nodded her head toward the bathroom. "Go then. The Mistress has important matters to see to but can't go anywhere without her bodyguard."

He grunted and rubbed his forehead into her stomach, rumpling the dark green tunic she'd chosen to go with the gray leggings she'd worn the day before. "The Mistress thinks very highly of herself."

Emry unfolded her arms and answered the urge to run her fingers through his black hair. She rubbed the tips of her fingers along his scalp, and he released a moan that made her laugh. "I'm not staying here all day. Go take your shower so we can go."

"Why are you in such a hurry?" His grumbling was muffled, thanks to his face in her stomach.

"Because I didn't sleep in," she retorted, shoving his head back with her hands. "Go."

"Fine." He stood, making her the one now looking up. *I didn't realize my Pair was so bossy.*

*I didn't realize mine was so lazy,* she snipped.

He grunted but bent his head and pressed his mouth against hers. "I'll be quick."

"That Teal speed has got to be good for something," she quipped at his back.

Emry watched him go. When she turned again to the kitchen, still grinning like a fool, Llydia was eying her. "Care to explain?"

Lydia had seen it all, Emry realized, and neither she nor Declan had remembered her presence. They'd been too absorbed in each other to remember they weren't the only ones there. They'd acted like ... like a couple. It was true, though. If this Pair thing was real, as it seemed both of them had come to accept, then they were as good as married. Even if they weren't really a Pair, which was highly unlikely at this point, Emry wasn't about to let him go. Especially not after he'd said he loved her, not after last night.

Declan's mother mistook Emry's silence for insecurity. "You know Levric and I both care for you. We have had our suspicions, ever since you arrived." She wiped her hands on a towel. "When were we going to be told?"

"All done." Declan strode into the kitchen. "I bet you didn't even miss me thanks to my Teal eyes."

"We're a Pair," Emry blurted to Llydia, stopping Declan in his tracks. "At least, we assume we are."

Llydia's eyes flitted to Emry's left wrist and back again. Emry frowned. Was that surprise in her gaze? "Why do you think that?" She asked them.

"Because I now have teal in my eyes," Emry said, sinking into a chair. She waved a hand at Declan. "And he has silver."

"And we can hear each other's thoughts." Declan laid a hand on Emry's shoulder. He'd shifted to stand behind her.

"The silence." Llydia blinked. "You were speaking to each other."

A knock pounded on the front door. Emry twisted in her seat as Declan moved to answer it. From behind her, Lydia said quietly, "Your Committee needs to know, Emry."

Emry nodded, her back still to her. "Once we figure out if we really are a Pair, I'll tell them."

"You're a Pair," she replied. "You just haven't completed the Pairing."

"What?" Emry whirled back around, but Declan had already opened the front door.

"My Mistress."

She stood and faced the voice. She didn't recognize the man, but she knew the black handkerchief around his neck – the symbol of her Eyes. Declan knew him. "What is it, Jed?"

The man stood with his feet apart and hands clasped behind his back, reminding her of the Challengers in her Trials. "I am to bring you to your Committee, my Mistress. We've received news from Breccan."

: : : : :

In Enlennd, there were two main harbors named, uninterestingly enough, North and South Harbor. Emry had always disliked the uncreative efficiency of her ancestors. The harbors were positioned exactly where their name suggested at polar sides of the region of Enn. North laid closest to Breccan, at the base of the Jeweled Cliffs – titled after her own royal bloodline as there were no precious gems ever found in those rocks. The South Harbor was much smaller than North and was not sixty miles from Quirl's Hade Harbor. Both were important ports of trade.

Apparently, Varamtha's invasion was to be, as expected, by sea. Thanks to some information discovered by Piran, Emry and her Committee now knew that the irritating Perth ambassador Emry had had to entertain had been at Vardin's side since the attack. Piran had taken it upon himself to discover why. After confronting the man, Piran learned of an armada of ships that should be docking in North Harbor any day now.

According to the report, Piran had broken the man as soon as he'd threatened to burn his face. The ambassador was no militant. He'd only been sent to update Vardin on Varamtha's incoming fleet. Vardin was the *someone* who Varamtha had promised Enn. He'd fulfilled his end of his bargain by incapacitating the Jewels, namely the king. With Emry in supposed hiding and Cit incarcerated within her own home, Varamtha was anticipating an easy conquest. She'd even said as much to Emry.

Also, from the mouth of the Perth weasel, Cit was only unharmed at the moment because Varamtha wished her to witness the destruction of Breccan before she was to become Vardin's personal plaything. Varamtha most likely chose North Harbor so that no other nations could come offer them aid in time. South Harbor would be close enough to Quirl that Varamtha could end up dealing with both nations. But in North ... Enlennd would be alone.

Such a bright future. And this was just what would happen in Enn. Those ships carried a vast number of soldiers no doubt, since Varantha planned to march them through all of Enlennd. To get to Quirl, most likely.

It was a mess. Emry massaged her temples while her Committee argued about the best course of action. All those months and years of scheming Emry had done to successfully reunite Enlennd without bloodshed had been thrown out the window just as she neared the finish line. It was depressing and infuriating.

This was precisely the outcome Emry had tried to

warn her father about over two years ago – when he'd told her his counselors could handle it. When she'd decided to take the welfare of her nation into her own hands.

"We need to move our troops towards Enn," Greggin – a stout man with an expansive mustache the same color as the long braid of hair down his back – told the table. They were in that middle room of Levric's forge again. Greggin Thawk, a Glav and Teal, had arrived bearing the news. He was the general of her forces in that region, while also unofficially over her generals in the other regions.

"They won't reach it in time." Emry didn't see who pointed that out.

"They should at least try," Greggin retorted to whoever had commented. "If only we had some sort of navy…"

Emry nearly groaned out loud as she sat back in her chair. "As I've said before, when I take the throne, I will grant you your navy."

Greggin grimaced. "If we survive this, you mean."

The room stilled, waiting for Emry's response. She repressed a sigh. Every member on her Committee was entitled to voice his or her thoughts. Honesty was what she strived for – was why she'd selected each one of them individually, including Greggin. He was an excellent resource with a background in merchant sailing. This outburst of gloom was not characteristic of him. He was afraid. Many of those at her table were. Emry could feel the dark emotion rippling off of them. They all had plotted with Emry for years, risking their lives in some cases. To have their goal so close only to be ripped from them at the last minute was heartbreaking.

She took a deep breath. "We will survive this,

Greggin," she told him quietly. "Even if I have to go and suck out every life myself – until I ooze shadow and my own soul is unrecognizable – I will do it for Enlennd. We can win this battle. We just need to be smart. Maybe enlist some unorthodox means."

Beside her, Declan cleared his throat. It was the first noise she'd heard from him since they'd sat down. "Our problem is getting enough warriors to the harbor in time, correct?"

"Yes," she said, turning to him.

There were a few squads stationed near the capital, but through the suggestion of Vardin, her father had given them two weeks leave following her Trials. Onyx had had no inkling of what Perth had planned. Vardin had told Onyx that should anything arise then his guards could protect Breccan. Lying bastard. And her poor gullible father. Emry frowned at the ache in her chest. When this was all over, she and Cit would mourn him. They just needed to get through the week...

"I have an idea that might help us," Declan told her.

"By all means." She waved a hand for him to continue, but he hesitated. *You're my Pair, Dec. I want to hear what you have to say,* she assured him.

"I believe the queen of Quirl has been training an army of blue-eyed assassins," he said.

*What?* Emry stared at him. *You told me you didn't know Fiona was queen.*

*I didn't,* he answered. *A year ago, when she told me what she was doing, I knew her as just Fiona.*

*And you didn't question* why *she was collecting assassins?*

*A girl's got to eat.*

Emry almost laughed out loud. She had to cover her mouth with her hand to keep it from coming out.

Across the table from them, Levric was nodding. "I've heard of her group."

*He's heard of them from me.* Declan grunted inside her head.

*He's trying to validate you,* she said. *He realizes Fiona might be one of the few options we have.*

"Are they stationed near North Harbor?" Greggin asked.

"I'm not sure," Declan admitted, "but where they're located is irrelevant. They travel by water and can be anywhere in the world within minutes."

The entire table was gawking, including Emry. Fiona was faster than Declan?

*Only in the water,* he retorted.

"How can we get in contact with the queen?" Levric was the first to find his voice. Emry didn't miss the sadness in his eyes. Most likely thinking about the torment that brought her to that point. The torment Declan endured.

"She can be summoned."

*Summoned?* Emry repeated, surprised.

Levric eyed his son. "Let's adjourn our meeting, so that Declan can summon the queen. She may be willing to help as her own country is also in danger."

"Agreed." Emry placed her hands on the edge of the table and pushed herself up. She turned to Declan. "I'll go with you."

She heard him chuckle inside her head. *Because you don't really have a choice.*

: : : : :

Emry walked with Declan to the stream behind his house. It was late afternoon, and the sun filtered through the trees above their heads. At least with the sun out there wasn't much of a chill in the air. They'd left the meeting and gone straight here. Apparently, Fiona liked secluded places when summoned.

The gravel path gave way to a pebbled bank. Declan, who'd been walking along with his hand in Emry's, pulled to a stop. He frowned. "I think you should stay in the shadows while I talk to her."

She blinked. "Why? I mean, I can. I'm just curious why you want me to."

He rubbed a hand against the back of his neck. "Fiona doesn't trust easy. It'd just be better for me to talk to her alone, at least at the beginning."

As one of The Stolen, Emry was sure Fiona had many reasons not to trust strangers. She nodded and became shadow before pulling back into the woods. Declan watched her go.

"Thanks," he muttered before returning his attention to the water. He stepped to its edge and laid one hand barely on its surface, so that his palm was the only skin wet. In a low voice, he said, "Find me, Fiona."

Emry wasn't sure how long it was supposed to take – Fiona coming. She was just about to question Declan down the rope between them, when the water in front of him bubbled up. Like a fountain. Emry stared as a woman emerged, replacing the bubbling water.

Fiona had long, shimmering white hair and honey brown skin. Her eyes were varying shades of blue, giving the effect of rippling water. She was almost as tall as Declan, coming to his hairline, and she wore a sort of bodysuit that looked to be made of some kind of pelt sewn together into clothing. It clung to her from her ankles, up to her neck, and down to her wrists. The fit left little to the imagination.

When her eyes landed on Declan, she quirked an eyebrow. "No weapons today?"

Declan grunted. "It's good to see you, too, Fiona."

"Are you wanting to work on fighting with your own hands?" Fiona's accent was most definitely Heerth – deep, rich, and luring. She grasped all her hair in one hand and wrung it out. "We both know, that's not your forte. Are you in the mood for a little humbling?"

He rolled his eyes. "I didn't call you here to spar with me."

Fiona frowned. "What's going on, Declan?"

"I have a message for you, from The Mistress," Declan told her.

"Ah." Fiona let out a short laugh. "And what does your famous leader have to say to me?"

"She'd like to meet with you and Rand."

Her eyes narrowed slightly. "You've told her about us."

He shrugged. "I think you should hear what she has to say. She's intercepted some information that might affect you."

"Affect us?" Fiona repeated evenly. "How?"

"That's for her to say," he replied, slipping his hands into his pant pockets. "Besides, it's been too long since I've seen Rand. It'll be good to get him away from those revenge dreams of his for a few hours."

Fiona was silent for a moment. Emry noticed the sudden distant look in her eyes. Then, it was gone, and she was frowning at Declan once more. "Meet me at the Kruth-Quirl border in thirty minutes. You know where. I'll bring Rand."

"Good to see you're still dragging him through the world," Declan mused.

"Always."

And then she was gone. She'd slipped below the surface as if the ground had given out beneath her. As if she wasn't standing in water that was less than knee-high.

Emry flung herself to Declan's side and solidified. "Can we make it there in thirty minutes?"

"We can if we leave now." He turned to her. "Is there anything you'd like to grab before we head out?"

She thought about a change of clothes, but it probably wasn't worth the effort. She'd already stuffed some food into her satchel that was strapped across her body. Enough for both of them, should they get hungry. So, she shook her head. "Lead the way."

He blinked. "I won't be carrying you this time?"

"No. We are both going to run," Emry told him. She wanted to practice using her new ability of speed, and she figured Declan could try to bolt through the world in bursts of shadow.

"That might make us late," Declan warned.

She let out a short laugh. "I doubt that."

"Alright." He smiled out the side of his mouth. "When you run, keep your eyes ahead of you. Focus on the spot you wish to travel."

"Then, for you, try to focus on pulling the darkness around you, like a cloak. That should help you become shadow again." She slipped her hand into his and glanced down at their threaded fingers. "Oh, and try to keep up."

With that, she shifted her body into shadow, releasing his hand, and tore off.

It only took Declan a heartbeat to catch up with her – black mist trailing in his wake. He'd done it again. He was that swirling, twisting blackness. He'd drawn from that bond that connected him with Emry. It'd been easy. The chain had become taut as they each tapped into the other's ability.

Beside him, Emry simply remained in shadow as she ran. One step was the distance she'd had her eyes on, just as he'd told her. Declan tried his best to do the same, keeping pace with her. She was going his speed – his unnatural Teal speed. And they prowled through the world as nothing more than shimmering smoke.

He knew Emry had never traveled so far on her feet in such a short span of time. She was feeling both thrilled and liberated in the way she blurred through the forest. Her excitement seeped into Declan. He grinned, proud of his own progress in remaining as shadow.

Neither of them spoke out loud. They had no need to with their minds interlocked. Declan knew where to go, and his knowledge led her feet, taking her almost unconsciously to their destination. Both he and Emry were panting and sweaty, even in the chilly air. But they were almost there. To the pond. Just a little further.

A moment later, Declan slowed and came to a stop beside the familiar starlit pond. Emry's own feet matched his. She stopped and placed her hands on her hips, gulping in the night air. She watched Declan as he dropped beside the edge of the water. He lifted his knees and rested his forearms on them.

"We're here now, Fiona," he called into the small clearing.

The water rippled from beneath, and Fiona's head popped up above the surface – white hair dripping. She'd changed into a gown that matched her hair since they'd last spoken. The soaked cloth was pasted to her body. Then, beside Fiona another head appeared, followed by the rest of his pale form. His tunic was the same color as Fiona's dress, Quirl's color – ivory.

Rand's dark hair sprayed water as he shook it. Fiona squeezed out her own hair once the water only reached her waist, which was just as Rand's gray eyes landed on Emry. Surprise filled them.

She smirked and, in her Enn accent, greeted, "Hello, Ryde. It's been a while."

# CHAPTER TWENTY-SEVEN

"Emerald." Ryde's eyes shifted between her and Declan, who was still on the ground. "You didn't mention you were bringing a princess."

"You look good, Ryde." Emry meant it. His dark hair was shorn at the middle of his ears. Barely longer than Declan's, who had cut his hair the morning after they'd arrived in Anexia. Rand had gained a thin inch long scar above his left eye, splitting his eyebrow. But it suited him. He'd always been handsome. Now, though, he seemed more so. He carried himself differently – more confident and with more grace. "It's good to see you."

Fiona was eyeing her from head to foot. "You're a princess?"

Emry nearly snorted. She doubted her wind tossed hair and rough tunic and leggings appeared all that royal. Declan pushed himself up to his feet with a groan and waved a hand back and forth between them. "Fiona, Rand – Emry. Emry – Fiona, Rand."

*I already know Ryde,* she reminded him.

*Yes, but I'm introducing you to Rand,* he replied into her mind. Out loud, he demanded, "When were you going to tell me you're royalty?"

Ryde's eyes flicked back to Emry. He grunted. "I was waiting for you to stop spouting your loathing for anyone with noble blood. And I did try to tell you once."

*What's this?* Emry quirked a smile.

*No one did anything to retrieve us, The Stolen.* He frowned. *I became a Rioter at heart in that camp.*

*I became one the night Ewan died,* she admitted. *When no one in my father's Court would listen to my suspicions that it wasn't either side.*

*Was that the night you chose to become The Mistress?*

*No, that came later.*

"Well, you're in luck," Declan told Ryde. "I no longer despise all royals."

"Good." Ryde wrapped his arms around Declan and both men pounded the other's back. When they parted, Ryde jerked his chin towards Emry. "I suppose she's the one to change your mind, *qippo?*"

Emry blinked at Ryde's use of the Heerth word. "Brother?"

"That's right," Declan replied. *It's the closest word we could find to describe our relationship.*

Love and joy filled him. Mingled with loyalty. Intense loyalty.

Fiona's lithe form hugged Declan next. "Where is that Mistress of yours?"

He kissed her cheek, ignoring her question. "Thank you for coming."

She huffed before turning to Ryde. She poked him in the ribs. "I'm ready to dry off."

Ryde nodded, and a whirlwind of hot air encircled just him and Fiona. Not twenty seconds later it stopped, revealing they both were now dry.

*I didn't know he could do that,* Emry mused.

*He probably couldn't when you saw him last.*

Five years ago. Before he became one of The Stolen. *Right.* Emry winced.

"Where is she?" Fiona asked Declan, but her gaze had drifted to Emry.

"Let's talk." Declan motioned towards some rocks that lined the pond, and they moved to sit down. Emry formed a ball of light and tossed it above their heads so they wouldn't be chatting in the dark. The heat from their run was wearing off. Emry rubbed her arms against the night's chill.

Ryde noticed. "Here, let me."

Almost instantly the air around them warmed, as if it were a mild summer night and not an autumn evening in the mountains. "That's a nice trick," Emry commented.

He shrugged but didn't say anything more. He and Fiona were waiting for an explanation. Declan leaned forward, clasping his hands between his legs. "I'm sure you've heard what's happened to Enlennd's capital."

"Just vague details," Ryde replied. "The palace overthrown from within. The King's death. A princess in hiding..." He trailed off as he stared at Emry.

"All true," Emry assured grimly. "Have you heard anything from the new queen of Perth?"

"Varamtha?" Fiona raised her eyebrows, and she exchanged the briefest of glances with Ryde. Emry wondered if she would have even caught it without sharing Declan's Teal abilities.

Declan rolled his eyes. "Whatever you're saying to each other, just spit it out." Of course he'd seen what Emry had.

Ryde's gaze snapped to Declan before his eyes glazed over. Then he laughed. A loud bark of startled laughter. "You're a Pair!" He blurted. "Of all the women to have been Paired with, you got stuck to a Jewel."

"She is, isn't she?" Declan winked at Emry, surprising her.

Emry bit the tip of her tongue. "Are the rumors true, then? You and your queen are a Pair?"

"We are." Ryde sobered. "How did the two of you become one?"

"He became my Knight," Emry said simply. "We think the Ruby did the wrong ceremony."

"Unlikely," Fiona quipped.

"There is only one ceremony in The Old Tomes that can bond one soul to another," Ryde explained, situating his leg on a short boulder beside the larger one he sat on. "A few centuries ago, those Trials Enlennd princesses have were set up as means of finding them a proper husband. Back then, all unions were Pairs. Over time, little things changed or were lost, and now Enlennd Trials are to find you a protector. But the ceremony has stayed the same, so I've been told."

"Why haven't I ever heard that before?" Emry demanded.

"Quirl has always been known for our very detailed scribes," Ryde boasted with a flash of teeth.

"Why weren't the last three princesses before me actually Paired with their knights?"

Ryde shrugged. "They probably never completed the Pairing."

"And how do you do that?" Declan asked.

His friend smirked and opened his mouth to reply, but Fiona was the one who answered, "To be Paired is to be married. You complete a Pairing the same way you would consummate a marriage."

"But my sister was married to her Knight," Emry pointed out. "They never had a rope of light connecting them."

Fiona gave her a polite smile. "Then, they weren't

really a Pair."

"Is that what you see?" Ryde cocked his head to the side. "I see a charge, like the two points that lightning flows between."

"With you a Gray, I'm not surprised." Emry leaned back against the rocks behind her. Declan was watching her. *What?* She asked.

He didn't respond to her. Instead, he turned to Ryde. "How are you able travel more than thirty feet from each other."

That was right. Fiona met them earlier without Ryde. Did it have anything to do with her remarkable ability to materialize out of any body of water?

"Pairings used to be expensive," Ryde told them. "Since they were the only accepted unions, parents would spend their entire life savings on finding matches for their children. Pairs were strong. Impressive pedigrees were formed. Small fortunes were spent. It got to the point that Pairs were political or financial alliances, between nobility and commoners alike. The thirty-foot leash was just a way parents protected their investments. To make sure the Pairing eventually was completed. They claimed it gave their children time to learn to love each other while eliminating their chance to run away from their chosen Pair."

Emry knew she was gawking but couldn't help it. That sounded barbaric. "When did Pairs start to fade out?"

He shrugged. "A couple centuries ago? When finding a Pair became so ridiculously expensive that people chose to simply marry those they loved. When it became more hassle than it was worth."

"But the two of you had the ceremony," Declan said. "How did you know that you were a Pair?"

"We started to share dreams," Fiona replied quietly. "Apparently, it is one of the first signs of a Pair. We would have the same dream and converse in them. Rand, the walking library, recognized what it meant and had us Paired."

"Walking library," Ryde scoffed. "I simply had a very expensive, thorough education."

Emry barely heard his rebuff. Her mind had drifted back to those months she'd spent in the Midlands. To the first time she'd dreamt of Declan. And then to all the other times.

Declan was watching her again. Shock not her own was seeping into her. She met his gaze. "Those dreams…"

"You fed me chocolate." His voice was soft at the memory. He remembered. He knew. He'd had the same dreams. All those conversations. Those moments that had first drawn her to him. That had made her fall in love with him.

Her fingers brushed over her lips. "I kissed you." She had. In her dreams. She'd had no idea he was experiencing the same thing. That it was real. The dreams were real.

*I told you I thought of you every day,* he whispered inside her mind, his voice a caress. Because he'd had his dreams while he'd endured that awful camp.

"We're a Pair," Emry breathed. There was no denying it now. And that pond … She scanned the one she now sat beside. The arrangement of the rocks. The trees. It had felt familiar when they'd first arrived, but she'd just assumed the notion had come from Declan. "We've been here before."

He gave her a small smile. *We have.*

Ryde lifted his scarred brow but didn't say anything.

Fiona cleared her throat. "You brought us here to meet with The Mistress."

"Yes." Declan turned. "First, we need to discuss Varamtha." He gave them a quick recap of what they'd learned of the Perth queen's plans – her intentions to invade the continent. He left out the bargain she'd tried to make with The Mistress. In fact, he left out any mention of Emry's other position.

When he finished, Ryde and Fiona were silent. After a couple minutes of no response, Declan grunted. "Did you forget we're here still?"

"What is it you want from us, Declan?" Fiona's tone was suddenly formal. The voice of the queen of Quirl.

"You know what I'm asking," he replied. "Would you send your water assassins to our aid? If they're ready."

"Of course, they're ready," she snipped. "I just want to know why you think Enlennd deserves any help when its nobility dug its own grave."

They didn't trust her, Emry realized. Just because she was their *qippo's* Pair didn't mean they thought much of her. Their pain and suffering as some of The Stolen, who nobility turned a blind eye to because only commoners – excluding Ryde – were taken, ran too deep. Even Ryde, who, honestly, she hardly knew, seemed to no longer count himself as royal, probably hated that he had any claim to it all.

*He does*, Declan commented. *There was shame in his eyes when he admitted what he was.*

*You've just got to skulk through my head, don't you?*

*If you didn't think so loudly, we wouldn't have this problem,* he shot back. *And relax, they'll help us. It's in their best interest. But perhaps The Mistress could do some convincing?*

Emry sighed. "A few of that same nobility have been trying for years to correct the mistakes made."

"What do you mean?" Ryde asked.

Going for dramatic effect, Emry pulled out the dark from her hair, making herself the ashy, silvery blonde. Then, switching to her Anexian accent, she told them, "The Mistress is to inherit the crown of Enlennd. What better way to unite both Rioters and Royals than by acknowledging they follow the same person. My father sat back and let others rule for him. He refused to let me get involved. Wanted me to marry a prince who could be my guiding consort – rule through me. So, I had to take matters into my own hands."

"You're the Anexian Mistress?" Ryde had a mischievous glint in his eyes.

"Half-Anexian," Emry corrected. "Don't believe everything you hear. Enlennd is stronger than it looks."

"Is it true The Mistress controls Enlennd's military?" Fiona asked.

"Yes."

Silence. Then, from Ryde, "Alright, *qippo*, when your Pair comes at me with a knife, where will she stab first?"

Odd question. Emry frowned as Declan glanced at her. He gave her a warm smile before turning back to Ryde. "Upward through the ribs, left side."

Emry blinked. It was true. Out of instinct she'd go for the most damage she could manage in an attack. But she'd never discussed this with Declan before.

But apparently it was the right answer for Ryde. A grin split his mouth, flashing his white teeth once more. "Very well. When do you need Fiona's fish?"

# CHAPTER TWENTY-EIGHT

By the time Declan and Emry parted ways with Rand and Fiona, it was well after midnight. Since they both were exhausted, Declan had suggested they spend the night in his cottage. It was much closer than his parents' house. She'd agreed, and just a few minutes later they were at his front door. That shadow shifting travel thing was useful. It allowed both of them to run at the same speed over a greater distance in one step. Not to mention, in the darkness they were near invisible.

The lock on the front door of his cottage gave way thanks to Declan's key he'd pulled from his pocket. He twisted the knob, pushed the door open, and held it back for Emry to enter before shutting it after her. By the time he turned back to her, she already had one of her light balls floating above them, brightening the entire cottage. Emry shucked off her shoes by the door and stepped to the couch.

She sank down onto it with a groan. "Why are my days too long now?"

He chuckled, leaving his own boots on the floor beside the door. "Good question. I feel like I used to have a lot more free time."

"What changed?" Emry tipped her head back against the couch and shut her eyes.

"I became your Knight. Or should I say Pair?" He dropped next her. "Either way, it's your own fault."

"I can live with that." She smiled, her eyes still closed.

"We should get some sleep." Declan leaned forward, his elbows on his thighs, and rubbed his eyes. "It's a safe bet that tomorrow is going to be just as long as today, if not longer."

From behind him, Emry let out short laugh. *No.*

*No?* Declan glanced over his shoulder at her, surprised. "No to what exactly?"

"I'm not going to sleep yet, and neither are you." She smirked at his raised eyebrow. With one hand on his shoulder, she pulled him back against the couch. Then, she angled her body towards him and slid her hand behind his neck. "If tomorrow is going to be longer than today was, we'd better make the most of tonight."

"Tonight," Declan repeated slowly, placing his own hands at her hips.

"I love you. You love me, so you say-"

"I do love you."

"And we've been married for more than a week now and hadn't even known it. Not exactly how I pictured my wedding growing up," she muttered.

He chuckled. "How exactly did you picture it?"

She leaned her forehead against his, ignoring his question. "I want us to become a fully functioning Pair, Dec. I'm going to need your strength to face Varamtha."

"Is that you attempting to be romantic?" He grinned.

Emry snorted and moved to shove him backwards, but Declan caught her hands in his own. He brushed his thumbs over her fingers. "And you're alright with being stuck with me forever?"

"Oh, Dec," she exhaled, her eyes locking with his own. "I've already told you, I'll always pick you. The only person who has witnessed me in both my roles and still wants to be with me. The literal man of my dreams."

"You saved my life, you know," he said quietly. "At the camp. The dreams of you kept me breathing. You made me remember there were reasons to keep living."

"I started loving you in those dreams," she admitted.

"I did, too."

She smiled. "When this is all over, I want a real wedding. One with my sister there. Your family. Friends. All of it. I want everyone to know I chose you."

"Whatever you wish." He pressed his lips to her forehead. "My Mistress. My queen."

"Emry will do," she retorted.

He grinned crookedly and pulled her closer. "I can do Emry."

: : : :

The caw of some passing bird outside woke Emry. She opened her eyes to a dimly lit cottage, thanks to the drapes that she didn't remember ever covering the windows. When she fell asleep the night before, she swore the windows were open to the stars and moon.

She shifted, stretching her back slightly. An arm around her middle tightened, dragging her backwards against a warm, sculpted physique.

*Declan.* That was right. They'd spent the night in his cottage. Their cottage. He'd said it was both of theirs now, and she'd laughed and said the same went for all of Enlennd.

Her eyes drifted to her left wrist. She smiled. It was now encircled by two cords – one silver and one teal – twisted together to form a sort of braid. A tattoo that had materialized on both her and Declan's wrists some-time during the night. A matching set. A Pair. The tingling from when it had first appeared was gone now.

She pulled her hand closer to her middle only to have it filled with Declan's. His hand had reached for hers. His tattoo pressed against her own.

*Has anyone ever told you that you think too much right after you wake up?* Declan yawned into her hair. *Could you keep it down?*

Emry grunted and elbowed him in the ribs. *You're so grumpy in the morning.*

He moaned, digging his face into her back. She giggled. Actually giggled. Something she hadn't done since she was a little girl. Yet, since they'd returned to the cottage she'd done it more times than she was willing to admit. She couldn't help it. Declan made her so … happy. She was happy.

*I'm glad I have that effect on you.* Declan chuckled and kissed the skin on the back of her neck.

She suppressed another giggle. *I'm going to put that mist back up.*

*Don't you dare.* The teasing in his voice was gone. *I hate that you even did it the first time. I like hearing your thoughts.*

*It doesn't seem fair,* she grumbled. *I don't ever hear yours.*

*That's because you're too busy thinking your own to ever take the time to hear anyone else's,* he retorted.

Emry turned into shadow and jumped to the edge of the bed, out of his arms. Or, at least, she tried to. Declan had anticipated the movement and done the same. Emry ended up on her back with Declan on top, pinning her down, hands on her wrists. He grinned down at her before pressing his face into her neck.

She squealed. The rough stubble on his face mixed with his warm breath tickled. He yanked back, staring down at her with a look of startled pleasure, and buried his face in her neck again. She struggled to shove him away between peals of laughter.

*Get off!* She demanded.

He flattened himself on top of her and released his hold on the bed so that Emry felt the full force of his weight. *Can't,* he said. *Too tired. I used up all my energy tormenting you.*

"Declan!" Emry's shout came out muffled thanks to his chest on her face.

*Fine,* he whined and rolled off, grinning like a little boy. It was the cutest she'd ever seen him. His black hair was standing on end in places, and his eyes were bright.

Emry returned his smile. "Good morning, husband."

"Good morning, wife." The boyishness was softened a bit by the deep hoarseness of his unused voice. "You're looking delicious."

"You would know," she retorted, "since you've already had a bite out of my neck."

*I found a weak spot.* He was thoroughly pleased with himself.

She rolled her eyes. Her gaze landed on the windows again, and she realized with a start that the light filtering through the gray curtains was much brighter than that of early morning. She sat up and the blanket pooled at her hips. "Wait. What time is it?"

*Don't worry. We still have time.* He reached out and

began lazily scratching her back. *You won't miss your reunion with the day to your night.*

"You said it wrong. I'm the night to his day," Emry corrected. Well aware of the twang of envy that shot through Declan. She glanced down at him. *You have no need to be jealous. I've never loved Trezim. He's a friend who happens to have a convenient collection of gold-eyed warriors I'd like to borrow.*

The Sun Soldiers. That was what Trezim had named his team. At Emry's random suggestion years before as a way for Trezim to feel useful, he searched for others with his own eye color and trained them in warfare. Even though Heerth and Perth had been on friendly terms for over a century, Emry knew that if she asked for Trezim's help he wouldn't hesitate. Originally, he'd been her makeshift mentor, but, over time, he'd transformed into her loyal ally.

Declan had learned Trezim's running joke, a play on their differing eye colors, last night. Before they parted with the Quirl sovereigns, Emry had asked Fiona to contact Trezim for her. To tell him that the night to his day wished to meet with him at noon tomorrow, which was today. Emry knew that would catch his attention. Apparently, it did the same for Declan.

*Sure,* Declan drawled. *I don't tell my friends that they're the night to my day.*

*That's because you're a Teal. It wouldn't make sense,* Emry replied matter-of-factly.

Emry let out a yelp as Declan yanked her back down beside him, nuzzling her into his chest. *You think you're so funny.*

She grinned smugly. *I think so.*

*You know, this was how you looked in my dreams.* He tugged on a chunk of her blonde hair.

*That's because I only dreamed of you when I was busy being The Mistress.* Emry brushed her fingertips over the crescent moon-shaped scar that encircled his right ribs – spanning from his front to back. She frowned. *This was fresher in my dreams.*

*Compliments of Rand.*

"Ryde did this to you?" Emry blurted.

"He did it to protect me," Declan told her quietly. "Did it so I would be out for a few days. So I wouldn't have to play with Torrek, a Backwards Ruby."

Backwards Rubys were the destroying kind. The ones who used their control over bodies for harm. In some nations, they were banned, Enlennd was one. In others, like Quirl and Heerth, they were trained as warriors or spies. Declan's wording, though, confused her. "Play?"

He grimaced. "It was what our captors called the maiming battles we each had to participate in. To get us to the point of desperation – to force us to push ourselves to the very limit of our existence. Over and over again."

Loathing and pain rippled through him. A few tendrils of shadow escaped out of his back, slithering over his shoulder. Emry bent and kissed his moon scar, gently grazing across it with her lips. She wanted to distract him from the memory she'd surfaced, but she did want to know the rest of the story. *So, Ryde fought in your place?* She selfishly prodded.

*He did.* Declan released a pent-up breath. *As the lord of lightning – his self-proclaimed title – he didn't have to touch the Ruby to beat him. I would have had to, though. The fights were always hand-to-hand combat. Abilities versus abilities. Rand saved me from the damage because even though we were slaves, we were investments. We were not forced to play while re-*

*covering from injuries.*

No wonder Declan still had nightmares. Emry rubbed her forehead against the broad muscles of his chest. "I'm sorry, Dec. I'm sorry my father failed you. That I failed you."

"How did you fail me?" He stiffened. His voice was barely more than a whisper.

"You never asked for the story of how I became the Mistress." Her lips brushed his skin with each word. "It started with your parents living in Breccan."

*What?*

*When I ran into your mother outside of the palace – literally and accidentally jumped into her path – she told me she and your father had been living in Breccan for two months,* Emry told him. *They'd been trying to gain an audience with my father. She'd looked so desperate that I told her I'd arrange one the next morning. I never asked what their business had been, but my father told me after they'd left that I was not to interfere with the affairs of the kingdom. That I was not to bring him any more peasants with silly requests. He was relaying the words of his ancient council, and it infuriated me.*

She winced. *Your mother had burst into tears when I told her I could set up a meeting. I knew whatever she'd wanted couldn't have been silly. Once again, I saw the divide between the noble Royals and the supposedly lesser, more common Rioters. And I knew that for the sake of my country and people something had to be done. So, I snuck out that night to see your parents and told them that I wanted to do whatever I could to help them. And your father, the clever man that he is, suspected my plot and aided me the best that he could to become The Mistress. The leader of both sects. The only way to bring Enlennd back together.*

*My parents went to Breccan for me, didn't they? To petition for The Stolen.* Declan was making idle circles on her waist with his thumb. Trying to be casual.

"I think so. They care very much for you." She frowned. "I don't know why they never told me you were Stolen. I would have put my plan in motion sooner. Trezim was the one who'd told me that The Stolen existed. In a way, he helped me concoct The Mistress. I should have acted sooner."

"Mistakes always look bigger in hindsight." He kissed the top of her head. "Thank you for helping my parents. You tried. No one else did."

"They're good people."

*So is the Royal who became a Rioter.* He squeezed her tightly before releasing her. *But come on, now it's time to get up.* "Trezim awaits."

Emry smiled out one side of her mouth and placed her hands on Declan's chest, forcing him still. "I think he can wait a little while longer."

# CHAPTER TWENTY-NINE

The designated meeting spot was the same pond as the night before. Declan and Emry arrived first, as they'd hoped. Declan called out for Fiona again, and she joined them. Then, just as the three situated themselves on the rocks as they'd done last night, a bright flash of light burst through the clearing, over the pond, and halted beside them.

Emry stood as the bright light dimmed and solidified into a brown-skinned, gold-eyed man with blond hair in a shade that matched his eyes. Sunshine bounced off of his shoulder-length locks, like light reflecting off a mirror. He had a firm, clean shaven jaw and an overall straight nose, except for a small crest in the middle of it. The moment his eyes landed on Emry, his mouth turned up in a grin that Declan could only describe as sultry. Declan frowned at him.

*No need to fret,* Emry assured across that span between their minds. *I love you. Not Trezim. Never Trezim.*

*Does he know that?* Declan grumbled.

"Well, dear lady of night, what need have you of your day?" Trezim had a deep voice, deeper than even Declan's, enriched by his Heerth accent.

"Cut the theatrics, Trez," Emry retorted in her Anexian accent. Unlike with Ryde, she evidently didn't feel it necessary to play the Enn princess with Trezim. "No need to put on a face here. You've already met our friend Fiona." She glanced at Declan and flashed him a smile. "And there are no secrets between me and my Pair."

Trezim's smirk dissolved into genuine surprise. His gaze dropped to her left wrist briefly. "You found a Pair? For you? Is he immortal?"

*What is that supposed to mean?* Declan blinked.

*He knows my well of power runs deep,* she explained. *For you to be my match, you would have to have an equal amount of strength. He's giving you a compliment.* To Trezim, she rolled her eyes. "Trez, this is Declan Sharpe."

The prince dipped his head in greeting. "I suppose a Teal would be the only one able to keep up with Emry. She has exhausted me on the rounds more times than I'd like to admit."

"For the most powerful of the Heerth princes, you do tire dreadfully quick," Emry simpered.

"Not prince. King," Trezim corrected her quietly.

"What?" Both Emry and Fiona blurted.

"You're looking at the newly appointed king of Heerth." Trezim pulled at the cuffs of his long sleeves.

Emry sank back down onto her rock and pointed to the spot across from her, near Fiona. "Sit. Explain."

They truly must had been friends because the new king didn't even blink at being ordered around by Emry. But then, now they were equals in rank. Trezim sat with a resigned sigh. "Remember the warrior of Perth I told you about years ago?"

"Varamtha." Emry nodded. "The current queen of Perth."

"Yes. Well, I strategically placed myself in her good graces over the past two years, and she decided recently to put me on the throne." Trezim grimaced. "Two weeks ago, my father and two elder brothers were traveling to our southern palace to survey the harvest, as is tradition. They were ambushed. No one in the traveling party was spared."

"And you think it was Varamtha?"

"I know it was her. She sent my father's head to me along with a note saying 'you're welcome.'" He snorted in disgust. "As if I'd actually wanted to be king."

They were all silent for a moment. Emry spoke first. "I'm sorry. I know you weren't particularly fond of the man, but it was still an atrocious act."

Trezim frowned. "Is it true? About your father?"

"Yes."

"He was a kind man," he replied softly. "I'm sorry."

She inhaled quickly. "Varamtha is responsible for his death as well. She's going to invade Enlennd."

"What do you need of me, Emry?" He tilted his head to the side, reflective.

"Your Sun Soldiers," she answered. "Could I borrow them for the next few days?"

: : : : :

Emry slipped her satchel over her head so that it strapped across her body. She watched Declan hug his mother before doing the same with his father. They'd returned to Declan's parents' home only a few hours ago, after making final arrangements with Trezim and Fiona. During a brief meeting with her Committee, she and Declan informed them of their alliance with Quirl and Heerth and announced their decision to return to Enn that evening. Her Committee agreed it was the best option. They would send messages to the Rioters closest to Breccan to join with Emry as soon as possible, while also preparing her troops for a possible invasion.

To the surprise of most of her Committee, Emry had declared Declan as her Pair. Stunned silence was really a better description to the reaction she received. Well, not her exactly. It was mostly aimed towards Declan, coming out something closer to awe. Her Committee knew her abilities were practically a bottomless source of power. For Declan to be her equal, that said a great deal about him.

Her Committee had accepted Declan as her Pair and another leader. It was a position Declan didn't particularly want. Yet, it was part of being with her – the titles, responsibilities. He understood the risks and still chose her. She'd never fully understand how she'd convinced him to love her.

*It wasn't hard,* Declan said. *You're easy to love.*

*When am I going to start hearing your thoughts?* Emry retorted, suppressing the grin that threatened to take over her face at his warm statement.

*I told you – when you stop thinking so much,* he flashed a smile at her. *You've got to work on gaining some quiet in that lovely head.*

She glared at him as she passed by him to his parents. To Llydia, she said, "Thanks for letting us hide out here for a few days."

Llydia released a surprised laugh, wrapping her arms around Emry. "You know you can come anytime."

Emry moved on to embrace Levric, her trusted second. "Until the next, Levric. Look for the harriers."

Levric nodded. "I'll be in touch." He glanced between them. "Stay safe. Rely on each other. Remember you're stronger together now."

Llydia bit her bottom lip. "Please be careful. I want to attend your Pairing party."

Declan chuckled and grasped Emry's hand, their fingers entwining. "We'll watch out for each other."

The plan was to travel as far as they could that evening – not desiring a repeat of their trip there to Anexia – and then hopefully make it to the palace by tomorrow night. They both would run as shadow as they had done to the Quirl border and back. Neither one of them were sure how long or far they could travel without exhausting themselves. So, this trip was going to be something of an experiment.

Then, once at the palace they would find Cit and Piran. From there, they'd take back Emry's home. After that – it all depended on when Varamtha's boats arrived.

*Ready?* Declan asked.

She nodded, squeezing his hand. The sun was about to set. As shadow, they could move fastest in the dark, blending in with the night. Declan gave his parents a sad smile. "Just another battle for our future. Nothing too serious."

His mother sucked in a sob. A few tears escaped down her cheeks. Levric laid an arm around her shoulders, pulling her against him. He dipped his head, a sort of bow. "Until the next, my Jewels."

He'd included Declan in the title. Emry could feel Declan's discomfort. She smiled and recited her usual farewell to Levric, "Watch after Anexia while I'm gone."

Before he had a chance to reply, Emry adjusted her eyes to see in the dark and became shadow, tapping into the speed that flowed from Declan. She took a step and the world slid by. Declan was right beside her. Not fully formed, but as mist. Hidden in the growing dark, neither of them released themselves from shadow as they ran. Unlike on the clay round at the cottage or even the night before, they didn't pop in and out. It allowed them to slip through the world swifter, easier. It took less energy.

Even though they both were soon panting, Emry wasn't tiring. Neither was Declan. And the distance between their steps was growing, going from feet to yards to miles. Once again, Emry trusted Declan to lead them. The green in his eyes directed his feet.

Above them, the moon drifted in and out of the clouds. It was nearly full again. Had it really only been a month since Declan had showed up at the palace for her Trials? As they moved, the world stood still. No one noted them as they passed in a blur of midnight black smoke.

Time lost meaning to Emry. It could have been minutes or hours since they'd left Anexia. The only constant was Declan at her side and the moon up above. Mountains, streams, lakes, meadows shifted in and out of each other.

Emry's legs began to burn. Sweat wet her tunic, her neck. It was odd that her body still sweat even while as nothing more than mist. Her body felt the exertion required to use both of their abilities at once. It was starting to get harder to keep moving. She needed water.

Declan heard her unspoken wish. He solidified off to her left. Emry did the same, releasing herself from shadow. Declan slowed, and she matched his pace. They stopped in an expansive meadow filled with moonlight. Emry bent over her hands on her knees. She didn't dare sit down, afraid she wouldn't want to get back up.

Once she caught her breath, she straightened. Declan handed her a water skin from the leather pack he'd strapped to his back. *Where are we?* She asked him.

He closed his eyes for a moment, searching for the answer from those green flecks in his eyes. *The Midlands-Enn border.*

*Already?* Emry returned his water skin to him.

He took a long swig from it. *We're moving straight across the nation. As smoke we don't need roads or even land beneath us.*

Emry glanced around them. There was no hint of life anywhere. *Do you think we could make it to palace tonight? I mean, if we're already at the Enn border...*

He frowned. *How are your legs? Tired yet?*

She grunted. He knew she was tired, but if they were this close then they should just finish the last span. They had less to go than they'd already traveled. Had they been on horse, they would only have a two-day ride to the palace. Enn was the smallest region after all. *I want to keep going.*

*You sure?*

*How are you feeling?* She shot back at him. *Can you keep going?*

*I can.* He assured.

She took a deep breath as he put away the water and swept her hand in front of them. *Lead the way.*

Her legs started to hurt again almost immediately. But she kept going. They were almost there. Almost to Cit. She could keep going.

She lost track of time again, but it did seem to move slower than it had before. Emry found herself focusing on breathing. Taking air in and pushing it out. It was better to think about filling her lungs than her pounding heart and weakening legs. She was nearing absolute exhaustion. Emry could feel it. At any moment, her muscles would seize up, and she'd collapse into a heap. It wouldn't be from a lack of her own power, though. No, she still had plenty to offer. It was from her own physical weakness. Her body wasn't accustomed to such an extended use of her abilities. She'd have to work on that later.

Once again, Declan heard her need to stop. Just as before, he halted, solidifying out of mist, and she did the same. This time Emry did sink to the cold, damp ground. She was barely able to brace herself up with her hands. Declan sat next to her, his knees raised and his arms draped over them.

For a long while Emry felt like she couldn't take in enough air. Her lungs ached, and her heart seemed like it might explode out of her chest. As for her legs, they were attached to her somewhere but there was no way she'd be able move them anytime soon.

Eventually, her heart rate decreased, and her breathing became more even. No longer feeling like she might die, Emry finally asked Declan, *Where are we now?*

He let out a quiet laugh. *Look up, Emry.*

She lifted her eyes from the dead leaves and dirt beneath her and glanced around. They were surrounded by trees on both sides, but only a few sat in front of them. On the other side of those were tall grass, but not really a meadow. Because across that…

Emry released a strangled cry. "We made it." She almost couldn't believe her eyes.

There was the palace. It had far more holes in it then she'd expected, but it was still standing. And Cit. She was inside. They'd made it. In one night. And neither one of them had passed out from exhaustion. Tears of relief blurred her vision. They'd made it.

Declan rubbed her back with one hand. *Rest. Once you can walk again, we can find a way inside.*

She already knew how to get inside. It would just require them to take a step upwards rather than straight ahead. *My rooms have holes in them. Access from outside.*

His hand stilled as he processed what she implied. Or probably just heard her thoughts. *Can we do that? Go up?*

*Let's find out.* Emry slowly eased herself up to her feet. Declan kept his hand on her back. He was there to steady her if she fell, but if they were to become shadow again, she needed to be able to get up on her own.

Once on her feet, Emry put one leg in front of the other and bent her knees, stretching them out a little. *Take your time,* Declan told her.

*Why don't you seem as tired as I am?* She retorted.

*I've run across the country with you on my back.* He shrugged. *This trip was easier than the last one.*

She stretched out her other leg and winced. Her legs shook a little, but she could survive moving at Declan's Teal speed again. She sighed. *Let's get this over with.*

Declan took her hand, surprising her. They had run separate all night. *I don't want you to get left behind somewhere,* he said. *This way I can pull you if necessary.*

*Alright.* Emry took a breath and dissolved herself into the night, becoming mist. Declan mirrored her, and they hurled themselves through the world to the base of the palace.

Staying as shadow, they paused for a moment before jumping up to the gaping hole into her room. It was an easy leap. At least, after the night of running she'd already done it was. They reached her empty, dark rooms and solidified.

Emry might have whimpered at the sight of her bed. Declan led her to it and had her sit down on its edge.

*I'm going to check to make sure we're alone.* He told her before pulling in the darkness around him, shifting into shadow. He was becoming fairly good at that.

He was back a heartbeat later. *We're good. Piran's asleep in your closet.*

*Really?* Emry nearly laughed out. *I guess this is where he's been hiding.*

*I grabbed us some fresh clothes.* He handed her a black satin shift. One she'd worn to sleep many times.

*Thanks.* She took it from him and ran her fingers over the soft fabric as Declan began to change. He'd selected a pair of his loose gray pants and a white, short-sleeved shirt for himself. She watched him for a moment, working up the drive to move again.

He yanked the clean shirt over his head and looked at her in surprise. She still hadn't moved. *Need help?*

She shook her head, frowning. *Tomorrow's going to be another crazy day, isn't it?*

*Most likely.* He chuckled softly.

*I don't know why I let you talk me into this.* Emry moaned, peeling off her tunic.

*Talk you into what? Coming here?*

Emry slipped into the shift, realizing that her room was very cold thanks to the holes in the walls. She pulled back the covers of her bed and quickly climbed onto the bed, yanking the thick blankets over her. Declan did the same on the other side before reaching for her.

As she nuzzled against him, into his warmth, Emry yawned. *Let's not travel again for a really long time.*

*Deal.*

# CHAPTER THIRTY

It wasn't the sun streaming through the holes in the walls that jolted Declan awake. He'd been too exhausted to notice. It was Citrine's voice. "When did you get here?" She demanded.

He sat up with a start but relaxed when he realized who it was at the foot of the bed. "Good morning, Cit," he murmured, rubbing his eyes.

Beside him, Emry stirred. She rolled onto her back and yawned into her hand. "Is it time to get up already?" She asked groggily.

"Your sister's here," he replied, scratching his fingers over his scalp.

That got her attention. "What?" She jerked up next to him, her shoulder brushing against his arm. Her eyes landed on Citrine in her maroon gown and carrying a platter filled with an assortment of muffins, meats, and cheeses. She raised her eyebrows. "You brought us breakfast?"

"This isn't for you," Cit snapped. "How long have you been here?"

*That depends on how long I've been asleep.* Emry moaned, massaging her eyes with hands.

Declan chuckled. *You do realize you didn't say that out loud, right?* She didn't answer. Instead, her mind began grumbling about how she was still too tired to care.

"You got tattoos?" Cit blurted. "It's been less than

a week, but you felt the need to get matching tattoos?" Her eyes were wide, shifting back and forth between them. "Are the two of you ... together?"

*Was that disgust in her voice?* Declan raised an eyebrow.

*Remember, Vardin murdered her husband far too recently,* Emry reminded him. Out loud, she said, "These aren't really tattoos. Well, not like you think."

Piran emerged from Emry's closet, looking like he'd spent the night on the floor, as he had. "Oh, you're back." His gaze landed on the tray in Cit's hands. He picked up a muffin and took a bite. "I didn't hear you come in."

Cit's eyes narrowed on him. "Had they been Vardin's dogs, you could have been injured."

"I heal fast." He shrugged, taking another bite. He waved at Declan and Emry and said casually between bites, "You two are a Pair?"

"What?" Cit hissed, whirling to her sister.

Emry lifted her left hand, flashing her tattoo. "That's what this means." To Piran, she tossed, "I'm surprised you know what marks a Pair."

He shoved the rest of his muffin in his mouth and shrugged again. "My parents are a Pair."

Both Emry and her sister stared at him. Declan felt how dumbfounded Emry was, and by the look on Cit's face, he'd say she was the same. Piran noticed them and rolled his eyes. "It's not like they hide it."

"Does his mother have something like this, Cit?" Emry pointed to her wrist with her other hand.

"Yes." Her sister didn't turn from Piran. "But hers is orange and purple. I had no idea it meant she's a Pair."

"If you'd asked about it she would have told you."

Piran snagged a slice of salami and a hunk of cheese. To Declan, he said, "I never thanked you for beating me at The Trials. I didn't want to be Emry's Knight."

"And she never wanted you to be it, either," Cit retorted, setting the tray down on the foot of the bed. She folded her arms across her chest and frowned at Emry. "I'm ready for you to explain."

"Explain what?" Emry yawned.

"Where have you been? Why have Piran and I been communicating with The Mistress's Eyes? And what gave you the idea to get yourself Paired without telling me?" Cit demanded.

"Ironic, since you eloped with Freddick," Emry shot back, pulling the blanket up around her shoulders. She was cold. Declan slipped an arm around her waist, pulling her against him.

Across from them, Piran stilled. "You were married to your Knight?" His voice had gone quiet.

Emry swore inside her head, surprising Declan. *What?*

*Piran's been in love with my sister for years.* She grimaced. *That was callously delivered.*

Cit's bottom lip trembled, and her voice cracked. "Well, it doesn't matter now, does it?"

"I'm sorry, Cit." Emry took a breath and released it in a rush. "It's been a very long week, and the next few days aren't going to be any easier. Forgive me for sounding inconsiderate. I'm sad about Freddick ... and our father."

Her sister grunted, angrily swiping at her eyes. "Just answer my questions."

Emry sighed. "Take a seat. As I said, it's been a long week."

: : : : :

Two hours later, after Piran, Declan, and Emry had all showered and were dressed for the day, they met in Cit's orange and red sitting room. As Emry lowered herself onto the couch beside Declan, she couldn't help but feel like she was meeting for war. She stared across the low table to her sister. Cit sat in a stuffed armchair and Piran occupied the one to her left.

They both were silent. Piran had accepted Declan's dropped alias easily. However, neither were taking Emry's revelation of herself as The Mistress very well. Cit had reacted the worst – she'd literally caught on fire, scorching her gown so badly she'd had to change as well. Piran had simply grown quieter and quieter until now Emry wasn't sure if he was even breathing.

*Of course, he's breathing,* Declan scoffed. *The man's not dead.*

*Was I asking for a commentary?* Emry shot back.

*If you were, I'd point out that Cit also singed your rug, and I'd make the connection that after the week she's had, you being the secret leader of Rioters was the final straw,* Declan drawled. *I can sympathize with the absolute betrayal and hurt she must be experiencing right now, as I've already gone through this myself.*

Emry was about to turn and swear at him when Cit broke the silence in the room. Her voice sounded strained, exhausted, frustrated, and resigned all at once. "What now, Emry? You said Trezim's Sun Soldiers and the Quirl Queen's Sea Serpents will be here by tonight, but what about you and your … Pair?"

"We're going to take back the palace," Emry said simply.

Cit snorted. "How? I've barely fought off my keepers just to have this floor to myself. Unless, you mean to…" She trailed off and concern took the place of the fatigue in her eyes. "Don't suck out their light."

"I wasn't really planning on that, but I will as a last resort." Emry shook her head. "No, I meant Declan and I will clear out the palace of Vardin's treasonous guards, and then we'll bring Vardin to you. And you may do with him as you please."

"Just the two of you?" Cit blinked.

"We just ran across the country in one night," Emry replied evenly. "You underestimate us."

Declan laid an arm across the back of the couch behind Emry and began scratching her shoulder. "What will you do with Vardin?" He asked Cit.

She shifted in her chair. "I don't know. I'm done with all of this. I don't like tossing flames at the guards who were supposed to protect me just so I can wander through the level that belonged to my family. I only learned to protect myself because Emry suggested it." She sighed and fresh tears spilled from her eyes as she looked at her sister. "I'm not meant for this, Emry. I'm tired of it. I'm so tired."

Cit was close to sobbing. Emry moved to stand, but Declan gripped her shoulder, holding her back. *Let Piran comfort her.*

*Why?*

*Do you love me more than your sister?*

*Yes.* She did.

*Then let him comfort her,* Declan said gently. *Trust me. At the moment, he's the one who cares for her most.*

It took a minute, but finally, Piran, moving slowly, knelt in front of Cit and pulled her into his chest. She cried against him for a moment while Piran rubbed her back. Then, he whispered, as if she were the only other person in the room, "Would you like me to take care of

Vardin for you? He can't drown me with my abilities."

His ability to heal abnormally fast. Declan remembered. Piran's lungs would empty the water Vardin put in them.

"You mean kill him." Citrine muttered into his shirt.

"Or bury him alive." Piran's tone was ironically gentle. "Whatever you wish."

Cit rubbed at her eyes, but didn't meet Piran's gaze. "I watched him fill Freddick's lungs until water bubbled out of his mouth. I saw the terror in Freddick's eyes, and I couldn't save him. Vardin put out my flames." There was a dark edge to her voice. "Part of me wants redemption, while the other never wants to lay eyes on that awful man again."

"We don't have to bring him to you," Emry said softly.

"No." Cit shook her head, raising her eyes to Piran. "Bring him. If I can't kill him, Piran will."

"Done." Emry tossed a glance at her Pair and stood. "Shall we begin?"

Declan blinked. "Now? You want to clear out the palace now? In broad daylight?"

"We don't need to rely on stealth for this. Your speed should be more than sufficient." She smirked. "Besides, I'd like to be done in time for lunch."

# CHAPTER THIRTY-ONE

Piran had brought a stash of knives and swords with him to the palace. He let Declan have his pick from the lot. Emry, too. She chose two short swords with thin, flat blades that were serrated on both edges. Enlennd blades. The brown, leather-bound hilts for them were small, fit perfectly to someone Emry's size – one of the reasons why she'd gone for them. Declan grabbed the larger, heavier twins to Emry's blades that he strapped to his back, thanks to more borrowed gear from Piran. At his belt, he stowed a couple throwing daggers and one small, black steel axe. When Piran noted the axe, he warned Declan to bring it back in one piece. Apparently, Piran never traveled without it.

Emry was struggling with the strips of leather that would attach her swords to her back. She was unaccustomed to the gear and was quickly becoming frustrated. Her brows were drawn together, and she was openly glaring at the straps.

*Here. Let me help you.* Declan took the bits of leather from her and began untangling them.

*I don't ever deal with these,* she huffed, placing her hands on her hips. *My shadow blades just dangle from my belt, when I have to be armed.* She bit the tip of her tongue. *I don't usually fight.*

*Where are your shadow blades?*

*Hidden here at the palace. Just not in my rooms. I had to*

*hide them from the servants.*

The straps were all straight now. Declan began the process of slipping them around Emry's abdomen, over the form-fitting Anexian tunic she'd worn here. It was muddy from their trip, but it was about to become much dirtier. From blood. Declan frowned. *Will you be able to do this?*

*You mean the killing.* Emry's shoulders stiffened a little. She was debating about how much to tell him. She was nervous about what Declan would think of her. He nearly rolled his eyes. When would she finally acknowledge how ironic it was that she thought she could have done anything worse than what he'd had to do on a daily basis in that camp?

She took a breath and said, *Trez taught me more than the Turanga. He introduced me to shadow blades and how to wield them. Then, one day, I learned how to fight my way free out of pure desperation – to ignore the scent of blood and the sight of gore because if I didn't, I'd be slaughtered.*

Declan's hands stilled. A sick feeling spread through him from Emry – for what she'd gone through, had had to endure. *Where and why?*

*I'll tell you the full story sometime,* she replied with the shake of her head. *But basically, Trez and I went out for a ride in the desert and were attacked by a rogue clan in Heerth. They wanted to use him for ransom and have a little fun with me. Trez and I barely made it out with our lives, but together we killed them. All of them.*

*You don't have any scars.* A fight like that should have left at least one. He finished tightening the last strap and slid her short swords into the scabbards at her back.

She frowned up at him. *Trez had a whole team of Rubys get rid of every single one. It took weeks, and was very expensive.*

*But no one could know what happened to us, especially not here in Enlennd. To keep up the ruse that I was two different people, one of me had to be unable to defend myself. Scars lead to questions. It's better to keep it all hidden.*

*And the clan? No one found the mess you left behind?* Because there would have been a mess.

*It's Trez's country.* She shrugged. *I let him deal with it how he wished. I was just happy to be alive.*

Declan glanced at Cit and Piran. They were talking quietly on a couch in Emry's front room. He and Emry were in the bedroom in front of the open door. *Does Cit know?*

*No.* Emry adjusted a strap on her shoulder. *She knows I can use shadow blades, that Trezim taught me. But she doesn't know what I've done. What I've become.*

*And what have you become, Emry?*

She hefted a throwing dagger from the edge of her bed, twirling it once in her hand, before slipping it into the straps she'd donned. She turned to him, locking her eyes with his. *Someone to fear.* He raised an eyebrow, and she smiled out one side of her mouth. *Well, by those who are dumb enough to prey on me or my own.* She glanced out at her sister. *She shouldn't have had to deal with this alone.*

He watched Emry for a moment, engulfed in the coiled anticipation she was experiencing. The dread and thrill that came before a fight. Then, he held out his hand for her. She took it without turning. His Pair. The more he learned of her, the truer that became. Now, it was time to move and act as one – as a Pair. He took a step toward the door, but Emry didn't move. *Are you not ready?*

Emry didn't respond. Instead, she closed the distance between them and pressed her lips to his. He wrapped his free arm around her, tugging her against him. When she eased away, he leaned his forehead on hers.

*Vardin has many guards.* She shut her eyes briefly. *One of us could be hurt.*

He let out a short laugh. *You traveled across an entire country last night, and you're concerned about a few guards?*

*I love you, Dec.*

*I love you, too.* He released his grasp around her waist. *Now, let's go reclaim Enlennd for the Jewels.*

She grunted. *And you call yourself a Rioter?*

"Will we be having a late lunch?" Cit called from the adjoining room.

Emry rolled her eyes and led the way out of her room, her hand still clasped within Declan's. "Being a bit pushy, are you?"

Cit stood and hugged Emry tight. "Will you be alright?"

"It's been a rough week," Emry soothed. "Don't worry. We'll run so fast they won't see us." She stepped back, her hands sliding down Cit's arms as they separated. "You and Piran keep this floor. Don't let anyone take it from you."

Piran bowed at the waist. "With my life, your majesty."

"So formal." Emry smirked. She turned to Declan. *Shall we?*

Declan headed for the main door of Emry's rooms, tossing over his shoulder at Piran and Cit. "Be sure to have a fresh, hot loaf of bread with plenty of butter ready for when we're done. And ham."

"Bread and ham?" Cit raised her eyebrows. "That's what you want for lunch?"

"And a giant bowl of grapes," Emry added as she joined Declan at the door. "Go ahead and order now with your maid. We should be finished by the time you get the food."

Cit eyed them suspiciously. "I can't tell if you're just trying to be arrogant or if you're actually being serious."

"We'll let you figure that out while we're gone," Declan replied and slipped into the hallway – Emry right behind him.

Emry closed the door and glanced around. The hallway was silent and bright from the two large windows at either end of it. The glass in these had miraculously been spared during Vardin's fireball attack. If Emry hadn't known better, her family's personal floor from here looked like nothing was wrong – as if her father would catch her sneaking around at any moment. But this wasn't the case. Her father was dead. Her palace had been overthrown. She was at war. Emry swallowed, pushing back the pain as she did. It still wasn't time to grieve.

*How will we know who's a friend to Vardin or you?* Declan's voice sounded inside her head.

*If they're still alive, I think it's safe to assume they're loyal to Vardin.* Emry began towards the servant staircase, keeping her steps light. Declan kept pace with her. *Vardin would've killed the ones still loyal to the Jewels, if there were any. He's been in charge of the hiring for years.*

They reached the stairs. The case that went up led to the roof. Emry glanced over the edge of the railing at the stairs below. *Down?*

*I figured you'd lead us.* He answered. *You probably know the palace better than I do.*

*Down it is.* Emry started their descent. *I know Cit claimed the floor, but she said she couldn't leave it. Where are the guards holding her in place?*

*Most likely on the other side of that door.* Declan pointed to the entrance to the floor below her family's.

*Right.* Emry sighed, unsheathing the swords on her back. Declan mirrored the motion. She rolled her shoulders a couple times in an attempt to loosen the tension in them. *I'm going to make it dark in the hall. Use my sight to see.*

*We can move faster than they can see,* he reminded her.

*Conserve as much energy as you can. We already ran all last night.*

*And you making it dark won't be using too much?*

*I don't think you understand how much power I've stored up.*

He rolled his eyes and gestured to the door they now stood in front of. *I'll follow you.*

Emry pushed it open with one shoulder, and black shadow streamed out of her. She cast the corridor into such darkness that had Emry not been able to adjust her eyes she wouldn't have seen her hand if it'd been at the end of her nose. From behind her, Emry felt Declan shift his sight, tugging on her ability.

Startled, frantic shouts sprang throughout the hallway. The very guards who had turned on her family only days before were now calling out for aid. Good, let the alarm sound. They'd murdered her father. It was time they paid for their actions. Emry sneered at the figures swinging their arms about blindly, and dove towards them.

The first two were easy. She stabbed them both in the chest at the same time. A little ahead of her, Declan took out two others. Further down, six others heard the gurgled cries of their downed comrades and began to retreat. Much too slowly. Declan took the ones in front this time, and Emry slipped past him to the remaining three.

One wide-eyed guard swung a sword toward the

sound of her. She sidestepped the blow and slashed her blade across his middle, burying it deep enough to damage organs. She momentarily acknowledged her prey doubling over before moving on to the next two frightened faces.

It wasn't until she'd finished with them that she realized none of the guards wore chainmail beneath their embroidered tunics. That was strange. They'd been armed but had worn no chainmail?

*It's because of your sister.* Declan pulled up alongside her. *These are her guards. They probably already learned Cit can heat their chainmail enough to burn them. I doubt those elsewhere will be as unprotected.*

That made sense. Emry continued forward. The rest of the hallway was vacant. Emry called back the shadows to her, restoring the light. She gazed along the doors to the many adjacent rooms and sighed. They would have to search each and every room of the palace.

*This is taking too long,* she grumbled. *It's already been ten minutes.*

Declan released a short laugh. *Then, Teal speed it is.*

They sped through the floor, splitting the rooms in half. They blurred past a few servants, but no more of Cit's guards. Deciding it was best to move on before the servants eventually encountered the bodies in the hallway, Emry and Declan made their way down to the next floor.

A heartbeat later they found a cluster of guards shamelessly flirting with a few maids. Emry adjusted her grip on her blades and frowned. *We need to draw them away from the girls.*

Declan loosed a loud, sharp whistle. The men spun in surprise, and the maids hastily ducked out of sight through some door. At the sight of Emry and Declan, they unsheathed the swords at their sides. These ones wore chainmail.

Emry tilted her head to one side. She was sure they recognized her and her Knight. What if these men could bring her and Declan directly to Vardin, and perhaps the majority of his followers. That would save time. She and Declan would have to exert a large portion of energy to fight their way out, but this searching room by room was tedious.

*We should let them capture us,* Emry mused. *I could easily feign incompetence with my blades and you could take on these four at normal Teal speed.*

*And let them overpower me,* Declan finished the thought. *Are you sure they'll take us to Vardin?*

*It's worth the try,* Emry returned. *If they don't, we'll become shadow, kill them, and move on.*

*Have you always been this bloodthirsty?*

She grunted. *Go play the part of my Knight.*

Declan stepped in front of her, and the four men glared. One was bold enough to speak. "You should have just stayed away, Emerald."

"That's Princess Emerald to you, swine." Emry clenched her jaw for show.

From that, they advanced. Declan bolted, taking on the first three and purposely letting one slip away. A black-eyed, red-haired man of Emry's height appeared in front of her. He swung at her leg, and Emry threw both of her blades into his to counter the blow in the most awkward way she could manage without him actually being able to harm her. From his lack of expected force – it was far too weak for a Black – Emry knew he was holding back. Maybe they'd bring her and Declan to Vardin after all.

The clanging of metal and grunting from off to her left assured her that Declan was still keeping them occupied. Her own opponent lifted his blade for another attack but stopped when freezing, biting ice enveloped both her legs and elbows, locking her in place. Emry whipped her head around to the smug face of one of Declan's guards. The pale, icy blue eyes were practically laughing. Pale-eyed – not really blue-eyed but not quite gray-eyed, dealing with the control of ice. In any other circumstance, the ice encasing her joints couldn't really contain her. She'd simply turn to shadow and slip out. But at the moment, she chose to stay in the bitter cold.

"Thane!" Emry cried out, adding an edge of desperation to her voice. He didn't realize she was calling him. *Dec, time to lose.* "Thane!" She yelled again.

He whirled. At the sight of her wearing ice, he legitimately gawked and backed up a step out of the grasp of his opponents. *Are you alright?*

*Fine for now. Think you can surrender?*

"Drop your swords, Knight, or I'll give her frostbite." The pale-eyed sneered.

Declan was fake panting. His gaze shifted between Emry and the pale-eyed a few times before a look of pure defeat overtook his face. Emry nearly laughed at his extensive effort. With a grimace, he tossed both of his blades at the Pale's feet.

"Good choice." The Pale smirked. He was clearly pleased with his supposed imprisonment of the princess. He turned to her in triumph. "There's someone who's been waiting for you to return."

# CHAPTER THIRTY-TWO

Declan and Emry were marched to the throne room. Both had their wrists encased in the same biting ice. He gritted his teeth. Along that chain between him and Emry, he could feel that this ice could not hold him. That it was his choice to remain bound. Yet, the still feral instincts of survival he'd gained while one of The Stolen were currently squealing out in protest. Demanding he free himself. He took a steadying breath. Just a little while longer.

*This isn't permanent,* Emry's voice assured him. *Almost there.*

And they were. They rounded one last corner, and Declan recognized the massive carved doors to the banquet hall and throne room. The guards didn't pause in front of them. Two of them pushed the heavy wood back, revealing the high-ceilings and extensive space within.

It was filled with people. Guards in Perth colors — wearing the same uniforms as the men currently escorting Declan and Emry — intermingled with courtiers.

Those in uniform were grinning and laughing … and drinking. That was ale sloshing around in their goblets — in open defiance of the Jewels' law of no alcohol at Court functions. Declan narrowed his eyes as the crowd parted for them. Some of the courtiers held goblets of their own, but most held wary looks in their eyes.

When their eyes landed on Declan and Emry, some showed open concern and fear. Fear for their princess, he realized. For her safety.

As they passed, the revelry of the guards and the murmuring of the courtiers fell silent. Declan held a few of the guards' gazes as he walked and was met with sneers. He tossed a quick glance at Emry to see who she might be glaring at and noticed her eyes were looking straight ahead, her back stiff. Outwardly she had the appearance of a princess, but inwardly she was seething. He could almost see the whirls of darkness building up within her, begging to be released.

An overwhelming rush of disgust suddenly saddled itself to Emry's rage. Declan whipped his head forward to see what had caused the emotion. Their path to the back of the hall had finally cleared, and there, lounging on the moon-pale throne of King Onyx – cape and all – was Vardin. He'd turned the banquet hall into a throne room.

A silver braided circlet sat on his head. It had belonged to Onyx. Declan remembered him wearing it during The Trials. No wonder Emry was disgusted.

Vardin's flat blue eyes landed on first Declan. The moment he recognized Declan's face, his gaze snapped to Emry, and he smirked. Without bothering to straighten on the throne, he waved them forward. "Emerald," Vardin greeted lazily, "I was hoping you'd come back."

Their escorts forced them to their knees. Emry knelt without complaint. She merely stared at the man before her. Vardin took her silence as grounds for him to continue. He gestured to the crowd behind them. "As you can see, you arrived just in time for our celebration. Today we feast, for tonight Enlennd as you know it will be no more."

*Tonight?* Emry hissed. *The ships arrive tonight?*

He frowned. *If they're not already in the harbor.*

Emry looked over her shoulder a moment, bordering on too long, at those standing behind her. Then, slowly, she turned back to Vardin. In her Enn accent, she called out loudly so that the entire room could hear, "If you wish to live, Royal or Rioter, drop your weapons now. My Pair and I have come to keep Enlennd from becoming a province of Perth."

"Pair?" Vardin frowned, his gaze drifted to Declan. "You made your knight your Pair?"

"No." She grunted. "The Ruby who swore him to me did."

A hushed rumble went through the hall at that. Vardin stood, his eyes narrowed on the Court before dropping again to Declan and Emry. "Pair or no, your attempts to keep the Jewels' hold on Enlennd are absurd. You have no power, Emerald."

She tilted her head to one side in her Mistress fashion. Even though she was actually looking up at him, it felt as though she was glaring down at Vardin. "I wonder what Cit will do with you for killing the two men she loved most."

Vardin's sneer faltered for the briefest of moments. Emry's threat from her knees, as a prisoner, had to have been at least a little unsettling. Vardin only knew the girl who sometimes avoided duties to tromp through the woods around the palace. To him, she was a small hindrance. He sneered. "I think the proper question is what will I do to her?"

"I hope she burns you alive," Emry said evenly. Then, louder, "You have my warning. Drop your weapons now. Or die."

And she dissolved into mist. Declan did the same, tapping into his speed just as he materialized. He slipped out of the ice cuffs around his wrists and was grateful to be rid of them. He felt more than saw Emry retrieve her blades from their captors before slicing their insides open. Declan first grabbed Piran's axe then his swords. He left the Pale for Emry to finish off before popping to the front of the hall by the doors. He and Emry could work their way towards each other.

*Don't kill any of the courtiers, not even the spineless ones,* Emry admonished him, her Anexian accented thoughts differing from the Enn voice she'd just used out loud.

*Wasn't planning on it.* Declan replied, slitting the throat of the first guard in Perth colors.

*Or any of the guards who dropped their swords, or look like they're about to drop them,* she added.

*Is that what you meant with that whole bit about dropping their weapons? I had no idea,* he retorted, stabbing two others in their chests. What were these blades made of? They cut through chainmail like butter. Or was it because of the speed at which he was traveling rather than the strength of the steel?

*You don't have to be rude about it,* she grumbled.

Declan smiled crookedly. He was almost to her now, having cleared out nearly half the room. *It doesn't seem to matter, though. I'm not finding any loyalists.*

*Me, neither,* Emry said somewhat sadly, *Vardin hand-picked his followers.*

They were done now. Declan sheathed his swords and extended his hand to Emry. They had to keep their feet moving or they would be seen. Together they blurred back to where they had been kneeling. The ice and guards were suspended in the air, not having had the time to fall. As one, they pulled to a stop just behind the ice cuffs.

The ice shattered at their feet and throughout the entire hall bodies collapsed. Shrieks and cries of alarm bounced off the walls and ceiling as the blood splattered. Vardin fell back a step at the sight of Declan and Emry. The only sign attesting at what they had done was the blood now dripping from the blade in Emry's free hand. She'd only sheathed one of hers.

Vardin's eyes were wide, and fear filled them. No, it was more like shock and horror. In barely more than a heartbeat, Declan and Emry had downed close to forty guards. Vardin saw what they were capable of. His mouth opened and closed a couple times in disbelief. Then, he pointed a finger at Declan.

Declan couldn't breathe. He was choking on fluid. He stumbled back a step in panic. In front of him Emry popped in and out of smoke, ending up on top of her father's throne. She had one arm wrapped around Vardin's chest, holding him back against her, and her throwing dagger pointed at his throat.

*Become shadow, Dec!* She ordered him. *The water is pinpointed on your location. Run, Dec!*

He obeyed, mustering the last bit of air he possessed. The moment he become a whirl of mist, the water inside his chest fell, sloshing onto the floor. Declan sputtered, sucking in air greedily as he darted to Emry, materializing beside her.

"It's over Vardin, and you know it," Emry hissed into his ear, no longer bothering to sound like an Enn. "Try one more stunt like that, and I'll yank your filthy soul out of you."

"Behold your queen!"

Declan's head snapped toward the courtiers. Piran was parading toward them, followed by Cit. He paused briefly at the dais before stepping aside for Citrine. She'd donned a tiara since Declan had last seen her. She smiled politely. "Sister, might we remove that treasonous snake from you so that your Court can properly bow to you and your husband?"

Emry blinked. She was feeling more like The Mistress at the moment than like the queen she was. Declan placed a hand on her back before peeling her arms off of Vardin. *You look every bit the leader you were born to be,* he assured her. *You just freed the palace and most likely Breccan.*

*With you,* Emry retorted, *I did it with you. You're just as much responsible as I am.*

Cit nodded at Piran. "Would you retrieve Vardin for me? There's a dark, damp cell I'd love to introduce to him."

Piran bowed at the waist. "Of course, dearest princess." He'd used the despised title on purpose, Declan realized as Piran stepped onto the dais. Emry was also in the room, but she was no longer a princess — she was the queen.

Without touching the man, Piran's outstretched hand lifted Vardin's wrists above his head. Declan stared in surprise. He'd thought Piran was only able to heal himself quickly.

*He can make appendages move,* Emry explained. *Not for very long and never a black-eyed. He used to make Cit spill her tea when she'd train with his mother.*

As Piran led Vardin out of the hall, Cit turned to the Court and repeated Piran, except she added two very important words at the end, "Behold your queen and king!"

Not consort. King. Was Cit insane? Or had Emry sanctioned this?

379

The Court, though, didn't seem to notice or hesitate. As one, the courtiers dropped to their knees. Cit faced her sister and Declan, then mirrored those behind her. "My queen and king."

It was a formal declaration. Enlennd Jewels didn't have coronation ceremonies. They were presented to their Court with their new title. Once the Court bowed, then the Jewel was considered crowned. Emry's Court had just bowed to them both. Emry was now queen, which meant that Declan was now her ... king?

He turned to Emry and noticed she was still standing on top of the throne, staring blankly at her Court. Her thoughts were still settling back into place after the killing. Their circumstances had shifted too quickly, leaving her mind to catch up.

*Emry?* Declan offered her his hand. She glanced down at it for a moment, her breathing still a little ragged, before slipping her blood-speckled fingers over his own. Without a word, he helped her step down from the throne before urging her into it. He then perched on one of its arms, still grasping her hand. He squeezed it.

*You need to be the one to tell them to rise,* Emry told him. *The Court needs to see that you're their king, not just my commoner consort.*

*So you were paying attention?* He blinked.

*I was the one who told Cit what to say when she arrived.*

*Taking a page from Rand?*

She glanced up at him briefly. *You're my Pair. My equal. So, you're my king.*

*Alright,* Declan suppressed a grimace. He hadn't planned on ever ruling Enlennd with her, but she accepted him as he was. To accept her was accepting that she was a queen — a queen who wished him to be her king. This had been his choice, being with Emry. He wanted her. All of her. So, he said, "Rise."

The Court all wisely obeyed. Perhaps the still fresh bodies scattered throughout the room, seeping blood onto the marble floor, was what convinced them. Today was not the day to argue.

"Might I be the first to wish you well?"

Declan turned just in time to see Trezim materialize out of the sunlight that streamed in through one of the windows. Declan blinked as Emry stood. "Welcome, King Trezim of Heerth. Late as usual, I see."

: : : : :

The throne room had been cleared of bodies, both dead and living. For now, the blood remained on the marbled floors – to be cleaned later by servants. The blood on Declan and Emry's hands had thankfully been washed off by wet towels brought to them earlier by a skittish footman.

Cit rested on the throne while Emry stood at the base of the dais, her hands on her hips. Behind her, on the two steps up to the dais, Declan was sitting with his weight forward over his knees. Trezim was helping himself to a plate of food from the refreshments table.

"Thirteen ships," Emry repeated slowly. She was keeping up her Anexian accent. "Perth sent thirteen ships. Did Varamtha send us her entire navy?"

Trezim snorted. "Unlikely. Perth is an island after all, and these ships aren't enormous. Medium sized, I'd say. They probably hold about three hundred soldiers each."

"So, Varamtha thought that she could take over the continent with less than four thousand soldiers?" Emry grunted. "I don't know if I should be offended or exuberant."

"Don't get too excited." Trezim left the table and dropped onto the steps at the opposite end of Declan with his spoils in hand. "Remember, before Varamtha became queen she ran Perth's military. The forces she sent are probably more like trained assassins rather than simple soldiers."

"And they're in my harbor." Emry swore.

"Just about," Trezim confirmed, taking a bite into a tomato laden piece of toast.

"Then, what do we do?" Cit asked, propping her chin up with her hand.

"Take a nap," Emry retorted.

"What?" Her sister blinked.

"We're going to do the same thing we had planned," Declan answered, his eyes on Emry.

"It's just going to be a little harder than anticipated." Emry frowned at Trezim. "I assume you didn't come here alone."

Trezim took another bite and winked. "Do I ever disappoint?"

"How many?"

"Sixty," he replied. "But we're only wondrous in the sunlight."

"Which is why you'll be guarding the docks and the beach with Cit," Emry told him.

"Come again," Cit straightened.

Emry bit her bottom lip. *We need cover. We need fog.*

"Rand should be here soon," Declan pointed out.

She nodded. "We need to gather some provisions."

# CHAPTER THIRTY-THREE

There were three main branches of docks reaching out into North Harbor. In between those were expanses of cream colored sand beaches. South Harbor was known for its silky smooth, cool, white sand and shell beaches, having a similar setup. North Harbor's sand, on the other hand, was coarse and clung to every single orifice.

Emry didn't mind the sand, especially not after spending so much time in Acoba, Heerth's northern, dry palace, with Trezim. Declan, however, was miserable. She and Declan were in the same clothes they'd worn all day and the night before. The sand rubbed at her skin, but she'd been covered in the blood of others for hours now. She felt grimy already. What was a little more sand? Declan on the other hand … She could feel his agitation mounting on top of itself with every movement. He was scowling at a soaked Fiona who had arrived only a few minutes ago and had done nothing to deserve his frustration.

Fiona was going over what information her Sea Serpents had gathered on Perth's fleet. Emry wasn't really giving them her full attention, as she was currently conversing with Ryde. Since she was constantly aware of Declan's position and mood, she couldn't help but notice the exchange.

"My Pair would like to know why yours looks as if he might stab her," Ryde said quietly after Emry glanced back at them for the third time. "He hasn't glared at her like that since we were at the camp."

She pulled a face. "It's the sand. He has a lot of it in his boots, beneath his shirt ... everywhere."

Ryde released a bark of laughter, which caused Declan's head to whip around towards them. Ryde raised his hand. "Don't worry, *qippo*, I'll be making the same face soon."

*Are you making fun of me?* Declan demanded.

*Me?* Emry widened her eyes innocently. *He was merely concerned that your last meal wasn't sitting well – with your face all scrunched up like that.*

He rolled his eyes, swearing loudly in his head, and turned back to Fiona. Emry smiled as Ryde asked, "How long have you been out here?"

"A little more than three hours," she replied.

Emry, Declan, Cit, Piran, and Trezim had arrived at the cove after quickly stuffing their faces and had been there ever since. Piran's mother, Moira, came not much longer after that. Emry left the palace in the care of Piran's father – to oversee the removal of all guards.

The cove lay at the most northern point of North Harbor, where the cliffs met the Kruth mountain range. A shoot of rock jutted out into the ocean, blocking the harbor from view of the calm beach. Its seclusion was perfect for their task.

They'd been carting in materials from the palace – about a thirty-minute wagon ride away from the cove – all afternoon. Wood, flint, weapons. There were now several large piles throughout the interior of the cove, awaiting Ryde's fog. The amount of trudging through the sand that had been required to get all the stuff in had left everyone coated in the coarse grains. As Emry watched Declan run a hand through his hair, she saw bits of sand spray off of him.

"I'm assuming you wish me to begin immediately?" Ryde glanced toward the harbor, as if he could see through the rock surrounding the cove. "Just over the water?"

"Ah, you were listening," Emry smirked.

"I see now why you're Dec's Pair," Ryde retorted. "Not that you may care, but I'll bring the fog in from the ocean so our Perth friends won't find it suspicious."

"That's very thorough of you." Emry just wanted some sort of cover and was willing to take what she could get at this point.

Ryde muttered under his breath, something about her being smart, and stalked off with a wave of his hand. "Be back in a few minutes."

Emry didn't bother wishing Ryde luck. Instead, she joined his Pair and her own. Declan's scowl had lessened a little. She hooked a hand into the crook of his elbow just as Fiona said, "I'll go call in my Serpents until we're ready to disperse them for battle."

"Let them take what little break we can offer them." Declan nodded. "If they're hungry, we brought some cheeses and bread. Have them eat their fill of it."

"I will. Thanks."

Once Fiona went off in the same direction as Ryde, Emry pulled Declan around to face her. He frowned. *I'm not really in the mood to be yanked about right now.*

*No?* Emry raised her eyebrows in mock surprise. *Whyever not?*

He blew out a breath and looked up at the late afternoon sky. The sun would be setting in just a few short hours. Emry could feel the tension in him. It wasn't anxiety, rather, resigned anticipation. He knew what was coming, what would be required of him, but wasn't looking forward to it. He'd do it, though. For Enlennd, for her, he'd fight the Perth fleet.

Not as King. That was a title he hadn't fully accepted in his head yet. He'd been declared as such too quickly and recently for him to think of himself as sovereign. She would bring that topic up at a later time. For now, let him simply focus on surviving the night. The future of the continent demanded that they succeed.

Declan let out a snort. *I can handle having a title now and still flay the Perths, Emry.*

*Well, you're fairly grumpy,* she shot back. *I didn't want to send you into hysterics over your new responsibilities.*

"Hysterics," he repeated out loud. "When have I ever-"

"Look." Emry cut him off, pointing to the edge of the cove.

Ryde had done well. Eerily well. A wall of thick, dense fog appeared to have been erected at where wave met beach and stretched outward into the sea. Within the fog there was little light, whereas, on the land the sun still shone.

"Is that good enough for your royal Pairship?" Ryde called out as he came back into view. He was followed by a dripping Fiona and her equally drenched team of Blues behind her. All of them, excluding Ryde, wore variations of those tight suits of skins.

"Took you long enough, *qippo*," Declan retorted. "Were you collecting seashells along the way?"

"Hermit crabs, actually." Ryde turned his back to them to shoot a blast of warm air at his Pair and her Sea Serpents, drying them before continuing on towards Emry and Declan. "You know me and my great love for carcinology."

Emry blinked, and Declan grunted, "Referring to Fiona as a crustacean now? Calling her a fish not working out for you?"

"No more than his pleading for me to call him my tempest," Fiona smirked, tossing her now slightly damp white blonde hair over one shoulder. She and Ryde separated from the Serpents to join them.

"Tempest?" Declan laughed, and Emry let his amusement trickle through her, easing some of her own tension.

Ryde grinned sardonically. "It's better than what she wanted me to call her."

"What would you like us to do now?" Fiona interjected to Emry, changing the subject before her Pair could embarrass her.

Emry partially wanted to Ryde to tell them the name anyway, but there was still work to do. So, she merely replied, "We have some fires to build."

: : : : :

The very last few rays of sunlight had turned the sky varying layers of orange, yellow, and blue. Night would fall in mere minutes. Then it would begin – the slaughter of the Perth ships. Declan had no doubt that it would be a slaughtering.

Trezim's gold-eyed force would protect the land with the help of Cit, Piran, and Piran's mother. Fiona's Blues would take the sea, damaging the ships and any rowboats that dared to head toward land. Ryde would do what he could with his weather elements. Then, Declan and Emry would travel from ship to ship.

It was a makeshift plan, but it was the best they could do. With no time or army, it was almost ridiculous for them to assume a victory. Yet, Perth wasn't expecting an attack. Varamtha thought she'd bargained for Enlennd's military. Many figured Enlennd was a divided, weak country of Rioters and Royals with two different leaders. No, Perth had no idea what was coming for them.

But now, in the fading light, he and Emry were making final preparations. Emry was in the thick leather armor of Quirl – a gift from its sovereigns. Declan had become accustomed to the tight pants and top long before, but Emry had never worn them.

The armor was an honor as much as a convenience. It was soft and flexible, fitting like a second skin, while near impenetrable from simple swipes. Naturally, there were a few differences in the black leather he wore and the chocolate brown on Emry. His short-sleeved shirt had fur lining the inside that touched his skin, and treated leather on top that had been quilted into diamond shaped puffs. The diamonds only covered his back and chest. The sleeves were smooth, flat fur-lined leather. On his forearms, he'd strapped black metal guards that nearly wrapped entirely around them. On his biceps were strapped small twin blades. Sand coated him everywhere.

Emry looked almost identical in brown except that her top plunged into a V and was laced all the way up her back. There was no mistaking her as anything other than female. She, too, had the guards on her forearms, but instead of actual blades on her upper arms, she had shadow blades hilts.

It was all very Quirl and reminded Declan of a different time – when he had had to battle his way to the top to receive such armor. There had been far less sand then.

At the moment, Emry was struggling into the straps for her weapons. The same ones she'd taken from Piran earlier that day. Declan grinned at the tangled mess she'd made of them.

*Can I help you?* Declan asked, not bothering to hide his amusement.

She sighed. "Fine. It's not worth the frustration."

As he began the process of untangling, he noticed her eyes drift toward the edge of the cove, by the water. Rand and Fiona were there, both in their Quirl armor. Rand was in black, the twin to Declan's, and Fiona was still in the strange pelt material she'd worn when he'd summoned her in Anexia – sleek and smooth, meant for the water. It most likely came from a sea lion, or something similar. She'd braided her long, white hair around her head. Emry in contrast had most of her hair down except for a single braid just above her forehead going from one ear to the other.

*I'm nervous,* Emry said.

*I know. I can feel it.* Declan held out the straps for her to slide her arms through. *We're going to do this side by side.*

*And if one of us is killed?*

He grunted. *I think you overestimate Perth soldiers.*

*Varamtha is a Silver—*

*Trezim said she wouldn't have deserted her throne so soon after gaining it,* Declan assured, tightening the straps around her. *But, if she is on one of those boats, we'll face her together.*

Declan turned her around to face him, gripping her by the shoulders so she had to look him in the eyes. *Let's get through tonight. For not just Enlennd but the continent.*

"Are you having some sort of staring contest?" Cit muttered from behind him.

"No, they're speaking mind to mind," Piran explained as Declan spun around to them. "Annoying, isn't it?"

"Don't fret, son," his mother joined his side, laying a hand on his shoulder, "we'll find you a Pair, yet."

Piran flushed as Emry stepped up beside Declan. "Thank you for coming, Moira, Piran."

"Of course," Moira gave them a scheming smile. Like her son, her hair was a reddish brown. They shared the same nose as well. But Moira's eyes were a flaming orange with ruby flecks. "I couldn't let my favorite student be the only Orange defending Enlennd."

"Aren't I your only student?" Cit retorted.

"Minor details."

"In case none of you have noticed," Trezim pulled up alongside Emry, "night has officially fallen."

"Such a bloodthirsty king you've become," Emry remarked.

"Right," he snorted, "because I'll be seeing so much action on the beach, surrounded by fire, a mile away from the ships."

"I must have forgotten your aversion to flames." Emry flashed him a sly smile.

"Convenient of you," Trezim said dryly.

"Are you having an impromptu war council without us?" Fiona asked as she and Rand flanked Declan's other side.

Emry tipped her head back and closed her eyes. Declan felt it, then. The light from the moon caressing his skin – tingling and invigorating. He blinked in surprise and cast his own gaze upward. Was this what Emry had experienced that night she ran out the stable door weeks ago? She'd said the moon had called to her.

"What are you looking at?" Rand glanced up.

"The moon," Cit answered quietly.

Declan's Pair lowered her head, eyeing the group, and grinned out one side of her mouth. "Let's go send a message to that Silver across the sea."

"For Enlennd." Piran nodded.

"For Quirl," Fiona added.

Trezim's golden eyes sparkled in the moonlight. "For our small portion of the continent."

"Ryde," Emry turned to the Gray. "Could you clear the fog?"

# CHAPTER THIRTY-FOUR

Side by side, Declan and Emry glided across the main dock of the harbor, one step at a time. As they passed each post, the lantern sitting at its top was lit by small balls of fire, the flames going from one wick to the next – courtesy of Cit and Moira. Neither Declan or Emry gave the lamps so much as a glance. Both kept their eyes glued to the closest ship, not fifty yards from the dock's end.

Declan kept his stride loose, unhurried, as Emry did the same at his right. He could feel the tension coursing through her – anxious, hot anger welling up within her. He had a feeling that the docile princess part of her was gone forever. She had no more need to hide behind the facade. The woman beside him was all Mistress – the queen she'd always wanted to be.

They stopped a few feet back from where the wooden planks gave way to the water. Declan felt as if they had a thousand eyes watching them. They probably did. Emry took a steadying breath before lifting her arm high above her head. In her hand was a small red flag. A flag of warning. Of impending doom. A threat. From their meager team to the Perth fleet.

No one believed the flag would actually intimidate the boats, but they figured it was worth a try to give them the chance to retreat. If nothing else, it was a dramatic symbol for the start of their upcoming fight.

Five minutes went by. Ten. Still no response. Then, a sudden shower of razor sharp icicles was flung from the sky above Declan and Emry. The ice met with the barrier of air encasing them and shattered into shards. Emry swore and dropped her hand. If Rand hadn't been protecting them with one of his weather shields, they would have been staked with ice.

"Well, there's our answer," Emry muttered, tossing the flag behind her on the dock.

"Brutal and to the point." Declan unsheathed the two blades from his back.

Emry whipped her head around to him, eyebrows raised. "Was that meant to be a pun?"

He blinked. "No…"

She chuckled as she pulled free two of the shadow blades at her hips. The empty hilts spouted smoke that solidified into straight black steel, serrated on either edge – the dark twins to the borrowed ones she'd used earlier. "You know, a month ago, I wasn't planning on being in this situation tonight."

"I definitely wasn't," he grunted.

Behind him, the beaches burst into flames. The bonfires had been lit, creating a perimeter blocking the only entrance to Enlennd for the ships. It was the signal.

Declan turned to Emry. "Don't leave my side."

"Better keep up, then." With that, she dissolved into mist.

: : : : :

It was a dance – to a song that hadn't quite been written yet. The steps were ones Emry had learned over the years, but the combination was something new. It was a sequence she knew from heart, practiced unwittingly day after day, night after night – all culminating into this moment.

Beside, behind, and across, Declan knew the steps as well. That rope of light between them had become taut, transforming into a beam – sharp and thin and indestructible. It was no longer a leash, but a tether, a beacon. It allowed them to swirl and twist in and out of their dance floor, amid their various partners, while always managing to know exactly where the other was. Bringing them back to each other easily. They weren't two separate beings, but one united soul.

Words weren't necessary. Emry knew Declan's thoughts, his actions, just as he did hers. Their steel whistled through the air. Their clashing beat a steady rhythm. Just as their hearts pounded in time within their chests. They spun and parried and advanced. All shadow and mist and speed. Such speed that the faces before them blurred into messy figures of purple Perth uniforms and flesh.

Emry was vaguely aware of others below the ships she and Declan danced across and within. Those others made the thick wood of the boat creak and moan, before exploding into splinters just as she and Declan moved onto another ship. And then another and another. Until Emry and Declan were nothing more than darkness on the roaring wind.

They were encased in a storm of lightning and enormous whitecaps – waves that should have been on deep water and not in a harbor. There was no rain. Just raw power splitting across a cloud covered sky, and through ice barricades that had been raised around a few of the ships.

Thanks to the waves and the wind, Emry was sufficiently drenched. Yet, that didn't slow her, nor Declan. His blades rang loudly, even over the wind and screams in her ears. Her shadow blades, in contrast, were silent as death. They were crafted from darkness, and darkness made no sound.

Minutes, hours, or days could have passed and Emry wouldn't have known it. She became a slave to the dance – to the instincts that had overtaken her body. Whether they originated from Declan or herself, she wasn't sure. All she knew was the song of battle as she faced opponent after opponent. Pale-eyed, blue-eyed, Orange, or Black … they all fell before her. Either too slow or too weak, it didn't matter. She and Declan were ushers of doom.

And then there were only three ships remaining. The others had been strewn across the harbor – any survivors dragged beneath the water, only returning to the surface when the light had left their eyes. Emry and Declan paused for half a breath, debating on which ship to jump to next. Two were already surrounded by Fiona's Serpents. One stood apart, entrenched in such thick ice that Emry was sure it went all the way to the harbor's jagged floor. Lightning fractured around the ice – multiple bursts battering the dense shield, sending sparks flying from wherever it connected. Yet, the ice still held. Neither the Sea Serpents nor Ryde could get through.

But Emry was darkness, and ice could not contain her. She and Declan could slip through the ice just as easily as the moonlight.

Again, words were not necessary. As one, Emry and Declan dove for the ice, becoming shadow once more. They hit the barricade at Declan's Teal speed. The ice gnawed into their exposed bits of flesh, like invisible clans running down the lengths of their arms. It was only a moment, though. They wisped through the ice, emerging on the other side as swirling smoke.

Then, came to an abrupt halt on the ship's deck.

There were only three figures visible. Two Pales positioned at the bow and stern. Both were focused on maintaining the ice walls, oblivious to Emry and Declan. But there, sitting at the base of the mast in the center of the boat was the shadow form of Varamtha. Just as she had looked in Anexia.

"Well, well, well." Varamtha eased herself to her feet. Her full-length, black gown of shimmering darkness floated over the aged wood where her feet should have been. "Why, must I ask, is my friend, The Mistress, standing before me?"

Now was the not time to gape, no matter how badly Emry wished to. Varamtha was not supposed to be here, but then, she wasn't really, was she ... Emry forced her face into what she hoped was determination with just a hint of mild surprise, and she dropped into her favorite Mistress pose. As she lowered her shadow blades to her sides, returning them to empty hilts, she urged her body loose. Despite her obvious panting, she willed herself to be casual.

Beside her, Declan made no such gesture. He held his stance, bloody blades still drawn. Emry tossed a glance around the ship before returning her attention to the Perth queen. "Is this your boat?"

"You know it is," Varamtha hissed through clenched teeth. "I should have known the treasonous leader of the Rioters wouldn't uphold our bargain. It was my mistake to assume you wouldn't go running to the very Royals you wish to overthrow." She slithered closer to them, but Declan stopped her with the tip of his sword pointed at her shadow face. She sneered. "You could have been my steward. Instead, you chose to *attack me!*"

Emry took a deep breath. "You have made a mistake, but it isn't what you think."

"We had a bargain!" She barked.

"Did we?" Emry tilted her head to the side.

"Don't play coy with me, Mistress," Varamtha seethed.

"Ah, and there is the mistake." Emry smirked. "My name is Emerald. Queen of Enlennd."

Varamtha's eyes widened, and she retreated back a step. "No…" She stared, and then cackled, long and loud. The jarring noise caused Emry to grit her teeth.

"Mistress and Queen," Varamtha chortled. "All this time, my spies led me to believe Onyx's heirs were docile. Vardin thought the same." She paused. "I hope you've already killed that fool."

If Emry hadn't promised Vardin's fate to Cit, she might have kept the man alive just for spite. "You should never have interfered with Enlennd, Varamtha."

"No," Varamtha's voice transformed into a low growl. "No, I shouldn't have underestimated a fellow Silver. I should have known you would be just as hungry for control, as I am."

Let the woman believe what she wished. Emry didn't particularly care about the Perth queen's opinion of her. She just wanted Varamtha and her armies out of Enlennd waters. Outwardly, Emry merely grunted. "Like I said, your mistake."

Varamtha's gaze drifted from Emry to Declan. "You are her Knight."

Declan's mouth curved into a predatory grin Emry had never seen him make. A look he'd crafted years ago

… during another time. "No, I am not her Knight."

*He's my Pair,* Emry nearly said it out loud, but the less Varamtha knew of them, the better.

A loud crack echoed within their chamber of ice, followed closely by another. The walls were splintering. Either Ryde or Fiona's Serpents were getting through. "Your time's almost up, Varamtha," Emry told her evenly. "Your army has been destroyed."

"Oh, Emerald, this wasn't one of my armies." Varamtha was on the verge of laughing again. "These were my *scouts.* Sent to get a feel for the terrain before I send in my forces." She sneered. "Now, I suppose I will just rely on my spies for that information."

"Scouts," Emry repeated slowly. Honestly, that made much more sense as to why she sent so few. Still, the thought of more coming, to invade with far greater numbers…

All at once, the ice around them shattered, exploding into pieces. Out of instinct, Emry raised an arm above her head to block herself from the shards, but none fell. The ice was blown away on the wind that now whipped at them.

Varamtha merely sighed. Her shadow form wasn't affected by the wind. "I suppose I must go, now. Until the next, dearest Emerald." Rage flashed across her face. "And I do mean that. We will be seeing each other again soon."

With that, Varamtha's shadow form dissolved, giving way to a sallow young woman with stringy brown hair. A Silver. The girl's gaze was distant as she backed up and sat down where Emry and Declan had found Varamtha. Emry stared at her. The Perth queen had once again connected her mind with another Silver, permitting her to shapeshift.

*We need to get off the ship.* Declan's hand on her elbow made her turn away from the girl. The boat was moaning as the others had done.

Emry nodded and whirled toward the shore. She and Declan became shadow and headed for home.

# CHAPTER THIRTY-FIVE

Declan didn't wake up until noon, not even with the light streaming in through the holes in the walls of Emry's bedroom. The only reason why he even awoke when he did was because Emry had jabbed him in the side with her knee. She'd said, too innocently, that it was an accident while trying to adjust her position, but Declan had felt how pleased she was when he'd opened his eyes. She was ready to rise and wanted Declan to do the same.

Once dressed, they sought out Cit and the other sovereigns. Not surprisingly, the others had barely dragged themselves from their rooms in search of food. Declan and Emry found them in the sage green breakfast room on the first floor, with a simple buffet set up for them against the wall opposite of a large open window that peered out into the gardens. The Pair filled their plates and sank into two of the empty seats at the pale wood rectangular table. The seats put them across from Rand and Fiona and beside Piran and Cit. Piran's parents were most likely asleep in their borrowed rooms.

"Sleep well?" Cit asked her sister between bites.

"Well enough," Emry replied, tearing open her biscuit to butter it. "I think my arms are a little sore."

"Have you not been keeping up on your exercises?" Trezim grunted as he strode into the room.

"Hello to you, too, Trez," Emry retorted, pouring syrup over her biscuit.

Rand watched Emry's movement with a raised brow. "Is this how you always eat those?"

"No, usually there's more butter involved," Cit answered for her.

"And where exactly did you learn to devour soggy biscuits?" Rand took a swig from whatever steamed in his cup.

"In a Heerth market." Trezim dropped into the seat next to Fiona with a loaded plate and full glass of juice that threatened to spill over its top. "Those are street food, but not ever with that much syrup smothering them."

Emry dug into the mess on her plate with her fork. "I've improved on their design."

Declan nearly laughed at the absurdity of their conversation. This was the first they'd seen each other since flopping into their beds late the night before, after their battle, and they were discussing food. It was all so … normal. They were all trying to be normal.

Everyone knew Varamtha would be returning with a host of destruction. That their lives had all become incredibly more difficult. That their three countries were now led by young, seemingly inexperienced kings and queens. That each country had its own internal difficulties to deal with along with the threat of obliteration from Perth. But today, for now, they would let all that fade into the background. They'd scheme later.

He watched their little group quietly as he ate. His friends. Emry's friends and sister. The people he and his Pair were closest to in the world. The ones Declan had a feeling he'd be fighting alongside again in the near future.

"My mother would buy one for my brother and I to split sometimes," Fiona told Rand with a small smile. "Whenever she had a coin to spare on market day."

Rand frowned at her but didn't say anything. Fiona laughed softly at whatever he'd spoken to her mind.

Cit's eyes rolled to the ceiling. "Oh, save me from Pairs."

"Don't worry, dearest princess." Emry grinned and repeated Moira's words from the night before, "We'll find you one yet."

Cit opened her mouth to retort but was cut off by Trezim rising to his feet. "Well, as charming as this has been," he drawled, "I must gather my Golds and begin the trek home. There's only so much sunlight left to-day."

"You sure you have the energy to travel?" Emry asked.

"Some of us are in better shape than others, oh queen," he smirked.

"Come talk to me when you can run across an entire country in one night, not just over a skinny little strip of Quirl," Emry shot back. She stood as well and popped across the table to Trezim's side, a swirl of mist in her wake. She wrapped her arms around him. "Thank you for coming, Trez."

He chuckled and squeezed her once before releasing her. "Of course. Anything for the night to my day."

Rand and Fiona pushed themselves up. "We need to get back home, as well," Rand said to Declan. "If Fiona's Sea Serpents stay too long in one place they begin to terrorize the fish."

"They do not." Fiona's eyes narrowed.

Declan reached across the table and clasped wrists with Rand. "Thank you, *qippo*. Want me to walk you out?"

"No, stay and eat." Rand shook his head. "I'm sure we'll be seeing each other again soon enough."

A few moments later, Declan and Emry were alone with her sister and Piran at the table. Cit leaned back in her seat and sighed. "So, what now?"

"We prepare," Emry replied softly. "Have you decided what to do with Vardin?"

The corners of Cit's mouth pulled down, but she nodded. "Fiona said she'd have her Serpents drop him at the bottom of the sea for me."

Emry blinked. "She did?"

"I told her he should drown as he's killed so many others, but I didn't know how to do that to a Blue." Cit glanced down at her hands in her lap. "So, Fiona said she doubted he'd survive in deep water."

A mercy to Cit. Declan recognized Fiona's behavior. She saw Cit's reluctance to deal with Vardin's brand of filth and agreed to dispose of the man for her. To shield someone from pain. It was what Fiona had always done, sacrificed herself over others. She and Emry were alike in that aspect, Declan mused. If Cit had said she wouldn't have anything to do with Vardin, Emry would have killed him herself.

"When did she say she'd take him off your hands?" Emry asked.

"She didn't, and I didn't care to know." Cit shoved back her plate and glanced at Piran. "I suppose you're going home today, too?"

He wiped his mouth on his napkin. "I was actually thinking of offering you my services." At the confusion on her face, he went on gently, "You no longer have a Knight. In the interim, I can fill the role, until another Trials can perhaps be arranged."

"I will *not* be having another Trials," Cit snapped. She frowned and took a breath. That must had come out harsher than she'd meant. "If you're offering to be my Knight for now, then just be my actual Knight."

Piran tossed a glance at Declan and Emry. "If my sovereigns permit it-"

"I was the one who sent you to protect her in the first place." Emry grunted. "Unless Declan has some aversion to it, I don't care. And don't ever pull that 'if my sovereigns permit' to me again."

"I don't care," Declan quickly added. "But, I don't think you should be sworn to each other."

"Oh, right." Emry shook her head. "Me neither."

"Why not?" Cit blinked.

"Because that's how we unwittingly became a Pair," Emry retorted, knocking back the last gulp of juice in her glass. Cit's face reddened, and Emry let out a short laugh. "Best to wait on that for now."

"Fine, then. Agreed." Cit stood, and turned to Piran expectantly. He pushed himself to his feet and Cit said, "I haven't sat at my piano in over a week. Care to see if Vardin's ilk destroyed it?"

Her new Knight inclined his head. "I will go where you please."

As they exited, Emry leaned her elbows on the table and dug her fingers into her loose hair. "I don't want to think about everything we have to do. I don't want to evict my father's council. I don't want to sift through our Court and figure out who supported Vardin. I don't want to send word to my Committee. Even though all of those things need to be done. Just not now. At least, not today. I have no taste for it today."

Declan laid a hand against her back, rubbing small circles with his thumb. "Then, don't. Not today. After last night, this week, we deserve one day to relax. And then we'll begin tackling everything else tomorrow."

"We," she repeated, straightening.

His hand stilled. "Do you not want my help?"

"Of course, I do," she faced him, smiling faintly. "I'm just marveling that you're willing to."

He leaned in and kissed her forehead. "We're a Pair."

Her grin spread slowly over her face, lighting her eyes. "Come with me?"

: : : : :

Emry led Declan out onto the roof, grasping his hand tightly in her own. They'd meandered through the palace and climbed the stairs at a normal pace, simply enjoying each other's company. Along the way, they'd encountered more than a few untended holes in the palace walls. Those would need to be repaired soon, before another infamous Enlennd autumn storm befell them. But she'd think about that later.

Today, she would do as Declan had suggested. Today they would do as they pleased. Which was why Emry had taken him to the roof.

She paused at the railing beside the vine ladder they both had climbed down only a couple short weeks ago. Declan frowned down at it as Emry leaned against him. She slid her hands up his chest, until they landed behind his neck. His own hands gripped her hips.

*You better not have brought me here to climb down this wall again,* Declan warned.

Emry pressed her lips together to suppress a laugh. *No, I had something else in mind.*

He raised an eyebrow, and she drew his head

downward. Their lips had barely brushed when his arms enveloped her, crushing her against him. She moved her mouth against his, savoring the taste of him.

This was her Pair. Her Declan. Her friend, lover, and confidant. His warm fingers slid to her neck, his palms and thumbs cradling her face. Emry felt his love for her thrumming through him.

*My Pair.* His voice echoed her own inside her head.

Eventually, he eased back and chuckled. "If you wanted to kiss me, I could have found us a better location than the roof. One more secluded."

"That's not why I brought you here," she poked him in the ribs. "Kissing you was just an added benefit."

*Why are we here?*

"To take your advice," she replied. "We deserve a day to ourselves. So," she paused and stepped out of his grasp. "You're it."

He opened his mouth to reply but before he could make a sound, Emry jumped onto the railing, her back facing the garden below. His eyes widened, and she dove backwards head first, becoming shadow in the air. She twisted through the world until she reached the edge of one of the orchards. Emry halted, solidifying once more, and grinned up at the palace's roof, to Declan. Except he wasn't there.

Emry frowned. And then was tackled to the ground. She released a startled cry as she landed. Declan straddled her, smirking and smug. "Now, you're it."

Declan planted a kiss on her mouth and disappeared into shadow. Emry laughed and rolled onto her feet. This was how she wished to spend her day. Tomorrow, she'd go back to being Mistress and queen.

For now, she was content to chase her Pair. She'd worry about the future later.

*Where did you go?* Emry sent down that rope that joined them.

"Come find me," Declan breathed into her ear. He'd materialized behind her.

She whirled, and he dissolved into mist once more. Emry grinned and became shadow. Then, dove after Declan.

# Also by m.l. greye

The Other World Series

*The Other Worlds*
*Ethon*

:::::

The Swift Shadows Series

*Of Rioters & Royals*
*Entwined Paths (coming soon)*

You can follow m.l. greye on Facebook, Twitter, and Instagram.

www.mlgreye.com

# ACKNOWLEDGMENTS

My first thanks goes to Bryce. My husband. My Pair. Thank you for being willing to build me a writing room with a view. I appreciate you listening to me talk through my story plotlines, even when I jumped around and you had no idea where I was going with it. You've always supported my writing, and I love you for it. You're my favorite.

Heather, no one could ask for a better editor or artist. Thanks for picking out every grammatical error and misplaced word. I'm even grateful for your weird obsession with commas. As for your cover art, you made a vague image in my head come to life. It turned out better than I imagined. It looks great and you're great. Thank you!

Hillary and Lauren, you're almost as entwined with this story as I am. Thank you for being my sounding board. For keeping me on track and consistent. For being my first fans.

A special thanks to my parents. You've been there to read my early drafts. I love you both and am so glad you encouraged me to write – going all the way back to my one-page series in elementary school. Thank you.

To my readers, you're wonderful. Thank you for giving me a try. You listened to my dreams and wild imagination in word form. I'll forever be grateful.

34832856R00255

Made in the USA
Lexington, KY
28 March 2019